CW00349564

MY ENEMY'S TEARS

MY ENEMY'S TEARS

THE WITCH OF NORTHAMPTON

A NOVEL BASED ON A TRUE STORY

KAREN VORBECK WILLIAMS

My Enemy's Tears: The Witch of Northampton

Copyright © 2011 Karen Vorbeck Williams. All rights reserved. No part of this book may be reproduced or retransmitted in any form or by any means without the written permission of the publisher.

Published by Wheatmark®

610 East Delano Street, Suite 104, Tucson, Arizona 85705 U.S.A.

www.wheatmark.com

ISBN: 978-1-60494-628-4

LCCN: 2011927538

Cover photography: Meredith R. Rubin

Rev201101
Rev201202

for my husband, Allen Burnett Williams (1918-2010)

Acknowledgments

First, I want to thank Phoebe Pettingell, whose knowledge of the 17th century and advice and interest in the project inspired me to get back to work on this manuscript. Any historical liberties taken are not her fault. Thanks also to my editors. Betsy T. White, was not only fun to work with but highly skilled and dedicated. The book benefited greatly from her input. Editor Dan Johnsen, with his quick mind and sharp eye, put the cherry on top. Thank you to Patricia Cumming and Lee Rudolph for our many years together as writers. To Phoebe Dunn and Deborah Lee I give thanks for their attention and for asking all the right questions. My appreciation goes to Julia Steiny, my astute, always helpful friend, who shares my love of the written word. My talented children David Ragsdale and Meredith Rubin have been a tremendous source of help and encouragement. Thanks to granddaughter Sophie Rubin for playing the part of Mary Parsons, her thirteenth great-grandmother, on the book's cover.

Gratitude must also be expressed to the 17th century writers who transported me to their world: Governor John Winthrop, who kept an almost daily journal that spanned the years 1630-1649; John Joselyn, who described so ardently the wonders of New England; Gervase Markham, who told me almost everything I needed to know about being a 17th century woman; William Wood, who captured in words the natural features of a virgin New England; Mary Rowlandson, for her faith and bravery; Anne Bradstreet, for her love of God and husband; and selected sermons of the Puritan Divines, especially Thomas Hooker. This book could not have come into being without my having reached, again and again, for books written by James R. Trumbull, Henry M. Burt, Perry Miller, Alfred A. Cave, John Putnam Demos, Roger Thompson, Stephen Innes, Ann Leighton and others too numerous to name.

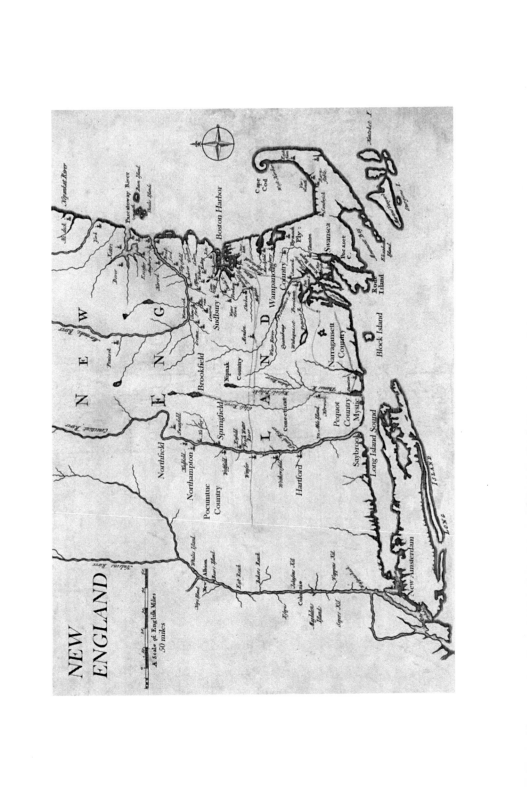

Deposition

William Branch of Springfeild testifyed on oath that when I lived at the long meddow & Joseph parsons lived there, a certain tyme Joseph Parsons told mee that where ever he laid the key his wife could fynd it : & would goe out in the night & that when shee went out a woman went out wth her & came in wth her but says Joseph Parsons God preserves her wth his Angells: & further the said William Branch sayth that while they lived together in the Long Meddow; George Colton told mee that he followinge Mary Parsons in her sift, he followed her thorow the water where he was up to the knees & shee was not wett : this thing I told to old mr Pynchon when he was here : who wondered at it but said he could not tell wt to say to it. Testified on oath before mee Elizur Holyoke

PART ONE
Journey Too Far

I

"Therefore, good sir, encourage men to come over, for here is land and means of livelihood sufficient for men that bring bodies able and minds fitted to brave the first brunts . . ."

—Richard Saltonstall (1586–1661)

Painswick Parish, England, 1633

MARY BLISS GOT it into her head that she wanted nothing more than to escape the nursery. She was supposed to stay with the other children and Nurse Bodwin, not wander off into the far reaches of the house, out into the garden, or off to the hills where the sheep grazed in summer. But that morning her curiosity got the best of her, and she devised a plan. The cook always brought them their afternoon repast just about the time Mary toiled at her sampler, before the younger children napped, when Nurse Bodwin would collapse on a settle by the fire and try her best not to doze. Mary figured that after a day of wiping runny noses and tears, and mediating squabbles between her brother and her cousin, the old woman would be worn out and wouldn't notice that she'd slipped away. She wanted to climb to the top of the stairs—to look out the highest window at the first snowfall of her ninth winter.

About the time Mary's stomach began to rumble, the nurse yawned, removed the handkerchief from her apron pocket, and wiped her eyes before folding herself onto the old settle to retreat behind closed eyelids. Then Mary had to decide what she wanted most—food or freedom. Perhaps if she was quick she could have both. She stole out the door and hurried past the kitchen, running as quietly as she could through the hall and past the door to the garden. Without stopping, she turned to look over her shoulder. The nurse hadn't followed her into the west wing.

As the ties of her white lace cap flew loose at her throat, she skipped rapturously on till she came to the foot of a broad staircase. Smoothing her apron, she lifted her skirts and began her ascent. Higher and higher she bounded, step after step, till at last she reached the third floor landing well lit by cold winter light shining through a casement with diamond-shaped panes.

She pressed her face against the frosty glass and breathed in the view. Far below lay her father's fields and paddocks, white with snow. She could see the bare orchards, the wild meadow, and rising above the valley, the high grassy hills of Painswick Beacon where the family went on summer picnics. From the top of the Beacon one could see the River Severn and the valley through which it ran. The summer before, Mary and her brothers had climbed to the highest point to explore the ruins of an ancient earthwork fort once used in defense of the hills. Below the Beacon lay the village of honey-colored stone, where the 600-year-old church building spread beneath its new spire that towered above everything else in the village. In summer, sheep grazed green fields outside the town. In winter, herds of deer came to the edge of the forested hills beyond, looking for tufts of grass to nibble through the snow. From her window Mary traveled to every corner of the only world she knew.

As the wind whipped the trees and whistled past the window, the sun hastened away behind a storm cloud. A dark-cloaked figure crossed the wild meadow and headed in her direction. Mary recognized the midwife, the old cunning woman, bearing the tools of her trade in a large soft-sided basket and doggedly making her way toward Bliss House.

Mary watched the old woman disappear into the house below. The midwife came when babies were born, that much Mary knew, yet so far as she'd been told neither her mother nor her aunt expected a child. She turned from the window and hurried down the stairs, the tap-tap of her shoes echoing in the hall. When she reached the second floor, faint but unmistakable cries reached her ears. Mary stopped short and shrank into the shadows as the midwife hastily approached a door and opened it.

"Lord, have mercy," Mary heard her mother pray as the heavy door wailed shut. Mary ran to peer through the keyhole. Pressing her cheek close under the latch, she saw her mother lying in bed. "Thank God you've come!" her mother said, as the midwife began her work at a table beside a roaring fire.

When Mary opened the door and ran to her mother's side, Margaret paid her no attention.

"Mother, are you ill?" Mary tugged at her mother's sleeve, concerned by her tear-stained face and hands clutching her belly.

The child watched the midwife pour boiling water over dried leaves, not knowing it for belladonna, a deadly nightshade with powers so great that folks knew the Devil himself kept a patch for his use. Steam curled into the cunning woman's lined face as Margaret wept and prayed, "Lord, have mercy!"

"Drink this, goodwife." The midwife handed her a cup. "Sure as day it'll stop thy labor." Margaret took the cup and raised herself up to sip from it as the midwife gently stroked her head. "Rest now, drink my decoction. Yer babe will not come today."

As if by magic, Margaret's fear soon calmed. As she finished her drink she smiled at her daughter and reached for her hand to kiss it.

"Why, Mary, you belong in the nursery. How came you? Never mind—I'm glad to see you here beside me."

When her cup was empty she heaved a sigh, closed her eyes, and, folding one hand across her breast, lay very still.

Mary touched her mother's cheek. "Is Mother dead?" she whispered to the midwife, for the words were too awful to say out loud.

The cunning woman reached to tuck a copper curl inside Mary's cap. "Nay, child, she sleeps. Fear not."

Mary brightened and turned her attention to the empty cup. "Show me your magic."

"Cry you mercy, 'tis no magic. The herb hath the power to calm a babe in the womb."

Mary's eyes grew wide. "She is with child again."

"Aye, and now, with God's help, it won't come early."

Her heart lighter, Mary returned to her mother's side. Margaret looked peaceful, eyes closed, her thick chestnut hair spread over the pillow.

The cunning woman sat down. "Ah, Mary," she said, her smile rearranging the web of lines on her face. "I shall ne'er forget the day ye was born. The wind blew soft and warm—'twas more like spring than the dark of winter—a harbinger, my child."

Mary came nearer, leaning close to gaze into the deep-set eyes. "Pray, what's a har-har-bin-ger?"

"A harbinger is an omen, a portent. When a babe is born on a rare day in winter 'tis a sign of good fortune. Why, ye shall be exceeding rich someday!"

Mary sat down at the old woman's feet, more interested in her own infancy than the nebulous future. "Was I very small?"

"Nay, ye was a lusty child, pink and fair as a rose, with the same great eyes I see looking at me now. Ye was born at twilight and came without a whimper. Quiet as a mouse—staring at me with those eyes—'twas a look I'll ne'er forget. In all my days I have ne'er seen such a look from a newborn."

Mary climbed onto the old woman's lap. "Show me! Let me see how I looked!"

"Cry you mercy, I cannot make such a face, but I'll tell you what that face said to me. 'This world is not what it ought to be!' And then ye began to wail, and from what yer mother tells me, ye hath hardly stopped wailing since!"

Mary laughed and took the cunning woman's hand. "When will Mother's new babe come?"

"In spring, if God wills."

"Did God will that her other babes die?"

"God wills all things, child. Fear not, your parents are still young, and 'tis my belief they'll have numerous more childer."

Mary looked at the old woman's knobby hand, preparing to count all the children on her fingers. "First came Tom and then Nathaniel."

"Tom was the child of yer father's first wife, who died giving birth to him. And then yer own mother had Nathaniel before she carried two babes dead in her womb. That's why they are over-thankful for ye. Perchance that's why they've spoiled ye something dreadful."

With one finger, Mary traced the knotted veins on the back of the old woman's hand. "Am I very spoiled, Grandmother?"

"Aye, but yer days as a princess are numbered. Two years after ye were born came Lawrence, and two years after him, this child. God will give ye little brothers and sisters to teach ye to be kind to them who's weaker and smaller."

"I don't love Lawrence, you know. He's very tiresome."

"Of course, you do. 'Tis wicked to say that, Mary." At the sound of horses approaching, a shadow passed over the cunning woman's face. She lifted Mary off her lap and hastened to the window. "I must away."

Mary ran to her side and gripped her hand. "Don't leave us."

"Yer mother sent for me, Mary, but there be those in this house who'd rather she sent for the doctor."

"I hate the doctor. He put a knife in my tongue to make it bleed."

The old woman bent low and kissed Mary's cheek. "Listen to me, child." She sprinkled more of the dried leaves into the empty cup and poured hot water over them. "When yer mother stirs, give her this to drink. Now stay by her side till she wakes." Quickly, she gathered up her basket and was gone.

The child set the cup carefully on the table and climbed onto the bed, resting her head on her mother's breast, quite aware that she was responsible for her well-being.

Later, when Margaret stirred, Mary sat up, glad to see that her pain had passed.

"Ah, child, how quickly I am restored. Why aren't you in the nursery?" Margaret threw back the covers. "I feel so much better—I must see to your father's supper."

"Nay, Mother, lie still. The cunning woman said so. Now drink of this cup and go back to sleep." Margaret obeyed Mary's childish command.

When springtime came, she gave birth to a nine-months' baby girl. The baby's father named her Hannah and blessed her with words from the Bible:

"And Hannah prayed, and said, my heart rejoiceth in the Lord."

MANY A TIME Mary had heard her kinsmen talk about wicked King Charles, debating among themselves the best way to pursue their Separatist cause. With scowls and angry voices, they described his cruelty, his hand of iron, his arrogance, his greed. The child didn't understand all that was said, but she knew that a great upheaval brewed in the land, and that the King hated men like her father. Men who desired to worship God without ritual, papist icons, or heathen feast days. And she knew that her father hated both the King and the Pope.

One night, after all the little ones were tucked into their beds, Margaret Bliss joined her husband and his kinsmen around the fireplace in the great hall. She allowed Mary to sit up for a while with the family as they settled in, surrounded by well-polished old furniture in the shadows along the paneled walls. They were glad of a fire, for a light rain fell outside, chilling the old stone house. Margaret had Mary sit between herself and her husband Thomas, who puffed thoughtfully at his clay pipe.

Thomas's face was sad. He shook his head, his heart seeming burdened.

"I know not—indeed, no man knows—how long we shall be allowed to remain here in peace. Others have left for Holland or New England rather than pay taxes to replenish the King's coffers and keep his French whore in lace and rubies. How long can we endure?"

Mary had never seen her good-natured father so troubled.

8

Feeling anxious, she moved onto her mother's lap, eager to understand why he thought they should have to leave home.

Her Uncle Jonathan spoke. "Neither the King nor the Archbishop has molested anyone here." Mary liked the sound of that.

Her mother stiffened. "'Tis not as if you are a minister of God, Thomas. Why should they trouble you? Here we live in peace with all our neighbors, whether or no they worship with us or in the King's church. None of the village folk will betray us, and you must admit that their minister, Mister Kittredge, has been kind."

What her uncle and her mother had said reassured the child. If only her father would not look so troubled.

Shadows from the firelight carved Thomas's face into a mask of sadness. "Things are getting worse. We are not prospering here like the old days."

Margaret drew her daughter close. "Those who have fled the country for Holland find their children forced to speak a foreign tongue and learn strange customs from the Dutch. I cannot suppose that you'd subject your family to that, nor menace us with wolves and savages at Plymouth or Boston. By what law— what right—may they force you from the land of your ancestors?"

Gleams of firelight lit her father's red beard as if it were ablaze, and his laugh, when it came, was bitter.

"The King and old Beelzebub of Canterbury make their own law. Damn them to Hell! I cannot live in a country where a man who does not swill his life away in drink, nor waste his time at playhouses, who works hard and abides by every Sabbath, is mocked with a sneer and called Puritan. Here folk think I am over-nice or suffer from melancholy humors."

Suddenly he stood up with his face to the fire and raised a fisted arm to shout, "I'll join them who march on London!"

Only the crackling of the fire echoed his declaration. Mary's Grandfather Thomas slowly closed his Bible. He was a man of eighty, bearded like his sons, with a face as wizened as wood left too long in the weather. Mary feared that his long silence and pained expression foretold argument between father and son, but her mother spoke instead.

"Ah, Father, tell him he is foolhardy! He cannot challenge the King. You, who are beyond youthful passions, know this is true. You are wise enough to see he must not tear us from our home."

Old Father Thomas ceased the thoughtful stroking of his white beard and crossed his arms over his broad chest. "We hath lived on this land since before the Normans did come. Here, where Bliss House was built more than three hundred year ago, we was once counted among the gentry. Since those days long past, our fortunes hath diminished. Now it is not so easy to put victuals on the table and coin in our coffers by keeping our sheep and thanking God for his goodness. As weavers and husbandmen we do not prosper here now. Inasmuch as the King hath abolished Parliament and our vote, we can no longer sit dumbly by. The time hath come for my sons to go to the New World. I shall not go with you, for I am too old for so great an adventure."

Mary's mother looked astonished, indeed frightened by the old man's words, while her father threw another log on the fire. As the coals tumbled over the hearth, the younger Thomas spoke.

"How shall we and our brothers in Christ counter the King's latest insult? William Prynne—how shall the King answer for what he did to Prynne?"

"Who is William Prynne?" Mary said. "And what has the wicked old King done to him?"

Thomas stared into the fire. "Put him in the pillory, then in the jail—but that satisfied him not—so he had the wretched man's ears off."

Mary shuddered and clung to her mother's neck.

"Aye, child, for speaking truth," her grandfather said. "Prynne took it on himself to write a book—most grievous to the King, it was. Therein he spoke plainly and in no pretty way about the Queen, who is French and a Catholic. Prynne rightly decried this ungodly union, for their heir—who will one day be our King—is sure to be a Papist."

"You'll give the child another nightmare." Margaret stood up, taking Mary by the hand. "Come, Mary, 'tis time for bed." She stepped toward the door, then stopped and looked to the men.

"How's a child to understand such things when these afflictions born of men's actions are fearsome to me? Why has the whole world gone utterly mad over religion?"

Thomas smiled. "You, my wife, are not worldly, nor should you be. England, Scotland, France—indeed the whole world—has been just so embroiled for a hundred years."

"Is the faith of the saints the one true religion? If only one faith can be right, then must it follow all the others are wrong? Yet just as we believe we are right, the Catholics and the folks who worship in the King's church believe their faiths to be true." Margaret pulled Mary toward the door.

Mary had a parting word. "I'm glad that poor, poor man wrote that book," she said. "It serves the King right!"

ON THE LAST night she would ever rest in Painswick Parish, Mary lay awake in the nursery listening to her mother's muffled sobs echo down the corridor from the Great Hall. Her parents were at work, hastily packing the last of their belongings. Her father's impatient voice came to the child's ear mingled with sounds of her mother's sorrow. Thomas had suffered enough from his wife's woe. His fortune was in ruin and he had taken as much grief as he could stand. He wanted to start over in New England. His wife wished to remain, to believe that they and the other Separatists could live free at home. She loved her large house and the help of servants. Thomas, on the other hand, saw the whole business as a blessing in disguise. They would sail to the New World, where he could live among other Saints, have plenty of land, and more easily remake his fortune.

They had already decided which of the possessions left to them would make the long journey to New England: one old chest large enough to carry clothes, linens, and other small items too numerous to fit in the family trunk; kitchen things like pots, pans, a kettle, and a churn. Their only concession to luxury would be Margaret's greatest treasure, the great carved bedstead. They would take a cow to be kept for the new farm, and chickens and rabbits to be butchered and eaten on board the ship during the long journey. Thomas had enough money for their passage and a nest egg to be used upon their arrival.

Out of the whole awful business Mary could fix on only one good thing—her longing for a first glimpse of the sea. From her little bed she listened to her parents quarrel. She welcomed the comforting blanket of violet light from the evening sky and a large cool-white moon which shone in at her window. She wondered what would become of her family. Would they survive the voyage to New England? And if they survived, how long would it take her father to make his fortune and build a fine new house?

"O Lord," she prayed. "If it is Thy will, protect us from drowning at sea. Protect us from sea monsters, the savages, the wolves, the snakes in New England."

The child wept, the full moon's buoyant light glittering through her tears. Not until the moon had risen high above Bliss House did she finally fall asleep. She dreamt of a house waiting for her family in Boston, a fine large house high on a cliff overlooking the windswept sea. She saw it, the beautiful sea, like millions of green rivers coursing around the great gray rocks that were the foundation of her father's house. The rivers of the sea flowed like the wavy locks of her mother's hair, and she heard the sound of women wailing. The wailing came again and again, rising to a great horrid pitch so loud that Mary sat up in her bed. She put her small feet on the nursery floor and fled the room. Through the hall and the kitchen, into the garden she hurried in her sleep, disappearing into the grasses and sedges down the cleave.

THE TAWNY OWL hunting leverets by the light of the full moon swooped above a white-gowned child standing alone on a stone bridge spanning a little stream. His silent passage went unnoticed by the somnambulant child. The night sky was clear, no wind roused the willows or the hollies, nothing stirred in the silkwoods where the lizards, cuckoos, badgers and adders slept hidden away from the owl's sharp talons. Soaring high over Bliss House, he headed for the open meadow.

· · · · ·

When she awoke, Mary found herself alone in the dark, sitting on the rutted road where her bare feet had slipped and she had fallen. She tried to collect herself, wondering what great hand had plucked her from her bed and set her down out of doors under the full moon. She remembered nothing, but she knew that in her sleep she had walked farther from her father's house than she had ever walked alone. Drawn by the thrill of adventure and the taste of freedom, she brushed herself off and continued on through the granite gateway, across the stile, through the thicket to the millpond that ran to deep pools swimming with trout now hidden under the dark water.

At last she stood on an ancient stone bridge looking up at the Beacon, smooth and round as a loaf of risen dough. "O night! I am moonblind!" she called, her small voice echoing down the cleave. The moon will light my way to the top, she thought, remembering the old story about the Nine Maidens and the ring of stones she would find there.

Mary hurried off, surprised at how strong she felt climbing the steep hill. Passing quickly over the grassy expanse, she found a gate in the stone wall built long ago to keep sheep out of the village. Mary opened the gate, then turned to look back across the cleave. Bliss House clung to the hillside, shining white in the moonlight like something from a dream. For the rest of her life she would remember this scene. Mary trembled, knowing that Bliss House had been taken from them.

The Beacon rose above her, a blue arc under a perfectly round white disc of moon. Feeling its pull, she slowly began her ascent, taking each step carefully, wanting to remember every moment just as it came: to savor the prickle of grass on the soles of her bare feet, the sight of the sky opening up above her, the gentle breath of wind that filled her shift, tingling her all over with goose bumps. She traversed the hill in what seemed like a moment, but at the top she looked back, amazed to see how high she had climbed. Looking ahead, she saw the gradual slope ending at the ragged edge of the ancient hill fort.

Again Mary thought about the story of the Nine Maidens and

began her search for the ring of stones. She remembered her nurse's words: "But it is true that, even today, under the full moon the stones up on the common come to life, and the Maidens dance once more."

Here there were no trees, nothing to obscure her view except for waist-high clumps of wildflowers and gorse, casting weird bent shadows over the grassy hill. Mary looked out to the valley below, an endless range of rolling hills and meadows, blue on blue under the night sky. Never before was there a night like this, she thought. With the moon at her back she could see millions of stars hanging close enough to pick like the cherries her mother let her harvest in June. No birds called, no breeze blew.

"What a sound is silence," she said aloud, her voice as alien as the little whirlwind that suddenly spun around her. She wanted to think about what it all meant, that quiet bottomless song sung under the stars. Was it the sound of God's dreaming? The stars blinked overhead like shimmering white sheep grazing on a heavenly meadow. She spun around herself, and the moon reeled in the sky, making her shiver as a cold wind whistled and whined through stiff twigs of gorse like whispers, like women beside their winter fires. Mary could not be sure if the night played tricks with her wits. As fast as it had come, the wind died away, then moments later came again with a new fury.

My bed is warm, she thought. How vexed Mother would be if she knew I was here. What's more, even in all this light I cannot see the ring of stones. Nurse must have made up the story. Maybe it's a lie. Mary turned away, retracing her steps back over the hill. She disliked the feel of the wind as it came and went, like a giant bellows huffing and puffing. Nor did she like the sound it made whistling, whispering.

She ran across the common, emerging breathless from behind a large clump of gorse to find herself at the edge of a wide open circle, smooth and bare like a little plain. In its center rose a perfect ring of stones of varying heights, most knee high, others low, smooth and round, but three as tall as grown women standing like ruined pillars washed in moonlight.

She did not move, nor could she breathe as she counted the

stones. There were nine, just as in the story her nurse had told. How I wish they would come to life, Mary thought, chilled as the wind came up again. Dare I go nearer? Then, on the wind came the sound of women praying, and the three tall stones slowly began to move. Mary ducked behind a clump of gorse, remembering the evil priest in the story. He had hidden and watched the maidens dance under the moon. He had been a sanctimonious rogue, overcome with jealousy.

"Faster and faster they twirled," Nurse Bodwin had said, "laughing and singing unto the harvest moon because, come winter, they would not hunger. But the priest was blind and saw nothing sacred—only wanton abandon and a joy he could not feel. In an instant, his heart overflowed with malice and hardened to stone. His soul cried out, 'Plague of God rot them!' In an instant the moon passed from view and the wind began to wail. Afeard of all that he had wrought, the priest ran away, his curse having turned the maidens to stone."

Mary watched as the maidens bowed toward the middle, then, moving to the center, they took each other's hands and began to sing and dance the ring. Their voices came low at first, clear and sweet as maidens' voices, but their dance was sad and slow, not wild and joyous like the harvest dance the priest had cursed. These maidens' clothes were not spun of silver satin, but of coarse cloth, dark like the hooded cloaks of winter. Their skirts swept the ground as they danced, yet Mary could not see their faces, for the hoods were drawn close about their heads as the song came and went on the breeze. She crept nearer, close enough to hear.

> The sun, the soul
> The moon, the spirit
> The body, the stone.
> Man is blind. He cannot see
> the river that springs from
> the foot of the tree.

The song was repeated again as they danced round the

15

ring. When the dance ended, the maidens bowed to one another, removing their hoods in unison as if this simple act had meaning, as if they had bared their heads to one another for hundreds of years in rituals hidden from the sight of men. Mary moved closer. Moonlight struck the dancers' faces, and she could see that each had a head of long, snowy-white hair, undone and loosed wild in the wind. Each had a face engraved by the ages, sunken mouths, faded eyes.

Mary pulled back into the shadows, then turned and ran toward home. The maidens had passed from the world, she thought. None were left to give thanks under the harvest moon, only darkly cloaked old crones who kept the rituals their great-grandmother's grandmother had taught them.

II

. . . if any come hither to plant for worldly ends that can live well at home, he commits an error, of which he will soon repent. But if (he comes) for spiritual reasons . . . he may well find here what will content him . . .

—Thomas Dudley (1576–1653)

Boston, Massachusetts Bay Colony

FROM THE TOP of the fort on the southernmost hill, Thomas Bliss looked out over Boston to the harbor where three years before they had disembarked from the ship *Regard* after a long sea voyage. Below him sprawled a bustling new town with winding cobblestone streets. Bound on two sides by water, a small bay to the south, and a river to the north, Boston was being built on several hills. At the top of a hill to the north, he could see the windmill tilting the breeze. He squinted through the chill air, hoping to count the forested islands floating in the bay, where men cut timber for lumber and firewood.

Land was already scarce, yet every day more pilgrims came. For his taste, Boston was overcrowded, becoming a center for government, shipping and trade. He had only been able to find five acres at Boston Mount. Furthermore, few meadows were left for grazing and the forests had already been cleared. He wondered how long it would be before those islands, too, were stripped bare of trees.

Disheartened, Thomas climbed down from the tower. He had gone there to think—away from the sight of his pregnant wife and disappointed children, huddled together beside the fire burning in his poor house. He mumbled to himself, despising himself, wishing he had never set eyes on Boston. "Because of me and my foolish dream, they dwell no better than poor country folk."

He shivered from the cold as he picked his way over frozen ruts in the muddy roadway. It was time to think of spring. How—what—would he plant? What little barley seed he had was the wrong kind. Fearing he could not survive another season here, he hunched his back and pulled his cloak tight against the frigid air. Thomas was a sheep farmer and weaver, like generations of Blisses before him who had raised wool and mutton in Painswick Parish.

He could not stop berating himself. What a fool I was to think I could make a profit raising barley, the only crop worth growing on so small a plot of land. My fields have grown lush with grasses and tares. The irony evoked bitter laughter, for Thomas was alone on the road with no one to hear. I have no choice. My nest egg is nearly gone. I must write to my sister Elizabeth at Exeter. She will send funds. We must go to Connecticut. There was no other help, for both his brother Jonathan and his father had gone to their graves.

SENT AWAY FROM the warm house to collect kindling for the fire, Mary and her brother Lawrence scattered over the yard toward the edge of the woodlot, picking up sticks and small dead branches blown down from the trees. Her hunger pangs nearly constant, the child was glad of only one thing—on such populous land folks were not troubled with rattlesnakes, wolves or bears. And as for Indians, she had seen very few. Her arms nearly full of kindling, Mary stood by as her little brother hurried along, stumbling over the frozen ground, trying to keep up with her.

"Take bigger steps, brother, for everything in this land is great in size. The natives are taller and broader than Englishmen."

"Nay, I say they are not."

"Aye, 'tis true, and so are the trees. I never saw trees so tall in England."

Lawrence looked ready for an argument. "Houses in England are greater than here."

They were almost at their father's one-room house, set in a bare muddy yard, when Mary answered. "Aye, 'tis certain, that, for in England poor folks live in houses like this."

She threw her kindling in a pile by the door. "At home we had great rooms filled with fine things. This little house is crowded, though we brought very little—just the great bedstead, little else. We have more children than anything."

Her brother's brown eyes were wide with concern. "Are we poor, Mary?"

"Nay," Mary said, for she believed that though they lived crowded into one small room, miserable and homesick, their condition was temporary. "We are not poor. When we move to Connecticut, Father will build us a fine house and he will make a great fortune."

From the door of the small hut Margaret called to her children. "Mary! Time to do the milking." With five children and another on the way, she needed all the help she could get from her eldest daughter.

At Bliss House, where they'd had half a dozen cows, Mary had watched her aunt milk, but no one had thought to teach her. It was different in the New World. Soon after they settled at Boston Mount, Margaret had taught Mary how to milk Cherry, the family's young Devon, so that afterward, morning and evening, in rain, snow, sleet or fog, the girl went to Cherry who waited in her lean-to, eager to be relieved of her milk. Now every morning at dawn she rolled off the straw pallet where she slept with Hannah and tucked the covers up over her little sister, careful not to wake her. Half asleep, she squatted over the chamber pot, then pulled on her stockings and several petticoats over her shift—how many depended upon the weather. Then came her yellow waistcoat and a white apron. Still yawning, she carelessly gathered her tangled red curls under a coif, put on her boots and tied them. At home I was never forced to go out in the cold, she thought, as she pulled her cloak around her and hurried through the snow to the cowshed.

After Mary had squeezed every last drop she could from the docile cow, she still had her part of the dairying to do. As her brothers rolled up their straw pallets and stacked them in the corner, Mary strained the milk through a fine linen cloth into the earthenware vessel she had washed, scalded and left to sweeten outdoors in the sun. She covered it with an oiled cloth and tied it with twine.

Margaret commended her daughter. "Now that you are skilled at milking and most of the dairying, when we get to Connecticut I shall teach you how to plant and tend a garden."

How miserable it is here, Mary thought to herself as she carried the milk to the cool, dark chest her father had built on the north side of the house, where it could be stored up to four days. Mary was still too young to churn butter or make cheese; Margaret did it herself when she had time or did without. All the same, she made young Mary watch and learn, preparing her for the day when she would have a woman's strength.

ON THE FIRST night after the new baby was born, everyone slept but Mary. Margaret lay cupped in the curve of her husband's body with the babe snuggled near her breasts. All three of her sons, worn out by hard work on meager victuals, slept nearby on the floor. But Mary was awake, watching embers from the fire glow in the dark. Her sister Hannah nestled against her back. She was unable to calm herself after the day's excitement—seeing the baby come.

Though she hadn't been allowed to watch, she was often close by, for she had been asked to help the four goodwives who assisted throughout Margaret's travail. She was given small tasks, finding the baby linens in the old chest, laying them by the fire to warm, serving cider to the women who had come for the birth. She'd seen lambs born, and kittens, but never a child, and was glad she had closed her eyes at the actual crowning of the head.

Her mother's pain had been a sore thing to see, and afterward when Mary was in tears Margaret had taken her by the hand to reassure her.

"Mary, my child, 'tis but a little pain given for a profound blessing from God. Go now, and hold your little brother, know this blessing for yourself."

Mary had lifted the infant into her arms, feeling his warm weight against her chest. On shaking legs she had carried him to the chair by the fire, where she rocked him and calmed his tears. She knew how to hold him, to support his head, how to keep him warm. She watched his lips quiver around his toothless mouth. I remember when I was a babe in my mother's arms, she had mused. She was sure of it. Her heart replete with love, she asked, "May I name him, Mother? We don't have a John."

"'Tis your father's place to name the child, Mary, but you may ask him. I like well enough the name John."

Mary had worked hard all day and was still hungry. Though she was tired and wanted to sleep, her excitement kept her awake. Her father had let her name the baby. And something else was keeping her wakeful, too. She did not want to know for certain if the warm dampness spreading under and around her meant that Hannah had wet the bed, though it would not be the first time.

FAR NORTH OF Boston, in the mists of a boreal forest, a sweet-water spring seeped from the hills into a bog of floating mosses. The first rays of morning sun spilled over the quagmire, lighting a small lake where great antlered moose grazed on the buds of pond lilies. On the murky shore, blackbirds swayed on tall reeds, and insect-devouring plants waited open-mouthed for their prey. Overflow from the lake flowed in a stream downhill toward a pond where a V spread on the glassy water in a beaver's wake, and a gray owl headed to his rest. When winter and spring had come and gone, the snow melted. The stream gathered and tumbled downhill until it grew into a river. Flowing south through more lakes, it collected and expanded into the wide Quinnehtukgut—"long tidal river" in Algonquian. More than four hundred miles the river snaked, finally reaching the fertile valley and forested homeland of Nipmucks, Pequots, Mohegans and Niantics. Through their lands, the river surged toward Saybrook, Long Island Sound and the ocean.

Having put their trust in God, a hundred somberly clad men, women, and children headed into this wilderness on an ancient Indian trail. Carrying no food, they drove 160 head of cattle west through the forest toward the Connecticut River. The milk from their cows and the daily hunt would sustain them. They had come from the Massachusetts Bay Colony, followers of a minister, Mister Thomas Hooker, who walked among them singing psalms. His presence comforted these wary people. The forest was a shadowy unexplored territory where wild animals and savages abounded.

But the Saints, as they were known among themselves, drew reassurance from Hooker's confidence that the journey was safe enough for his own family. While most wives walked, infirm Susanna Hooker rode in a horse litter. The Hookers' children were among the travelers, four daughters and a three-year-old son. On this long walk, which would take at least a fortnight, these sojourners would never be overwhelmed by fear, for they believed God walked with them.

Thomas Hooker was in his late middle years, a commanding presence in his dark beaver hat and cloak, his white ruffed collar signaling that he was of a higher class than most of his followers. His eyes were a gentle blue, and he wore a handsome moustache and short-cropped beard salted with white. His was a profoundly intelligent, compassionate face, unblemished by evil emotions. Responsible for all the people in his care, Hooker understood the risk and believed their travels worth it. They would all find greater freedom on the Connecticut River than in the Bay Colony.

Hooker's unfailing energy had surprised even himself. His little band had been walking now for twelve days, and though he was not a young man, he felt like a youth moving among his people, encouraging them forward, his eyes alert as an eagle's. His heart beat fast, not from overexertion but in anticipation for the adventure at hand. These last years had not been easy for the preacher.

He'd had to part company with his friends John Winthrop and John Cotton after sailing with them to the New World in 1633. He'd lost the battle with his fellow divine John Cotton, who wanted to found a colony where suffrage would be allowed only for men in good standing in the church. Hooker had argued that every land-owning man should be allowed to vote, whether or not he covenanted with the church. His own experience in England had taught him that blending of church and state led to oppression.

The minister's mind burned with a passion for the new colony he and his followers would create, a colony most like God's kingdom on earth. As they built a plantation religious—not a plantation of trade like Boston—they would live in love and peace with their neighbors and become an example of true reformation for all of Europe to see.

Thomas Bliss and his wife Margaret, who carried his sleeping infant son, were among these pilgrims heading into the unknown. Their sons Tom, Nathaniel, and Lawrence, and daughters Mary and Hannah walked beside them. Thomas had grown used to upheaval, yet with every change, every new disappointment, he heard his wife sigh and saw her wring her hands as she struggled to keep her thoughts from becoming hot coals in her mouth.

"Where will you move us next, Thomas? I pray to the God of all good that you shall live in Connecticut in peace with yourself."

He watched helplessly as Margaret toiled along the narrow trail like a hen trying to keep her brood in hand. The strain of their long sea voyage followed by disastrous failure in Boston had caused the whole family pain. Yet, optimistic still, Thomas believed that the frontier would provide them with plenty of good land and a new beginning. He felt blessed to follow Mister Hooker, the most famous English preacher to come to New England. Back in Painswick they had lived a good three-day ride from Chelmsford, where Hooker had preached, but even in the hinterlands they had heard of him. His Separatist preaching had electrified the English countryside, winning converts by the thousands. Thomas Bliss had followed the news of his trials with Archbishop Laud, who would not let Hooker rest. Thomas knew of Hooker's near-arrests, his months in hiding, his escape to Holland. A copy of Hooker's book *The Poor Doubting Christian Drawn unto Christ* was tucked in among his own things.

Late in the day, three-year-old Hannah, cold and tired of walking, insisted that someone carry her. Tom, Nat and Lawrence were already carrying heavy burdens, and Margaret had the baby to look after.

"Mary, you carry her awhile," her mother said.

Mary was glad they'd left Boston Mount, and with a joyful heart she had helped her parents to pack for their long trek west. Handing her own bundle to her brother Tom, she lifted the child into her arms, knowing that she would not be able to carry her very far. Little Hannah rested her head on her big sister's shoulder and snuggled into her neck.

"Listen well, Hannah," Mary whispered, "you must do your part. We are walking to a new land where Father will build a house like the one we had at home—nay, even grander. There we will live in exceeding joy. You do want to get there soon—I know you do."

"Aye," Hannah whimpered, "but the way is rough, and I am small."

"Even small children can be brave if they truly want." Mary kissed the little girl's cheek. "Now, I shall carry you for two long minutes, and then I shall put you down. So rest yourself while you can, then walk beside me. I shall hold your hand."

Hannah's small body went limp as Mary hummed a lullaby, wondering where she got her strength. Dusk was approaching, and they had been on the stony, root-tangled trail since early morning. Mary's head filled with visions of the new land as her heart swelled with love for the sweet bundle she carried. She walked on, unaware that she had fallen behind.

As the sun fell behind the hills a tall figure appeared at Mary's side, and she heard a deep voice. "Let me carry your sister." She looked up at the man towering beside her. Gently, he took the sleeping child from her arms and settled her on his chest. On his head he wore a dark beaver hat, and under its brim his clear blue eyes smiled down on her.

"Mister Hooker, I do thank you. You must have known I was growing tired." As he nodded, she took his hand and picked up her pace, keeping stride with the great man.

"Soon you shall rest," he said. "All of us, too. The forward men have found a suitable campsite."

Night came to the forest, and the company of pilgrims settled down beside a stream. They built a dozen fires for protection from wild animals and assigned watchers to tend them through the night. Men took turns sleeping and watching over the cattle and the camp. Half a moon was barely visible through the trees, and when all human voices finally fell quiet, the only sounds were those heard since the beginning of time: the flutter of wind rustling the canopy, the trickle of water over the streambed, the crunch of deer hooves in the leaf litter, the bone-chilling howl of wolves.

All the children were asleep, but Margaret lay awake listening to the sounds of the night. Even with her husband's arms around her she could find no comfort. A stone dug into her hip, a twig stabbed her shoulder. Already weary of the New World, she gave thanks nevertheless that their small party would not be alone on the frontier. In 1633 the English had settled Windsor along the great river. The same year, the Dutch had built a fur-trading post at the junction of the Connecticut and Little rivers, and in 1634 more English had settled Wethersfield.

Men from Hooker's congregation had ventured ahead of the rest to make the beginnings of a town across the river from the Dutch fort. Margaret would not allow herself to consider the fact that these few Englishmen—hardly a handful—would share the territory with thousands of Pequots and Mohegans.

THOUGH MOST OF the people and livestock came to the frontier on foot, most everyone's household belongings, including Thomas Bliss's bedstead and loom, came up the river by ship. Those who arrived the year before had built small one-room log houses with thatched roofs. Of those who came later, some had used bent saplings to build English wigwams around a stone fire-place, covered in bark and walled with reeds. Margaret Bliss had already told her children that the house their father was building was a temporary shelter. It would keep them warm during their first winter on the frontier, so they had best not grumble about how it looked or how small it was, only thank the Lord that they would not freeze to death come winter.

"Your father will build a real house when spring comes," she reassured Mary, "like the ones you see in the village—or bigger." Inwardly, she felt sorry for her children. Outwardly, she had to show strength and expected them to do the same.

"But 'tis no more than a fruit cellar!" Mary complained, as she watched her father and brothers hoist seven-foot logs into position. They had already excavated one side of a little hill and were bracing what would be the back wall of the house.

"Next year's cellar, Mary. But first it will be our home. Come winter you'll be warmer than you'd be in a tent or one of those foolish wigwams. Now get yourself down to Little River and fetch me some water."

"I hate it! How can you ask me to sleep in a hole?" Mary jerked the yoke and two leather buckets onto her shoulders and stomped barefoot down the road toward the river. Witness to her daughter's fierce anger, Margaret knew it was directed at her. She wants me to feel sorry for her—and I do. The poor child is hungry and disappointed. Indeed, are we not all so?

Mary headed down the road cursing her life. "Like moles in a dirty hole, we shall dwell—no windows—only a fire-pit with a hole in the roof."

The three years since their arrival in the New World had been unspeakably hard, but her father had promised they would do better at Hartford. He was full of hope again and ready to joke about the whole experience.

"God created the earth in seven days, but it took me fourteen days to move one man, one woman, four sons, two daughters, one sow, one cow, and four sheep to Hartford."

Mary had to put her trust in her father—the one she loved most. Other fathers beat their children, but Thomas was kind and patient. He disciplined with gentle reprimands or long speeches, liberally sprinkled with passages from the Bible meant to teach his children and put them on the narrow path. Mary had overheard her mother say that his soft heart would ruin every one of his children.

Across the road, she saw the Bartletts' house and beyond it the Richards' closed in by dense woodland. She longed for the open windswept fields and green hills of Painswick, where the sky was wide and open. Past these houses, the cart-way cut through the forest. Shivering, she walked faster, imagining Indians hiding in the underbrush. She'd heard how a brave would tie branches on his body to be taken for a bush, how they lay in wait for children, how they stole away English women and made them slaves. Yet only a few of these great swarthy men had ever crossed her path.

The English called the Indians around Hartford the Podunk people. They spoke an Algonquian dialect and for the most part stayed to themselves, only occasionally venturing down English cart-ways or into the village. But Mary had got a good look at natives on the streets of Boston. She'd never seen such tall men with straight backs and even darker skins than the Spaniard her father had pointed out. Unlike Englishmen, whose heads were blond or red, brown or black, with eyes of various colors, all natives had black hair and black eyes, high foreheads, and well-oiled skins glistening with the fat of bears. She wondered how the children could tell which man was their father and which woman their mother. She'd heard they lived in mean little houses made of sticks, wore skins, ate only one meal a day. Until they'd tasted English beer and spirits, they drank nothing but water. She had asked her father many questions. Why are they so tall and lusty with healthful bodies, and though they be fifty years old the hair on their heads is not gray? Why do the women labor long hours while the men go hunting?

"The savages are not weakened by hours of labor like we English, nor do they abuse their health," he said. "'Tis a shameless thing—men sporting through the woods hunting deer while their women labor clearing and planting fields."

She was glad when she reached Little River, which wound its way through the forest and meadows from the west. The smaller river emptied into the great river at the south end of the village, near where the Podunks had their summer lodges. The Indians used Little River for bathing and fishing, while in separate reaches English women scrubbed their clothes and collected water, though none of them bathed. Taking a bath, exposing one's skin to the elements, could cause illness except under certain careful conditions.

At the river Mary wiped the sweat from her brow, kilted up her skirt and petticoats by her apron strings, and knelt by the water's edge. She scooped water into cupped hands and drank thirstily, as a delicious chill hit the bottom of her empty stomach. Gulping ravenously, she quenched her hunger and washed her face in the river. Then she pulled off her boots and with the yoke on her shoulders waded in. Along this stretch, the river's edge was gentle. She moved easily through the current, carrying her burden, her bare toes grasping the slippery rocks. Water coursed around her calves as she filled her buckets and struggled back to shore.

The leather buckets were heavy, but Mary was growing tall like her father and strong for her age. She put her boots on and adjusted her clothes before starting a slow walk back, hating every step of the way, stopping often to adjust her burden, knowing she would have to return to the river before dark. Her family would soon use up all the water she carried. She prayed for the day when her father would dig a well.

III

These Indians being strangers to arts and sciences, and being unacquainted with the inventions that are common to a civilized people, are ravished with admiration at the first view of any such sight. They took the first ship they saw for a walking island, the mast to be a tree, the sail white clouds, and the discharge of ordnance for lightening and thunder, which did much trouble them, but this thunder being over and this moving island steadied by an anchor, they manned out their canoes to go and find strawberries there.

—William Wood
New England's Prospect, 1635

A SMALL BARK ON a trading mission bound for Long Island sailed into the Sound. Choppy waters glistened in the sun as a fair wind from the north sent her speedily toward her destination. Captain John Gallop and his crew of three had sailed from Boston bearing trading cloth and iron pots, hoping to exchange them for the Montauks' furs. A sudden change of wind from the west sent the bark off course toward Block Island, where the captain spied a pinnace anchored about two miles offshore. The ship looked familiar. It belonged to a man he knew, John Oldham, a fur trader out of his fort at Wethersfield on the Connecticut River.

Signaling to Oldham's vessel, Gallop sailed closer, but as he approached the pinnace he was horrified to see its deck swarming with savages. He counted fourteen in all. Some hurried to set sail, as others paddled a canoe laden with trade goods toward the shore.

The only means of defense Captain Gallop had on board were two muskets and some duck shot. Fearing Oldham had been killed, he fired on the Indians, who scurried around on the deck hoping to escape. Though his firepower was wanting, Gallop kept firing as the pinnace lurched toward the island. The spattering of shot across the deck frightened the Indians into the hold.

With that, Gallop turned his bark to let the wind fill its sails, returning at full speed to ram the pinnace with a deafening thud. As Gallop's vessel nearly capsized Oldham's ship, wood collided with wood and a terrible screech rose above the rushing sounds of wind and sea. Six frightened Indians leapt overboard, and though they struggled mightily to swim ashore, all drowned.

Gallop stood off again, catching the wind, crashing once more into the pinnace. Sticking fast to her, his men pummeled the deck with duck shot. Breaking free, they sailed off again, rammed again, and fired on Oldham's little ship as four more Indians jumped into the sea to evade the gunfire. The captain and his men watched as one by one the savages sank under the waves.

Having counted the enemy, the captain now believed there were only four Indians left on board, so he and his men boarded the vessel. They had hardly set foot on the deck when two frightened English boys ran out to greet them. Oldham's young crewmen had hidden among the barrels of goods still on the quarter deck.

"Where is Oldham?" Gallop asked a tall, fair lad who looked barely old enough to shave.

The boy looked ashamed. "I cannot say. We hid ourselves when overrun by hostile Indians."

Another boy, a red-headed lad who looked only slightly older than his companion, stepped forward. "We are unarmed, sir, and could not aid our captain."

"Come, then, and help us look for him." Gallop beckoned to his men to join him and Oldham's young crew for a search. "Watch out—there be four Indians still hiding aboard."

Just two days before, young Joseph Parsons had boarded Oldham's ship at Wethersfield and signed on as an apprentice seaman. A year before, he had come alone to New England from Dorset, eager to make his fortune. Already he found himself in the midst of a great adventure. In sailing down the Connecticut and into the Sound, he had served like a man as he worked with Oldham's two Narragansett Indians and young Tom Bliss, the red-headed lad they'd picked up at Hartford. Young Bliss's father had given him permission to make a few trips with Oldham in the hope that he would soon earn a wage.

The two young men headed toward the quarter deck right behind Captain Gallop. When one of the hostile natives stuck his head out of the hatch for a look and came face to face with the captain's pistol, the Englishmen seized him, tied him up, and tossed him below. When a second surrendered, he too was tied up, but Gallop was afraid to put them together.

"They are clever," he told his men. "They know how to untie themselves and disappear and reappear at will. Take these savages and throw them into the sea!"

Upon a further search of the ship they came upon the bodies of the two Narragansetts who had sailed with Oldham, and then a trail of bloody footprints leading to a blood-smeared spot where John Oldham's warm corpse lay hidden under an old fishing net. He was naked, his head split open to the brain, his hands and legs cut through as if the Indians had been interrupted in dismembering him.

Gallop ordered his men to bury Oldham at sea, then once again search the ship. Finding that two Indians armed with hatchets had hidden themselves in a small compartment in the hold, the English feared they could not remove them without injury or loss of life. They loaded Oldham's sails and the remains of his cargo onto their bark, then tied on the pinnace and towed her east toward Boston.

Night approached on a brisk gale, and to keep from capsizing the bark they were forced to turn the pinnace loose. Wind and water would set her adrift toward the shores of Narragansett Bay.

More's the pity, thought Gallop, the Indians hiding below would soon have their freedom.

ONE EARLY AUTUMN evening after their meal, the Blisses built a fire outside in the yard where they had made a sitting circle from stumps and sawn logs. In good weather they liked to get out of their cellar and watch the sun slip behind the forest. This evening they had visitors, and Thomas had brought out a jug of cider to share. Their next neighbors, Robert Bartlett, his wife Ann, and their infant son Samuel, had joined their circle, helping the whole family to a light-hearted mood.

Tom Bliss and his new friend Joseph Parsons had returned to the village after an unscheduled trip to Boston with Captain Gallop. Since the village folks had made the boys objects of interest and curiosity, both had grown weary of questions about their adventures.

Frontier settlers were always eager for news, and on this night it was Goodman Bartlett who had some to relay. Bartlett had been among the first to come to Hartford.

"A reckoning's in store for us, I'll warrant," he said. "Soldiers have retaliated against the Block Island Indians for the murder of Captain Oldham."

Young Tom spoke up, impassioned. "He was a good man, a respected trader, and he did not deserve to die."

Margaret noticed her younger son wandering and called to him. "Lawrence, don't be a temptation to wolves. Get back to the fire." Like the rest, she wanted to hear all that Bartlett had to report.

Joseph said, "What have you heard about the fight?"

"Just yesterday I went to meet the supply ship and heard from Master Stone about the raid. The Bay Colony sent Captain Underhill and John Endecott and his army to attack Oldham's murderers. Stone said two ships sailed to the island, in the midst of a gale."

Younger than Thomas Bliss, Bartlett was a tall, burly man with intense dark eyes and a short-cropped beard. He had on the clothes he'd labored in all day, his long dark hair swept under a knitted cap. Though Mary was glad she wouldn't have to wash his filthy linen shirt, she found his conversation riveting.

"They reached the island just before night and tried to land in the storm. Able warriors—fifty or sixty—tall and straight as those trees at the edge of your woodlot, rose up from behind an embankment and showered them with arrows."

"Cry you mercy!" Mary said. "How many soldiers were killed?"

"Only one was stuck in the neck by an arrow that entered his flesh to a good depth," Bartlett said, "but Master Stone said he will live. Endecott himself was hit, 'twas his heavy cloak and armor saved him." He scanned all the faces around the circle intent on this news.

"Now, remember, our men were still in that furious sea. The shallops rolled and tossed so, those on board could not stand steady enough to take aim with their firearms. Forced into the surf, they waded to the beach where, with feet planted on solid ground, they finally fired their weapons. Bullets flew around and about the heathen, but they ran, laughing at the soldiers as they disappeared into the swamp."

Lawrence's eyes grew wide. "Why did they laugh?"

"Crafty devils they are," Bartlett said, "who fancy more than almost anything making fools of Englishmen."

Mary could scarcely sit still. "Let's be thankful they ran away, then, and no more suffered their arrows. I wish I could go into battle."

"Hush, Mary," Tom said. "Let Goodman Bartlett finish the tale."

"Now, as it was getting dark, Underhill's men and Endecott's moved a short distance inland, where they made camp for the night."

Mary hugged herself and shivered. "I'd be afraid to fall asleep in such a place."

"Aye, Mary," Bartlett said, "but they set up sentries and kept careful watch all night."

"Don't forget, child," came her father's gentle voice, "God was there to protect them."

"In the morning," Bartlett went on, "they searched the island

and found two Indian villages at some distance one from the other. There were about sixty wigwams, some very large, and hundreds of acres of corn, some already gathered and shucked, the rest standing ready to harvest. But the natives hid in the swamp, and none could be found in the villages.

"Next day, the soldiers tried to scare the Indians out of the swamp but still could not raise them. The soldiers, ordered to kill all the men and enslave the women and children, were enraged, as all they could do was burn the villages to the ground, kill stray dogs, and spoil the crops before leaving for Saybrook. "

"Mary, Lawrence—go to your beds." Margaret feared that her children had already heard enough to give them nightmares, nor did she approve such wanton waste, even if it was Indians who would starve. "And take Hannah with you."

Mary hadn't moved from her seat. "Oh, Mother, please let me hear what happened next."

Thomas was quick to support his wife. "You heard your mother."

Mary sulked off, pulling Lawrence by one hand and Hannah by the other. Inside their hovel she would put little Hannah to bed on a mat under the table. Lawrence would unroll his mat, which was standing upright beside the door. Mary would take off her petticoats and crawl in beside her sister, hoping Hannah would not wet the bed.

Once the children were out of earshot Bartlett went on. "Well, now, where did I leave off? Upon leaving the island, Endecott sailed for Fort Saybrook hoping to attack a nearby Pequot village, but those devils espied him as he came and escaped into the forest, so that all Endecott and his men could do was burn their village and their crops. Come winter, they'll starve." He didn't appear to regret it.

Thomas loaded his pipe. "Where's Endecott now?"

"They've sailed for Boston, wouldn't you know, abandoning all our river towns to a pack of angry wolves ready to surround and devour us."

Young Joseph Parsons fretted. "Those soldiers from the Bay

come down here for one reason—to kill Indians. They spoil their crops, then retreat to the safety of Boston, leaving us here to endure the Indians' revenge."

Thomas cast a fond look at his son's young friend. "Surely Gardener at Saybrook and Pynchon at Springfield can get the Bay Colony to send soldiers for our protection. You shall see Pynchon soon, Joseph, I'll warrant, and learn of his plans."

"Ha!" Joseph scoffed. "'Tis true I return to Springfield day after tomorrow, but Pynchon does not speak in confidence to me."

Bartlett was puzzled. "What is your connection to the great man?"

"A family friend, he helped me come here from Beaminster. It was he who got Oldham to take me on."

Margaret said, "Pray tell me, why all this trouble now?" She found the ways of all men, savage or civilized, confusing.

Thomas smiled at her. "Indeed, wife, how could you know? Now that the Dutch and we English have come among the Indians, the Mohegans and Narragansetts trade with us, while the Pequots trade with the Dutch. The Narragansetts liked it not that Oldham stepped out with the Pequots.

"And I heard another reason, given by Master Stone, though I don't know if it can be believed. He said that after the Indians came down with that plague of smallpox and so many died, they blamed Oldham for bringing it to their villages. The only Englishman ever to visit them, and they had no smallpox before he came."

After Thomas threw another log on the fire and passed the jug of cider around, the talk turned to local politics. New laws had been posted on the Meeting House door. Now every man must plant flax or hemp for the good of the town, and all were forbidden to entertain Quakers, Ranters, Adamites or other notorious heretics for more than a fortnight.

"Goodman Bartlett," Thomas said, with a chuckle, "have you ever known a heretic of any stripe?"

"None save our King, if such he be," Bartlett said with a chuckle of his own, knowing they had the sea between them.

Margaret and Ann huddled close, each glad for another

woman's company, quite aware how little knowledge they had of worldly things and thankful for it.

"Have you heard," Ann said to her neighbor, "Thomas Richards's wife, she who lives down the road toward the village, is with child, and they do say her travail is near. Do you feel settled enough to lend a neighborly hand?"

"Aye, of course I do. 'Tis no more than any of us would offer."

As Tom and Joseph headed off toward the cowshed to the nearby tent where they slept with Nathaniel, Tom asked his friend, "Will you live at the Pynchons' when you get back to Springfield?"

"For a while. I must find work again, and Pynchon will help. But, Tom, if there's war, I want to fight. How about you?"

"Aye, we shall be soldiers!"

VERY LATE, WHEN there was hardly a moon—just a thin silver slice drifting along in a universe of blinking stars—Mary stood alone in the middle of the cart-way, her white shift catching the breeze, her head lifted to the stars. Her eyes were open, but she did not see. The poor child was asleep.

IV

The Pequts heare of your preparations [for war] *and Comfort themselves in this . . . a witch amongst them will sinck the pinnaces by diving under water and making holes* [in their bottoms] *. . . as also that they shall now enrich themselves with store of guns but I hope their dreames (through the mercie of the Lord) shall vanish, and the Devill and his lying Sorceres shall be Confounded.*

—Roger Williams (1603–1683)
From a letter to Governor John Winthrop

A S WINTER APPROACHED the tiny village of Hartford, Thomas Hooker's flock prepared for the cold dormant season to come. Dwellings were finished and tightened against the weather; squash, turnips, cabbage, dried corn and beans were stored away in the rafters. On the way to their winter camp deep in the sheltered woods the Podunks stopped by the village with their surplus dried fish, a gift ensuring that none of the settlers would starve.

After the flaming scarlet and gold of autumn laid the trees bare, the vibrant green grasses turned brown. After the last of the geese flew, the river grew silent and white. Then the Blisses huddled together in their dark den like a family of hibernating bears. Under baskets of corn and beans hung from the rafters, they waited for the wind and snows to abate. Gifts of winter squash and dried peas were shared by their more established neighbors.

Some day, when they were able, they would repay every mouthful, for while often forgiven for years at a time, debts and kindnesses must be repaid.

For three months the family faced darkness and paralyzing cold. On the coldest days their fire did little more than cast bright shadows across the floor. Inside they had no privacy, and though they tried to keep up the children's lessons and read stories from the Bible, they all suffered greatly from crushing boredom. With scarce work to do—even hunting was impossible when the snow was deep—the ceaseless darkness sent them to their beds and Margaret dreamt she'd been buried alive.

Mary, on the other hand, found the cold white silence of the wilderness oddly appealing. It was the opposite of life inside their hovel, where endless darkness and the constant bedlam of caged children nearly drove her mad.

She confided to her mother, "If I must choose between freezing in peace outdoors or warmth, foul smells and noise, I choose the cold. Let me go out for kindling. Please, let me go!" She was already dressed in her long wool stockings, every petticoat she owned and a woolen doublet. After she pulled on her boots, wrapped a shawl around her shoulders, and covered all with a hooded cloak, Margaret sent her off with a blessing.

Reflected sunlight dazzled her eyes, and frigid air bit at her lungs as she stepped out into the cold. She wrapped the shawl tighter around her throat and walked behind the hovel toward the edge of the forest. She heard only the sound of her own footsteps crunching the snow. She bent to look at wolves' tracks. In the night she had heard their soulful howling with no idea that they'd come so close to their hut.

Alive with the thrill of danger, she moved her feet in lock step beside the wolves' tracks toward her father's woodlot. She remembered the day when she and the other children had run down the road to Goodman Bartlett's wolf pit. A large gray she-wolf had fallen in, and as Bartlett raised his long gun and took aim, Mary had looked down into her fiery eyes and understood for the first time what it meant to be wild.

AT LAST SPRING came, bringing such heavy rain that the rivers overflowed, sending its waters among the trees at low places along its banks, making quiet pools where Mary went to fish. She felt favored, for a change. She would much rather fish than do laundry at the river. While the shad were running, her mother had given her a job she enjoyed. She had caught three of the silvery, fat-bellied fish, so large and full of fight that she had to leap into the shallows to land them. Waiting for her pole to lurch again, she let her toes play in the water eddying around the large stone where she sat.

The day before, Captain John Mason had left Hartford with ninety colonists including Mary's brother Tom. They had sailed for the fort at Saybrook where they planned to join Bay Colony troops under the command of Captain John Underhill, the Mohegan sachem Uncas and eighty of his warriors. Every time she thought of her brother fighting the Indians she said a prayer. Mary hoped that if she was good, Divine Providence would protect him. She also knew that if she tried very hard, she could be pious for as long as it took to bring him home.

From her perch she watched Podunks paddle upstream in dugout canoes filled with beaver pelts, scattering cormorants, mute swans and great blue heron. An eagle dropped out of the sky, plucking a fish from the river. Across the water the Dutch fort loomed at the top of a rise. An imposing structure surrounded by a stockade with cannons menacing from its earthwork walls, the Dutch called it House of Hope. Though village folks had warned her away from the Hollanders, she longed to see behind its mysterious walls. The Dutch never came into town, for their supplies arrived on ships sailing up from New Amsterdam. Mary had heard of fights between the Dutch and the English. She had no idea why they were unfriendly, though she thought it had something to do with Indian trade and which ones had settled here first.

Tired of her thoughts, tired of waiting for another fish to bite, she strung her fish together with a line through their gills and hoisted them over her shoulder. Her skirt was wet and muddy to the waist and smelled of river water. As she hurried toward home, thinking about how her mother would prepare the fish, her mouth watered. First Margaret would scale and wash them and put them into a deep pewter coffin to cook with sweet wine and a large lump of butter. She would sprinkle them with herbs, and when they were done, strew minced hard-cooked egg all over their tops. And then, laying them on a platter with herbs all around, she would serve her hungry family. That was how Mary imagined it would be, though she couldn't imagine where her mother would find sweet wine.

THE CONNECTICUT TROOPS had sailed to the fort at Saybrook in a trading shallop belonging to William Pynchon. A two-masted pinnace and a small square-rigged vessel called a pinque waited on the far side of the river to take them to war with the Indians at Mystic.

Tom Bliss, his mind filled with his mother's worried eyes at their departure, would long remember the overcrowded shallop and Captain John Mason. The imposing young commander of the Connecticut forces inspired confidence in the men just by his presence. A bear—that's what Captain Mason looked like to Tom. He was both tall and broad, with a barrel chest, a wide back and shoulders. His great head sported a shock of thick dark hair, an abundant moustache and beard. Although the swollen river, the infant green of the forest and the salmon leaping upstream also etched memories for Tom, it was Captain Mason's gigantic frame, his immaculate armor and manly self-assurance that set his imagination on fire.

Before the soldiers left, the town had requisitioned rations for them: pease, oatmeal, four gallons of strong water, two of sack and a hogshead of good beer for the captain, the minister, and those who were sure to get sick. Knowing that the rest of their supplies would be issued at Saybrook, Thomas Bliss had seen to it that Tom had gunpowder, shot, twenty bullets and a musket. Though both Tom and his father had trained with the militia, the elder Thomas was kept back for the home guard, the younger man deployed for battle.

Tom removed the itchy metal helmet he had borrowed from his father to let the breeze cool his head as he toyed absently with his thin young moustache. In going off to fight the Indians he felt vitally important to his people. He was glad to greet his friend Joseph Parsons, who had sailed down from Springfield, and before they set sail with Mason the two young men joined the others in worship at the wharf. Master Samuel Stone, who would go to battle with them, encouraged the troops with these words: "We are called to execute those whom God, the righteous Judge of the world, hath condemned for blaspheming His sacred majesty and murdering His servants."

Prayerfully, Tom thought of John Oldham—the man's butchered body haunted his dreams—and of the men and women at Wethersfield murdered in their fields, though he had no sympathy for the latter. They had broken their promise to the natives, stealing land from its rightful owners, and thus provoked their own disaster. Immoral and foolhardy though their behavior had been, these massacres could not go unpunished. He thought, too, of the kidnapped maidens, still living as slaves among the Pequots. Such threats to English safety must not go unanswered, for to do so would be to invite more of the same.

At Fort Saybrook, Lieutenant Lion Gardener and his men, Mason and the Connecticut troops, and Uncas and his Mohegan warriors welcomed into their midst young Captain John Underhill and his nineteen men from the Bay Colony. Underhill, only twenty-eight years old, was already a storied military leader, having received his training from the Prince of Orange in Holland. Despite heroic reports of his valor in battles abroad, on this side of the water young Underhill was relatively untried. Mason, similarly trained, was quite aware that Underhill's recent foray with John Endecott to punish the Block Island Indians for Oldham's death had been a failure.

As Underhill and his men drilled with the Connecticut forces, a bemused Uncas with his eighty warriors settled outside the fortress walls. Uncas's tawny army wore a strange array of animal skins and feathers—some with yellow paint on their heads, some with chests painted red, some wearing English coats. From their location just outside the fort they grinned behind their hands as they watched the English drill. Uncas himself was a giant and of royal blood, having descended from Woipequand, Grand Sachem of the Pequots. Three years before, he had been passed over when his cousin Sassacus was made Grand Sachem of the Pequots. In a fit of rage, Uncas and his followers had broken from the tribe, naming themselves Mohegans—Wolf People.

Every man in the English contingent at Fort Saybrook was uncomfortable with the Mohegans' proximity. Lieutenant Gardener, their commander, was not pleased that his fort had been selected as a place of rendezvous for the Mohegans and the English forces. Because he knew that many of the natives biding their time outside his fort had kinsmen among the people they had promised to attack, he didn't trust them. That very morning his men had reported seeing six Pequots in a canoe on Bass River, at an inlet just off the Connecticut.

This intelligence had given Gardener a brilliant idea.

He searched for Uncas among his encamped warriors and found him alone in the shade of a tree, preparing to lash an iron arrowhead onto its shaft with a strip of sinew. As Gardener approached, the Indian looked up from his work, nodding in recognition.

Without greeting, Gardener said, "You say you will help Captain Mason."

"I have said so."

"I need proof." Gardener trusted no Indian. "Send you now twenty men to the Bass River where you'll find six Pequots. Fetch them here, alive or dead. Only then shall you go with Mason."

Uncas's black eyes flashed angrily at Gardener, then he held his arrow to his eye to check its straightness. It seemed to Gardener that Uncas must be making up his mind. Uncas still did not bother to look at the captain.

"When the morning sun rises, I will see Bass River." That was all he said.

. . . . .

After training all morning, Tom and Joseph paused for the midday meal at a table with Master Stone and some others of the Connecticut troops. They drank ale with a coarse brown bread and stake-roasted salmon. The neophyte soldiers ate in silence, listening as the militiamen talked among themselves. Days had passed since Uncas had left Saybrook with his men, presumably for Bass River. He had been expected before now.

A veteran of Indian battles who wore an eye patch looked worried. "Uncas will turn traitor, I'll warrant ye."

His remark seemed to alarm a young soldier from Wethersfield. "Surely he will not desert us."

The veteran snorted. "More likely that blackguard will be back with hundreds more of his kind to slay us all."

"Nay," said another hardened soldier, "he'll go with us into battle, then in the midst of the fray join with the Pequots to destroy us."

Neither oracle appealed to Tom, who hoped the older soldiers were simply doubters or else egging them on. When he had eaten, his food rested like a stone in his stomach, and he welcomed a prayer from Master Stone. "O Lord God," the young preacher said, standing with bowed head, "if it be Thy blessed will, look with favor on Thy poor distressed servants. Manifest one pledge of Thy love. Confirm to us the fidelity of these Indians who pretend friendship and service. Encourage our hearts, O Lord, in this work of Thine. Amen."

Then, as if in answer to the prayer, Captain Underhill appeared, helmet in hand. In an urgent voice meant for all to hear he called out, "Brethren! Uncas has returned with proof of his loyalty, bringing the heads of four Pequots, one Pequot mortally wounded, and Kiswas, a traitor!"

Joseph turned to the man with the eye patch. "Who is this Kiswas?"

"A rascal well known to the men at Saybrook. He had lived a long time among them and turned traitor, spying on the English for the Pequots."

To a man, the enraged soldiers rose up and hurried outside, Tom and Joseph among them. Caught up in the angry mob, they burst into the yard eager to face Kiswas. "Let's see the traitor!" someone shouted as they ran.

Presently a wild man painted red, a wolf etched in black on his muscular chest, was dragged into the yard. His head was shaved except for a scalp lock: a hank of hair for taunting his enemies: "Take this, if you can!" was its message.

"Dare not kill a Pequot!" he yelled in defiance, a terrifying light burning in his eyes.

Lieutenant Gardener, furious with the man he'd once trusted, forced his captive at gunpoint into the Mohegan camp.

"Kill this traitor," he called to Uncas, who towered over him robed in raccoon skins with eagle feathers trembling in the breeze. "Let us know your allegiance. Kill Kiswas!"

Uncas did not flinch. He looked Gardener in the eye as an equal and directed his men to tie one of Kiswas's legs to a post. Tom, who stood at the fringe of the crowd, was pushed forward with curious soldiers who cheered as one of the Indian's legs was tied.

"Dare not kill a Pequot!" Kiswas taunted again, mocking them as his other ankle was bound with a rope, and twenty Mohegan warriors took hold for a tug-of-war.

While Kiswas took his torture in silence, soldiers cheered his tormentors on. And then, in a sudden moment of horror, a hush came over the mob. Tom, knowing what was coming closed his eyes. In the time it takes for a man to heave a long sigh, Kiswas's body split in two from his crotch to his breastbone. Still alive, still silent, with bubbles of blood coming from his mouth, Kiswas was relieved of his suffering by Underhill's bullet to the head.

As some retched and groaned with horror, the soldiers silently drifted back inside the fort. Dazed and sickened, Tom and Joseph walked away toward the wharf. Speechless, overwhelmed with confusion, Tom dared not look at his friend. To see his own revulsion mirrored in another's eyes would only confirm what had just happened.

At the river, Tom gazed across its wide expanse. It never halts, he thought. "Nothing can stop the river coming by here," he murmured. He picked up a stone and threw it hard, far out over the moving body, watching it arc then fall and splash into the water. He dropped down to sit on the wharf with his head in both hands, aware that Joseph had sat down beside him. At length they looked at one another. Why? Tom's eyes asked of the blond, fresh-faced, young man at his side.

"Why?" Joseph voiced, his face mirroring Tom's horror.

Moments passed, then Joseph spoke again. "Uncas had proved himself, you know. Did he not bring Pequot heads and Kiswas here to the fort?"

Tom had fixed his gaze on the river. "Aye, he did the lieutenant's bidding. Why, then, did he have to further confirm his loyalty? Why did the men cheer, as if pulling a man to pieces were great sport? I've never seen one so brave—to suffer so, and in silence. Some say the Indians are not human. This day our English had not a human heart among them."

Finding no answers, the troubled lads looked toward the anchored ships waiting for the wind to rise. "And we," Joseph said, "here we wait. When shall we go to war?"

The air was as still as the hush that held them.

Finally Joseph said, "At Pynchon's bidding, I've had dealings with the Indians at Agawam. They are peaceful men—not like these Mohegans."

With nothing more to say, the two young soldiers kept to their places on the wharf. They could hear the soldiers drilling: the drumming, the commanding officers' shouts. Tom remembered the first time he saw Joseph, on the deck of Oldham's pinnace. Only two years older, he felt protective toward the lad.

"Let's make haste, Joseph, before they discover our absence."

Topping Captain Mason's list of grievances was his general irritation with Lieutenant Gardener. Mason found the lieutenant's vociferous praise of the Indians' prowess in battle annoying, treasonous even. Gardener, who would not be going into battle with them, repeatedly reminded him how these natives had been savage fighters from their youth and how much he esteemed them above all other warriors—even the Spanish.

"They know the trails, the plains, woods, and brooks, while we English wander—lost as lambs," Gardener said. "They run swift as deer, while we are weighed down by armor. Without Uncas's help, the whole lot of you shall perish, man and mother's son."

Mason's instructions from the Connecticut court directed him to proceed to the Pequot River to attack and destroy Sassacus's settlement there, yet his vessels had been becalmed at Saybrook since Wednesday and could not move. And there was something even more troubling, something that had him paralyzed. He and his co-commanders could not agree on how to proceed. Mason knew that until they were of one right and true mind, God's wind would not fill their sails. Furthermore, he was not convinced that the Connecticut court knew what it asked. Mason believed he had a better plan.

In considering the course the court had ordered, Mason had argued with his co-commanders that he dared not sail his little flotilla up to the fort in broad daylight.

"A direct attack on Sassacus's village is a disaster in the making," he said, as the commanders met yet again in Gardener's private quarters. "The Indians have a few guns with powder and shot. They will be on land, and being fleet of foot, will much impede our landing and possibly dishearten our men. Let us not forget that they outnumber us. We need to come upon them at Fort Mystic unawares."

Gardener refused to heed Mason's words. "If one of our guns is as good as ten Indians with bows, then you be not so outnumbered."

Mason shook his head in impatience. "We've heard you say, Gardener, what fierce warriors they are. Make up your mind, man."

Captain Underhill agreed with Mason. "Sassacus keeps watch on that harbor day and night. He'll see us approach—they won't expect us by land. But we cannot willfully disobey orders from the court and march to Fort Mystic instead."

"I have a plan," Mason said, "if you'll hear me out. Let us sail past Pequot Harbor on to Narragansett Bay. There we may recruit a party of Miantonomi's Narragansett warriors, take on supplies of food and water, and attack the Pequots at Fort Mystic by surprise from the east."

"That's well enough," Underhill said, "but how long an overland march would that be?"

"Four . . . five days. But Miantonomi will resupply us."

Again, Gardener scoffed. "And should things go wrong, what shall you tell the court then?"

"We must have discretion to decide for ourselves," Mason insisted. "Nobody far removed from the scene of battle can foresee all accidents and occurrences that fall out in the pursuit of war."

Underhill set his jaw and folded his arms. "I'll not violate orders."

"Then let us ask our chaplain," Mason said. "Let Master Stone commend our condition to the Lord. Let the Almighty direct how and in what manner we should proceed."

That seemed to settle the question, and all present agreed Master Stone should be asked to pray for guidance.

That night the chaplain sat up late, praying in his quarters on board the pinque. By morning he had his answer, and after making his way to Mason's cabin, he informed the commander that God's wishes would be best served if they sailed to Narragansett Bay and mounted their attack on Fort Mystic from the east. When Mason let Underhill and Gardener know of the chaplain's communiqué from the Lord, they had to agree to Mason's strategy. Truly they and the Connecticut court could not argue with God Almighty.

North of Saybrook, a late-May breeze gathered and blew through the forest, rustling the pines and new leaves in the hardwoods. An eagle picked up the wind for a ride, soaring high above the river. Rushes and cattails bent along the banks as a milkmaid in the meadow pulled her shawl tight around her shoulders. At Saybrook, seagulls shrieked and dove around a pinnace, a pinque and a shallop running full speed into Long Island Sound, their sails puffed like cumulus clouds. On board the three, nearly a hundred English soldiers and seventy Mohegan warriors were armed and ready for battle.

THROUGH HIS INTELLIGENCE, Sassacus had known for some time that the English planned to attack his fort at the mouth of the river. His lookouts had been in place for weeks, and when they saw three English vessels approach from the west they knew that today they would kill Englishmen in battle. The alert was sent out and hundreds of armed warriors moved into position behind the palisades. But then, to their surprise, the English ships sailed downriver toward the Sound.

A cheer went up from the warriors. "The English are cowards! They are afraid to fight!" The Pequots believed that when the English saw their well-manned fort they had sailed on in fear. That night, and for nights afterward, the Pequots celebrated with bonfires; they danced and sang and laughed at English cowardice.

V

. . . the Indians shewing us a Path, told us that it led directly to the Fort. We held on our March about two Miles, wondering that we came not to the Fort, and fearing we might be deluded: But seeing Corn newly planted at the Foot of a great Hill, supposing the Fort was not far off . . . gave the Word for some of the Indians to come up: At length Onkos [Uncas] and one Wequash appeared; We demanded of them, Where was the Fort?

—Captain John Mason
A Brief History of the Pequot War (1637)

UNDER A FULL moon, on the eve of the Sabbath, the English and their Indian allies sailed into Narragansett Bay. On Sunday they did not disembark but stayed on board for rest and worship. Monday and Tuesday gale-force winds battered the ships, so no men went ashore. When the winds abated, Mason and his men marched to Miantonomi's camp seeking help in the form of both rations and warriors, but the Narragansett chieftain offered little support. He sympathized, but claimed not to have enough food or manpower for the fight.

Hoping to gather larger forces, Mason marched twenty miles to a Niantic village, where once again the English were refused the help they needed. These Indians' demeanor toward their cause was so guarded as to be hostile, and Mason quickly posted English guards around the camp, warning the head of the clan that if the Pequots got word the English were on their way, the village would be sacked and all would be killed.

Carrying only meager supplies, including what little Miantonomi had provided, Mason, Underhill, Uncas and their men marched overland for six days toward Fort Mystic. The weather turned from unseasonably warm to brutally hot and humid. Along the way, grasses and tares wore cloaks of dust and new leaves on the trees had wilted. The air was laden with moisture, and the men breathed heavily as they marched. Mason worried that on low rations and under such conditions his troops could not endure the beating that lay ahead.

In the midst of their trek, an advance party of Narragansetts rode up from the rear in clouds of dust with the news that a large army of several hundred warriors followed on foot. All wanted to serve with them and gallantly promised to kill Pequots. With all the commanders' approval, the Narragansetts joined the march.

In such fierce heat, as some English soldiers suffered fatigue and heat prostration, it seemed to Mason that all the rest were disheartened, beaten before the fight. When they reached a broad shallow river, Mason encouraged them to rest a while, cool off, and drink their fill. After an hour, their spirits lifted and they forded the river to march on.

Uncas, who recognized that spot in the river as the place where Pequots often fished, told Mason they were not far from their destination. As word spread among the troops, the Narragansetts appeared frightened and began to disappear in throngs, but Uncas and his men remained steadfast.

The sudden desertion of the same men who had, only days before, crowed about their eagerness to fight Pequots puzzled Captain Mason. He turned to Uncas. "What will *your* men do now?"

Uncas, always straight in body, drew himself higher. "What I said at Saybrook the Mohegans will do." Then he smiled slyly. "But of the Narragansetts—all will go."

That night, believing that they were very near the fort, the assault party camped in a small swamp between two hills. To avoid attracting attention, they kept silence and bedded down with rocks for pillows. Mason planned to sleep for a few hours, then muster his forces to attack just before sunrise. The sound of the Indians' drums beating in the distance kept many awake for hours. In the morning they failed to wake until roused by the sun.

With the sun still low, Mason could see his objective—a walled fortress upon a hill surrounded by acres of newly planted corn. Tom Bliss, who had remained by his friend throughout, gazed toward the well-defended fort and poked an elbow into Joseph's side.

"That's it, Joseph. Bigger than I expected. What say you?"

As Joseph studied the palisade, his eyes widened. "I've never seen so large an Indian fort. Three acres inside, I'll warrant you."

At least the morning was cool. Tom couldn't tell whether the pain in his stomach was hunger or fear. The men had not eaten since the midday before, and that meal a meager one.

Suddenly Lieutenant Gridley, a weathered soldier, approached the two young comrades and pushed a flask of strong water at Tom. "Drink this." He stared at Tom until he did as he was told. The fiery liquid ran down his throat and hit his empty stomach like a torch. "Drink more, son—it bestows courage." Tom drank again, spewed, and pushed it away. "Here, bear up," the lieutenant insisted. "It deadens pain." After Tom forced himself to take another swig, Gridley turned to Joseph and bade him do the same.

The fort had been built of small trees and half trees, twelve feet high, four feet deep, packed with mud. Openings left between the stakes served the bowmen's needs. The fort had two entrances, one on the southeast, the other on the north. The attacking force couldn't see that within the palisades there were more than eighty wigwams, covered with rush mats skillfully woven by Indian women to make the dwellings impervious to rain and wind. Nor could they see that on deerskin robes inside the wigwams nearly five hundred Pequot men, women, and children lay asleep. Nor did the English commanders know that another 150 warriors from another encampment had arrived the day before and were still asleep.

After the scouts Mason sent ahead had returned, Underhill and his men headed toward the southeast gate, and Mason's troops moved to the north entry, where they found brush piled neck-high blocking the entrance. Quietly, so as not to rouse the Indians, Tom and Joseph helped to untangle the brush and threw it out of their path. But burly Mason, impatient with their progress, fell upon the brush, trampling it underfoot, and motioned his men to follow. The young soldiers climbed over the barrier at their captain's heels, to find themselves inside the fort.

A dog barked.

A Pequot brave ran into the yard shouting in Algonquian, "English! English!"

Acting on instinct, Joseph and Tom ducked behind a wigwam. Joseph's mouth was dry. He looked at his friend. "I've got to piss." Tom had the same need, and fumbling around with their breeches, they relieved themselves in the dust. A hail of arrows fell suddenly from the sky, striking two soldiers near the lads. One of them fell at Tom's feet, another who'd just entered the gate also crumpled. As more arrows fell, scattering other soldiers, Joseph sprinted for cover.

"Jesus fights with us!" someone yelled.

The Indians, dashing in and around the wigwams, were too far away for the attackers to engage with their swords. Following their commander's lead, the young soldiers took cover behind another wigwam. Each volley of incoming arrows brought more cries and curses of wounded to their ears. Arrows rained all around Joseph. Why had he not been struck?

The wind came up to fan the sweat on his face. He heard Mason shout orders and saw the flash of muskets firing on a band of warriors who appeared in the alley between the wigwams ahead. Not yet having fired his weapon, he raised it and aimed at a warrior who came screaming toward him with his hatchet raised. Joseph fired. The warrior collapsed and died without another sound.

Mason, saved from a flying hatchet by his helmet and armor, reloaded his gun and fired it time and again as fast as he could.

Joseph followed his example, keeping an eye on Tom. Soon, with no Indians left standing, Joseph had seen for himself that, horrifying though they may be, hatchets and knives were no match for guns.

As Captain Mason approached a large wigwam he motioned for the men to follow. With two others at his side and Tom and Joseph behind, the five of them left the bright sunshine to enter the dimly lit structure, where armed braves sprang to the attack. As the English and native warriors struggled wildly, fighting for their lives, the captain's sword laid open one warrior's face. Joseph buried his sword in a brave's belly and spun in time to stop another coming up behind him with a knife. He had to fight down nausea as the reek of death rose off the bodies of the slain and mortally wounded. By the time all the braves inside the house lay dead, Joseph's legs were drenched in red. As they prepared to leave, he glimpsed a squaw lying under one of the beds. With pleading eyes, she held her hand over the mouth of a small child. Joseph turned away.

Having finished off those warriors, the Englishmen stumbled back outside, immediately confronting another large band of Indians. Sweat dripped into Joseph's eyes, and his bowels griped. He could scarce believe how many Indians they faced, nor could he believe it when they turned and ran. On all sides, Pequot warriors tore through the crowded alleyways, fleeing gunfire, terrified by the sight of gun-carrying soldiers. Because no women or children were among those who ran away, Joseph guessed that they, like the squaw he'd seen, still hid in the wigwams.

In the melee of confused soldiers and running Indians, Joseph and Tom followed Mason and several others in pursuit of a gang of warriors. At the end of one alley they came upon still more Indians, armed with knives and stone hatchets. One band of fighters was as horribly surprised as the other. In the ensuing fight the English killed seven Indians, though the rest escaped. Joseph, tallying up, didn't know how many of his bullets had found their mark, though so far he had single-handedly killed five savages in close combat.

Joseph believed he still lived only because he had stayed close to his commander. Frustrated by being penned in, he wondered if Mason also hated fighting the Indians in such close quarters. The big man was breathing hard as he ran, his heavy steps jarring the ground. Joseph guessed that his captain would rather fight face to face in an open field. Having to dart in and out of wigwams and race down narrow alleys was no way for an Englishmen to fight.

Joseph and Tom kept close at the captain's heels as his pace eased to march his men slowly along the alley, pausing each time they came to another of the narrow passages. Then all at once Mason ducked into the nearest wigwam, out of sight. Puzzled, the soldiers looked to one another. Should we follow?

Before they could act, Mason suddenly reappeared, carrying a firebrand. He plunged the smoldering stick into the dry mats covering the wigwam, and in an instant it caught fire. The wind fanned the flames and spread them until all the nearby wigwams were ablaze.

Mason yelled, "Fall off and surround the fort!"

The two friends raced with the others for the gate. In the rush, Joseph dropped his weapon, and when he stopped to pick it up an arrow found his shoulder. His knees buckled, yet within seconds he found strength enough to stay on his feet and run for his life with the rest, the arrow so painful he feared falling in a faint. Tom, seeing what had happened, dashed back to Joseph's side to support him.

In minutes, every wigwam inside the palisade was ablaze. The English outside the fort fired on those who tried to escape. Very few made it safely to cover. Terrified of the English guns, some of the braves ran straight into the flames. Warriors climbed to the top of the fortress walls in a desperate attempt to engage the enemy. As the flames mounted, the warriors' bowstrings caught fire and they could fight no more.

It was all Joseph could do to stay on his feet. Paralyzed with awe, he stood with Tom watching the fort burn as doomed Indians tried to escape the inferno. The cries of burning women and children rose on the heated air. In a moment that seemed to rush upon them, both young men knew that the fight was over, that they would not be defeated. They would not perish in battle. Though nearly all the Narragansetts had fled, Uncas and his Mohegan warriors had not betrayed them.

Having retreated to a safe distance, mute soldiers and rapt Mohegans continued to stare into the flames. There was nothing left to do. Faint from thirst, hunger, horror, and the amazement that he had killed and survived, Joseph stumbled and reached to touch the arrow stuck in his shoulder. Tom led him to the edge of the cornfield where other wounded had gathered.

"Bear up, my brother," Tom said, as he eased his pale friend to a seat on the ground where the arrow in Joseph's shoulder would be removed and his wound tended.

When Tom returned to stand with the troops and the Mohegans, he heard Uncas complain quietly to Mason. "You English fight too furious. You slay too many."

Tom moved into a gathering of shocked younger men as an older soldier jeered, "Ah, yer maiden battle, I'll warrant ye. Hurry on home, ye mother's babes."

The victors waited. No more Indians came into view, and within the hour there was only smoke, the stench of roasted human flesh, and unholy silence.

VI

Married Persons, (by the blessing of God) have Issue, and become Parents. The Father, begetteth and the Mother beareth Sons and Daughter (sometimes twins). The Infant is wrapped in Swadling-cloathes, is laid in a Cradle, is suckled by the Mother with her Breasts, and fed with Pap, Afterwards it learneth to go by a Standing-stool, playeth with Rattles and beginneth to speak. As it beginneth to grow older, it is accustomed to Piety, and labour, and is chastised if it not be dutiful. Children owe to Parents Reverence and Service. The Father main-taineth his Children by taking pains.

—John Amos Comenius
Orbis Pictus, published in English in 1659
The first picture book for children

IN THE VILLAGE it was common knowledge that deep in the surrounding forest Satan danced with savages by the light of the moon. Even in the dusky gloom of daylight demons hid inside wild animals, ready to jump from their skins into the bodies of foolish wandering children. Mary was forbidden to go into the forest, though her mother had sent her to gather fiddleheads at the edge of the wood just off Bartlett's field. In one hand she held a basket, and with the other she pulled at the plain white cap hiding her copper curls. A lovely head of hair like Mary's was seen as a conceit, and covered for modesty's sake. Though her hair was thick and wild and her curls were forever escaping, she was glad to have a coif and wished for a new one. This one was too small and should be passed down to Hannah.

Only a few steps inside the wood she found a vast stand of fern—curled green heads snaking up through spring mud under a budding canopy of hardwoods. Quickly she filled her basket, quite unconcerned that with each fistful she had moved deeper into the forest. Through the trees she saw the road and the Bartletts' house across the meadow, looking small nestled near its farm sheds, a thin line of friendly white smoke rising from the chimney. Outside in the greened-up meadow it was sunny, but cool and dark under the trees. The wood seemed a friendly enough place with bright sunlight piercing the chestnuts and pines, sending thin shafts of light to the forest floor. Mary looked down at the ground pine, wintergreen and bright mosses growing in a patch of sun. Awed by their perfection, she went to her knees, collecting tiny pines, miniatures of the giants towering near. With grimy fingers she pried velvety mosses loose and tucked them under the fiddleheads. Before she turned to go, she looked toward the deep wood where a path curved through the shadows under the canopy. Someone had walked there. Her eyes traveled the length of the needle-strewn way to a pool of light so brilliant she found the courage to risk going nearer.

She remembered the story her father had told about the folks at Wethersfield who had stolen land from the Indians, and how afterward the Indians had killed nine settlers and taken two young girls captive. Having every reason to be wary, she looked back over her shoulder toward the meadow and the comforting sight of her neighbors' house. Pushing forward, she soon came to the edge of a small, sunlit glade. Pausing to let her eyes adjust to the radiant light, she stepped into the clearing, a nearly perfect circle where strangely shaped and colored mushrooms grew on a rotting log, and dark-winged butterflies flitted over the grasses and wildflowers. The clearing buzzed with winged creatures, bees—and three fantastic birds. Tiny things, with fiery red breasts and iridescent green bodies, hovered in the golden air at the throats of flowers. Although her father had described these magical birds of New England, this was the first time Mary had seen them. Swinging and dipping in astonishing aerial display, they hummed as they flew.

"Humbirds!" she cried aloud. At the sound of her voice the tiny jeweled birds flew straight up to vanish in the air.

Mary's gaze alighted on curious low-growing yellow flowers scattered under a pine. She went to her knees for a close look at their funny faces, flagged by two brown wings on either side of a pouch, when suddenly she scampered to her feet. Someone was watching. She could hardly breathe. She scanned the shadows under the trees and, seeing no one, her mother's voice came quickly into her head: *Mary, you'll scare yourself out of your wits with your wild imaginings!*

Anxious all at once to be back at home, she looked for the path, remembering the stand of arching green wands that marked the entrance to the glade. But in their place she saw a tiny old woman, standing motionless in the shade. Her first instinct was to run, until the little woman smiled at her.

Moving forward with her hand extended in friendship, she wore a long dark-green cloak with the hood drawn over her head. Her voice was strangely soothing.

"Prithee, why is a young thing so far from home?"

"Mother sent me for fiddleheads. If you are from the village, goodwife, I beg you, don't tell my mother you saw me in the wood. I'll be punished, though I've done no real harm."

The old woman regarded her intensely. Feeling awkward, wishing to fill the silence and distract her, Mary handed her the yellow flower she had just picked. "Pray, do you know this bewitching plant?"

"Aye, it be good for the pain of thy courses. Ah, but neither of us hath need of it, for thou art too young and I too old."

The aged woman came closer, her breath sweet with herbs. "Thou art a comely lass—hair like the fire of poppies and eyes as green as grass. Why, I think there be none so fair in the village. What be your name, child?"

"Mary, daughter of Thomas Bliss." Though she found it difficult to follow her strange speech, coming in a voice as thin and small as the woman herself, Mary had lost her desire to flee.

The old woman's smile broadened. "My name be Mary too, but the village folk call me Goody Crespet. Come, let us rest our feet." She took gentle hold of Mary's hand and drew her to a large flat stone, where she sat down.

"Settle down beside me, tell me the story of thy life."

Mary sat. "'Tis not a grand story, for I'm not old enough to have one."

"Thou hast crossed the sea and come to the New England— there's a story in that, I'll warrant."

"Aye," Mary ventured, "we came from Painswick Parish where we lived in a big house, and once, when I was very small, I climbed to the top of it." She was warming to her tale, for she loved nothing more than daydreaming of England. "Shall I tell you about our father's land?" Her voice grew lively with enthusiasm. "I could see the whole of it from a window at the top of the house, and from there I saw for miles in every direction—all the way past the church tower out to the sea."

Mary couldn't resist embellishing, even though the River Severn, carving its way through little hills, was the only body of water anywhere near Painswick Parish. "In those days we journeyed far and wide to wondrous places," she went on. "Often Father took me to visit the great city of Gloucester. I saw the abbey, and the castle walls, where no one enters except through its gates. He took me to every shop filled with rare goods from all over the world—beautiful cloaks, jeweled rings, bright polished boots, shoes of every color under the sun."

The old woman's eyes sparkled with interest.

Mary was borrowing from stories she had heard or imagined so often they seemed real to her. "We wanted for nothing. We had fine things to wear. Once we went to a pastry shop where they sold sugar-plum cakes covered in sweet cream and pastries stuffed with strawberries all thick with honeyed almonds, and we ate all those delicious things." Suddenly her eyes filled with tears.

"Prithee, you must think me foolish, but I think of home every day. I hope I shall never forget."

"Of course not, child. Hast it been so very hard since thou came?"

"Aye, we sailed first to Boston, but my father's crops failed quite miserable there. Our first house here was dug into a hill—like mice we lived, all winter in a hole—I hate that dark smoky place, but now it's to be our root cellar, for Father's house is almost built."

"So thou hast a proper house at last?"

"Aye, Goody, but we have six children, and any day my mother expects another. Yet Father says we shall prosper here, for he has more land than he had in Boston, and he's learning to grow flax and barley. Before, he was a weaver by trade. Now he's busy in his fields with my brothers Nat and Lawrence, for my brother Tom has gone off to fight Pequots. Mother and I keep up on the weaving."

"Why, Mary, thou art too small for a weaver."

The girl smiled, proud of her skills. "Just the same, I am a weaver. Mother is teaching me. But it's working in the garden that I truly love. I like everything about it—hoeing, raking, even weeding, and I like planting and watering and watching things grow most of all."

The old woman's wrinkled cheeks flushed as pink as a baby's. "Then thou art like me in that way. My husband, the dearest man who ever married, was one of the first to settle here by Little River— across from the Dutch Fort. Such an effort was too great for a man of his age"—she sighed—"but God sustained him long enough to finish his house. Then he left me to go home to the angels, where I shall find him one day."

"Oh, my. How do you get on without him?"

"The way a lone woman doth—bringing babes into the world, preparing the dead for burial. Oft I am called to the sick. I hath knowledge of herbs, and folks pay in trade. I hath what I need."

"Where are your children?"

"I be childless."

Mary didn't know what to say. She had just felt sorry for the poor woman's loss and now, learning that she was childless, cast her eyes down.

"Do not grieve for me, for I hath loved other people's children and I hath all this and more." The wise woman gestured toward the glade and the open sky above. "And there's my love of God. If the day should come that thou wants to know the wonders that sustain me, ask, and it shall be given thee!" She smiled at her own boldness in using the words Jesus spoke on the mountain. "But hark, child, 'tis time I showed thee out of the wood. Come, we must away." She took Mary's hand and led her back toward Bartlett's field.

On the long walk home Mary decided she'd never met anyone like Goody Crespet and that she hoped to see her again. When she entered her mother's kitchen, long past the time she was supposed to be helping with supper, she was in trouble again.

"Mary! You are an affliction on me!" Margaret's face was red with anger. "What kept you so long?"

"I stayed to frighten crows out of Father's field," she lied. "I chased them till I was near to a faint. You can thank me for saving his crop."

Margaret still fumed. "How long could that take—if it happened at all?"

"And after that, Mother, when I could find no fiddleheads on our land, I walked to the woods across from Bartlett's—there I found them. It was a long, long walk and I stopped to visit with—"

"Mary, if I have to listen to any more of your lies, I'll encourage your father to whip you. Now get those fiddleheads cooked before they wither."

"I hate fiddleheads. I hate this evil place! I care not if Father whips me. I care not for anything at all!" Mary was afraid to say all the rest—that she hated her mother and father for bringing her to New England.

VII

Mr. Ludlow, Mr. Pincheon [William Pynchon], *and about 12 more came by land from Connecticut and brought with them a part of the skin and lock of hair of Sassacus and his brother and 5 other Pequod sachems, who being fled to the Mohawks for shelter, with their wampom (being to the value of £500) were by them surprised and slain, with 20 of their best men. Mononottoh was also taken, but escaped wounded. They brought news also of diverse other Pequods which had been slain by other Indians, and their heads brought to the English; so that now there had been slain and taken between 8 and 900.*

—Governor John Winthrop
August 5, 1637
The History of New England 1630–1649

FOLLOWING THE FIGHT at Fort Mystic—where Pequots lost over 600 to the two English deaths—Tom and Joseph, along with other young and wounded soldiers, were loaded into a shallop and within days arrived back in Hartford. Joseph was too ill to travel much farther, and Tom took him home with him after convincing his superior officer that Margaret Bliss was the one person on earth who could heal his friend's wounds. After they arrived Thomas sent word to William Pynchon at Springfield that his young charge would remain with them until he was well enough to travel.

Joseph's high fever worried Margaret, so she sent for the cunning woman.

When Goody Crespet came, she tended his wound with an herbal balm, hot oils, and vigorous prayer, voicing a caution. "Goodwife Bliss, 'tis a dangerous wound. The furious fever is an ill omen, yet sometimes with hot oils and prayers for God's mercy, such fevers abateth. If so, he will live."

While Goody Crespet nursed with the quiet concentration of a contemplative, Joseph tossed deliriously on sweat-soaked sheets, his complexion a deathly pallor. He lay so still and breathed so shallowly that Margaret feared he had gone to his maker. By my life, she said to herself, never have I seen one so ill. God have mercy on him. She thought he looked doomed, though she said nothing to alarm Tom.

After three days of delirium, Joseph woke cool and thirsty, barely aware of what had happened, wondering why he was in a strange, dark room with light coming from behind a half-open door. Is this my grave? Is that the door behind which God waits? To him the place felt like the tomb where Jesus had lain before the stone was rolled away.

Yet on the other side of the pallet where he lay, Joseph saw a young girl, sitting on a stool, stirring hot coals on the hearth. He rose up on one elbow. When she saw him she ran into the light, calling out the door, and he knew her for Tom's sister Mary.

"He wakes! Mother, he wakes!"

Seeing the light like a red halo about her curly head, Joseph remembered all the redheaded children who had gazed down on him from a dream.

That night, gathered around a bonfire under a clear early-summer sky, Thomas led the family in thanksgiving. "O, Lord God, 'tis right that we bow our heads to thank You for blessing us with young Joseph's life. 'Tis right that we thank You for delivering Your servant, for he shall live to serve You here on the frontier. Keep us ever mindful of Thy love and goodness towards us. Amen."

Mary had given up trying to find out what had happened to Tom and Joseph at Fort Mystic, though she was sure they had a secret. Hearing news of their victory after the battle, the whole town had celebrated, and Mister Hooker had preached a grand sermon extolling the bravery of the English soldiers and God's mercy toward them. She had heard that of the Pequots all but seven had perished, yet Tom's silence confirmed her belief that something still troubled him.

Around a crackling fire, with the delicious smell of fish roasting Indian-style, everyone talked of Joseph's impending return to Springfield.

"What became of the maidens from Wethersfield?" Mary asked. "Are they dead or living as slaves?"

"They are free," Tom said. "The Dutch secured their release from the Pequots most cleverly. They captured some of their warriors and offered to drown them at sea unless the maids were set free."

Joseph had more information to impart. "The Pequots made a trade—maids for warriors. The poor things were taken first to New Amsterdam to be questioned, then to Saybrook. They had dwelt so long with the enemy that they had knowledge of their movements and the location of their camps."

What neither Tom nor the other villagers knew was that they had also been questioned at length about their treatment. The authorities especially sought to know whether they had been polluted and had learned that the maids had been treated humanely.

THE MONOTONY OF winter was followed by Mary's fourteenth spring. Two things had changed for the girl. First, the house was finished and already seemed too small, and, second, she spent her days buffeted between a barely submerged anger and a terrible wanderlust. One day while Margaret was at the loom, blue skies and warm sunshine materialized from behind mountainous clouds, and Mary escaped. She flew down the road toward Little River, cutting across Bartlett's cornfield, her feet barely touching the ground, promising herself that she wouldn't be a minute. She knew that a big basket of laundry awaited her at home, but she ran down the road anyway, like a young colt bolting into the meadow. She had to run; it was as if she had a fire inside that would consume her if it smoldered for another moment. Though she had work enough to tire her, it brought her no peace of mind, for her heart and her head longed for something she could not name. She did not want a life like her mother's, yet, as far as she knew, all women led the same lives, and so would she. The thought terrified her, yet she dreamed of love, of marriage, of having children—but mostly of love.

Mary had become a great mystery to herself, for something primeval had snatched her heart. From ancient times hearts had beat faster in the springtime. With the return of the sun, human-kind praised the gods and rejoiced. Dancers and lovers frol-icked in the meadows. Once, within Mary's hearing, Margaret happily recalled how, when she was a child, folks in her village tied gaily colored ribbons, laurels, and flowers to a tall pole and danced around it on the village green. For days, couples feasted, took strong drink, and disappeared into the bushes. The Protes-tants banned the practice wherever they could, even though King James—and King Charles after him—thought spring frolics per-fectly natural and a fine way for malcontent peasants to let off steam. But Mary wasn't thinking about maypoles or frolics in the meadow. She wasn't thinking about anything. All she knew was how good it felt to stretch her legs and open her lungs to the next breath of green-scented air.

At Little River the waters moved slowly through the forest, carrying the blue sky and a few wispy clouds on its surface. Ducks swam in idle circles where Mary stopped, out of breath. She caught a glimpse of a doe with her twins across the water. How she longed for a friend, someone her own age to talk with. She didn't even have a big sister—just a younger one, plus big brothers and noisy little ones running around underfoot. If she had a friend, she would meet her here by the river, and they would talk and laugh and tell each other secrets. Even though she was supposed to be at home helping her mother, she decided to stay, to lie down in the grass and watch the clouds drift by. She didn't care how harsh her punishment would be when she went home.

Immersed in early summer, she walked beside the flax fields—blooming bluer than the sky—and through Little Meadow and down to the river for a look at the Dutch fort looming on the far side like an English castle. Not that the fort actually looked like a castle. To Mary, it was the only structure on the frontier that let her imagination travel back to England. Sometimes, sent into the heart of the village to shop for her mother, she walked around the edge of Meeting House Yard, staring at the wretched sinners on display in the pillory and stocks, wondering if she'd end up the same way. Mary had heard often enough that her saucy tongue and lack of piety would be her ruin.

The town had no shops yet, but on Thursdays, before and after Lecture, folks gathered in the same yard where Podunks displayed their wares on bearskin robes spread on the dusty ground. Mary was fascinated by the Indians' clay pots and wooden bowls, sometimes decorated with carved animals. Hunters and farmers crowded the market to hawk their surplus in summer, along with river travelers who came to buy and sell everything from produce and fish to gold jewelry. In the open market there were people to talk with—people with news fresh from England, or Boston, or the territories where Indians had caused trouble for the English. To talk, to listen—conversation with people outside her family—Mary longed for it.

One day on a trip to Meeting House Yard, she saw Simon Fisher clapped in the stocks and knew why. He had run off to live with the Indians, which was against the law. No doubt he'd chosen an easier life with the natives because Puritan laws were so strict. Mary felt sure she'd never be so tempted, as their wigwams were said to be full of smoke and fleas, and she'd been told their habits were contrary to civilized life.

She found a crowd at the pillory. A large bonfire burned nearby, and cruel boys had collected in a noisy mob to throw cow piles and stones at the miserable wretch whose head and arms the pillory held tight. A placard nearby gave his name and described his crime: Aaron Stark, for unclean practices.

Just as she came upon the scene, the peg-legged constable approached, waving a glowing branding iron. "Out of my way!" he barked at the mob. "Here's yer mark," he sneered as he burned an R on the offender's cheek. As Stark screamed and jerked in pain, Mary heard skin sizzle and smelled the stink of burning flesh.

The mob jeered and laughed. Someone yelled, "Now ye won't be after Jane Holt so soon!" Mary had heard gossip about Jane Holt, a poor servant girl pregnant out of wedlock who claimed Stark had raped her. Her stomach turned at the sight of Stark's runny nose and mouth, his uncontrollable shaking, his pitiful cries. She walked away and headed toward the Meeting House, confused by her sympathy for the brute. Hurrying off toward a swarm of folks gathered in front of the Meeting House, Mary tried to find a way through the scattered edges of the crowd.

Tom Judd set down his bushel of alewives to scold her. "Wait your turn, Mary Bliss!"

An old woman with a hump on her back rasped, "Some of us has been here near half of the hour waiting *our* turn."

Mary sniffed, then came back at her accusers. "I only wanted to see! What on God's good earth do you wait for?"

"Why, to see the bloody head of the Devil hisself," the old woman hissed.

Judd laughed. "Aye, and ye should be afeard to see it, I'll warrant you."

"Nay, child," another voice said, "you'll give yourself nightmares."

The voice sounded quite familiar. Mary looked around to see her neighbor, also waiting for a look. "Goodwife Bartlett, tell me. What is it?"

"Why, 'tis the head of Sassacus, brought here by Mohawks."

"Up from the Hudson River Valley they brought it," the old woman chimed in. "That's where he tried to hide, and now the war is over for sure, and we shall hear no more their name."

Mary was puzzled. "Their name?"

"'Tis now forbidden by law to say—it." Ann Bartlett cupped her hand to whisper in Mary's ear. "Their tribal name—Pequot. It has been banished by law from all of Connecticut."

The old woman was eager to tell all she knew. "True, they are no more. Those what was now live as slaves among the Narragansetts and the Mohegans, and they must take the name of the tribe that's enslaved them."

Tom Judd summed it up. "Aye, let that be a lesson to all savages who plot to destroy the English!"

"Oh, I do wish to see it," Mary said. "I've never—"

Quickly Goodwife Bartlett took her by the hand. "Mary, I know your mother well, and she would not want you looking at a severed head. Let's walk home together. I shouldn't fill my mind with such things either. He was, after all, a man who lived like other men, and for all I know has a wife and children who cared for him."

Mary hadn't thought of Indians like that—as men like her father, with wives and children. She'd considered them more like the wolves or the bears of the forest.

Ann Bartlett, who was a few years younger than Mary's mother, led her away from the crowd. Mary was torn, feeling sure the goodwife was right and that she should be thankful for her deliverance, but her curiosity was powerful. "I've never seen anyone dead."

"Mary! What a thing to say! Do not wish to see the face of the dead, child—that will happen soon enough, I'll warrant." She hurried Mary toward the road to Little River.

As they walked, Mary noticed for the first time that Ann was with child. "Ah, Goodwife Bartlett, when will your babe come?"

"I expect about harvest time." She smiled, looking grateful for her full belly. "Now, Mary, tell me about your mother. Is she well? Her travail must be near at hand. And how do you like your father's new house?"

IT WAS DARK, and the loft where Mary's big brothers slept was empty of winter stores. Downstairs the floor was strewn with small children asleep on pallets and straw mattresses. Mary sat on the edge of her parents' bed beside her mother, who was so big with child that everyone guessed she carried twins. Her father slept on the other side, his snores a source of merriment for his wife and daughter. Mary jerked and moaned as Margaret brushed her tangled curls.

"Hold still, Mary," Margaret whispered. "If you took a few minutes to brush your hair every morning, I wouldn't have to work so hard at the snarls every Sabbath eve."

"No one asked you to brush my hair," Mary said. "Neither God nor I care about snarls."

Margaret stopped brushing, closed her eyes a moment, and dropped her head, resisting the temptation to slap her daughter's face for the second time that day. Over the past year her eldest daughter had turned into an angry shrew with a penchant for driving her mad. Margaret had news for Mary, and this seemed as good a time as any to break it. Bracing herself and taking a deep breath, she said as quietly as she could, "Mary, the time has come for you to go into service."

"Nay!" The girl was incredulous. "How could you say such a pitiless thing? I am far too young."

Thomas stirred.

"Mary, lower your voice. You are not too young. You, more than any other maid I have known or heard of, are in dire need of proper training from an impartial master. You are spoiled and willful, and your tongue wants a soaping. Your father and I agree it is for your own good."

"Nay, I won't!" Mary jumped up, hands on her hips, to glare at her mother. "I want to dwell here, with you!"

But when Margaret glared just as firmly back, Mary burst into tears and clung to her, burying her face in her mother's nightdress. She hopes to soften my heart, Margaret thought. I mustn't weaken.

"Mister Lyman has come to see your father. His wife is weak and sickly and needs help with the house and garden. And there be none more suitable in the village than you. He has agreed to take you."

"Ah, Mother!" Mary burst out crying. "How can you be so cruel? How could you say yes to that man?"

Thomas opened his eyes and rolled on his side. "Keep your voice low, Mary. You'll wake the whole house."

Margaret sputtered under her breath.

"'Tis already settled. You shall work days at the Lymans' and sleep here at night. Though I told him you were skilled at your chores, I did not spare him knowledge of your faults."

Mary's whimpering and the pitiful look in her eyes were hard to stand up to. "He has agreed to rescue you from your wickedness," Margaret said, "and in exchange for your labors he will give us five pounds a year—six, once they are satisfied with you."

"But, Mother, you'll need my help when the baby comes."

"You are little help, Mary, what with all the squabbling I have to endure. Hannah is old enough to help. Lawrence too."

Mary shook her head. "Hannah is so slow, she'll be no help at all. And Lawrence? He's useless!"

"They are good children, my dear. It is settled. Nothing you may say will change a thing." Defeated, Mary clung to her mother and wept until Margaret let her fall asleep in her arms.

Soon the little house filled with the breath and sighs of sleepers as moonlight seeped through a crack in the door. The oiled paper covering the windows glowed from without, their light falling on the children's angel faces, but, before the moon had risen high in the sky, Mary was gone. She walked quietly in her sleep out into the night, where she would wake up and find herself staring at the moon.

VIII

On Sleeping During Sermons: *"We may here take notice that the nature of man is woefully corrupted and depraved, else they would not be so apt to sleep when the precious Truths of God are dispensed in his Name, Yea, and men are more apt to sleep then, than at another time. Some woeful Creatures, have been so wicked as to profess they have gone to hear Sermons on purpose, that so they might sleep, finding themselves at such times much disposed that way."*

—Increase Mather (1639–1723)

THE MEETING HOUSE was properly set in the center of the village, surrounded by a large open yard. On the hard-packed dirt loomed the stocks, the whipping post, and the pillory, encouraging every sinner to a sober demeanor. Nearly always occupied during the week, these instruments of correction were abandoned on the Sabbath, for criminals were obligated to attend Meeting along with everyone else.

"How ready is the Lord Jesus Christ to save the souls of sinners that affectionately look unto him!" Thomas Bliss said to his children every time they passed the pillory.

Built of clapboard, the Meeting House had many windows, and on its roof a small cupola waited for a bell. The massive front door was nearly invisible under notices, military orders, town regulations and bills. On either side of the door and under every window hung wolves' heads, dried blood from their severed necks darkening the unpainted boards. A dead wolf brought ten shillings from the town.

The Meeting House windows had no glass, but in summer wooden bars kept out wild animals and witches' familiars who had taken wing. In winter the windows were covered with oiled paper and shuttered to keep out the wind. At first the building went unheated—fires belonged in Hell, not in Christ's house. After the Saints put up with one New England winter, this custom vanished. The men sat on one side of the room and the women on the other, all on rows of rough wooden benches. Mister Hooker had to climb steps to reach the pulpit, fashioned with raised oak panels and elevated above the worshippers' heads.

Mary, already favorably impressed by all the stories of Mister Thomas Hooker's bravery and courage, was certain he bore a great likeness to God. Sabbath day, to her, was a mixture of freedom and bondage, of fascination and boredom, endurance and rest, of quiet, and the most conversation she would have all week.

"I take my text this morning from Ezekiel, chapter 11, verse 19," Hooker declared on this particular day. "'I will give them one heart, and put a new spirit within them; I will take away their stony heart, and give them a heart of flesh.' It is true, that we have no sufficiencies in ourselves, yet the Lord Jesus hath enough; the spirit is able to do that for us which we are not able to do for ourselves."

A long pause followed as Hooker waited for the men to stop their conferences, the women to cease their gossip, the children and servants to sit down and stop moving about the room. Sitting between her mother and Hannah, Mary settled herself to listen, for her father might test her on the sermon when she got home. While there was no punishment for not remembering its key points, she would have to respond well enough, else her father would do his best to preach the sermon all over again.

Finally the room fell silent.

"It is a fine passage of David. 'Lord,' says he, 'teach me the way of the Spirit,' as if he had said, 'Lord, I have a naughty spirit,

I have a naughty heart, but Lord, Thou hast a good Spirit, lead me by that good Spirit of Yours in the ways of uprightness. Thus do you wait upon God in His ordinances and say, Lord You have promised that You will put a new soul into Thy people, and create a new heart in them, and throw their sins into the bottom of the sea, and that You will cause them to walk in Thy ways—"

Mary wished for a psalm to sing—some bright song praising God. She fidgeted in her seat thinking about her naughty spirit and her naughty heart. Soon her mother prodded her with a warning elbow.

"You have promised to give Thy Spirit to them that seek it, Lord, make good this promise to me; take away this wretched sinful heart of mine, and create a new heart in me, and direct me by Thy Spirit to walk in the ways of Thy commandments—"

The preacher had lost Mary. She was fixed on a spider waiting patiently in its clever web spanning the corner of a window.

"It is true, Lord, a leper cannot take away his sores, a blackamoor cannot change his hue, but, Lord, You can make a blackamoor white, and You can cleanse the leper; though I be a dead man You can put life into me, though I can do nothing, yet You can do all things—"

Distracted from the spider, Mary's gaze followed the squirrels hopping over the rafters then returned to settle on a fly caught by its wing in the same spider's web. It struggled as the spider wound her web like a fisherman's line. The fly looked as though he would gladly sacrifice a wing to be free.

"I am a blackamoor, but You can make me of a white hue, I am a leper, but You can take away my sores; I am natural and carnal, in me there is no good thing, but, Lord, You can make me entertain spiritual things—"

The spider had closed in, the fly had ceased his struggle, and Mary had shifted her attention to the loft where the town had heaped up its surplus grain and the militia kept its gunpowder store. A beam of sunlight lit up a bale of straw, dust motes billowed like smoke in a radiant shaft of light.

"Therefore begin speedily to attend upon God's ordinances—"

Mary couldn't take her eyes away from the sight, imagining a little flame in the straw. She envisioned the straw smoldering, catching a blaze to quickly run rampant throughout the loft. She saw herself stand and shout, "Fire!" But no one responded, for they were all spellbound by the voice of their beloved preacher. The fire raged on, smoke swirled above their heads, and only Mary saw the caskets of gunpowder blow the roof away.

There were two sermons. Mister Hooker's lasted nearly three hours, and after the midday recess Mister Samuel Stone preached for two. During the break, families spread cloths on the grass, opened their picnic baskets and shared food with their neighbors. Children ran and played, goodwives exchanged news, and their husbands discussed trading deals and unmended fences. And of the second sermon Mary Bliss heard scarcely a word, for she fought throughout it to keep from falling fast asleep.

WITH EVEN MORE than her usual anticipation, Mary set off to visit Goody Crespet. Ever since the day they met in the woods, Goody had been her secret friend. On the road to South Meadow she passed the Podunks' summer camp, some thirty wigwams in the meadow where Indian women had planted corn and were busy tending their field. In passing, Mary nervously looked their way, then, remembering what Goodwife Bartlett had said, she smiled and waved as if they were village women. The squaws seemed pleased and waved back, giving Mary even more new thoughts to ponder about Indians.

She turned off the road onto a footpath winding up the hill above the great river. Sweating from the heat of the day, she was glad for the shade of her hat's wide brim. As she approached Goody's little white house, the sight of her roof, now green with fresh grass shoots and spotted with yellow wildflowers, made her smile. No one else had a house like that anymore, built under a ledge with a grassy hill as a roof over her one room.

Glancing down at the path, Mary stopped dead in her tracks at the sight of a snake sleeping in the warmth of the sun. It wasn't the biggest snake she'd ever seen, but it had a diamond pattern running the full length of its back. It looked like a rattler, though she wasn't sure, because every time her father had killed one she ran away without taking time to study it. She stood still, debating how she should pass. On one side was a barrier of steep rocks, while the other side fell off to the river below. Doing her best to keep calm, she decided to inch her way past on the river side of the path, but as she drew near, the snake reared its head, hissed, and lurched at her, bringing forth an earsplitting scream.

Goody Crespet must have heard Mary's cry from inside her house, for she appeared at her window. Mary went on shrieking at the top of her lungs for Goody to come, while the snake recoiled and puffed itself up. Then all of a sudden it shivered, fell to the ground, rolled belly up, and lay perfectly still.

"Lord have mercy!" Mary cried as Goody reached her side, having run from the house as fast as her short old legs could carry her. "I've killed him!"

"Why, that's Gawain," Goody said. "I haven't seen him all summer." She took hold of him just below his head and lifted him, stroking his long body gently with her little herb-stained fingers.

Mary shuddered. "How can you touch that vile thing?"

"He's not dead, Mary." Goody laughed and gently laid him down on a sun-warmed rock. "Thou frighted him, and when he's afeard he feigns death in the hope that thou wilt go away and leave him alone. That's what he's wishing now, lying there so still on the rock. Shall we take leave of the poor fellow?" She reached to take Mary by the hand.

Mary pulled back, thinking that the same hand had held the snake. "He must not be a rattler—is he?"

"Nay, he be a hognosed snake. Harmless he is—save to a toad. He's been around here many a year. A rattler would shake his tail."

"What name did you call him?"

Goody smiled. "Gawain. I named him for a fearless knight, hoping a brave name would help him to courage."

After the heat of the sun Mary was glad for the shadowy coolness of Goody's little house. "Sit thee down, Mary. After such a fright I'll brew something to calm thee. Tell me, why hast thou come?"

Mary obeyed her friend and took a seat near the open windows. Unlike windows in any other house in the village, they were set side by side, giving a wide view of the river flowing far below. Enchanted by the curious room, she sat quietly taking everything in.

Like every house in the village, its floor was strewn with bits of wormwood and herbs to sweeten the air, and in the dim light of the rafters hung bunches of drying herbs. And there the resemblance to other houses ended. Three speckled eggs lay in a nest on a table strewn with objects which must have been picked up on Goody's walks—weathered sticks, a collection of wild bird feathers, several seashells, the foot of a rabbit and a strange necklace made of rawhide and bear claws, like Mary had seen squaws wear.

A small carved crucifix of great age hung on one wall near an ancient mirror with a long crack running through the middle. These last two things, Goody had told her, came from her husband's family, who were French and Catholic. On another wall a gaily painted charger hung over a two-drawer chest painted black. On the chest rested an oaken coffer with a lock, and next to it a Bible. A blanket chest sat to the right of the fireplace below the tinderbox and a small shelf full of books. Across the room in the shadows stood the bedstead, under a blood-red coverlet. Mary was so taken by the room and the questions it evoked that for a moment she forgot why she had come. Expecting to see Goody's pet crow, she looked up into the rafters. She had seen him the first time she had visited. His name was Uther, and he had been with the old woman ever since his mother was shot in a cornfield.

"Where's Uther?"

"Ah, he's out, taking the air," Goody said. "He won't be long. Now, tell me why hast thou come?"

Just then in a whoosh of black wings Uther flew in through the open window. Cawing and calling "Hello!" he landed in the middle of the table, disturbing the still-life of bird's eggs, twigs, and feathers.

Delighted, Mary held out her hand to him, wondering about

his timing. Strange things happened when Goody was near. "How ever did you teach him to talk?"

"He's a good listener and learned on his own."

"What words can he say? Could I teach him to say my name?" she asked, as Uther stepped onto her hand.

"Try, if it pleases thee," Goody said with a smile.

"Mary. Say Mary," she coaxed, as Uther cocked his head and stared at her like she was daft. "Ah, Uther, can't you say Mar-y— Mar-y?" she begged, as the bird turned his head and flew up to the rafters.

Though disappointed, Mary quickly lost interest, for she remembered what brought her here in the first place. Her eyes filling with tears, she brushed them away to confess, "Mother and Father say I must go into service."

"Where, Mary?"

"At the Lymans'. Do you know Richard Lyman?"

"Only by sight—and his sons and his daughter Sarah. I hath seen them at meeting, but never been called to their house."

Mary wondered if she'd seen the slightest shadow of concern pass over Goody's face. "Mother says I need training by an impartial master, for I am spoiled and willful. She thinks she and Father have loved me too much."

For a moment Goody was silent. "Thou hast many fine virtues, Mary."

"Ah, Goody Crespet, you are deceived. I am the most selfish, willful, spoiled and wicked maiden in all the world."

Goody laughed. "Mary, I am not deceived. Thou art none of those things. Why, what is known as willfulness, in time, may become thy greatest strength. It is true—thou art still young and must yet learn how to use thy will for good. And it is possible that the Lymans be the ones to teach thee. But accept this new turn of events as a blessing, child, for surely your parents love thee so well and know best."

IX

And surely there is in all children . . . a stubbornness, and stoutness of mind arising from natural pride, which must, in the first place, be broken and beaten down; that so the foundation of their education being laid in humility and tractableness, other virtues may, in their time, be built thereon . . . For the beating, and keeping down of this stubbornness parents must provide carefully . . . that the children's wills and willfulness be restrained and repressed, and that, in time; lest sooner than they imagine, the tender sprigs grow to that stiffness, that they will rather break than bow. Children should not know, if it could be kept from them, that they have a will in their own, but in their parents' keeping; neither should these words be heard from them, save by way of consent, 'I will' or 'I will not.'

—John Robinson (1575–1625)
Pastor of the Pilgrims' Church at Lyden

HALF GRUDGING, HALF afraid, Mary walked the mile to Richard Lyman's house. From the road she saw a two-story clapboard dwelling, painted gunmetal gray, sitting properly at the front of thirty acres with fields, a young orchard, and a large woodlot at its back. Determined to make the Lyman family sorry they ever laid eyes on her, she knocked on the front door and was ushered inside by a young woman who wished her "Good morrow." Mary had seen Sarah Lyman at meeting and in town and was immediately taken by her gown with a long, pointed, white collar and blue skirt with black braid at the hem. She was further dazzled by the thin cord Sarah wore around her small waist from which a pair of bright new scissors dangled like a fine piece of jewelry.

"Good morrow," Mary echoed, dropping a little curtsy in deference to Sarah's position and greater age, for she looked all of twenty.

Sarah invited her into the small entranceway, closed the door, and offered to take Mary's shawl, but Mary chose not to part with it.

"Our family is small," Sarah said. "I am the only daughter living at home—with my brothers John and Robert and Mother and Father we are five. Though you need not consider them, I have another brother and a sister as well, both married and living away from this house."

As she spoke, Mary noticed her controlled expressions, the modest lowering of her eyes, the pretty pursing of her lips.

"The work of this house involves diverse duties, but I shall work closely beside you, Mary."

"Mother has trained me well," Mary said. "I weave, mend, and sew—of cookery I am also well learned, and have gardening skills." She did not mention her experience as a laundress, the work she hated more than any other, hoping her duties here would not include the washing.

Sarah said, "If you have no knowledge of spinning, baking or laundry, Mary, I shall teach you."

"I forgot to mention laundry," Mary said to the floor. "I do know how to scrub the clothes clean." Her attempted deception hadn't worked, and heat rose in her face. The ability to deceive, she feared, was the skill she had practiced longest, yet here it did not avail.

"And spinning or baking?"

"I've had little practice. Mother and I are weavers—and we've had no oven at home—until now." Mary assumed that the Lymans spun both woolen and flaxen yarns and sent them to be woven by others, such as the Blisses.

When Sarah moved toward a door, Mary prepared to follow.

"Before I show you the house, I must introduce you to my mother, who is waiting for us behind this door." Sarah's voice was quiet, and she lowered her gaze as slowly she opened the door to the parlor. Her solemn demeanor told Mary that she would do well to steel herself.

Entering the room, Mary could hardly see, for dark loden curtains were pulled closed over both windows. She held her breath, waiting for her eyes to adjust to the gloom, and soon she was able to make out a corner cupboard filled with pewter and brass and a chest with an old Bible resting closed on top. The fireplace centered a blue-paneled wall with several closed doors that she presumed concealed shelves. Two carved and joined stools rested beside the fire. The massive bed filled one end of the large room, larger than any of the Blisses' or their neighbors' rooms, its furnishings so fine they took Mary's breath away.

The mistress of the house was ensconced atop a feather bed in the middle of a large bedstead curtained in indigo serge. She was a pasty, gray-looking little thing, dressed in an over-laced cap, her two white collars and laced cuffs standing out from her dark-gray gown.

Sarah almost whispered. "Mother, Thomas Bliss's daughter is here. Mary, meet my mother."

"How do you do." The woman sighed weakly, looking over her spectacles at Mary. As if Mary was too witless to answer for herself, she directed her question to Sarah. "What's her name?"

"Mary—Mary Bliss, Mother."

Mary couldn't guess what burdens of body and spirit weighed the mistress so mightily, though she suspected some tragedy had overwhelmed her, her face and body wore such a heavy mantle of sorrow. The meeting was brief, mere dutiful inquiries from Mistress Lyman as to the health of her mother and father. Satisfied with Mary's replies, she dismissed the two. "Sarah, show the maid the rest of the house."

The kitchen, with its massive fireplace, had a gigantic stone hearth on its way to a rich patina from fat sputtering off roasting meats spitted on two long, hand-turned rods. It was a large new room, running the width of the house with a small dairy room at its north end. Work would be a pleasure in such a fine kitchen, where wall shelves were laden with platters and chargers, vessels, a chafing dish, and an old wooden firkin. With seven rooms and an attic, the house was large for such a small family.

Within an hour Mary was thoroughly charmed with the house and its young mistress and fascinated by old Mistress Lyman. She could almost smell the mysteries hidden behind the closed doors around the parlor fireplace. Even the clean-swept floorboards reeked of secrets. Forgetting her resolve to make the Lymans miserable, Mary determined to become indispensable to the family, to learn all she could about the house and its strange mistress.

DURING THE DAY Mistress Lyman never moved far from her bed or chair. No matter the weather, she wrapped herself tight in a heavy shawl. She did no work, and she slept for hours. One day, about a fortnight after Mary first laid eyes on that house, Sarah told Mary she had spinning to do and asked her to make jelly. She supplied her the calves' feet and asked her to wash and scald them. Mistress Lyman had dragged herself into the kitchen and pulled up a chair by a window, apparently so she could watch Mary work.

Mary went to work scalding the feet, then splitting them with a hatchet, all the while offering her mistress a stream of polite, friendly chatter. But Mistress Lyman said not a word. Eventually Mary continued her work in silence and before long felt she was walking on eggshells, wishing she were invisible, growing cold in her mistress's gaze. The old woman stared shamelessly, offering no instruction or pleasant conversation. Mary put the calves' feet to boil in an iron caldron, covered them with clean water, and prayed the old woman would fix her eyes on the book lying open in her lap and stop molesting her with her gaze.

That night as Mary snuggled beside her sister in bed her dreams were filled with sorrowful eyes—the same haunting, dark-blue eyes that had watched her in the kitchen. She woke in tears and climbed into bed beside her mother, waking her.

"Mary, have you had a bad dream?"

"Aye, Mother, I beg you, do not send me back to that house where my mistress's sorrow is blacker than night. My dream is a bad omen—I know it."

Sorrow was no stranger to Margaret. "Pay her no mind, child. There's nothing you must do in that house but your work. You're not responsible to cheer her. Some folks are thin and melancholic. Be thankful for your own more sanguine nature and be of good cheer."

In the morning Mary pled her case once more. "Mother, I do beg you, have mercy." She wept, and when that altered nothing, tried another tack. "I have too many mistresses in that house. I am beneath them both."

Margaret made no reply, but the glimmer in her eyes let Mary know she hadn't an ounce of sympathy for her plight. No doubt she believed such a low position was exactly what a haughty maiden like Mary needed. After a breakfast of bread sopped in warm milk straight from the cow, she sent her daughter off for another day at the Lymans'.

As the only daughter at home, Sarah was required to do some of the work. Often she worked with Mary in the garden or kitchen; but the day came when she wanted Mary to do her share of the spinning. The Lymans had a great wheel for wool and a small one for flax, so both young women could spin.

Taking shelter from the hot sun in the shade of an old tree, Sarah, with her round, creamy face, slender body, and fine obedient, honey-colored hair, and Mary, with a face full of summer freckles, hair wild as a spring gale, and a ripening figure, began the spinning lesson.

"No matter how often you watch, Mary, you shall never learn without practice," Sarah said, sitting at the Saxony wheel with a handful of well-hackled flax. Mary watched her turn the wheel with one hand, drawing the fine long fibers into a uniform, continuous yarn. Her fingers moved quickly, gracefully drawing the web.

"Yesterday," Mary said, "you promised to tell me about your childhood in England." She was imitating Sarah's spinning hand motions.

"Mother said I was born in the dark of the moon in February, the same year the Pilgrim Fathers landed at Plymouth." Sarah kept her eyes on the bobbin as she talked. "It was during the reign of King James. I took a long time coming, nearly killing poor Mother. I grew to a maid on a great estate outside High Ongar. Our home lay all the way across the water meadow from the village, where the townsfolk lived in little houses crowded along narrow streets."

She sighed, her delicate fingertips effortlessly guiding her web. "To this day, if it is very quiet and I close my eyes, I find myself back there." The way she said it echoed Mary's own longings for home—for England. "I wish we'd never left that heavenly place," Sarah said, then stopped spinning to look at her pupil. "Now, Mary, let me watch you spin."

Already seated at the great wheel with tummed and carded wool in her hand, Mary set the wheel spinning, drawing out the wool with her fingers as the spindle twirled it to yarn.

"Go steady—not too taut," Sarah said. "Your wool is coarse, so from it you must draw a coarse thread."

Mary eased up on the wool and felt the spinning go more easily. "How far back can you remember?" She called up her own favorite memory—the view from the top floor of her father's house.

"'Tis hard to tell, but I remember the day Father took us through Epping Forest on the way to visit our cousins at St. Albans. I was small enough to sit on Father's lap." Sarah smiled at the thought. "Our carriage moved swiftly along a narrow highway through the dark forest. I still hold my breath remembering how the horses ran through the fearsome darkness, to a place where the forest gave way to a clearing. There we saw King James with his hunting party."

Mary was amazed, even a little jealous of Sarah's good luck. "I can't see how you know it was the King!"

"Father said so." Sarah sounded a mite irritated. "Besides, everyone knew he rode a tall black horse and was a great hunter; and there we saw the same, along with other riders, and a pack of hunting dogs." She paused to take a breath and temper her excitement. "The King smiled at me as we passed, and I waved to him. I shall never forget how it felt to be smiled upon by the King. I was bewitched, though Father said he was an evil man. He was an enemy of our religion, and when he died soon after, I was glad of it."

Mary feared she'd never get to tell her memory, for Sarah went on and on, mentioning every one of her ancestors, most notably her uncle Sir John Lyman, the knight merchant who'd become Lord Mayor of London four years before she was born. Her brother John had been named for that same great man.

As Sarah talked, Mary learned that the Lyman family had sailed from London to Massachusetts Bay on the ship *Lyon* when Sarah was nearly twelve years old. "Sailing with us were distinguished men," she said, "the great preacher Mister John Eliot, and the wife and son of Governor John Winthrop. We arrived to cheering crowds, for our coming reunited the governor with his family. Celebrations and prayers of thanksgiving were offered throughout the town," she said proudly, her bobbin now full of fine-spun flaxen threads.

The difference in their stories stung Mary hard. No one had noticed the Blisses' arrival, and furthermore, the Lymans had come to the New World by choice, not in desperation, settling first in Roxbury, where John Eliot was minister. Their youngest son, Robert, was born there. But after only four years Richard Lyman had sold his property, trekking west with a group of Saints bound to settle Connecticut. He was among the first to arrive at Hartford.

As Sarah talked on, they spun their threads and Mary seldom got a word in. This must be good training, Mary admitted to herself, for someone as proud as I. At home, among her siblings, she was always in command. And what was more, she had to admit that she took pleasure in watching her young mistress, hoping one day to grow half as lovely as she.

. . . . .

As for young Robert Lyman, Mary had finally met someone more selfish and spoiled than herself. A fat, lazy, incorrigible boy, he ordered Mary around like his private slave. Strangely, when his demands were directed at someone else, she found them fascinating, for he was brash enough to carry them to elegant extremes. He seemed not to care a whit what anyone thought of him. She soon discovered he had a knack for disappearing just when there was work to be done, though his absence was such a great relief that Mary never minded his slacking.

Margaret, for her part, fulfilling everyone's predictions by giving birth to twin girls, loved to hear Mary's stories about the Lyman family, though she always prefaced her questions warning that by gossip they trod a dangerous path.

"You must not tell tales out of the Lyman house, Mary, especially not to wives in the village. Idle talk is a sin, and I do not approve."

It was late in the evening, and one of the new babies, Hester, had begun to fuss, so Margaret removed the sated twin, Elizabeth, from her breast. She laid the sleeping baby in its cradle, lifted the other, and put her to the full breast.

"Now, Mary, tell me what befell that house today."

"No one could find Robert," Mary said, happy to have her mother's attention. "I heard my mistress tell Sarah to fetch him, for Robert is just of an age to help his father. But all the day long he was nowhere to be found. Late, as I was about to set out for home, here came Robert driving a sow down the road, cursing her and hitting the poor beast on her back with a long staff, as she squealed and tried to run away. His father, all red-faced, dealt with the lad about where he got the sow, but I heard not what he answered, for they sent me away."

"He stole it, I'll warrant you!" In saying such a thing Margaret shocked herself, thinking the worst on no better grounds.

EVERY AFTERNOON BEFORE the sun got too low, Mary set out for the long walk home by the road to South Meadow. After a day's hard work she hated tramping home in all kinds of weather, arriving just in time to help her mother with supper. Goodman Lyman had told her about a path through the woods to the road, and one day she decided to try the shortcut.

It was a fine early autumn afternoon, and after crossing the hayfield and the orchard, Mary stepped onto the path through the wood, looking up to watch a flock of snow geese cross the sky. Maples flared scarlet and gold beside rusty oaks and chestnuts, the pale gray of shaggy birch trunks and vibrant green spruces. She walked happily along, thinking of Sarah: What she needs is a husband, and a home of her own. Mary worried that her young mistress's spirit was too permeable, constantly subject to her mother's melancholia. I know well how Mistress Lyman's gloomy countenance weighs on me, and I'm not so easily moved as poor Sarah.

Suddenly frightened, she halted. Have I strayed off the path? She looked around and saw no path either coming or going. To calm her fears, she took her bearings. She was traveling south, for the sun was low in the west. If I keep the sun at my right shoulder, I'll come out of the woods at the right place. Heaving a sigh of relief, she walked on for a while, and when she saw the road in the distance through the trees began to run. But the moment she did so the earth beneath her feet gave way and she fell, plunging through darkness into the hard cold earth at the bottom of a deep hole.

When she awoke she had a terrible headache and no knowledge of how long she had lain there. Through the jagged opening above, she could make out the darkening sky. She reached to soothe the pain in her knee, then stood up, touching the wooden support beams that surrounded her. Now she knew full well where she was. Mary had watched her father dig a wolf pit just like this one—deeper and wider than a grave, lined with stripped planks too slippery for a wolf, or for a maiden, to scale. She knew that wolves hunted at night, and only when morning came would the maker of a wolf pit go to check his trap. Furthermore, she knew that at this hour Goodman Lyman, whose pit this surely was, had just finished supper and was lighting his pipe.

"O, Lord," she prayed, knowing there was no chance for escape before morning. "Don't let a wolf fall in beside me." Though calling for help was useless, she hollered at the top of her lungs until she made herself hoarse. Weeping, she remembered the day she had looked down into Robert Bartlett's wolf pit to see the red-hot terror in a trapped bitch-wolf's eyes. Best not to think of that now. She found it a comfort to sit down and let herself sob. With a bright full moon in plain view it seemed to her that it was a fine bright night for a nocturnal hunt. So as not to attract wild beasts, she decided to make herself very still. Crawling out of the pool of moonlight at the center of the pit, she curled up out of sight in a dark corner and began to pray.

"Lord, You are my rock and my tower. Deliver me," she whispered softly, finding comfort in the words so often sung at meeting. "Help me, Lord, if it be Thy will, for I cannot find my way out of this hole." Exhausted, she closed her eyes and slept for a time without dreams, her head resting on one bent arm.

"Good even!" came a rasping voice from on high. At first Mary was not certain she was awake at all, for the voice was strange indeed. She could see no one, only bright moonlight streaming in through the hole.

"Good even! Mary, Mary!" came the ragged voice once more.

She struggled to her feet to stand. "Who calls?"

The voice she'd heard was strange and inhuman, but too high-pitched and indelicate to be the voice of God. Then suddenly she saw something move at the top of the hole.

"Who's there?" Frightened, she moved back into the shadows.

"Heh-heh-heh-ha-ha!" The voice was unmistakable.

"Uther!" She was astonished to see the black crow—a silhouette against the moonlit sky. "Uther!" she cried again. At the sound of her voice the crow took flight.

"Don't leave me! Uther, come back," she called, straining on tiptoe, hopeful for another glimpse. But he was gone.

"Surely I am the unluckiest, most miserable soul on earth," she said aloud.

A long spell of quiet followed, and then the crunching of dry leaves as something approached the wolf pit. Mary held her breath, sure that her heart had stopped. Something trod softly above her. It was not a great thing, for the earth did not shake, but something small and wary.

"Dear God," she whispered, "save me." She slid back into the darkness just as a shadow fell over the hole. Though she wanted to scream, she clapped both hands over her mouth. The shadow receded, leaving nothing but night sky above, and then a dark form blotted out the moon.

"Mary?" This voice was soft and small.

At once Mary knew who it was. "Goody Crespet! You found me!"

"'Twas Uther who found thee," she said, as he landed in a flutter of wings on her shoulder.

"I have a rope, but first I must tie it to a tree, for I lack strength enough to haul thee up." She disappeared for a time while Uther perched at the edge of the hole, impatiently pacing and cawing.

Goody came back, lowering a rope tied with several large knots. "Let us hope thou art a strong one and can pull thyself up," she said.

"I've never scaled a rope before," Mary said, thankful for the chance.

"Use the knots to brace thyself and shinny up."

Gripping the rope between her knees, Mary grabbed with both hands just above one of the knots, then another, until she had struggled slowly to the top, where Goody Crespet waited to greet her.

"Praise God!" Mary cried. "How shall I ever thank you?" She hugged the tiny old creature around the neck. "I thought I would perish for sure." She sat down suddenly, overcome with sobs.

"Now, now," Goody said, "'tis not all that fearsome a place, a hole in the ground. I'd rather be there than in some goodwives' kitchens."

Mary was amazed, believing she had been in great peril. "Why on earth?"

"One day thou shalt hear the hateful sound of gossip and know what I mean."

Goody offered Mary a hand to help her to her feet and they began to walk through the woods, the old midwife now no taller than Mary's shoulder. She understood what Goody meant, for she had already heard plenty of gossip about Goody Crespet. And what if she does practice witchcraft? She has saved me. She only uses her magic for good.

"Now I am weary," the old woman said, out of breath, "but my house is very near." Tonight thou shalt sleep at home with me. There are wolves in these woods, and I cannot ensure thy safety tonight. Never fear, I'll wake thee at dawn."

Mary was not concerned about Goody's plan, for now and then when the Lymans had great need of her she stayed the night with them. She knew that her mother would not worry. Holding Goody's tiny rough hand, she trudged along with her through the dark wood, the full moon barely lighting the path. Very soon they came upon a bright clearing, and through the trees Mary could see Goody's little white house shining in the moonlight, a lazy stream of smoke rising from its chimney. The clearing itself was small and perfectly round with a series of flat stones set in a circle around kindling wood laid for a fire. Goody stopped and, kneeling, lit the fire.

"What is this place?" Mary asked. Clearly, her friend had come earlier to lay the fire.

"This is where I come the first night of every harvest moon. I always celebrate this night alone, but tonight"—she smiled—"I shall have company. Here"—she indicated one of the stones—"sit thee down beside me."

Mary sat down as the fire began to catch. Uther, who had flown off, returned, descending into the circle to stalk around the fire like a stiff-legged old man muttering under his breath.

Mary, relieved, was finally able to laugh. "He sounds like an old man cursing!"

"He is," Goody, said, setting herself off on a fantastical torrent of laughter.

Mary listened as her merry convulsions bubbled like song. Most goodwives titter, Mary thought, but not Goody. When the old woman was composed at last, they sat silently staring at the moon. How still was the night, no sound but the crackling fire as sparks flew skyward and the silvery moonlight sent thrills up and down Mary's spine.

At length she broke the restful peace. "Why do you come here?"

"Because of the moon."

In silence Mary gazed at it for awhile. "Oh, Goody, how lovely and mysterious and ancient is the moon."

"Aye, sunshine gives life, but moonlight is a source of wisdom. I come here to remember, Mary."

"To remember?"

"My grandmother. Her wisdom came from the moon, and it was she who taught me."

"How I wish I had a grandmother." Mary believed that grandmothers loved their granddaughters absolutely.

"Thou hast such a one, Mary, if it is thy wish."

Touched, the girl whispered her thanks as she took Goody's hand. "Will you teach me everything your grandmother taught you?"

"Nay, I cannot. 'Tis forbidden. When I was a child I lived in a land ancient and hallowed—it was a different time. Here the old teachings will die with women like me."

"They won't if you give me your knowledge."

Goody patted Mary's hand and smiled to herself. "Throughout thy lifetime, moonlight shall quicken thy wisdom. Thou must remember this and hearken unto the moon."

Though Mary did not understand her words about moon wisdom, she understood that her friend had refused to teach her what was forbidden. She wondered if Goody Crespet's secret knowledge had something to do with witchcraft. She wanted to ask but was afraid to put the question.

"Dost thou know, Mary, that there's more than one kind of witchcraft?"

"And is it evil?"

"Witchcraft is evil if it is used to pervert nature for personal gain."

"I have never heard one thing about witches that was good."

"Knowledge is neither good nor evil. It is all around us and may be used by both good and evil folk. Now, child, we must be silent"—Goody raised a bent finger to the moon—"and let her teach us."

Doing just that, they sat in restful silence for a long while more. Mary guessed that the old woman was waiting; she waited, too. When the fire had died to coals and only the moon lighted their faces, a breeze stirred in the trees, rattling dry leaves, filling their noses with the smells of a forest sleeping. The breeze hurried on, and the air grew still and quiet, as a large white-tailed stag with massive antlers walked into the clearing.

Goody Crespet clasped Mary's hand tight.

The stag looked toward the old woman and the maiden huddled together. He raised his head to sniff the air, then walked toward the center of the clearing, stopping a scant distance from the ring of stones and the dying embers.

Even though she sensed that Goody had no fear, Mary's heart began to pound. The tiny wise woman's face lit up with a quiet smile. The gigantic buck stood boldly towering over them, his head held high while the moon seemed to rest in his antlers. For what seemed a long time to Mary, they sat hand in hand facing the stag, who bore his rack like a crown. At last he backed away. He lowered his head, snorted in the dust, then slowly turned and walked back to the cover of the trees.

"Oh, Goody," Mary whispered, "look at him go. He looks like a mighty king, so proud, and strong. Have you seen him before? Do you know him?"

"Nay, Mary. He came unexpected. I believe he is very old and soon to die. In days of yore, people lived more at peace with wild places. That was before preachers gave us to fear the natural world."

"You are not a Christian, are you, Goody?" she asked, frightened to hear her answer. She loved the old woman, and to be other than a Christian was a great sin.

"I am a Christian. I believe God came down to earth to live as man, and I believe all that He taught us. I believe His holy spirit is with us here now, that He dwells in every house, weeping tears for the bitter way we treat one another." Her voice strangely firm, she stood up, her white hair glowing with the moon at her back. "Now I am weary, child. We must leave the moonlight and go to bed."

Moonstruck, Mary felt no hunger, but before they slept Goody Crespet insisted that she eat bread and honey washed down with a strong hot drink—delicious but foreign to Mary. Pouring a large basin full of hot water, Goody persuaded Mary to wash her face, hands and feet.

"Aren't you afeard I'll catch my death?" Mary's mother would never have allowed her to bathe at night.

"Nay, child, after a day of hard work, thou must wash if thou wishes to live healthy. These days folks are superstitious about bathing. Why, I've always kept myself well scrubbed, and 'tis plain to see I have outlived everyone I knew in my youth and am now so old I know things nobody else remembers."

Mary looked at her hands, with black dirt from the wolf pit embedded under her broken nails, and plunged them into the basin of hot water. Shivers of pleasure ran up her arms and all the way up her spine.

Goody Crespet handed her soap and a towel. "These will help," she said, leaving Mary to her task. She turned away and went to open a small box on a table beside the fire.

Mary took the strong-smelling soap in her hands and scrubbed them well, then rubbed soap on her face and splashed it, enjoying the feel of warm water on her skin. When she had finished, the old woman helped her lower the basin to the floor so that Mary might wash her feet and ankles before drying herself with the towel. She removed her outer garments but was ashamed for her host to see her dingy old shift. Originally white, little washing and constant wear had aged it to a dull gray.

Goody had noticed. "I have a fine large piece of bleached linen I shall give thee for a new shift," she said. "I would sew it myself, but my hands are too stiff for sewing." She showed Mary where she must sleep and kindly pulled the covers down. "'Tis late, my child. Now get thyself into bed. I have a thing to give thee." She took something shiny from her pocket. "Open thy hand, Mary." When Mary did, the cunning woman placed something in it. "Here, I've had this since I was a young maid."

Mary looked into her palm to see a fine silver chain. When she lifted it, a silver ornament adorned with curious markings dangled from it. In its center was a large cross with a circle over it and two strange words, *Sola Gratia*, then at the bottom three crosses and what looked like a snake. She turned it over to see that the back was shiny, as though rubbed to a polish. "How comely. What is it?"

"'Tis for thy protection. I've had it near all my life."

"What does it say? I do not know these words."

"You've no need to know the meaning tonight. Wear it under thy shift and show it to no one."

"But I want to know. And why should no one see?"

"Such things are not allowed in this place. If thou dost not want to wear it, then keep it safe hidden—it will still protect thee."

Feeling like a princess, Mary climbed into bed, her newly scrubbed skin tingling, her nose filled with the smell of soap. Reeling with excitement and the wonder of the night's events, Mary slipped the silver chain around her neck and hoped her mind would let her rest in such a large bed. She settled in under the sheets and snuggled up to a mountain of soft pillows. Above, Uther perched in the rafters, and Goody was still busy beside the fire. "Thanks be, Goody."

"Sleep, Mary. I shall wake thee at dawn." The old woman sat down in her three-legged chair.

"Aren't you coming to bed?" Mary yawned, suddenly so drowsy she could hardly keep her eyes open.

"My body is tired, but my mind wants to read for a while," Goody said, her voice distant and small as she picked up her Bible.

"Thank you for finding me and—" Mary was fast asleep, dreaming that Mary Crespet was a young maiden of her own age. She saw her standing before a blazing fire as she loosed her long, shining black hair. Dressed only in her white shift, she lifted it over her head and let it drop to the floor. Naked, except for something silver glittering around her neck, she was no more than a thin, wavering silhouette against the fire, so transparent she glowed like a finger held close to a candle. She raised her arms heavenward, her voice like a song as she prayed. Suddenly a small radiant creature, flying in circles around the room, landed on one of her outstretched hands. Stroking the thing, she spoke to it softly. The dreamer could not see what it was, but it was not Uther, nor any other bird she had ever seen.

X

He brought children: Phillis, Richard, Sarah, and John. He was an ancient Christian, but weak: yet after some time of trial and quickening he joined the church. When the great removal was made to Connecticut he also went, and underwent much affliction; for going toward winter, his cattle were lost in driving, and some of them never found again. And the winter being cold, and ill provided, he was sick and melancholy. Yet after, he had some revivings through God's mercy . . .

—John Eliot (1604–1690), writing of
Richard Lyman (1580–1641)

B Y LATE NOVEMBER, with the country covered in snow, it was agreed between Mister Lyman and Mary's father that, except for the Sabbath, she was to stay at the Lymans'. She did not mind sleeping in the straw bed at one end of the kitchen, the warmest room in the house.

From early morning till dusk Mister Lyman's days were spent in his orchards and fields. He had several acres of maslin, a mixture of wheat and rye from which most of their bread was made, more acres of summer wheat and oats. Smaller fields were used to grow peas and barley, and in the largest he grew Indian corn and feed for livestock.

Mary came to know the master of the house when they gathered for catechism after the evening meal. She couldn't help comparing Richard Lyman to her father. Her master was a quiet man—more placid than Thomas Bliss—much smaller, with a full head of graying blond hair, a near-white beard, and blue eyes reddened by the sun and wind. He rarely showed his temper. Mary considered him fine-looking, for an old man.

Beside the kitchen fire on winter evenings, with the young people gathered around, Mister Lyman read from his Bible. His voice was low and melodious, and he read as if he had written the words himself. We are all perfectly able to read for ourselves, Mary thought, but the warmth of the fire, the well-schooled voice, and the gathering of souls seemed as important to her as the holy words. Though the law required that the head of household teach weekly catechism, Mister Lyman counted these hours with his children among his favorites and called them to the fireside nearly every night without fail.

Mistress Lyman never joined them in the kitchen. She haunted them through the open door as she sat alone in the parlor, reading in the glow of that fire. Mary noticed how kindly her master treated his wife, attending to her wishes, and allowing her to rest when and where she wanted. Sometimes, if the young folk had caused no conspicuous worry and appeared in no immediate need of scriptural attention, they could get Richard Lyman to tell them stories about the wider world or his own adventures. One night he chose to tell them about something that had happened in Hartford.

"Today the General Court met to adopt The Fundamental Orders of Connecticut. Does anyone know what that means?"

John leaned forward, glad he knew the answer. "Yes, Father, we heard Mister Hooker's sermon. The governor and magistrates have used his ideas to draw up orders for the government."

"Right you are, lad. At the opening session, Mister Hooker spoke about freedom. He said 'the foundation of authority is laid in the free consent of the people.' What is the meaning of these words?"

Not sure, Mary took a chance. "Does it mean that free men

must chose their own government? Like here—where we live—that we in Connecticut must not live under the rule of the King?"

"Aye, in part, Mary, and those Fundamental Orders lay out a plan for just such a government. Nothing like it has been written before. Through it we shall have regular elections, and magistrates sworn by oath to administer justice according to the laws established *here*. It has been ordered that no man stand as governor for more than two years at one time, and that standing courts shall meet twice a year, and that the towns will send deputies to represent them at court. My children, these are significant times."

To Mary, Goodman Lyman seemed as good as a preacher, better even, for his eyes danced with enthusiasm for the ideas he shared. He spoke of things spiritual. He delighted in commenting on the meaning behind the Bible stories and welcomed the children's questions, while Mary's poor father pulled out the Bible and, in a weary voice, did his duty after too many long hours of hard work.

Throughout the whole conversation, wayward Robert Lyman had fidgeted and squirmed, yawning as his eyelids drooped with boredom.

The elder Lyman eyed the indifferent boy. "Robert, what say you? We have heard nothing from you."

Robert looked defiant. "I want to go to bed."

Mary had seen the look often, usually just before he bolted for the door. She braced herself for the storm that was sure to follow.

But Lyman said, with measured calm, "Very well, after a closing prayer, we shall all retire for the night." He closed his eyes and bowed his head, a signal for all to do the same.

"O Lord, bless this house and everyone in it, especially Robert, who does not understand that he must lead his life straight. For on the Day of Judgment we all shall stand not only before God but our parents as well. Amen."

Mary knew what that meant. God listens to everything your parents say about how good or bad you are and puts you in Heaven or Hell based on their references.

Lyman raised his bowed head to gaze intently at his stubborn youngest son. "What are children by nature?" he asked.

Robert yawned again. "Children are sinful by nature."

"Well, then, if that is true—which it is—how do children achieve salvation?"

At least Robert knew the right answer. "Salvation comes through knowledge of God and his laws and through diligent prayer and catechizing."

"Salvation is impossible without knowledge," Lyman went on. "And knowledge is impossible without attention, Robert. With knowledge, your corrupt nature will be redeemed and one day you shall become a fine Christian man." He looked tired. "Now, it is late—we shall retire for the night. I want each of you to think on Satan and how he is at work in your lives, for tomorrow night we shall speak on sin."

Mary, who felt she had spent her whole life getting into trouble, already knew far too much about Satan's work with children. Since she had been with the Lymans she had noticed that Sarah seldom got into trouble. But when she did, Mary envied her ability to turn white as snow and look chastened near to death. In the face of such contrition, her parents always forgave her, and she went unpunished.

IN MARCH, MISTER Lyman came down with the rheum. Sarah and Mary nursed him for the accompanying flux, fever, and coughing. Though they gave him nutmegs, aqua vitae, rose-water, and every other medicine know to them, he did not revive. When Mary suggested that they call Goody Crespet, Sarah seemed put off by the idea and sent for the doctor instead. The man, one Rosseter by name, had to come all the way from Windsor, arriving late in the afternoon. Mary was shocked when she saw how young he was. How could one so young know anything about illness? She longed to be able to convince Sarah to send for Goody, for she had every confidence in the cunning woman's skills.

Sarah's face was pale and drawn with fatigue as she explained to Mary what the doctor had done. "After bleeding Father and giving him a vomit, the doctor instructed that his diet be nothing but broths and pottages seasoned with hot and dry herbs. 'Tis late, Mary, and Mister Rosseter cannot travel all the way back to Windsor. He must stay the night here. Please change the sheets in the small chamber upstairs and build him a fire."

The doctor had been gone three days, and though Mary and Sarah had followed his instructions exactly, Mister Lyman was no better. A heavy pall of sadness fell on the house, and Mary longed to go home. She wanted desperately to sit beside her mother and tell her all that had come to pass since she'd seen her last Sabbath. Every night Mary sat on her bed in the kitchen and, after prayers begging God's mercy for her master, wondered if she should go against Sarah's wishes and ask Goody Crespet for help.

On the fourth night the house shook as sleet and wind loosed their fury. Mary pulled her blanket close, listening to the walls creak. A loose shutter banged somewhere outside, probably on the dairy. As she often did when she felt lonely or ill at ease, she reached for the silver amulet Goody had given her to keep around her neck. She always found comfort merely from the weight of it in her hand.

Just then, through the open door to the parlor, she glimpsed the pale glow of a moving candle. Mistress Lyman was pacing the dark room. All day long, Mary thought, she is naught but a sick weak little thing, yet well enough to march up and down once the sun sets. As her mistress approached the kitchen door, Mary watched the light from her candle fall across the kitchen floor, its flame like a single star in the night. And when Mistress Lyman turned, her shadow blotted out the light and fell close over Mary's face like a smothering hand. Back and forth she paced, the light pouring over the floorboards just before her awful shadow descended.

Why, Mary asked herself, does she frighten me so? I don't believe she is ill; she pretends to be frail so that all will pity her. As the candle approached once more Mary shrank back, and this time when Mistress Lyman stopped to look into the kitchen, Mary held her breath and half-closed her eyes.

Raising her candle to better regard her young servant, Mistress Lyman stood a long time watching Mary. The flickering candle-light turned the old woman's face into a baleful mask of light and shadow. One eye, shining from its dark pocket, reflected the flame in her hand as her thin lips twisted into a grin.

Mary's heart leapt into her throat. Why does she look at me like that? I've never seen her look so long, with such interest, at anything else before. I know not what sad old women think to themselves, but she frightens me. Is there nothing in her house, indeed her life, to enthrall her except me? Through her half-closed lids Mary saw her mistress turn and walk back into the parlor and watched her blow out the candle and sit down by the fire. At least for now her pacing was at an end.

Mary pulled the covers over her head and struggled to soften her heart toward Mistress Lyman. She made herself remember what Sarah had said about her sad life: *Ill fortune has followed her most of her days. I believe she suffers from a broken heart.*

Poor soul, Mary thought, wondering why her own mother, who had also suffered the loss of her home and infants in the childbed, was able to replace her grief with hard work and some gift for happiness. No matter how long she thought about these mysteries and how much she wanted to understand, she could not. She lifted the silver amulet into the light from the open door. *Sola Gratia.* Mary had again asked Goody the meaning of the words, and she had answered, "Grace alone." And when Mary had asked what it meant, Goody answered, "We are saved by God's grace. Not by anything we do to deserve salvation." Mary kissed the round silver disc, which had grown warm in her hand, and tucked it back inside her shift, reassured that though she was surrounded by mystery, she was safe.

All week long as they bustled from task to task trying to run the house and care for the ailing master, Sarah's impatience came down hard on Mary. One morning after she had scolded Mary again Sarah burst into tears of frustration. "I shall die if I have no rest," she wailed.

Mary gave her a glass of sack and insisted that she lie down, offering to make the midday meal. Grateful for her help, Sarah lay down on Mary's bed in the kitchen, so fatigued that the sound of clamoring pots did not disturb her sleep.

On the Sabbath the younger Lymans went off to meeting, leaving Mary at home to tend to the ailing master and mistress. This pleased Mary not at all. It was her agreed-upon right to go home with her parents after meeting each week, to rest and eat her mother's cooking, perhaps to laugh, to be out from under the melancholy of the Lyman house. But she was needed and would not have a day of rest this week.

Mary took a tray to Goodwife Lyman in the parlor where she slept, resting after her nighttime promenade. She returned to the kitchen and prepared a tray for her master, with naught but wine and clear pottage, and carried it upstairs to his room. She found him propped up in bed with a mountain of pillows at his back. The chill room smelled of frankincense and sage simmering in a kettle over the fire. Mister Lyman stared straight at the wall, his eyes oddly glazed, his complexion bluish, his breath rasping and painfully labored. As she approached, he tried to speak but was stopped by a coughing fit.

"Don't try to talk," Mary said, going to his side, patting his back until the fit ran its course.

Gratefully he took her hand and with enormous effort said, "Mary, you must bring me something solid to eat. Say not a word—they're starving me to death."

"What have you eaten today?"

"Only clear broth—that's all they've allowed since first the doctor came."

"But the doctor said—"

"Damn the doctor! Bring me some meat," he gasped, coughing again.

Mary returned to the kitchen. She sliced a piece of mutton from the bone, and with some bread and butter in hand, hurried back to her master's room. While she buttered his bread, she made him drink his broth, then allowed him the meat. He ate, relishing every bite, smacking his lips, licking his fingers. Satisfied, he sank into his pillows and sighed.

Mary feared she had taken too much on herself. "We must be careful not to overfeed you. The doctor said—"

"May he rot in Hell! 'Tis your mutton that has saved me, for this hour at least."

Mary decided to risk a question. "Mister Lyman?" When he looked at her as if granting permission for her to speak, she said, "I know a cunning woman—she's very wise. Since you seem to have no liking for the doctor, may I fetch her? I have so much trust in her, she might prevail where he has not."

Lyman smiled weakly, showing a trace of his former self. "You are a good girl, Mary, I cannot imagine why your parents think otherwise. If you value this woman, then send for her. I would trust my life to her before that quack." He reached for Mary's hand and gave it a gentle pat of dismissal, then closed his eyes to rest.

When Sarah, John and Robert came in from meeting, Mary was washing up the dishes, deep in thought about Mister Lyman.

Sarah took off her cloak and hung it on the peg by the door. "How is Father this afternoon?"

"He is resting now, Sarah. He is discontented with the doctor and has asked me to fetch Goody Crespet."

"What! Why would he even think of sending for that woman? You tried to convince him, didn't you?" Sarah threw herself onto a chair, regarding Mary with contempt.

"Nay, I only mentioned her."

"You should know better, Mary. I'll not have to do with that woman or her remedies." Sarah stood, her angel face twisted with hatred. "The blare-eyed witch does the work of the Devil— everyone says that!"

Mary, who was now as tall as Sarah, drew herself up to her greatest height. "Your father has asked for her himself. He knows that the doctor has failed."

"How dare you twist the mind of a dying man?" Sarah raged. "He is fevered out of his wits and would agree to anything."

"'Tis nothing but gossip you've heard about Goody Crespet. I assure you, she is kind and wise—I know it as sure as I know the same of my mother. If you do nothing and he dies, you will have yourself to blame." Mary reached for her cloak.

"How dare you speak so to me! You've been tricked, Mary Bliss. The witch is a practiced deceiver. The Devil follows her wherever she goes. Why, she's been seen in both Hartford and Lyme on the very same day—impossible lest one flies on a broom staff. I forbid you to bring her into this house. Why, with my own eyes I saw a black crow following her on the road."

That's just Uther, Mary wanted to say, but she dared not. She did venture, "Say what you will, I'll not believe it—you repeat nothing but wicked gossip and lies."

With no venom left for a fight, Sarah collapsed to her knees, buried her face in her hands, and wept. Disgusted by her intolerance and her weakness, Mary put on her cloak, took up her muff, and walked out of the house, caring not at all what punishment she faced upon her return. I would not return at all, she thought, if my master were not in need of me. She headed down the road to South Meadow to Goody Crespet's little house by the river.

"Why, child, thy hands are cold as ice." Goody bade Mary sit close to the fire.

Uther hopped from the back of a chair to perch in Mary's lap.

"I've come for help," Mary said as she smoothed the crow's silky black feathers.

Looking concerned, Goody Crespet poured Mary a few drops of sack and said, "Goodman Lyman is very ill."

Her remark did not surprise Mary. Goody was aware of everything that went on in the village. "He is. They sent for the doctor."

Goody shook her head. "And he cannot save the man's life."

"Nay, he cannot. My master is worse than before. That's why I've come, Goody." Mary searched her friend's face, wondering if she was aware of all the horrible things people said about her. "Will you come to him, or else tell me what I must do to heal him?"

"Thou hast done all that can be done, child. Goodman

Lyman shall not live." The cunning woman lowered her eyes in resignation.

"Nay, Goody, don't say that. He is such a dear, good man and not so old—not ready for the grave."

"Mary, that is as easily said of infants and children who are called home." Goody shook her head sadly and eased her small frame into a chair.

"Why?" Mary's heartfelt question came with tears, as she remembered those she had lost: Grandfather, Uncle Jonathan, her mother's babies whom she was taught to love, though she had never known them.

"God is a welcoming father, child. Death is nothing to fear."

Mary sobbed. "I hate God for being so cruel!"

"God shall survive the wrath of Mary Bliss." Goody smiled quietly, as an agitated Uther began making sounds not far from a giggle.

Mary stood to leave, forcing Uther into flight. He landed in the rafters where he began pacing and crying, "Good even! Good even!"

"Fool crow," Mary said, "'tis afternoon, not even at all." She looked to the window to see that no light radiated from the other side of the oiled paper. The sky was darkening and night was well on its way. She pulled on her cloak. "Nay, 'tis I that's more the fool," she said, grabbing her cloak. "A fool for coming here at all, for getting myself into trouble again."

Sorrowfully, Goody lit a lantern and offered it to Mary. "Thou shalt need it to light thy way."

Deeply saddened as well, Mary accepted the lantern and turned to go.

"Forgive me, Mary, 'tis wrong of me to say things thou canst not understand. Believe me when I say it, if I could save Mister Lyman from his fate, I would—if only for thy sake." Goody stood on tiptoe to place a kiss on Mary's cheek.

Ashamed of her outburst, Mary embraced the old woman. I love her, she thought, no matter what nonsense may come out of her mouth.

. . . . .

As word of Richard Lyman's death spread throughout the town, Mary was asked to help the Widow Doty prepare the body for burial. Out of concern for her daughter, Margaret Bliss came to help. Mary did her best not to fly into her mother's arms and beg to be taken home, welcoming her instead with a glad heart and a touch of her hand.

After warming water at the hearth, Mary poured it into a pail and took it to the waiting women, who had stripped the corpse of clothing. Dizzy and with shaking hands, she helped them wash the body and dry it with a towel. She wanted to pray, though prayers for the dead were thought useless and not offered. This was her first corpse, and Mary looked furtively at her master's face. His eyes had been closed at the time of death, but his mouth was open and dry. She wept to see his body looking so still and vacant.

Margaret felt sorry for her daughter. "Go, child. Ready some refreshment for the widow—"

"Nay! I want to help, Mother."

Widow Doty looked at Mary like she was a weanling and showed her black teeth in a smile. "Have ye a penny at hand?" she asked Margaret, who did not. She turned to Mary. "Go, ask the young mistress for the same."

When Mary came back with a penny she saw that while she was gone, the women had rolled the body onto a linen sheet. She dropped the penny into Widow Doty's outstretched palm and watched her stuff it into the master's open mouth. "For Saint Peter," the widow mumbled.

Margaret sniffed, as if she did not approve.

When Widow Doty asked for a needle and thread, Mary ran to fetch it. When she came back, the widow said, "Give it to yer mother. My eyes, they are dim. She must sew 'im in."

Mister Lyman's body had been washed and wrapped in a winding sheet, provided with a penny for Saint Peter. Their work was done. Mary served sack and cakes to the two older women, and later the men arrived with a wooden coffin. Near dusk, goodmen and goodwives came from the village to call, bringing condolences and gifts of food.

Mary clung to her mother's arm. "Pray, Mother, do take me home."

"I cannot, Mary," Margaret whispered. "Sarah and her mother need you now." And in a few minutes she kissed her daughter and bade her goodbye.

XI

The Carpenter: The Carpenter squareth Timber with a Chip-Ax, whence Chips, fall and saweth it with a Saw, where the Saw-dust falleth down. Afterwards he lifteth the Beam upon Tressels, by the help of a Pully, fasteneth it with Cramp-irons, and market it out with a Line. Thus he frameth the Walls together, and fasteneth the great pieces with Pins.

—John Amos Comenius
Orbis Pictus, 1659

SARAH WATCHED THE young man from the doorway of her father's house. He didn't seem to notice her or the rain as he worked to build a house on a small parcel of land almost directly across the road. She had never seen him before and wondered who he was. The rain was relentless, day after day adding to her feelings of loss. Glad to have something to distract her from the memory of her father's death, she watched the young man's progress with interest.

Toward the middle of May the earth dried out, crops were planted, and curiosity forced Sarah to walk past the new construction. When the young man saw her he stopped work and smiled in her direction. She nodded in a neighborly way and quickened her stride as though she had urgent business elsewhere. Hastening home by a circuitous route on the footpath through Arnold's woodlot; she entered the house from the back.

The moment she was inside she called, "Mary, he's alone—I saw no one else about." Sarah sat down by the window and, full of questions, picked up her mending to ask the first one. "Does a young man build a house unless he intends to marry?"

Mary had been busy kneading bread and had three pies waiting their turn for the oven. "Well, he'd best not try to dwell there, or the selectmen will be at his door," she joked, for it was against the law for a single man to live alone. "I wonder if he's betrothed."

Sarah, a little ashamed for plotting what would happen next, decided that it was Mary who encouraged her boldness. Before she came into service, Sarah thought, I was modest and shy, maybe even prim, and now I take the steps of a wanton.

As the summer wore on, Sarah found excuses to walk past his property nearly every day. "I must hasten to the mill, Mary," she'd say, or, "Goody Arnold is ill. I'll take her a pie."

One morning she had a favor to ask of Mary. "Will you come with me? I want to make a social call."

Mary looked puzzled, as well she should, for Sarah had never invited her anywhere.

"Don't refuse, Mary, for to be sure, I can't just walk across the road and shamelessly knock on his door. We can carry him something warm from the oven—just Christian neighbors. Why, we've already put off being neighborly far too long."

Mary baked a pound cake for Sarah, and while it was still warm Sarah instructed her to wrap it carefully in a white towel. In the spirit of the adventure, Mary covered a pitcher of cool milk with parchment and tied it with a rawhide string. Eager for a look at Sarah's young man, she packed a basket with two glasses and plates, a cloth and a knife. Sarah dressed herself carefully, and Mary remarked on how well she looked.

The maidens crossed the road together. Sarah's stomach was full of butterflies as she walked a pace ahead. Mary followed carrying the basket. Seeing them approach, the young man came down from a ladder, looking pleased.

"Good morrow," Sarah called with good cheer. "I ought to

have paid a call long before, but I have been in mourning, my—my father died."

"I am sorry to hear it, Goodwife." He looked embarrassed, uncomfortable and shy.

"Praise be," Sarah said, "I am not yet a wife."

The young man blushed and said nothing.

Sarah felt sorry for him and her shyness disappeared as she introduced herself and her servant.

"Pleased to know you," he said, offering his hand. "I'm James Bridgeman. You live just across the road, I'll warrant." He gestured toward the Lyman house.

Close up Sarah saw he was of a moderate height, with light brown hair, a beard, and gentle curls around his neck. His eyes were a temperate hazel, his face sunburned from long hours of work out of doors. She liked his looks and felt herself blush.

"Mary has baked a cake for you, and I've brought fresh milk to wash it down. Are you hungry?"

"Aye, starved, if truth be told. Come inside."

Once inside, he showed Sarah about his rooms as Mary spread the cloth on the floor and unpacked the basket. She cut the cake and poured the milk, and they sat down on the floor to eat. Sarah and James, both falling silent and shy, tasted their first bites of cake.

Sarah noticed all of a sudden that something seemed wrong. "Mary, you look unwell."

"Will you excuse me, please?" Mary said, "I feel quite ill and beg to go home."

"Why, Mary, poor thing," Sarah said, "I shall come with you."

"Nay, stay and finish your cake. I'll be fine, but I must lie down."

Something about Mary's eyes reassured Sarah, and she guessed Mary was pretending to be ill, plotting a way for her to be alone with the young man. "Quite sure?"

"Quite." When Mary got to her feet, bade them goodbye, and set off across the road, Sarah noticed her gait was as lively as ever.

Sarah stayed for an hour, and when she returned to the house she cried out with joy, "Mary, you are a shameless liar! I had no idea you were so clever! We could not have carried it off so well had we conspired to deceive him." The two young women laughed and embraced warmly.

"Very well, you may pay me now," Mary said with a smile. "Tell me what happened. Where did he come from?"

"Saybrook—he's a carpenter by trade." Sarah was clearly overjoyed. "Why, we passed the time quite easily—most pleasantly once we began to talk."

"Is he betrothed?"

"I did not ask."

Mary looked skeptical. "Why ever not? At least did you ask why he is building a house?"

"I could not bring myself to pry." Sarah had been too afraid to ask, fearing the answer. So long as she didn't know, she was free to imagine he was building the house for her.

Seeing that Mary looked ready to ask another question, Sarah suddenly liked her questions not at all. Mary had become too familiar, too saucy for a serving girl. Sarah withdrew to the parlor where she could stare out the window to catch glimpses of James Bridgeman as he worked.

As the days passed, each visit with James helped to mend Sarah's grieving heart. She was no longer tormented by thoughts of her father, dead and rotting under the ground. Sarah worked hard to push off the thought that she may have caused his death by refusing a witch's help. For weeks after their meeting she was happy to live with the mystery of James Bridgeman's house.

By the time the rains began again in September the house was nearly finished. During a weeklong soaking the weather was so wet that she did not visit him, but finally she could bear it no longer and threw on her cloak. Running through the pouring rain, she found James alone inside, trying to build a fire with wet wood.

He stood up when he saw her. "It must be an angel come to cheer me!" He pulled back the hood of her cloak to better see her face and looked at her with affection, his gaze so warm that her cheeks burned.

"I'll have Mary fetch you some coals from our fire," Sarah said, as he touched her shoulder. He took her into his arms and held her in silence for a time. Neither of them spoke, but she felt his heart beating against her breast, and finally she heard him say, "Sarah, be my wife."

He had come to Hartford to build his house with nothing more than faith and hope that God would send him a wife.

Very soon James posted the banns on the Meeting House door. The date for the wedding was set for May—the following spring.

With Sarah's betrothal her mother, confident that her youngest daughter's future was secure, was finally free to die. She wrote her last will and testament. Her words were concise, for she had little energy for writing.

> As I am soon to di, I bequeth all tht was wiled to me by my late husbnd, R Lyman, equal to my sons, Richard Jr., John, and Robert. Excepting for the contents of this howse to be shard by my daughters. Sarahs haff to be held as a dowrey. I put my hand to this last wil and testament on this day, 6 July, 1641.
>
> Sarah Osborne Lyman

The old woman stopped eating and drinking, and within days she was dead. She would suffer no more. Sarah sent Robert to tell Mister Hooker and busied herself helping Mary with supper. That evening Widow Doty came to wash the body and wrap it in a winding sheet for burial. Few tears of grief were shed in that house, for all felt relief at her passing.

Within two days Sarah Osborne Lyman was carried to the graveyard. Only then did Sarah weep bitterly at the sight of the first shovelful of earth thrown on her mother's coffin. She wept not for her death, but for the sorrow that had been her mother's life. With her mother at rest, Sarah begged Thomas Bliss to let Mary remain in service at the Lyman house. But Mary did not wish to stay, and Goodman Bliss took his daughter home. Sarah was furious. She believed that Mary had betrayed her, and vowed never to speak to the Blisses again.

John, Sarah, and Robert Lyman were now living in a house with no parent. Thomas Bliss and others in the village brought the Lyman children's condition to the attention of the townsmen. At their next meeting the selectmen considered the "complication the Lyman deaths had created for the town."

"For the town? Upon my soul," Sarah railed to her brothers, "I have never heard anything crueler—for the town, indeed!"

They ordered her to remove to the home of William Hill, where her sister Phillis was mistress, and ordered John and Robert to take shelter with their brother Richard at Windsor. Until it was sold, the Lyman house was locked and the windows barred, leaving Sarah bereft. Mary tried to visit, to sympathize, but Sarah could not bear the sight of her and angrily sent her away.

ON HER WEDDING day Sarah pinched her cheeks to a throbbing pink. Tears of gladness came as she dressed. With her pale skin, the redness from tears always showed long after Sarah wept, and there she was, red-faced, expecting her bridegroom at any moment.

With a glad heart and a borrowed white mare, James arrived to take Sarah to the magistrate's house. The day was clear, and sunshine warmed the air. He helped his bride to a seat on the mare and led the horse down the road and over the bridge by the mill. Town folks greeted them from their dooryards, some joining in, and soon a jovial parade followed. Vows were spoken at the magistrate's house, and Sarah's sister and brother-in-law provided the wedding feast. By law, they would not be wed until the marriage was consummated in the dark of the nuptial bed.

Following the wedding feast, Sarah's sister Phillis gave the bride a posset of warm spiced wine to relax her. As she sipped and smiled at her beloved, he looked at her tenderly.

"I shall never forget how you look today, Sarah," he said, "as chaste and pure as an angel sent from heaven."

But Sarah longed for James to take her home, to lay her down on the bed, to possess her.

When it was dark, the couple walked home to the new house, now furnished, stocked with food, and ready for the newly-weds. While wedding guests made merry down the road James laid a fire. A bewitching lightness still in her head from the wine, Sarah lit a candle on the bedside table. The large bedstead had belonged to Sarah's father, but the featherbed was new, cloaked in a burnt-orange coverlet. Sarah could hardly wait to snuggle under its covers, pull the curtains to shut out the light, and in the darkness find her husband. To herself she confessed shyness, hoping he would not force her to see him naked, though she felt certain that as time passed she would think nothing of seeing him thus. Removing her coif, then her clothes, she looked back on the day—the happiest, most perfect day in her life.

"Tonight, Lord," she prayed, "quicken my womb. Let me give my husband a son." Stripped of everything but her shift, she felt as light and gay as a child as she climbed into bed.

As though waiting for the right moment, James turned from the fire to walk toward the bedstead, then hesitated. "How lovely you are, my Sarah, my wife," he whispered, removing his blue wool doublet strung about the waist with red and green ribbon bows.

As he removed his shirt and undid his breeches, Sarah closed her eyes and did not open them until she felt him slip gently in beside her. She went into his arms, snuggling close, touching the soft hairs of his curling beard. She wanted him to kiss her and waited for his lips. They had tasted a thousand loving kisses during their betrothal, and the memory of his lips excited her desire.

"Ah, Sarah," he whispered, taking her face in his hands. "You have made me happy beyond anything I can say." He drew her to him, gently placing a kiss on her lips.

"From this day forward I shall never be unhappy," she sighed, her heart full.

"I know how wretched you have been, but from now on you shall dwell with me—under my protection. I shall let no trouble—no evil—spoil our bliss," he said, bringing her hand to his lips and kissing it.

"Don't talk now," she said, wishing he would crush her in his arms. He looked at her in the candlelight as though she were a child who depended upon him for food and shelter. And then he looked away.

"James, what troubles you?"

He settled back on his pillows and stared at the shadows flickering across the ceiling. "Give me your hand—all the night long I shall hold it, lest we wake to fear that we have parted." He kissed her hand again. "Now, let us sleep—today has been blessed enough. Tomorrow we must go to our housekeeping, and I am weary." He closed his eyes with her hand still in his.

She flattened herself against the mattress, refusing to swallow the knot that lay on her throat, knowing that if it dissolved she would disgrace herself with tears. Why? Why does he not desire me? She knew that a bridegroom, much more than a bride, looked forward to the heat and darkness of the marriage bed.

A MONTH AFTER the wedding Sarah was harvesting peas outside the new house her husband had built in the hope of finding a wife. She looked across the road at her father's abandoned house. There the fields had not been plowed. She knew they would soon return to meadow and, left long enough, to forest. 'Tis best that the place remains abandoned, she thought, filling her basket with the crisp green pods. I would rather it fell into ruin. How cruel if strangers lived there, strangers with a yard full of children, a goodwife spinning in the shade of the oak, men at work in the fields. It would be as if my father had never lived.

Distracted by such imaginings, she abandoned her work to cross the road. She had not set foot on the place since the day she was forced to leave. The house was shuttered tight, the doors sealed by the town. At the well, she lowered the bucket, and drew it up for a drink. Though the water was refreshing, she had difficulty swallowing, and tears filled her eyes. What am I to do, she asked herself, taking a seat on the old bench in the sun. I have no mother to advise me, my only sister is as good as dumb. To Sarah the bench felt haunted. A hundred times she had sat there with Mary Bliss, talking and carding wool, telling stories, laughing.

Feeling Mary's eyes upon her, Sarah hurried away. Forcing her from mind, she unlatched the gate and entered the paddock. She's nothing to me, Mary Bliss! Nothing! She closed the gate behind her and headed toward the orchard and the wood. Apple and pear trees were fully leafed, with tiny fruits beginning to swell. And I have no child in my womb. Not once had James sought to plant his seed. She had tried to reason with him, and when tearfully he told her he could not bring himself to desecrate her, she had begged him.

"I am no angel, just a wife who wants children." She had done everything but throw herself at him wantonly. Sarah shuddered, remembering how he had turned from her and wept like a boy. He slept little ever since they were wed, and though she pretended to rest, neither did she. There must be something, someone who can help me, she thought, letting the tears come.

In blind distraction, she approached the path to the woods. There must be some simple to cure him—or a charm. She shivered, knowing perfectly well that the cunning woman who lived down by Little River had the knowledge to help. Wondering if the Evil One had put that thought into her mind, she felt afraid and quickened her pace. No wonder Satan tempts me! "It matters not how hard I pray," she said, aloud. "God has forgotten me!"

"God forgets none of his children, Sarah." The gentle voice came from very near.

Sarah clapped both hands over her mouth to stifle a scream. She looked all around and, seeing no one, cried, "Am I not alone?"

"'Tis I." Goody Crespet moved out of a stand of fern onto the path. "I saw thee approach. I spoke out when I heard thee cry."

Sarah was dumbfounded. "Why, 'twas only a moment ago

that you came to my mind, Grandmother." She was frightened, wondering if she had unwittingly summoned a witch.

Goody Crespet smiled her warmest smile and looked Sarah kindly in the eye. "I am not what thou fearest, child, but I have knowledge to help. And, if I am not mistaken, thou art in need."

"I have nowhere to turn." Sarah glanced nervously around to make sure no one saw her with the old woman.

"We are alone," the cunning woman reassured her. "Now tell me what troubles thee."

"As you may know, I was recently wed, and my husband—" Sarah's gaze fell to her clenched hands.

"I am listening, Sarah—what of thy husband?"

"Well, praise be, he thinks I am too pure for a wife and has trouble—well, you know—he has trouble—uh—in the bed." Sarah was mortified.

"Ah, I see. That difficulty is not new to me, and there be a remedy for it."

"There is?" Sarah brightened. "Just today I thought there must be."

"Aye, 'tis simple enough—but only the wife can do it." Goody moved closer.

"Tell me then. What I must do?"

"Dost thou have oil of violets somewhere about thy house?"

"Why, of course, everyone has oil of violets."

"Well, my dear," Goody whispered, "'tis the very finest remedy for his problem."

Sarah was intrigued. "And how must I use it?"

"To make a man eager for his wife, she must rub his stones very slowly and gently with oil of violets. Then, my dear, your prayers will be answered." Goody patted Sarah's hand for a tiny moment before she disappeared into the woods.

XII

One Hopkins, of Watertown, was convicted for selling a piece and pistol, with poweder and shot, to James Sagamore [an Indian], for which he had sentence to be whipped and branded on the cheek.

—Governor John Winthrop
The History of New England 1630–1649

COLD NORTH WINDS blew down early. Winter was on its way, and Margaret had asked Mary to close off the windows. As she mounted oiled paper over a front window, she looked across the dooryard to her mother's raised beds. After a sudden killing frost, the remains of the garden lay withered, and across the road a cold misty fog settled over Bartlett's field.

Three years had passed since Mary left the Lymans—hard years. This year alone had begun with a devastating earthquake, which shook Hartford almost to ruin, and in its aftermath came the rains and spring floods, followed by summer dampness and a mildewed harvest. Last year Thomas Bliss had managed to add a workroom to the back of the house, and his new loom kept both Margaret and Mary busy. Still, his flax fields were poor and his wheat poorer.

For a while everyone came to life over the news from England. Civil war had broken out between the Parliamentarians and the King's supporters. King Charles had shut off emigration and the flow of English goods to the colonies. Fear of warring Indians was the foremost concern for the people of Hartford and territories as far away as New Amsterdam. In Connecticut, the Narragansetts led by Miantonomi and the Mohegans led by Uncas had been at war against one another. The Dutch were in the fight of their lives with tribes of the lower Hudson River valley. Short of soldiers, they had put up money to entice English soldiers from Massachusetts and Connecticut to fight the Indians.

The mist had spread out of Bartlett's field onto the road and crawled toward the Blisses' door, enveloping the kitchen garden. The faint glow of late afternoon sun veiled by haze lit the sky at the end of the road, silhouetting the dark image of a man on horseback. Mary trembled at the sight and drew away from the window, then admonished herself and returned to look again. What reason had she to feel such apprehension?

The sizable, dark-cloaked man stopped in front of the house, tied his horse to the post, and walked up the path toward the door. Tall as an Indian, he moved purposefully, his brown cloak cutting through the gloom. Mary did not recognize him and left the window to wait for his knock. At first she was afraid to answer, then chided herself, opening the door just wide enough to see a bearded man on the doorstep, his face in the shadow of his broad hat.

"Is Goodman Bliss at home?"

"He went off to his woodlot after dinner." She answered guardedly, for he was armed to the hilt with a matchlock musket, a sword, and across his breast a bandolier filled with charges. "My mother will have to do—I'll fetch her." Mary thought quickly, closing the door, then ran toward the kitchen calling for Margaret.

Margaret hurried to see what man was at the door and, opening it, broke into exclamations of joy. "Praise be, 'tis Joseph Parsons!"

"Praise be, indeed, my dear Goodwife Bliss, for a kind welcome from *you*, at least." He gave Margaret a bow and Mary a frown.

Humiliated, Mary looked hard at the stranger's face. Sure enough, it was Joseph. I can do nothing right! she thought. If he had been a masquerading Indian I would have merrily invited him inside to murder us all.

"I beg your pardon, Joseph, I did not recognize you. You sent no word and were not expected," she added, not willing to accept all the blame. Mary had not seen Joseph Parsons for eight years, not since her brother Tom had brought him home following the battle at Fort Mystic.

"True enough. I am just returned from battle and could not stop in Hartford without calling to see the good people who saved my life." Joseph smiled, remembering the moment he awoke from his fever and saw Mary's caring face. Being with Mary and Margaret in that room again made him realize that he still dreamed that scene, the light pouring through the open door, the bright-headed maid calling, "He wakes! Mother, he wakes!"

Margaret took Joseph's cloak and hung it on a peg by the door, then welcomed him into the kitchen, where she had just begun to think about supper. "Come, Joseph, sit you down by the fire and Mary will serve you a drink. Mary, fetch the sack—or would you rather have beer?"

"Beer—I'm thirsty!" Joseph said as Mary handed him a full cup of beer. "Why, Mary, you knew my wants before I knew myself."

Just then Thomas Bliss and his sons came in from the woodlot, happily surprised to find such a welcome visitor beside the fire. They greeted him with shouts of joy and warm handclasps. All with cups of beer in hand, they sat down in the kitchen as Mary and Hannah helped their mother prepare the evening meal. Margaret, in a festive mood, decided that instead of serving the usual leftovers from dinner she would roast the pigeons Tom had shot the day before. To sauce them, Mary stirred vinegar and butter together in an earthenware pipkin over the fire.

Thomas lit his pipe, and Joseph was eager to tell them about his adventures as a paid soldier, fighting the Indians with Captain Underhill for the Dutch.

"I had wanted to go to war," Tom said, his disappointment obvious.

"He stayed home with the militia," his father explained, "and I am grateful for it, being short of grown sons."

Thomas seemed to ponder for a moment, then turned and grinned at their visitor. "Ah, Joseph, fighting Indians is profitable work, or so I've heard." Goodman Bliss's eyes glinted merrily. "Indeed, they tell me Connecticut has given Captain Mason five hundred acres of Pequot land."

Joseph returned his smile and nodded. "I too was well enough paid."

"Husband," Margaret said, "I do hate to say it again. I wish you would not smoke in the kitchen.

Mary, though busy slicing the apples she would dip into a batter and fry, couldn't stop staring at Joseph. No more a lad, he was a man full grown, and a handsome one.

Supper was soon ready, and Hannah had spread the table with a cloth. With wooden trenchers in hand, the youngest children huddled in the chimney corner or beside the fire, wherever there was room. Thomas knocked the ashes out of his pipe into the fireplace, Mary and Hannah served, and grace was said.

"Now then, Joseph," Tom said, "tell us where have you traveled and what you have seen."

"I sailed to Long Island and marched to New Netherlands." Joseph looked around with a grin. "Such a distance to learn that after all, the Dutch are good enough people."

"And the war between the Mohegans and the Narragansetts? What have you heard?"

"When our troops left Connecticut to fight for the Dutch, Miantonomi saw his opportunity to attack the Mohegans, even though he had treated with us and promised not to fight Uncas without bringing his complaints to the English first. Miantonomi is nothing if not a villain." Joseph shook his head, concerned. "He means to cause trouble where he can."

Mary could scarcely eat for the excitement, but had a question. "Then what profit is there to allow our soldiers to leave the territory?"

That brought a hearty laugh from Tom. "Why, silly, the profit is in the soldier's pockets!"

Eager to be taken seriously, Mary said, "I believe that Indian Miantonomi has long resented Uncas for his service to the English."

Joseph nodded. "Right you be, Miantonomi is not to be trusted. Remember, Tom, he came to our aid as little as he could at Fort Mystic?"

Tom reached for another piece of bread. "'Tis true, for all the provisions he furnished we might have starved. In Miantonomi's attack on Uncas, then, what came to pass?"

"The Narragansett brought warriors—a thousand in all—into Mohegan territory." Joseph paused to gnaw the last tasty bit off a pigeon bone. "Though Uncas had half as many men, *he* won the battle."

Mary said, "Pray, how could that be?"

Good-natured Joseph shook a finger at her and winked. "If you be quiet and let me finish my story, you shall hear." He knifed another helping from a charger stacked high with roasted pigeons and dropped it on his plate.

"After we had fought along with the Dutch for a month, Captain Underhill sent a few of us on a mission back to Connecticut. On our way we came upon Uncas and a small party of his men, armed with guns and leading their captive, Miantonomi himself. We were welcomed and followed them here. At this very moment, Miantonomi sits in Hartford jail. And that, my dear friends, is why I now enjoy your hospitality."

As if she could bear to hear no more, Margaret put down her knife. "Joseph, you saw the Indians with guns?"

"Aye, we saw a number with muskets and powder."

"Are the English not forbidden to sell them these things?"

"Some men love gold better than they love their lives," Joseph said as a matter of fact.

"Aye, 'tis nothing new." Thomas Bliss licked his fingers. "Name a law writ by God or man, and we English shall break it. Ah, Mary, this sauce is masterful. Learned at the Lymans', no doubt."

Mary colored at the compliment.

Hannah spoke up for the first time. "The law says that no man shall let an Indian come into his house, yet I saw Old Joe go into Goodwife Bartlett's back door."

"Tut, Hannah," Mary said. "I wouldn't think much of that. He's a kind old fellow—a follower of Christ."

Tom downed the last of his beer. "Some folks think to make servants of them, but not I, for they are lazy and willful, not fit to serve."

Leaning back on his chair, his powerful hunger slaked, Joseph smiled at his hostess. "I do say, Goodwife Bliss, I've dined at the Pynchons' and diverse other places, and never have I had a better meal."

"Why, thank you, Joseph." Margaret ducked her head modestly. "Mary and Hannah did their part, too."

"Then thanks be to you." He bowed to Hannah. "And to you." He winked at Mary.

Thomas pulled out his pipe, with Tom and Joseph following his cue.

Emboldened by the compliment, Mary returned to the subject of law. "While we speak of the law, must you smoke in the house? 'Tis against the law for a man to spoil the air for those who would not taste that foul weed."

Joseph began to fill his pipe, darting a bold look of mock defiance at his young critic. "As for me, I would taste it, gladly, for tobacco bewitches me."

"All of you, now." Margaret shooed them out of doors. "Out of this kitchen with your foul-smelling pipes."

Long after the sun had set, Mary sat listening to the young soldier, her brothers and her father talk beside the fire. Her mother and youngest siblings had gone to bed. Ever since Joseph's arrival Mary had studied the young soldier's face. Goody Crespet was teaching her the art of physiognomy, and from her Mary had learned that when the corners of a man's mouth are upturned, like Joseph's, it is a sign of an amiable and pleasant nature. And he does not laugh uproariously, she noted to herself, showing he is indeed steadfast and laborious. By firelight she studied Joseph's brown eyes, which were open and peaceful. The eyes, she thought, of a man who is good-tempered, loyal, and of fine intellect. She wondered whether once the Indian troubles were settled she would ever see him again, and if she did not, how she should ever know if she had read his features correctly.

He was telling the story Uncas had told as they camped beside the great river on their trek to Hartford. "One of Uncas's scouts saw Miantonomi and his thousand warriors approach. He ran to alert his comrades, whose numbers were half that of the others. Knowing a surprise attack was their only hope, Uncas moved forward until he came to the great plain by the Shetucket River, where he halted on a low hill. There he gave instructions to his men, revealing his secret order for attack."

"Secret?" Tom said. "At Fort Mystic Captain Mason *shouted* orders. Why keep it secret?"

"He could not shout—you shall see. The Narragansetts had forded the river and had come in wide array to the bottom of the descending slope, just below the Mohegans. Uncas sent one of his men to ask for a meeting with Miantonomi. When his request was granted, the two chieftains met in the middle, the warriors on both sides remaining within bow-shot of the others. Uncas tried to convince Miantonomi that it was madness to waste their warriors' lives, when a fight between just the two of them could decide. 'Let *us* fight it out,' he said. 'If you kill me, my men shall be yours, and if I kill you, your men shall be mine.'"

Thomas roared. "Such a solution would never come to the mind of an English captain, I'll warrant you."

"Right you are!" Joseph chuckled at the thought. "But Miantonomi refused. Not for a moment did Uncas think his enemy was afraid to fight him, for he was as tall and strong as Uncas himself. He refused Uncas's offer because Miantonomi had more men, and he knew he stood a better chance of winning the battle."

Mary sat transfixed. "What a clever one."

"Just you wait, Mary, and see how the story turns out. I haven't yet told you about Uncas's plan to deceive them—the secret signal."

"Tell us, Joseph!"

"To signal the moment of attack, the crafty Uncas fell to the ground like a dead man, astonishing his enemy. His men attacked, hitting the Narragansetts with a deluge of arrows. Then Uncas leapt to his feet and led his warriors in a battle cry—a terrible sound many men have not survived to hear a second time. His warriors raised their hatchets and rushed against the confused enemy, so overwhelming them with surprise that they ran away.

"The Mohegans pursued them through that country like a pack of wolves chasing a herd of deer. Miantonomi tried to flee with his warriors, but he was wearing a corselet he got from the English and could run no better than we can. Two of Uncas's men captured him."

Mary leaned forward, clasping her hands under her chin. "What is Uncas like? You must know, for you marched with him yesterday and fought with him at Mystic." She still hoped to learn, at last, what had happened in the deciding battle of the Pequot war.

"Ah, he's a wily one—a good ally, because he knows he's fighting with the stronger force. He wants to win. He knows that in any given battle between the English and the Indians, the English may lose, but in the end the English will triumph."

"And Miantonomi?" Mary said. "What of him?"

"As we trekked north toward Hartford with Uncas, I never heard the captive utter a single word. He walked in his chains, head down, like a man in a dream. And Uncas asked him, 'Why do you not speak? If you had taken me, I should have besought you for my life.' But Miantonomi made no reply."

Thomas had noticed that Mary's eyelids were drooping. "Tomorrow at first dawn, Mary, you shall pay for the loss of your sleep. Best take to your bed."

As long as the men talked of war she longed to listen, but now she wanted her sleep more. Leaving them reluctantly, she crawled into her low kitchen bed. In that house of close quarters, sleepers fell easily to rest in the firelight, accustomed to the voices of those not yet asleep.

As Mary settled comfortably into her bed and drifted into that strange place just before sleep, she cursed her full bladder. Sleepily, she got up and stuck her feet back in her boots, wrapped herself in her cloak, and opened the kitchen door. On any other night she'd have lifted her shift over the chamber pot, but unlike her youngest brothers and sisters, she would never relieve herself in the house while a guest was there—especially Joseph.

A light snow had fallen over the yard and the fields, and above the white the full moon cast a dazzling light nearly bright as day. Why, she wondered, when no one else cares, do I love the moonlight so? A shivery chill passed through her body as she thought of her friend Goody Crespet, wondering if just now she too looked at the moon.

But it was cold outdoors, and the house was warm. Mary crept back into the kitchen, and as the firelight died away, the men went to their rest and Mary fell into a dream. Slumbering in Goody Crespet's large bedstead, she smelled the sweetness of strewn fragrant herbs and longed to tell her friend something of great importance. Inhaling again, the air struck her lungs like a knife, for it had grown suddenly rank and befouled. Some great force, perhaps her own terror, flung her from the bed to the floor, where her body rolled down a steep slope coming to rest against something cold and soft. Though it was dark, she knew it was Goody Crespet, lying dead on the floor.

Mary woke with an unvoiced scream in her mouth, her heart pounding as though she had run a mile. I must go to her now. Dreams were not to be taken lightly. They were forewarnings, portents, guidance from God himself. She rose quickly to dress. It was still dark, and she had no idea of the hour. She grabbed a half-eaten loaf of bread and her cloak, unbarred the door and hurried outside again.

The full moon lit the snow-covered country like a great lantern held aloft by the hand of God. Mary hurried down the road to Goody Crespet's, praying her dream had come soon enough to save the old woman's life. The wind skittered through the forest as she ran past flat fields white with snow and darkened dwellings where her neighbors slept unaware of the miracle of the night. So enchanted was the night that in a space of a few breaths, it seemed, she found herself at Goody Crespet's door.

She entered the dark house. Cold rank-smelling air forced her hand over her nose. "Goody," she called, coughing, stumbling around in the dark. "Goody, where are you?"

"Aaaahk!" came a scream, with a cold stirring of wings from the rafters.

"Uther!" The bird had startled her near to death.

"What a ruckus," Goody croaked weakly from her bed. "Mary, hast thou come to me?"

"Aye, Goody, I must let in some light." The room was cold as the outdoors and so dark that she could barely see the outline of the bedstead. She ran to the window and opened the shutters, letting in the first light of dawn and a view of her old friend buried under quilts and a counterpane. It was obvious that Goody was sick and unable to do for herself. "I'll light a fire."

"Aye, child, praise God thou hast come." Her old voice cracked in tearful relief.

"Aaaahk!" Uther cried, pacing over the counterpane, his black feathers glistening in the moonlight.

Mary found the jug and poured a tumbler of angelica water for her friend. "I had a dream, Goody," she said, as she headed for the woodbox. "Do you have a fever?" She was already laying wood for the fire.

"The fever hath passed. It left me too weak to get out of bed. I had no food yesterday, child."

"As soon as the fire burns, I'll give you something to eat and to drink." Mary made a nest of small sticks and dry grass, and from the tinderbox removed a char cloth, placing it on top of her nest. With flint and steel she struck her spark. A spot of red glowed on the char cloth and, blowing gently, Mary lifted the nest into the air above her head. Her tinder burst into flame and she quickly placed it under the kindling wood.

Then she gave the old woman a piece of the bread she had brought from home and helped her to another drink. "Now sleep awhile, and I'll see to everything," she said. On her way to the woodpile she emptied the chamber pot, then hauled wood inside and stacked it into the empty woodbox. She boiled up a skillet of pease and from Indian meal made unleavened bread fried in hot fat on the griddle.

As morning approached, she woke her sleeping friend and washed her face with rosemary water. "Now, that should help you feel better. I must away, but first I want you to eat." She helped Goody sit upright against her pillows. "How do you feel? Will you eat?" She placed a tray with cornbread and pease on Goody's lap.

"'Tis better—well enough for thee to leave me."

"I must. But one of us—Hannah or I—shall return in a few hours. Are you hungry?"

"I shall eat and then I shall rest."

"Promise that before you sleep, you will eat the pease and the bread," Mary said, kissing her. "If only I'd come earlier."

"Do not worry thyself. God provided me with all I needed— including thee."

As Mary walked past the stubble left in a Podunk cornfield, the Indians milled around their wigwams breaking camp, preparing to leave the meadow for their winter quarters. Thinking of the long, hungry winter ahead, she heaved a sigh and walked faster, wondering what lie she could tell her parents when she got home. As she turned on the road from South Meadow, the sun was well over Little River, and just ahead came a rider on the road.

Mary had no doubt who it was. Joseph appeared to be getting an early start on his way into town. He reined in his horse and stopped, seeming surprised to see her. "Why, Mary, you are missed at home. They have guessed every likelihood except for the one I see before me. Where have you been, and where are you going?"

"To my father's house," she said, not wishing to answer his first question.

"Here, climb up behind me—my horse will carry you faster." He offered her his hand. "Put your foot on my boot and I'll pull you up."

"Don't mind if I do." She took his hand, eager for a ride on horseback.

"Swing your leg over his back," he said as he hoisted her up.

As she tried to mount, she felt the horse stiffen and step aside. Her leg got tangled in her skirts, her hand slipped from Joseph's, and she fell to the ground.

"Mary, are you hurt?" Though his words expressed concern, she heard telltale laughter in his voice. He jumped down and helped her to her feet.

"Nay, I am just fine." For a long moment she brushed the snow from her cloak. "I think two things. You laugh at me and you've never asked a person in skirts to ride with you before. I'll walk— your horse would rather not carry me."

"I'm not laughing," he said, though they both knew he had. "I'll help you up myself." He lifted her by the waist, setting her down sidesaddle as though she were a feather. Mary knew she was blushing, feeling a sudden thrill in her belly. She adjusted her skirts and tried to compose herself.

"You shall ride like a queen," he said, merrily, "and I shall walk like your servant."

The last time Mary had ridden a horse was as a child long ago in England. She had clearer memories of riding the cow. Cherry's back was wide and not so tall, her movements slow, while the horse felt spirited beneath her.

"'Tis plain to see you won't tell me where you got off to." Joseph's warm breath came in a frosty cloud. "Or why you put yourself in danger, leaving the house by night. You are more than two miles from your father's house, and who knows where you've been?"

Giving in to his curiosity she gave a guarded reply. "I went to Goody Crespet. She was ill."

"Ah, yes, that kind old woman. I remember she nursed me after I'd been shot. But could it not have waited until daybreak?"

"It could not."

A silence fell between them. The only sounds were those of the horse's hooves falling on the road and Little River flowing past. Mary wondered why she felt so honored to be riding while he walked, so cherished by his concern, so aware of his handsome profile, his wide shoulders. She looked away. I should be thinking what I'll tell my parents. Suddenly chilled at the prospect of what she might face at home, she glanced at Joseph to find him gazing at her. When she smiled, he quickly looked away. I care not. I am finished with childish lies, she told herself. I shall tell the truth.

"I had a dream, Joseph, a portent," she ventured, her voice soft. "Goody lay dead on the floor of her house. When I went to her, I found her sick, without food or a fire, and in need of help."

"And you took care?"

"She is my friend."

"Then she is fortunate in your friendship." His face spoke his respect. "But we progress too slowly. Now I shall ride, and you shall ride with me." He handed her the reins, then sprang up to a seat behind the saddle. With his arms around her, he took back the reins, surrounding her with his arms, the sound of his voice close in her ear. "Your parents have worried long enough." And with that his heels told his horse he meant to cover the distance at a fair pace.

XIII

Beat them, whip them, pinch them, punch them, if they
resolve not to winch for it, they will not. Whether it be
their benumbed insensibileness of smart, or their hardy
resolutions, I cannot tell . . . but a Turkish drubbing
would not much molest them. And although they be nat-
urally much afraid of death, yet the unexpected approach
of a mortal wound by a bullet, arrow, or sword strikes
no more terror, causes no more exclamation, no more
complaint or whinching than if it had been shot into the
body of a tree.

—William Wood
On the Hardiness of Indians
New England's Prospect, 1634

JOSEPH, WHO HAD permission to be away from his duties for a night, returned to town that morning in time to rejoin his commander and fellow soldiers. The final decisions about Miantonomi's fate had been made. Uncas had brought his rival to Hartford for one reason—to seek permission to execute him. The English, in treaties with the Indians, had successfully sought control over native movements in territories with settled English towns, and Uncas was unwilling to take action without English support. Unprovoked, and against agreements made with the English, Miantonomi had attacked the Mohegans. The crime was plain for everyone to see. The Narragansett chieftain could not deny his actions. Only one thing was left to decide. Where would Miantonomi die?

Joseph was glad to see Hartford again, for it had grown into a larger, livelier place. On his way to the ordinary he rode into Meeting House Yard, which already bustled with tradesmen setting up for the day and Podunks eager to sell their surplus. Joseph knew that the presence of even friendly Indians annoyed the townsmen. Sometimes, either out of curiosity or with intent to rob, Indians entered the village houses and shops, frightening the English.

But not Joseph. He took pleasure in the very sight of them. Something struck his fancy in their mysterious countenances, their exotic dress, and their willingness to expose their skin to the sun. He was never happier than when he had ridden with Uncas and his men, making camp in the forest or beside the river, fishing for their supper, sleeping under the stars.

He loved nothing more than to sit around the fire at night, listening to Uncas tell his stories in broken English. Once the sachem had offered Joseph a pipe of tobacco, and at times he was willing to teach him more of the Algonquian language, which varied little between the different river tribes. After fighting beside the warrior at Fort Mystic, Joseph felt indebted to him.

Uncas was wily, to be sure, and had motives no Englishman could know, but he had laid his hand over his heart and professed to John Winthrop: "My heart is not mine but yours. I have no men, they are all yours. Command me in any difficult thing, I will do it."

Joseph rode up in time to see Uncas standing beside Governor Haynes and the assembly gathered in the yard as soldiers from Joseph's detachment led Miantonomi out. Dismounting, Joseph approached his commander, Lieutenant John Hazard, who stood in a cluster of soldiers and motioned him forward.

"Parsons," he said, "two must accompany Uncas. He's taking Miantonomi back to Mohegan territory, by order of the court." Though Joseph did not grasp his superior's meaning, he asked no questions, for Miantonomi stood nearby looking directly at him with eyes of steel. "I must have two volunteers," the lieutenant said.

Silence followed until a middle-aged soldier, known simply as Chase, stepped forward, and it dawned on Joseph that he was about to lose a chance for adventure. He spoke up without further thought. "I, too, Lieutenant."

"Excellent!" Hazard said. "Your duties are simple. You and Chase are to go behind. Chase will fill you in on the details. Make sure Uncas follows orders, then report back to me here. The governor has asked us to stay on. I expect you to be gone no more than three days."

Included in the party marching south, tethered to the prisoner by a rope, was Uncas's younger brother, Wawequa. Behind Uncas on his stallion, their company included fourteen Mohegan warriors on foot. Miantonomi walked in chains, followed by Wawequa, also on foot. All wore bearskin robes and deerskin leggings. Wrapped in heavy winter cloaks, Joseph and Chase on their mounts brought up the rear. Uncas's orders were simple: kill Miantonomi and bring back his head. There was to be no torture, and the act itself had to be carried out in Mohegan country, not English territory.

As they marched, Joseph could not keep his eyes off the doomed man. What would it be like to walk in his shoes? Perhaps he hopes for mercy, for the two sachems have been brave and potent in battle. That alone is reason for common admiration. Joseph knew from his own experience in battle how one comes to be in awe of the enemy. Did Miantonomi hope that underneath all their struggles the sense of brotherhood between the two chiefs endured? No, he told himself, Miantonomi knows he is a dead man.

As they traveled, they retraced the same route Joseph remembered having taken to Hartford. The trail led them through the forest to the open banks of the great river, then into the forest again. They spent the first night in a small clearing under a cloud-covered moon. The air was cold, and they slept by their fires wrapped in cloaks and blankets. Joseph slept while Chase stood sentry, then, when Chase could no longer keep his eyes open, he woke Joseph to watch the rest of the night.

Memories of his recent adventures kept Joseph awake—the Indians he'd killed in close combat with the Dutch and in his first experience of war, at Fort Mystic. Still disturbed by what he and Tom had seen and done there, he remembered how Captain Mason had materialized with a firebrand in one hand, how he had set the wigwams on fire, the terror that followed. Though he did not like to think about the battle at Mystic, he could not forget, and many nights since then his dreams had been filled with the cries of women and children in flames.

He watched the Indian sentries change guard. A rested brave moved into place with a musket in hand and propped his back against a tree. Sudden melancholy overcame Joseph, and as a remedy he turned his mind to the money he had earned as a soldier: enough for a beginning. He wanted more land, a house, and a family. But he wanted more than that. Joseph Parsons did not intend to hitch himself to a plow forever, or pursue a trade, and he had no interest in the church.

Not yet sure how he would achieve it, he meant to be every bit as rich as William Pynchon. Pynchon had a son, John, who would one day inherit his father's wealth. Joseph, not so lucky, knew he would have to make his own way. Nevertheless he promised himself a fortune that would turn heads. He wanted more than most men, and that included a beautiful woman. Already he had one in mind, for nowhere had he seen a maid more to his liking than Mary Bliss. He tried to guess her age—eighteen, maybe nineteen? He spent the rest of his watch thinking of Mary's light-filled green eyes, the freckles across her nose, her rosy lips, her cheeks brushed by wayward curls, her smile—and her terrifying frown. He smiled to himself remembering how he'd appeared at her father's door and she hadn't recognized him, thinking him a menace. That frown had come again when she fell off his horse.

Another day's travel and another night's watch brought the death march to the Shetucket River's wide estuary, below the plain where Miantonomi and his thousand men had attacked the Mohegans. The place itself must have been the signal, for they had gone only a little way farther before Joseph saw Wawequa raise his tomahawk from behind and bury it in Miantonomi's head. Except for the release of his breath, the Narragansett sachem made no sound as he crumpled to the ground, tomahawk still embedded in his skull. The Mohegan warriors cheered as Uncas claimed the hatchet, then took his knife and cut a hunk of flesh from his enemy's shoulder. He held it aloft for his warriors to see, declaring, "This will be the sweetest meat I ever ate! It will make my heart strong." To Joseph's revulsion, Uncas consumed it with gusto.

XIV

*. . . James Everel, a sober, discreet man, and two others
saw a great light in the night at Muddy River. When
it stood still, it flamed up, and was about three yards
square: when it ran, it was contracted into the figure of a
swine: it ran as swift as an arrow towards Charlton, and
so up and down about two or three hours.*

—Governor John Winthrop
The History of New England 1630–1649

THE CRUEL WINTER led villagers to cut down large sections
of the forest to burn for warmth. Repeatedly, blizzards buried
the town. The difficulty of movement in deep snow meant that for
weeks no one ate fresh fish or game. Dried fish and salted meats
went first, and after that the Blisses had nothing but cornmeal,
pumpkins, squash, and dried peas and beans. Mary and her
brothers and sisters groaned at the sight of another meatless plate.

"At least you'll not starve," Margaret said. "Give thanks for
your blessings."

Mary cleared plates at the end of the meal, her stomach half-
empty. My blessings, indeed! Her bones were wracked with cold,
and she was so thin that her waistcoat no longer hugged her body
but hung like a sack from her shoulders. And to think, she told
herself, that I used to envy Sarah Lyman's lithe body.

Worried about Goody Crespet alone and so far away in her
little house above the river, Mary and Hannah had tried to reach

141

her after the first snows. Up to their knees in the drifts, they had to turn back in defeat, comforting themselves with the knowledge that the old woman had survived legions of winters without any help from them. She would surely survive this one, too.

After the rigors of winter the loons came back to the marsh, their eerie demented laughter an accompaniment to the song of marsh wrens, the drumming of grouse, the trickle of water seeping everywhere as the snow melted. Flocks of wild turkeys sunned themselves on a bank below a blazing grove of red-twig dogwood and at the feet of pussy willows. The spring brought sun and moderate rains, and with them, hope. By June the fields and the kitchen garden were filled with tender young seedlings, the miracle Mary loved most. "From little yellow seed to great cornstalk grow," she sang at planting time. After the planting she waited, running to the field and garden every day for signs of first leaves pushing through the soil. Then she felt blessed, rewarded.

Mary walked carefully across rows of lush young corn, lifting her skirts to keep from bruising them, heading for the edge of the woods to gather hellebore root for Hannah's toothache. As she entered the path through the brush, a thrush's sudden brilliant song took her breath away. Clear it was, and sweet, like a bell ringing high in the canopy. Such a merry sound charmed her. She looked up, hoping to see it, only to encounter a giant spider's web suspended by thin silken threads hanging close over her head. She arched her back, shading her eyes for a better look at the web, a precision miracle glinting in the sunlight, now bowed and strained by a sudden breeze.

Then she saw them. Thousands of caterpillars covered every inch of the massive trunk of a beech tree. She looked overhead at pine branches, and they too were covered, and then at the chestnut grove, and leafless shrubs both low and high, smothered with millions of sleeping caterpillars. Nearly every bit of green had disappeared from the woods. Was it only yesterday, she thought, that I looked with fondness at the newly green forest? Surely such devastation had taken more than one night. And now with their gluttonous stomachs full the caterpillars slept. There were so many, and the destruction they had wrought was so complete, they had left themselves no place to hide. Mary looked down at the forest floor to see that she was standing on caterpillars. She screamed, and her mouth filled with bile. Dizzy, she ran toward home calling for her mother, trampling her father's cornfield.

Everywhere throughout the plantation, folks talked of nothing but caterpillars. No one had seen a worse infestation. The people knew no line of defense, nor did they know what course the pestilence might take. Soon sated, the horrid worms began to drop from the trees until it seemed to rain caterpillars. Folks untangled the detestable creatures from their hair or scraped them off their shoulders. One could not step out a door or walk on the road without crushing the monstrous things underfoot. At night villagers lay in their beds unable to sleep for the noisome sound of caterpillars chewing the meadow grass, the fields of barley, corn, and wheat. The goodwives wept at the loss of their kitchen gardens. Every man alive felt helpless and utterly hated by God.

On the Sabbath Mister Hooker wept in his pulpit. "O, how a soaking shower of righteousness would settle our shaking times, repair our losses, and restore the years which the caterpillars, the sword, and the mildew have taken from us!"

After meeting, Goodwife Knapp said to her husband, "With the Devil's help, she'll ruin us all."

"Aye, 'tis the witch's work," Goodwife Olmstead said to her neighbor.

"Why, I saw her on the meadow with her walking stick—herding caterpillars, she was," Goodwife Bunce told the fishmonger. "And before my eyes she raised her staff and spoke to the evil hordes, whereupon they turned from their path toward Searle's cornfield. An hour later he hadn't a seedling to his name."

On his way out the door, Goodman Bunce said to Deacon Mygatt, "Long have I known that the Devil keeps her company."

The deacon nodded, eager to add his bit. "When I went to fix her roof I seen a broken mirror and a cross on her wall."

"Did you know she keeps a black crow?"

"She has knowledge of palms, you know."

"I saw her fly on her broom staff high over the road and across Little River."

The town quickly stirred to frenzy, and the magistrates brought Goody Crespet to trial. The hearing lasted less than a morning, with testimony about a magic walking stick, a forbidden idol, a familiar spirit in the form of a crow, and Goody Crespet's preternatural ability to fly. After the "evidence" was collected, the magistrates gave Goody a chance to confess.

"Thou hast promised me life enduring if I confess to these crimes," she said in her small voice. "I cannot confess to lies. But it is a very small thing that I should be judged by thee or by any human court. I am not aware of any wrong I've done, but I am not thereby acquitted," she said. "'Tis the Lord who judges me. There is not one among thee who can promise me anything on God's account. I feel Christ lifting my soul!" she cried. "Little care I what thou dost with my body."

On the day of the trial Thomas Bliss forbade his family to go near the center of town, nor would he go himself. He had heard gossip enough from the Bartletts and knew perfectly well what was happening. He refused to allow his wife to testify on Goody's behalf, though both Margaret and Mary begged him to let them tell the town how mistaken they were about this kind-hearted soul who would not raise her hand to hurt a fly. Thomas held firm, for he knew the mood of the town. Their testimony would make Margaret and Mary suspect as well. He had heard Mary's tales about the old midwife and knew they would only confirm some of the charges and condemn Mary too.

Mary wept bitter tears. "But Father, who will save her?"

Her mother answered. "Listen to your father, Mary. It would be their chief desire to try you for witchcraft right alongside her. Many folks know that you are acquainted. Mary Crespet knows that you cannot go to her defense—if she were here now she would beg you to stay at home and pray for her deliverance."

Though her parents succeeded in frightening her, Mary would

not be comforted. Her mother stayed by her side all day, trying to console her, offering her sips of sack.

And then, when hardly a blade of grass was left, gigantic flocks of birds blackened the skies. The awesome whirr of their dark wings and the sinister bedlam of their cries frightened the villagers, who ran indoors, falling on their knees to pray for deliverance from yet another terrifying pestilence from God.

As the shadows grew long in the dooryard and the birds flocked to the woods, Goodwife Ann Bartlett came to the Blisses' door with news. What was left of Goody Crespet's mortal remains could be found high over Meeting House Yard, swinging from the hanging tree. Until after the Sabbath Goody's meager body would hang in plain view, her pecked hands and face, her broken and stretched neck a warning to witches and any who would befriend them.

As long as Goody Crespet's body swung in Meeting House Yard no one in Hartford could find a caterpillar anywhere. Goodwife Knapp summed up the widespread belief: "The witch is dead, and all the caterpillars have followed her to Hell."

Mary, with Margaret at her side, looked out at the meadow. "Mother, the caterpillars are gone. The birds have eaten every one."

Thomas having given his permission, just after dawn Mary and her mother set out to look for Goody's grave. Because of her supposed crime, her body could not occupy space in the Christian burial ground, yet secretly word of the grave's location had come to the women. Poor Goody had been laid to rest in the nearby woods, just off the burial ground.

"'Tis fitting enough," Mary said, "for she found solace and strength in the woods."

Margaret had insisted that they go early, before the market filled with people. Mary had wanted to bring wildflowers or a bird's nest, something for Goody's grave.

"Nay," Margaret had said, "we'll carry no pagan objects."

Mary held her tongue, though she knew that Goody would have seen such things as small wonders of God's Creation.

They entered the burial ground and anxiously headed toward the woods. At the very edge of the trees Mary spied a place where the weeds and wildflowers had been trampled down. They hurried in under the trees and were quickly hidden by the underbrush. After a short walk, when they came to a bed of pine needles under a pair of ancient white pines, nearby they saw a clearing surrounded by an oak grove.

"Look!" Margaret whispered, pointing at a mound of fresh-dug earth.

Slowly, reverently, they approached the place, and when they reached it Mary went to her knees. "She lies here. Oh, Mother, I know it. Look where she lies. I kept it secret, but the first time I met Goody was in the woods—in a place like this."

Margaret knelt beside her.

"I want to pray, Mother."

"Aye, you are the one who loved her best."

"O Lord, give rest—sweet and blessed—to Thy friend, Mary Crespet," she said through her tears. "Take her to Thee in heaven where there is no sorrow—where she will forever live in the light of Thy kindness. Amen."

"'Dust thou art, and unto dust shalt thou return,'" Margaret whispered, taking Mary's hand to help her stand.

Mary looked around at the place where her friend would sleep for eternity. "She belongs here where the birds sing—away from those who hated her."

XV

How much better is thy love than wine!
And the smell of thine ointments than all spices!
How fair is thy love, my sister, my spouse!
Honey and milk are under thy tongue;
And the smell of thy garments is like the smell of Lebanon.
Thy lips, O my spouse, drop as the honeycomb:
A spring shut up, a fountain sealed.
A garden enclosed is my sister, my spouse . . .

Song of Songs 4:10-12
The Holy Bible, King James Version

THOMAS CAME HOME, weary from a day's work in his woodlot and field, to find his elder daughters sitting beside a window with the mending. He was pleased to see how far Hannah had come in her stitchery, for she was simple and slow and good as an angel. He was amazed by how different the two girls were. Smiling, he remembered Mary's various comments on women's work:

"The best part of winter is baking bread, for I am warm by the fire."

"Some chores are loathsome—beating flax, churning butter, scrubbing laundry. They take the strength of a man, and afterwards I am pleased to sit down with the mending."

To his mind, Mary was too preoccupied with her own comfort, but his heart filled with joy every time he saw her—like now—

sitting peacefully in the light of a window, her mending just lowered to her lap as she greeted him with a smile.

Though he was tired and dirty, he felt an unfamiliar lightness in his heart. As he came closer he tried to attract her attention with the gay little tune he whistled.

She returned his smile. "Father, 'tis plain to see, you have something to say!" then bent her head to her work again.

"Indeed, I do, but you must beg to hear it." Thomas did not often tease.

"I care not, one way or the other," Mary teased back, and Hannah laughed at her sister's boldness.

Her father took Mary's hands, pulled her up from her seat, and danced her around the room. "You are such a pretty rogue—but stubborn and willful and so mightily mean-hearted—I can't imagine why he wants you."

"Wants me?" she cried, "Prithee, Father, who wants me—and for what?"

Out of breath, Thomas brought their jig to a halt. "He wants you for his wife."

"For his wife? Who?" Mary seized his shirt as if to shake him like a rag.

"Nay, I thought you didn't want to hear it."

"Now then, Father, stop your jesting. Must you be so wicked?"

"Very well," he said, "sit you down and be very serious and I'll tell." After Mary complied, he revealed the secret. "As I was working in my far field, a fine young man approached on a handsome bay. He had ridden here from a distant village, just to see me. He said that as I was the father of one Mary Bliss, he had come to ask for my daughter's hand in marriage."

Mary looked astonished. "Prithee, who was this fine young man?"

"He's a young farmer with forty-six acres."

"I care not for his acres! What is his name?"

"Joseph Parsons!" Thomas shouted, so loud that Margaret burst in from the kitchen.

"What's all the fuss? Is Joseph here?" She was wiping her hands on her apron.

"Nay, but he promises to come tomorrow," Thomas said. "Well, Mary, what do you say?"

"What do you say, Mary?" Hannah echoed.

Looking dizzy, Mary hugged herself, saying nothing.

Margaret was at a complete loss. "Thomas, say about what? Have you seen Joseph today?"

Mary found her tongue at last. "I cannot think what to say, Father, I am too astonished. Do you jest?"

Margaret could scarce contain herself, looking first at Thomas, then at Mary. "Why is she astonished?"

Thomas went to stand at his wife's side. "Joseph has asked for Mary's hand. Would you love him, Mary? Would you be happy as his wife?"

"Of course she will," Margaret blurted. "He is dear to all of us."

"Dear to all!" Hannah chimed.

There was no danger that Thomas Bliss would marry his daughter off to a man she did not love. Without love there could be no fulfillment, no union with God, and certainly no children.

It was more like summer than fall on the day Joseph came to call. White and violet asters bloomed amid goldenrod in the uncut meadow grass. Inside, Mary waited for him, wearing her best yellow waistcoat and dark-green skirt. As her mother tidied up near the fireplace, she sat primly passing a needle through linen stretched on a frame. She was singing softly, her voice light and sure.

"He'll come through that door before you know it." Margaret was nervous. "Now, I want you to keep a civil tongue and an open mind—and stop that singing. You behave like such a wretch at times Mary, I fear for your very soul." It was all Margaret could do not to smile at her daughter, who stitched and sang her psalm as if she was truly pious.

"For beast he makes the grass to grow, herbs also for man's good: that he may bring out of the earth what may be for their food." Mary rolled her eyes and looked heavenward fluttering her eyelids, teasing her mother.

"Wine also that man's heart may glad and oil their face to bright; and bread which to the heart of man may it supply with might," she sang with mock sanctimony.

"Ah, Mary," her mother said, "the Devil will have you yet."

Mary gave her a cheerful smile.

While Margaret knew how much Mary enjoyed the attention, she knew too that her daughter never would come out and say how much she looked forward to seeing Joseph again, or how thrilled she was by his proposal. All at once the embroidery fell to the floor as Mary jumped up from her chair to dash to the window, Margaret at her heels.

They saw a rider approach, kicking up dust on the road. When he tied his horse at the gate Mary pulled back from the window. Margaret guessed she didn't want to appear overeager.

"He comes," Mary whispered. "He looks very handsome. Was he so handsome the last time he came to call? Tell me quickly, Mother, shall I sit and sew, or stand like a fool by the door?"

"Sit and sew," Margaret commanded. She ran to the door herself, opening it before Joseph could knock. "Oh, Joseph," she feigned surprise, "'Tis good to see you!"

"Good morrow, Goodwife Bliss." Hat in hand, he bowed, then stepped into the room, his eyes searching for Mary, who sat by the window. "You look well, Mary."

"And you, Joseph. Come, sit you down." She kept her seat and pointed to a chair.

Margaret's thoughts rushed hither and yon. Surely everything is different now that Joseph has made his intentions known. Why should I be so anxious? He's never made me so before. Smiling, she bustled around serving cider, the anise-seed jumbles she'd made that morning, leftover gingerbread from the day before. Why, oh why, does Mary just sit there with nothing to say, leaving all the work to me? "How fast the summer has flown," she said, smiling again, certain that she had never smiled so often in a seven-day week.

"Indeed, Goodwife, it has." From Joseph they gleaned quite a parcel of news. He told them he'd acquired land and built a house

150

in Springfield. The townsmen had elected him highway overseer, a job that required him to keep the roads and byways of the town passable in every season. And he was now a fur agent working for William Pynchon.

"We've not journeyed to Springfield," Margaret said, a proud thought coming to mind—a man wasn't usually asked to hold public office until he'd been a householder for five years.

"Are you acquainted with James Bridgeman?" Mary said. "He and his wife Sarah removed from Hartford to Springfield not long after they married."

"Aye, the carpenter built his house north of mine on Town Street."

"I knew her when they were here," Mary said. "And what of the town?"

Margaret got up to fetch a bottle of sack, having seen that Joseph had drunk up his cider.

"'Tis a fair piece north of here on the Boston side of the great river, with two large rivers to the south and many brooks and streams—all filled with fish and beaver ponds. To the north lies the Chicopee plain, and above that the wilderness, full of beaver for the taking."

"But what of the town itself?" Mary leaned forward to hear as Margaret offered Joseph a glass of sack.

He received the glass with a nod of thanks. "'Tis smaller than Hartford, but of late many have come. There's a meeting house, to be sure, and an ordinary—and a new sawmill."

After more polite conversation, mostly about the progress of the Blisses' fields and crops, Margaret pressed Joseph for word of Springfield's most prominent citizen. William Pynchon was famous throughout the colonies. Some folks called him the Baron of Springfield.

"He's a fine fellow," Joseph said. "Most all the men in the town work his fields, or at his sawmill, or raising his herds. He ships beef as far away as England. And he has agents, like me, working in the fur trade, and canoe men to haul furs and supplies. It was he who single-handedly led the cause for Springfield to secede from Connecticut." He chuckled, taking a sip of his drink. "Massachusetts was glad to welcome us."

"Pray, Joseph, tell us why?"

"I'll not bother with particulars but, chiefly, Pynchon and the Connecticut court disagreed about the price of corn." His face broke into a pleasing smile. "Pynchon won!"

Margaret smiled. "And he is friend to you, Joseph?"

"Aye, he has been charitable toward me. He helped me when I came."

"Then you knew him in England?"

"Nay, we have a mutual friend who, in corresponding with Pynchon, mentioned my desire to come to New England, and he agreed to welcome me. These ten years, he and his son John have been as good as family to me, though I have repaid him in full by my labors."

Margaret was thinking what a blessing it was to have such a powerful and charitable friend. Satisfied at last about Joseph's prospects and well aware that Mary wanted him to herself, she suggested to the young couple that they go for a short walk. "Just don't stray too far or stay gone too long," she said. She shook a playful finger at them. "I shall expect you back well before the sun disappears behind Bartlett's woodlot."

Joseph and Mary walked out on the road to Little River, and as soon as they were alone, to Joseph's puzzlement, Mary fell silent. Had she not been told of his intentions? But his tongue was likewise tied, he could not say what was on his mind. For the moment he wanted nothing more than to press her into his arms, to kiss her, to bed her. He tried to make himself think of something else.

They walked on awhile in silence until Mary said, "Pray, Joseph, have you fond memories of England?"

He shook his head. "Nay, I think not of the past, for my happiness is here."

Mary looked puzzled. "Happiness? I wonder, has anyone ever said such a thing to me?"

At a spot along the river where an old tree had fallen over the water, she hesitated, and he took her hand.

Quite sure of herself she said, "Only God may assure our happiness. We have no power over such things."

Joseph let go of her hand to step up onto the fallen tree trunk. "I do believe we have," he said, walking out over the water as Mary watched from the riverbank. Suddenly he turned to look at her. "See that wilderness out there?" He pointed north toward the forest. "It's waiting for me—full of riches beyond the dreams of anyone in England." With that, he dashed back along the stout tree trunk and jumped to the ground. "And I am here, Mary!"

Though she shook her head, she smiled at him. "You expect too much from this life!"

Her lips looked so tempting, he wanted to bite them. "And I like it well!" he exclaimed. When he reached for her, she stepped playfully away.

"This life is mine to do with what I will. I shall make my fortune here!" He took her hand, small and soft compared to his.

She stared at him just long enough to raise his hopes of a kiss, then turned her face away. "Winter's coming on," she said, a touch of sadness in her voice. "The cruelest season."

He lifted her hand to his lips. "It will be hard for us to see one another." Was she thinking the same thing? "Has your father spoken to you?"

Mary turned in surprise at the sight of a bright bittersweet vine growing on a nearby tree. She reached to touch it as if were a jeweled necklace. "Aye, he said you want me to wife."

"And your answer?"

Her eyes twinkled. "I haven't made up my mind."

But Joseph read the answer on her face—yes.

The path took them up a lightly wooded hill high above the river. They walked for a while in silence, the song of the river below, when the sound of laughter drifted up to them. They looked down to see a small group of Indian women, bathing in a little cove. The women had no idea they were being observed. Quickly, Joseph pulled Mary to crouch with him behind a bush. "Hush," he whispered.

The naked women were young and supple. Their long, black hair fell over their backs and breasts as they talked and laughed and splashed one another. Joseph smiled to himself, for he understood most of what they said as they jested about a certain brave and his sexual prowess—a subject he knew he must keep to himself.

"Have you ever seen nakedness before?" he whispered.

"Only babes and children." Mary blushed and ducked her head.

Finding them comely, Joseph wanted to watch. "Look, Mary, how free they are, how they move and play in the water," he whispered.

"Nay, Joseph, let's away." She tugged at his shirt, but he did not move.

Feeling like a sneak-thief, Mary moved out of the underbrush and fled down the hill. Walking faster, she looked over her shoulder to see that Joseph had not followed. Anger rose in her breast as tears filled her eyes. She walked on, wondering what her father would say when she told him. Hoping Joseph had come to his senses, she looked back, but she was alone on the path.

As she turned on to the road for home she heard him call to her. "Mary, Mary, wait up!" Running, finally he caught up to her. But when he took her by the hand, she yanked it away.

"I'm sorry!" He laughed. ""I am sorry, truly I am."

She turned to face him. "How dare you touch me? Sorry? You're not sorry at all! I never want to see you again!" And she set out at a clip toward home.

Using long strides he kept up with her. "Ah, Mary, don't be a prude." He took her arm, turning her firmly to him. "I harmed no one."

Her fury mounted. "Prude?" She raised her fist as if to pound it against his chest.

"Pray, don't strike me." He pretended to cower, then leapt out to seize both her wrists. "You frighten me, Mary. Such anger— you look ready to tear my heart out." He pulled her close to peer intensely into her eyes.

She struggled against him. "Let me go!"

"I'll never let you go," he said. "I want you more than all the riches in this New World. I'm sorry I grieved you, truly I am. 'Twas only a callow interest in the wonders God hath wrought."

She was almost ready to forgive him when she saw mirth lurking at the corners of his eyes. "Remember, God looked and saw that it was good." Joseph's smile was both mocking and warmly engaging.

Confused, Mary backed away. She longed to kiss him, yet she wanted to slap his face. Trembling, she looked down to study his dusty boots planted close to the hem of her skirt. He thrilled her, yet what he did—tempting her to look at nakedness—was wrong. This time, when he pulled her to him by her wrists, she did not resist.

"Look at me!" he commanded. The longer she stared at his boots, the closer he pulled her until his arms were around her, and his face was a breath away. "Look at me," he whispered. She could resist no longer, fixing her gaze on his warm brown eyes until her anger vanished and she grew easy in his arms. Suddenly he lowered his arms, freeing her.

"There," he said, still gazing into her eyes. "Tell me what you see."

"I see *you*, Joseph, a man who knows what he desires and will stop for no one."

"Is that so terrible?"

"I know not. But I pray to God that I am never the poor wretch who stands in your path." To her dismay, she desired him ardently. He would be her husband.

He reached for her. "May I kiss you?"

"Nay, Joseph, I've had quite enough excitement for one day."

"Do you hate me, then?"

"I don't hate you, nor will I say I love you. 'Tis a long courtship we must brave," she said, taking his hand, leading him toward home.

XVI

The man whose heart is endeared to the woman he
loves . . . dreams of her in the night, hath her in his eye
and apprehension when he awakes, museth on her as
he sits at the table, walks with her when he travels . . .
She lies in his bosom, and his heart trusts in her, which
forceth all to confess that the stream of his affection, like
a mighty current, runs with full tide and strength.

—Thomas Hooker (1586–1647)

THAT WINTER WAS long and severe, endless for Mary.
Because of all the snow, Joseph had been able to visit her only
once. He stayed at the Bartletts' across the road, and in Mary's
presence he managed to conduct himself with propriety, changing
her opinion of him a great deal for the better. Mary kept their
meetings on as lofty a plane as she could manage, insisting on
discussions of important topics such as his plans for expanding
the fur trade, gossip about all the important people in Springfield,
and particulars of his travels north, where he lived and worked
with the Indians.

On one occasion they went for a walk through the snow,
and though he asked, she would not allow him to kiss her. She
explained her reason sweetly.

"There will be time for that soon enough—*if* we marry."

Joseph was impatient, but his love for her had grown so ardent
that he allowed her to control the progress of their courtship.

SPRING CAME AS it always had, barely in time to save humanity from madness. As soon as the trees filled with bright new buds and the grasses on the meadows grew sweet and tall, Joseph returned to Hartford. A gentle breeze freshened the air in the Meeting House, where windows had been flung wide to the sound of birdsong. No longer did Mary lament her lack of piety. Though in hearing distance of a great preacher, she preferred to sit across the room from the man she loved, listening to the birds sing, wrapped in daydreams.

The night before, giddy and breathless, she and Joseph had run through a moonlit pasture, away from family and friends gathered at a bonfire. Standing ankle-deep in new grass, he had stopped to embrace her. And this time he asked no permission but kissed her feverishly, again and again, as Mary felt her feet leave the ground and the stars wheel overhead. When the kisses stopped, she broke from him and looked across the pasture at the figures silhouetted against the fire. "We must go back, Joseph."

"Nay." He pulled her closer. "Stay with me." He kissed her, letting his tongue slip gently between her lips, then kissed her again more passionately, bringing them both to their knees. He laid her down in the grass and covered her with his body.

She could feel his weight, knew how perfectly he would fit her. "They will see us, Joseph."

"It is dark. Nobody sees." He pressed hard against her.

"God sees in the dark," she said, and pushed him away. She got to her feet and turned to run, then looked over her shoulder. Joseph still lay in the grass, his arms flung out to his sides. She ran on.

Joseph rolled over on his belly and buried his face in the new grass to breathe in its earthy smell. Overwhelmed by desire for Mary, he let out an anguished cry. "I must have her or die!"

THOMAS BLISS HAD come to doubt he would ever support his family adequately in New England. Most years he had to write to his sister for help, and he felt her resentment growing with each reply. He walked across his rain-soaked field quite aware that he had failed, remembering the hope, the faith he'd put in a new life. Yet nothing much had changed for him. After all these years he was still walking home each evening exhausted, knowing he had been wrong. Margaret had been right. He had believed and had followed his heart, but his heart had led him to these sodden fields where his crops were rotting. He'd believed he could reclaim his family's position and wealth, had convinced his wife to trust him, yet all he'd done was barely keep his family fed.

Aware of her father's troubles Mary felt ashamed of her happiness. She was in love and lay awake nights summoning up Joseph's kisses and the look on his face when he held her. 'Tis delight and longing I see in his eyes. He wants to bed me. She knew nothing of such things, yet she found her own stirrings enticingly potent.

Thomas took to sitting up late at night reading the Bible by the light of the fire. At first Mary found it difficult to fall asleep, for his presence made the room gloomy. One night as she watched him from her bed she thought he looked old, the lines on his face sagging downward, his lips glistening with ale. He slumped in his chair, no longer strong and muscular. His red hair had turned white, his tall body had thinned.

She got out of bed and went to his side. "You look tired, Father," she murmured, sitting down at his feet. "Go to bed now and rest."

"I shall rest when the rain stops, but I will go to bed after we speak of Joseph Parsons," he said, his voice low.

"What would you have me say?"

"You've seen him many times now. Does he please you?"

"Aye, Father. He does."

"Could you grow to love him, Mary?" he asked, stroking her hair.

She looked up at him. "Aye, my heart leaps when I say it out loud. I love him well."

Her answer seemed to disturb him. "You must not love him too well," he said. "Your first love must be kept for God. Mother, father, husband, and child—all will be taken to the grave. Save your best love for God alone—only He will not die."

IN SUMMER, FOR all the world to see, Joseph posted the banns on the Meeting House doors in both Springfield and Hartford. His announcement gave the date as 26 November, 1646, naming his intended as Mary, daughter of Thomas Bliss of Hartford. The wedding day would follow the long, hard work of the harvest.

While happy that their daughter had found a promising young man to marry, the elder Blisses had difficulty accepting that she would move thirty miles upriver to a village they had never seen. After their son Nat had married, he took his bride to Springfield. They would have to be content that their eldest son, Tom, and his wife still lived in Hartford.

Shortly before the wedding, Thomas voiced a particular concern to his wife. "Have you spoken with her about her wifely duties?"

"Aye, she knows how to bake and spin." Margaret was satisfied that she had taught Mary all she needed to know. "And you'll not find a better gardener in all of New England."

"That's not what I mean, woman. What does she know of men, the marriage bed—of being with child?"

Margaret considered for a moment before she answered. "Aye, in truth, I may need to tell her a thing or two before the wedding day. "But, my husband," she propped her hands on her hips and cocked her head to one side with a smile, "I shall do it in my own time and the place of my own choosing, without any prodding from *you*."

The time and place came on a bright, cool day in October. Mary and her mother were tidying the raised beds and harvesting the last of the cauliflower and beets. "'Tis my duty to talk to you, Mary, about what will happen after your wedding—on your wedding night," Margaret began.

"I know all about it, Mother," Mary lied.

Margaret straightened up to lean on her hoe. "Now where would you have learned such a thing, if not from your own mother?" She gave Mary her don't-try-to-fool-me look.

"Well, I know that, well, babes come and all." Unwilling to meet her mother's gaze, Mary glanced up at the clouds rolling by.

"Tell me, then. I want to hear it from you."

"Well, you know," Mary said blushing.

"Of course I know. I've given birth to eleven babes, and before I did, my mother told me what I should expect. Now will you listen to your mother or not?"

"Aye, tell me what I must know." Mary gave her mother a hug.

"Let's gather up the beets and things," Margaret said, "and take them to the keeping room. I think this talk deserves a drink of sack."

By the warmth of a fire and over glasses of sweet spirits, Margaret began anew. "After you are wed, Joseph will share a bed with you and take his pleasure. 'Tis important, Mary, that the wife also find pleasure from lying with her husband. If, for some reason, the husband does not please the wife, she will be barren. Her body will not give off its seed, and it is from the seed of both the husband and the wife that a child is sown. Now, child, do you understand?"

"Aye." Mary took another swallow of her drink. Though she believed she understood her mother's words, still she did not know what, if anything, she was supposed to do.

"Let me tell you how you will know that your seed has been given off," Margaret said, emptying her glass. "At that moment, you will be overcome with a bewitching pleasure, like nothing you have ever felt before. And Mary," she added, "a wife must not let her husband withdraw too quickly, lest the seed catch cold."

It appeared that her mother had more to say, for she poured a wee bit more sack into both their glasses. "If a wife has difficulty conceiving even though she has lain with her husband successfully, then she may see a cunning woman for a remedy against barrenness."

Thoughts of her old friend sprang to Mary's mind. "Goody Crespet must have helped many women," Mary said, wishing she were here to share her happiness.

"To be sure," Margaret said. "I have never had difficulty conceiving and most likely neither will you. Now, I have one last bit of advice. You must try never to refuse your husband when he wants to lie with you. On the other hand, he must never force you against your will or treat you cruelly. And if he should, you are not bound to stay with him."

As the two exchanged a loving look, Mary reached across the table gratefully to touch her mother's arm, feeling deep affection for this good woman in whose care God had placed her.

The marriage rite was short, unblessed by prayers, a simple civil ceremony conducted in the earnest hope that the affection the bride and groom shared would not excite God's jealousy. Their covenant was sealed. The day was so pleasant and rare for November that folks thought it a sure sign the marriage would be blessed. A feast was laid on a long table in the sun, near a tall maple tree that still clung to a few bright red leaves. In the distance haystacks looked like golden cones of sugar against a sky of blue.

With help from their neighbors, Mary's family prepared a feast. The two pigs Thomas had killed roasted on spits over a pit of coals. A still life of roast fowl, baked squash and pumpkin, corn pudding, succotash, fried parsnips, baked beans, sweet Indian pudding, and a staggering array of breads covered the table atop the Oriental rug the Bartletts had lent. A children's table was laid nearby.

All the adult guests gathered at the large table. At the head sat Mary and her bridegroom, listening as their honored guest, William Pynchon, proposed a toast.

"Let us salute this fine young couple and bless them," he began, as all the company rose to their feet. "To your prosperity, Joseph, whom I have taken to my heart. And to the fair Mary, his wife. May God grant you good health and earthly riches. May you be fruitful, as God commands, and bring children to fill the earth—" he looked over all the happy faces, "well, perhaps filling Spring-field will do."

Mary blushed as cups clinked and hearty cheering followed. She reached down to clasp Joseph's hand as laughter bubbled up and down the table.

Joseph smiled, well at ease but quite aware that his bride did not like merrymaking at her expense. Throughout the day he'd been helpless to keep his eyes off her in her new gown. Her auburn curls, though held by a lace coif, were allowed to flow down her back. The rose-colored silk gown had been sewn by her mother's loving hands, its deep lace collar fastened with tiny bows to match the gown. She was too thrilled to eat, though Joseph ate ravenously and drank thirstily.

Cup in hand, he turned to his bride and raised it. "At last I toast my wife," he said quietly, to her alone. "I can say no more of my love for you here, Mary," he murmured, then drank again and reached for her, kissing her lightly on the lips.

The wedding feast was a great success. Thomas had so much to eat and drink that Margaret put him to bed halfway through the party. After the older guests had gone home, Margaret embraced her daughter and said goodbye with a kiss. Some of the company followed Mary and Joseph across the road to the Bartletts' house, where they would spend their wedding night in a spare room on the second floor. The younger guests crossed the road singing rowdy songs and shouting, as the young couple ran ahead.

> I put my hand all on her toe,
> Fair maid is a lily O,
> I put my hand all on her toe,
> She says to me—

Mary looked back over her shoulder, then to her new husband. "They wouldn't behave like this if Mister Hooker was here, I'll warrant. Make them go away, Joseph, please."

Joseph laughed. "Nay, they're just being merry."

> 'Do you want to go?
> Come to me quietly,
> Do not do me injury,
> Gently Johnny, my jingalo.'

When they reached the house, Joseph stood on the threshold and turned to face their tormenters. "You have given us a merry send-off. For that we thank you, but good night!"

Everyone cheered as Joseph took Mary by the hand and pulled her into the house.

While three of the Bartlett children hung from the stair rail for another look at the bride, Goodman Bartlett poured Joseph a drink. Goodwife Bartlett carried the baby up the stairs, pushing past her gawking brood—Samuel, Abigail, and wide-eyed Nathaniel, his thumb stuck in his mouth.

"Follow me, Mary, I'll show you the way," she said, beckoning. The goodwife settled her guest into the room that would be theirs until Joseph took Mary home to Springfield, wished her good night and closed the door behind her.

Mary went to the window. How odd it felt to see her father's house across the road, smoke rising from the chimney, dimly lit windows inviting. Her mother was still up. Suddenly she felt an urge to go to her. Where was Joseph?

Downstairs in the parlor, Robert Bartlett laughed and patted the groom on the back. "Get upstairs to Mary, lad. You don't want to spend your wedding night with me!"

"How right you are, good fellow." Joseph laughed, tossing down the last of his wine. "I'll thank you and bid you good night."

He found Mary standing beside the fire. He came to her just as she removed her lace coif, just as all that glorious hair fell around her shoulders. "I'm glad you are still gowned, for now I may untie all those bows," he said, his eyes shining with wine and desire.

"Pray, what makes you think you know how to undress me?"

"I've plotted it ever since I first saw you." He took her in his arms, kissing her tenderly. She trembled as he reached for the bows on her collar.

"Joseph," she whispered through his kisses, "Joseph, wait—"
He was moving too fast for her.

164

"I've waited too long." He covered her mouth with his as he pulled at the fastenings on her gown, then lowered it from her shoulders and let it fall to the floor. He raised her shift over her head, covered her breasts with kisses, and brought them both to their knees.

Swept up in something too strong for her to either desire or to resist, she pushed back. She wanted to talk to him, to calm him.

"Don't pull away from me. You are mine now," he said, his voice soft but firm, picking her up and carrying her to the bed to lay her down. She watched him open his breeches and climb on top of her, still wearing his boots. She was not afraid and said no more, for she was curious to experience his passion. He entered her sharply, moving hard against her.

"I've waited too long," he cried again, this time rapturously, and soon rolled off, collapsing on the bed beside her. Reaching for Mary, he drew her to him and held her close. Within a few breaths, he was sound asleep.

Light from the moon streamed in through the window. She lay beside her husband and watched him sleep, his tousled curls falling over his forehead, his mouth innocent as a babe's, lips parted as he took in her breath. He lay sprawled across the bed, his boots sticking out from under the coverlet. She got out of bed and pulled them off, letting them fall to the floor. He did not wake but rolled over on his stomach and buried his head under a pillow.

Feeling disappointed and lonely, she wondered what the morning would bring. When something wet came out of her body she knew it was his seed. Not knowing what else to do, she slid the chamber pot from under the bed and cleaned herself with the towel her hostess had left for them.

Joseph woke early and put wood on the fire, encouraging the flames with a bellows. Rising from his task, he went to the window and opened the shutters on a dreary morning with heavy ground fog hovering over the pasture. He looked across the room at his sleeping wife and the towel lying on the floor, stained by her virgin blood. Shivering from the cold, he closed the shutters and crawled back into bed. Bundling her into his arms he kissed her mouth softly.

"Mary, I can wait no longer for you to wake."

She yawned. "You are an impatient man, Joseph."

"Aye, I do confess it. Last night I was too full of wine and too eager to bed you."

Mary studied his face, brushing a lock of hair from his eyes. "Last night you made me remember my duty as a wife, Joseph. Your duty as a husband is to be patient with me."

"Is that what your mother told you?"

Looking hurt and confused, she turned away.

"Forgive me, Mary." He crawled over her, lying close so she had to face him.

"I know my duty," she said. As he tried to protest, she covered his lips with her fingers. "Joseph, answer me. Would you rather have a dutiful wife or a willing wife?"

He laughed heartily, unable to be serious. "I want both."

Mary seemed bewildered by his teasing. "I hope you are laughing at yourself and not me, for you have spoken more truth than is prudent. You reveal yourself as a man burning with self-interest."

"Ah, my bliss, I am only interested in you," he said, pulling up her shift, covering her belly with kisses.

PART TWO
Good Men, Good Wives

I

December 26 [1696] We bury our little daughter . . . Note:
'twas wholly dry, and I went at noon to see in what order
things were set . . . the coffins of my dear father Hull,
mother Hull, cousin Quinsey, and my six children . . .
My mother's lies on a lower bench, at the end, with her
head to her husband's head; and I ordered little Sarah
to be set on her grandmother's feet. 'Twas an awful yet
pleasing treat; having said, 'The Lord knows who shall
be brought hither next,' I came away.

—Samuel Sewall (1652–1730)

Springfield, Massachusetts Bay Colony

EXCEPT FOR THE crystal moonlight passing in and out of
storm clouds, it was a melancholy hour. The houses on Town
Street were dark, while in the snow-covered forest to the west
fires burning inside Nipmuck longhouses sent curls of smoke into
the sky.

Springfield's main street ran north and south, with fifty-nine
house lots settled between the great river and a long narrow band
of wet meadow. In summer, when still air lingered above the
soggy ground, marsh gases ignited into ghostly blue lights and
hovered like flickering lamps—part of the natural order of things,

like wolves howling in the forest, and bears prowling the edge of the village.

The bulk of the houses on Town Street were alike: a single room with oiled paper and shutters covering the windows, a large chimney at one end. Some houses had three rooms with a center chimney, but few could afford two stories or glass in the windows. Inside, weary goodwives had gone early to bed. Their husbands would rise before dawn and, after an hour or two of work, come home wanting breakfast.

Protected by a tall wooden palisade now banked in snow, William Pynchon's general store stood like a fort on the west side of the river. It was the chief retail and wholesale market in the upper valley, and at that location accessible to river traffic. Here the Indians brought their furs to trade, and people from neighboring towns found European goods: cloth, farm and household implements, boots, coats and blankets. Pynchon had thought of everything, even the manufacture of wampum. The store was, at heart, a company store. Most everyone in town worked for its owner. Springfield, unlike Hartford, was founded as a trading post, and its soul resided in commerce, not in the building of a Christian utopia. In general, men with skills were most welcome there, whether or not they brought their virtues.

As the moon disappeared in a whirl of clouds, the languorous river flowed past frozen fields, now deep with snow. Across the river in the orchards, the arms of trees reached to capture falling white flakes. Now deserted, Town Street was intersected by four rutted roads. One traveled through the marsh, onward for a three-day journey to Boston. Another ran down to the field where the militia trained and on to the burial ground at the river's edge, where gravestones chiseled with skulls lay buried in snow. Churchyard burials were thought too papist. Up and away from the burial ground sat the Meeting House, and farther on the ordinary, where men gathered to talk and drink ale, brandy and Spanish wine. All the important gossip—men's gossip—was heard at the ordinary.

It was late when the innkeeper said good night to the cooper

170

John Dover, one of his best customers. He snuffed out all but the last candle and locked the door. The candle would light his way up the stairs to the rooms where his family slept.

Outside, carrying his long gun, John Dover turned south on Town Street, the only man left on the streets at that hour. After an evening at the ordinary and a snoot full of ale, he walked as swiftly and steadily as he could down the snow-glutted street. Besides making barrels for everything from beer to beef, he crafted shingles and picked up odd jobs gardening and mending fences for Pynchon and others. He also served the town by beating the drums on Sabbath mornings, rousing the faithful in time for meeting. At his house near the bottom of the street, his wife Susannah and two small daughters waited for him in their sleep.

The farther one walked up Town Street the larger the house lots and grander the houses became. The first noticeably large parcel belonged to the minister, George Thatcher. Tonight, indeed every night, the tall, skeletally thin man slept in good conscience cuddled against his warm, fat wife. He was Cambridge-educated and proud that the settlers never occupied a foot of the territory called Agawam without paying the natives their due. In 1636, the land on both sides of the river had been bought from the Indians for ten fathoms of wampum and ten coats, hatchets, hoes and knives. It was Thatcher's calling and duty to convert these children of sin to the gospel, that they might no longer be the Devil's vassals but suitable neighbors for the English. As one of "the godly" he hated sin and battled against it wherever it existed in the heathen encampments or among his own people.

Only weeks after their wedding and removal to Springfield, Joseph Parsons and his wife Mary had settled into a small center-chimney house with three rooms and a loft, just two lots north of John Dover. Wind-driven snow buried the little house in a grave of white, while a fire burned warmly inside, gilding the room where they slept.

From the moment he took shelter from the storm Joseph wanted her. "Stay with me, my bliss," he said, lifting Mary to the bed. "By morning we'll be snowbound. I'll not oversee the highways of Springfield nor go out to hunt. We'll not have to part."

Snug in their warm bed, they rolled together for hours. In the pale light Joseph finally got Mary to take off all her clothes and let him look at her. At his bidding, she stood naked in the middle of the room, turning so he could see every curve of her hips and buttocks. He gently pried her hands from her breasts and with his kisses made her nipples shiny and hard. Burrowing inside her, he wished never to leave her. He wintered over in her long thick hair and felt it whip across his chest as she rode him like a stallion, ruby sparks dancing between her curls and the firelight.

After two days, when the snow and the winds abated, Joseph dressed to go out, and Mary knew she had conceived. She said nothing of it to her lover but let him go into the bright white day to help clear the roads. She closed the door behind him and turned to look at his little house, dark and warm like a womb. She felt a great power had possessed and changed her forever. She thought of Goody Crespet and went to the shelf near the fireplace. From a little wooden box she lifted the silver amulet, kissing it before she put it back in its hiding place. Then she took dried angelica and rue, and, with a prayer on her lips, scattered bits of both across the doorway and all around the room.

AFTER THE MEAN winter came the spring rains. James Bridgeman's young wife Sarah gloomily pulled away from the door she had opened only a crack. She had gone there to look at the beds of lettuce drowning in her front yard. God has sent rain again today, she thought, with no thought for the planting season. It wasn't as if the heavens hadn't opened wide every day for nearly two months, leaving her confined indoors with her two-year-old son, John, and four-year-old daughter, Sarah Jr.

The rivers had overflowed their banks, flooding the villages from Springfield to Saybrook. The day before, the water had been knee-deep over the road to the mill. For everyone living along the Connecticut River, the endless rain was making life onerous and dreary. After the winter their stores were low, and it would not be time to plant the fields until the next full moon.

From his pulpit Mister Thatcher warned of disaster if evil were not exposed and routed out. From every New England pulpit a new law was proclaimed: One day each month to be set aside as a solemn day of humiliation, when the Saints would be called to humble themselves and to fast. These past years had seen Indian troubles, earthquakes, hurricanes, excommunications, and widespread crop failure. It seemed God was not pleased with the people of New England.

"God promised Noah that never again would He flood the earth, but He knew not the wickedness of Springfield," Mister Thatcher had proclaimed from the pulpit on the previous Sabbath. "We are a burden to God. He cannot bear us—and will think His troubles well over when He has destroyed us."

Sarah shivered whenever that sermon came to mind. She was not sure what to make of it, though she was certain of the good Mister Thatcher's wisdom. She was with child and had spent most of the morning at the spinning wheel beside the fire, remembering another spring six years before when God had smiled upon her with the greatest gift of her life—a young carpenter building a house across the road. As rain pelted the roof overhead she tucked little John in for a nap, then returned to her wheel.

Sarah looked lovingly on her daughter as she played beside the hearth with her new poppet. But thoughts troubled her mind. Why is God so mysterious in His ways? Surely if people are good, God should reward them and not be so fierce in His judgment.

Moments later Sarah realized she had stopped spinning, wasting time in her reverie. Scolding herself, she gave the wheel a turn. But her mind would not stay in the present. Here there was little to think about except the rain and her worries. Promising to keep her hands busy, in her mind she revisited Hartford and the memory of her father's and mother's deaths, the misery that had followed when the town forced her and her siblings to leave their home.

It was at that time that Thomas Bliss refused to let Mary remain in her service, and he had been among those who persuaded the town to shut up the house. And now Mary Bliss Parsons was living no more than a mile down the street, on a larger plot of land than James Bridgeman's. Sarah saw her almost every Sabbath, at meeting with her handsome husband. And only last week Mary had appeared to be with child. Though they had often greeted one another during the break between sermons, Sarah did not engage with Mary in any sincere way. She could not.

The door opened, and a gust of wind sent a shower of raindrops over the floorboards. Sarah's husband stood before her soaked with rain. James Bridgeman looked at his wife as if she was out of place. "Sarah, I'm ready for supper."

Sarah could see he'd had all he could take of the rain and needed the comfort of a fire and warm food in his belly. She helped him out of his sodden coat. "Ah, where has the time gone? Here, let me put your coat by the fire. Warm yourself and I'll get you something to eat," she said, bustling off to the kitchen.

She had forgotten the hour. The baby woke in his cradle and began to cry. She started for him. It was time for her husband's supper, yet she had sat all afternoon at the wheel with little to show for it, and now the baby had picked this time to fuss. Sarah Jr. ran to his cradle and tried to lift him.

"Nay, Sarah, you'll drop him on his head!" she cried, lifting the baby into her arms. "James, take him, please, while I get something for you to eat." She handed him the whimpering child. From a cask she poured his beer into a tall cup and cut some bread and cheese to hold him off for a bit. "Sarah, come," she called. "Take this to your father." She tried to remember what she had quick and ready for supper, as she watched little Sarah carry the plate into the parlor. James stood near the fire, warming his backside, as little John toddled around the room. "Start with that," she told him, turning to go.

Just then a familiar pain shot through her back and she clasped her full belly. It was too soon for the baby to come. James, who had gladly accepted the plate, took no notice of his wife's distress. Sarah caught her breath and eased back to the kitchen in the grip of sudden apprehension. The pain seemed the same as the other times—just before her babes were born.

In the ashes she found two roasted eggs left over from the midday meal, and beans in the oven, barely warm. Thankful that her pain had passed, she put on her cloak and hurried outside to the box on the north side of the house where she had saved a section of alewife pie. From all these ingredients—eggs, beans and pie—she made a plate for her husband.

James accepted the food gratefully and held out his empty cup. "I'll have another."

Though suddenly overcome with a terrible desire to lie down, Sarah obliged him. Then she put the baby in the wooden walker her husband had built. "James, I beg your understanding. I am not ill, but I do feel the need of rest. Will you excuse me? I want to lie down."

She sometimes found comfort in resorting to the great Lyman bedstead she had inherited and brought with her from Hartford. Proudly displayed in the parlor, it was the finest object in her husband's house—indeed the whole village, if you didn't count the furniture at the Pynchons' or the Holyokes' or maybe the Smiths'. She felt no pain and no hunger and settled with relief into the featherbed, resting her head on her mother's pillows and bolster.

Sarah had thought that once she was married her happiness would be assured, but she had been disappointed. Life was difficult no matter your condition; she knew that, and reminded herself that she must give thanks for any moment of happiness. The worst times, she believed, were times when we expected to be happy but for some twist of events or disappointment could not be so.

Sarah lifted a hand mirror and gazed at her face. I am set to wonder, she mused, every time I see my face. If nothing else, God has blessed me with beauty. See, my hair glows with a golden light. Yet when there is no mirror in my hand I think my hair thin and dull like something soon to die. See, my face is alive, my skin white as milk. Yet away from my mirror I feel my face as blank as an unwritten page.

II

It was a woman child, stillborn, about two months before the just time . . . it had a face, but no head, and the ears stood upon the shoulders and were like an ape's; it had no forehead, but over the eyes four horns, hard and sharp; two of them above one inch long, the other two shorter; the eyes standing out, and the mouth also; the nose hooked upward; all over the breast and back full of sharp pricks and scales, like a thornback; the navel and all the belly, with the distinction of the sex . . . between the shoulders it had two mouths, and in each of them a piece of red flesh sticking out; it had arms and legs as other children, but instead of toes, it had on each foot three claws, like a young fowl, with sharp talons.

—Governor John Winthrop
The History of New England 1630–1649

MARGARET BLISS CAME upriver for the birth of Mary's first child. The Widow Marshfield was called, and neighbors came. Goodwives Joanna Branch, Blanche Bedortha and Hannah Langton performed the rituals necessary for the delivery of a healthy infant son, who would be named for his father.

It was a dangerous time to be born in New England. For a month an influenza epidemic had swept through the towns along the Connecticut River. "And there is no sign of it letting up," Margaret said, whipping a vial of syrup of violets from her pocket and administering a teaspoonful to all present. She brought news from Hartford. Influenza had killed dozens of people there, including their leading citizen, Thomas Hooker. Mary had wept for that loss.

"Our best luck is to keep it from us," Margaret said. "If a good man like Thomas Hooker cannot survive this visitation of God, there's no hope for anyone." On a mission to protect the Parsons' house and all who dwelled there, Margaret sent Joseph into the woods to collect hemlock boughs, while she and Mary filled what cracks there were around the shutters so that no air or light could get inside. She swept the floor and threw southernwood into the fire, filling the room with the pungent odor of bruised artemisia. She hung hemlock boughs over the door and ground some of the leaves in a mortar and pestle to brew a bitter tea.

"We must stay indoors and drink of this at least three times a day till the influenza has passed from our midst," she told the young couple.

Not far away, Sarah and James Bridgeman lost their battle with influenza when their infant son Thomas was taken from them. Sarah mourned her third-born, sometimes consoled by thoughts of her baby going to heaven in the arms of Thomas Hooker and the others who died with them. A long chain of Saints, hand in hand, rising through the clouds with their beloved preacher and little Tom clasped to his heart, guiding them toward Heaven. Here was an image she could not shake, nor did she want to, for she remembered Mister Hooker with affection.

Out of rhythm with Springfield women who fulfilled their destinies to give birth, nurse, conceive, and give birth again, usually on a two-year cycle, Mary conceived a second time when Joseph Jr. was only four months old. But Baby Benjamin was born too weak to suck and soon died in her arms. Again, Margaret came up from Hartford, this time to cradle her broken-hearted daughter in her arms and help in the house until Mary recovered enough to let her mother go.

. . . . .

Near the wet meadow at the southernmost reaches of Town Street, Eunice, wife of the bricklayer Hugh Pierce, had put six-month-old Josiah in his cradle near the hearth. His fever blazed, and Eunice was frightened out of her wits. All day long she had given him doses of monkshood, to no avail. He would not stop crying. Eunice, a frail little thing with burning blue eyes near the size of saucers and the face of a child herself, was perpetually frightened and grieving ever since her toddler Samuel's death nearly two years before. It seemed to her that she had sorrowed ever since she was born, her mother's scrawny eleventh child. Her first husband had been an old man, and worse, a Catholic her family had pressured her to marry so they would no longer have to feed her. He had been so old that during their seven-year marriage he never lay with her once. Foolishly, she had admitted to a woman friend that even though she was married she had fornicated with Hugh Pierce, and—she wished she could remember whom she told—was glad when her decrepit husband died. Why? Why, she asked herself, do I go around saying such things to people I cannot trust?

Yet her grief was only a small part of her trouble. After her marriage to Hugh and her child Samuel's death, she had also carelessly voiced her belief that the Widow Marshfield had caused his death through witchcraft. The widow answered with a slander suit, and the verdict came down against Eunice, who was sentenced to the whipping post—twenty lashes by the constable at the center of town. An alternative sentence had been offered, payment of three pounds to the widow toward reparation of her good name, but Eunice's husband Hugh said he would as soon have his wife whipped as part with three of his hard-earned pounds. Finally, after Eunice begged him on her knees and appealed to his mercy, he did pay the widow an equivalent of three pounds, in the form of twenty-four bushels of Indian corn. Since the town took the widow's side and turned against her, Eunice was now an outcast.

Hugh Pierce was a cruel husband. Eunice thought he cared

little for her or his children. He was ambitious and greedy or, as she put it, "eager after the world." When their son Samuel was ill, Hugh had forced her to work in his field harvesting corn. She believed he wanted the child to die, freeing her to help with his work.

And now it was little Josiah who suffered. Poor Eunice could not decide what to do. She could not think. The baby would not stop crying. Surely he would drive her mad. She envied her husband, who had drunk himself into a stupor and, undisturbed by the baby's cries, snored on top of the covers. Thankful that his hateful black eyes were closed, she looked at him with a mixture of fear and loathing, wondering what she had ever seen in him, ugly as he was with his lantern jaw, his head of wild dark hair, and that horrible red beard.

Evil thoughts tramped through her head on demon legs. The Devil had her, though she struggled not to listen. "Get some rest, Dearie," Satan was saying. "Just press a pillow over the little imp's face and muffle its cries."

Panicked and in a sweat, Eunice ran toward the meadow. Her skin ablaze, she looked up at the sky. Tearing at her shift, she let cool air beat about her throat and her breasts.

As the sun dawned over the planting grounds across the river, freshly stoked and fed fires burned in every house along Town Street. The goodwives put on their aprons. Joanna Branch stood at her door wondering what Eunice Pierce was doing on the street at that hour of the morning. Shuddering at the sight of her, she watched her approach carrying a package under her arm, glad she wasn't inside the woman's shoes. Of all the wicked creatures the world had ever seen, the Pierces were the ones she feared most. As the thin, forlorn figure neared her door she pulled back from view, hoping Eunice would not see her and want to stop for a visit.

Eunice passed the ordinary and the Meeting House, trudging on toward the magistrate's house. With many eyes upon her, she did not look toward the shadowy figures standing in judgment behind their doors. At last she reached William Pynchon's house, and even the grandness of that place did not shake her resolve. She walked boldly to the front door and, as if her life depended upon someone's answering, pounded with a fist. Soon the door opened, and a startled servant woman found Eunice with a bundle in her arms, begging to see Mister Pynchon. Reluctantly, the servant ushered her into the kitchen, as the front room was reserved for respectable guests. If it weren't for Mr. Pynchon's official position in the town, she'd have turned the woman away. The servant tried to take Eunice's cloak and relieve her of her bundle. Babbling about nothing any sane person could comprehend, Eunice refused to part with either. The servant's offer of common courtesies seemed to agitate her more.

"Sit yerself down, Goodwife Pierce," the servant said. "I'll see if my master will attend ye so early in the morning." She hurried off to fetch Mr. Pynchon, to confront him with news she knew would add to his already agitated state.

Pynchon had recently received the bad news that his first book, *The Meritorious Price of Our Redemption,* was in the hands of the court and was scheduled for burning. Printed in England, hardly anyone in the colony had seen it except for the members of the General Court, who had branded it heretical and ordered Pynchon to recant. Pynchon could think of nothing else. His reputation as a theologian was in shambles. Sleepless nights had left heavy pouches beneath his dark, penetrating eyes. He wore a worried face, dominated by a broad nose, dark moustache and long pointed chin. He was a short man—with no visible neck— but his girth and commanding demeanor gave him a powerful appearance.

Concerned about his book and the horrible business in Boston, Mr. Pynchon stepped into the kitchen to confront a wailing Eunice Pierce.

"You will be glad of this day," Eunice cried, her unearthly blue eyes about to pop from their sockets, "for I bring you a witch!"

As a member of the Court of Assistants in Boston, Pynchon

had on a number of occasions been called to sit in judgment of witches. Perhaps Eunice had come to the right man. But so early in the morning Pynchon was unprepared to meet a crazed woman, pacing in a convulsion of pent-up energy across his kitchen floor.

"My husband has murdered his own flesh!" she shrieked.

The horror of the spectacle before him made him reach out to touch her shoulders, hoping to steady her. "You are overwrought, Goodwife, and quite unintelligible."

"I seen him do this vile black thing," she said, unwrapping her bundle, handing it to the stunned older gentleman.

Pynchon accepted the burden, suddenly realizing that wrapped in a blanket was the body of an infant about six months old. "Dear God!" he cried, then called his servant woman to help him determine if indeed the child was dead.

"It were last night he done it!" Eunice raved, as Pynchon and the servant labored over the body, listening for a heartbeat or a whisper of breath coming from its open mouth.

"The child is cold," the servant said. "'Tis lifeless, poor thing." And she whisked it off to the keeping room as though she were tidying up.

Weak in the knees, Pynchon sat down by the fire to study the agitated woman. She was still raving, saying things he found impossible to comprehend.

"I dreamt that his spirit rose up out of him as he slept and went to the cradle," she cried, flinging her arms this way and that, spinning as she paced.

"Goodwife Pierce," Pynchon said, "I can see your anguish, but will you kindly calm yourself enough for me to understand what happened to your poor child? And why, prithee, it is to me and not the constable, you have appealed?"

"Begging your pardon, Mister Pynchon," she said, as if suddenly awakened to understand where she was and to whom she spoke. "'Tis just as I believed, Mister Pynchon, my husband Hugh Pierce is in league with the Devil. I've known it for a long time but was afeard to say it, because if he's hanged, me and my baby will starve."

Pynchon leaned forward, intensely interested. "What makes you think so ill of your husband?"

She lowered her voice as if imparting a confidence. "Under the last full moon he led me to the Devil."

"You've seen the Devil in Springfield?"

"Aye, good sir. We—and Bessie Sewell and Goodwife Merrick from the village—was in search of some good cheer." The memory seemed to revive her panic, and she clapped her hands over her mouth, stared at him as if shocked, then lowered her hands to go on with her tale.

"We built us a fire late at night in the woodlot and drank sack and danced barefoot, sometimes as ourselves and sometimes as cats. Since then—while he was drunk asleep—I searched his body for signs of witchcraft."

"And what did you find?"

She threw her hands into the air. "Why, nothing, Your Honor, for 'tis not always so that a mark be apparent." Looking trapped, she hugged herself and began to rock back and forth. "Oh, why do I say that? I know nothing of these things! I have no skill in witchery or knowledge of its workings, though 'tis true that I think I should have been a witch sometimes, but I was afraid to see the Devil."

Pynchon was losing patience. "You think you should have been a witch? Such thoughts, woman."

Suddenly ensnared, she looked ready to run. "The Devil told me I should not fear him—that he would not come as an apparition, but only into my body like the wind. He said he would trouble me only a little while and go forth again, so I consented, as did my husband. But then, Mister Pynchon, I did repent of it and sent the Devil away. 'Twas my husband saw him more. And last night as he slept, I saw his spirit rise up out of his body and smother his son with a pillow."

III

. . . If we may believe the Indians who report of one Pas-
saconaway that he can make the water burn, the rocks
move, the trees dance, metamorphise himself into a
flaming man . . . in winter, when there is no green leaves
to be got, he will burn an old one to ashes, and putting
those into the water produce a new green leaf which you
shall not only see but substantially handle and carry away,
and make of a dead snake's skin a living snake, both to be
seen, felt and heard. This I write but on the report of the
Indians, who constantly affirm stranger things.

—William Wood
New England's Prospect, 1635

WHEN PYNCHON AND the magistrates questioned the Pierces about the death of their son, the news spread like wildfire. Everyone in town had an opinion as to whether or not the Pierces were involved in witchcraft, and people had stories to tell. Both Mary Parsons and Sarah Bridgeman were present when Goodwives Branch and Bedortha discussed the case. Joanna Branch described an argument her husband had with Hugh Pierce, saying that the fierce little bricklayer had threatened to get even with him.

"That night after my husband went to bed," Joanna said, her eyes round and animated by the tale she was about to tell, "he was awakened by a light all over the chamber like a flame, and there came a thing upon him like a little boy, with a face as red as fire. And he felt something like scalding water on his back, and then he heard a voice saying, 'It is done, it is done!' And he thought of what Hugh Pierce had said to him and wondered if this was his way of getting even."

Sarah looked shaken. "What a fearsome thing for him to behold!"

Blanche Bedortha, a plump woman with coal-black hair and skin as white as her apron, had a story of her own. "One day last spring, Hugh Pierce came by to deliver the load of bricks my husband had ordered. He dumped them all over my garden, and when I asked him to pick them up and pay for the damage, he refused, saying, 'Gammer, ye need not have said anything. I shall remember ye when you little think on it.' The look of hatred in his eyes froze my heart." She shivered. "And soon after, not long before my travail, came a pain in my stomach so tedious that it was like the pricking of knives, so that I durst not lie down. My thoughts at the time were that this evil might have come upon me from the threatening speech of Hugh Pierce."

"I would die if he spoke like that to me," Sarah cried. "Praise be that neither I—nor James—ever had dealings with that odious little man."

The women looked to Mary, hoping she too had a story to tell about a run-in with Hugh Pierce, but she gave them no satisfaction. "We mustn't add kindling to the fire," she said. Though frightened of the man herself, she determined to bring reason to the conversation. "There may be other causes for these happenings. Why, Goodwife Branch, perhaps your husband had a nightmare, for they can seem real as life itself. If there had indeed been a flame in the room, surely you'd have seen it. And as for your trouble, Goodwife Bedortha, I too had such pains late in my term, and when I went to the Widow Marshfield for a remedy, she told me it was only a grief in my stomach and gave me a decoction of endive and mints."

Disappointed by her reply, the women looked chastened, and considering what had happened to Eunice Pierce after she had called the Widow Marshfield a witch, they quickly reconsidered their own positions.

Johanna Branch said, "Tell no one of this conversation, Goodwife Parsons, I beg you, or we shall be whipped for telling tales, and Hugh Pierce will dance with joy round the whipping post."

After Benjamin's death, life for Mary and Joseph changed. To Mary, everything seemed sullied. The marriage, motherhood, life itself mocked her. One night not long after the baby was carried to his grave Mary woke up with her bare feet deep in the ooze of the wet meadow. Now conscious and shivering with cold, she fully understood the implications of that moment. She had left her husband's bed; though no longer a child, she had walked in her sleep. Shocked to realize she wore nothing but her shift, she ran toward home, praying no one had seen her. Quietly she opened the door and slipped inside, hoping not to wake Joseph or their son, who slept between them. Feeling like a naughty child, she slipped under the covers and, trembling with cold, curled her body against the soft warmth of her sleeping baby. But she could not rest. She had her babe to grieve, and now her sleep to dread.

The next morning at breakfast she thought Joseph looked at her oddly. For days he'd had little to say and seemed withdrawn. She told herself that he was also grieving, that she had nothing to fear. Still, she could not escape the feeling that some evil had come between them.

Her work and the witch excitement provided her with brief distractions, and by the anniversary of Benjamin's death she was pregnant again. For long stretches of time now Joseph was away trading with the Indians, and when he came home he was hungry for her. Yet out of their bed he seemed distracted and cold, and she feared he no longer cared for her.

On two more occasions that she could remember, she walked in her sleep. Both ashamed and exhausted because of her restless nights, she had nowhere to turn. She could not tell her friend, Joanna Branch. The woman was too self-assured and disdainful of human frailty to be trusted with her shameful secret.

THE MASSIVE DUGOUT canoe was loaded to the gunwales with household belongings. Two of Pynchon's canoe men, one an Indian and the other a coarse-looking man called Sam Terry, helped Margaret Bliss, her boy Samuel and her daughter Hannah to seats in the center of the craft. Barrels full of Margaret's kitchen and fireplace implements, linens, clothes and dishes were packed side by side, having replaced a shipment of naval stores brought down from Springfield the day before. Over thirty feet long and five feet wide and deep, the canoe was supplied with paddles, oars and poles. The bedstead, furniture, and four of her children had gone ahead to the house her sons had built for her at Springfield. All her children had worked hard to give her a new home.

Margaret sighed and turned for a last look at the wharf and the town. Thomas had died in the spring. Though Hartford had been her home for fifteen years, if she had learned anything in life, it was to expect change. She looked out over the broad river, a good third of a mile wide, and up the banks to the wharf where her eldest son, Tom, waved a cheerful goodbye. She was only going thirty miles upriver, and it would not be long before he would greet her again. As the canoe men paddled toward the center of the river Margaret cast her eyes north, to the broad span of silt-colored water flowing out of a long, gradual bend through the forest and down to the sea.

"I can't see home anymore," Samuel cried, looking back.

Hartford had disappeared from view, and Margaret, suddenly overcome with sadness, wiped tears from her eyes. Hannah put her arm around her mother's shoulders and whispered, "Father wants you to weep no more."

When Thomas Bliss had lain ill, word sent to Springfield had brought Joseph, Mary and their sons, little Joseph and the third one, John, downriver for a last visit. The sight of his beloved Mary and the gentle touch of her hand had revived Thomas's spirits for a time, but soon he wanted to talk about his impending death. Sadly, Margaret asked him how he wished to dispose of his estate.

"'Tis all for you, my wife—there is so little." Tears had welled in his eyes. "We took a journey too far from Painswick Parish—I never prospered—you and the children suffered hardship. You were right."

Margaret protested. "Ah, Thomas, don't say it."

"You have labored hard, Margaret, and I would leave all to you," he said, reaching for her hand.

She drew his hand to her lips. "You are a good husband and father. And your sons, would you leave something for them?" With her other hand, she wiped tears from her eyes.

"My children know their mother's due," he rasped, and with his eyes fixed on Margaret's sorrowing face and his big rough hands now clinging to both his wife's and his daughter's, he died.

Soon the tidal river would lie behind. Ahead, the river stretched wide into low places in the forest. Overhanging limbs trailed their branches, making wakes of their own. Margaret looked upriver and thought ahead to her new life. She had nine loving children and so many grandchildren coming she had to stop and count. She knew her blessings. Springfield beckoned to her, just as resoundingly as Hartford had said, "Go in peace, you were a true and loving wife." I have life yet to live, she thought. When the harsh glint of sun on the water dazzled her eyes, she looked toward a shady swamp at the river's edge. She was glad to be out in the breeze at midstream, away from the swarms of mosquitoes that hovered in the shallows. She could hear birds singing gaily in the trees, and her heart filled with promise and joy, for soon she'd be settled near her children.

Margaret thought back to the recent past. Four years ago, King Charles had been clapped into prison, where he sorrowed for two years before they took off his head. Now the Puritan Oliver Cromwell ruled the Commonwealth. Glad to be free of the King, many Separatists had gone back to England. After Thomas died Margaret had let herself dream of her own return, but she knew she could never leave her children.

"Look," Samuel cried, "an island and a big river." He pointed to a large intersecting river and a narrow channel separating the island from the mainland.

"It won't be long before we get to Windsor," Margaret said. Distracted from her thoughts by the sight of men fishing below fields of corn and barley, she mused how that very river had shaped their lives. The fish have fed us, she reflected, and the floods have starved us. It is both the edge of our world and our road to the world outside. Though she wore a broad hat, she closed her eyes for a moment to rest them from the sun's glare. She had traveled this river for the birth of Mary's sons, and wondered if today would be the last time she saw Hartford.

When a cool, sweet-smelling breeze came to her from the forest, she opened her eyes. Here the river seemed less full, for a network of channels and sandbars was visible below the water's surface. On the western bank Windsor rose on a bluff. Near the mouth of the Santic River their dugout passed the sawmill, then the ferry landing and the house where the ferryman waited to take passengers across to Windsor. Samuel had fallen asleep, his head resting in Hannah's lap.

From up in the bow, Sam Terry called out. "Fair warning, the rapids are around the bend."

"Hear that?" Margaret woke her little son. "Hold tight, Samuel, we are in for a ride." Samuel stretched and rubbed his eyes, then stared straight ahead and stood up for a better look. "Nay, sit you down!" his mother ordered as they cut through a torrent hell-bent on reaching the sea.

Samuel's constant pestering "Where?" and "How far?" made it seem a long time before they saw the first sign of white water. Terry and the Indian rowed straight into the rushing current, then both stood and lowered long poles into the water. The dugout twisted and rolled in the boiling river as the canoe men righted the bow to point straight into the current, slicing the water like a knife through butter. The rapids' deafening roar filled their ears, and briefly Margaret was afraid. Lord, preserve us for Your use, she prayed. Keep my children safe. She regarded her last child, his eyes wide and fearless, though Hannah's pale face looked stricken, damp with river spray as she clung to her mother.

Despite her own anxiety, Margaret reassured her daughter. "Fear not, Hannah. These men never lose a shipment, or they would have to answer to old Mister Pynchon. Look!" she shouted over the roar of the raging rapids. "The waters here abound with fish!"

Silvery alewives, shad, and bass swam just under the surface, their mouths open wide to catch smaller fish. All at once above the roar gulls cried. Overhead, dark cormorants and white-bellied osprey dove, cormorants headfirst, ospreys pulling up at the water with their talons lowered. Long-legged heron waded in the shallows along the shore, gulping down as many fish as their bellies could hold. Avoiding the rocks, the canoe men skillfully guided their craft straight on through the rapids. As they bucked the waves, Margaret and her children hung on for dear life.

In time, when they slowly emerged into a calmer river, green and wide, the men shipped their poles and picked up their oars again to row toward a warehouse above the east bank. Here Pynchon stored hundreds of pelts: beaver, otter, lynx, bobcat, bear, wolf, moose and mink. Indians who paddled upstream and down in fur-laden canoes stopped here to trade. Below the warehouse, men labored to carry barrels on board a large flatboat surmounted by a mast.

The great river curved gently, and as their canoe moved around the bend, the Agawam River spilled into the Connecticut from the west. On its banks rested the general store, gristmill, and the planting grounds. A little farther upriver the Mill River flowed in from the east alongside the sawmill and, at last, the wharf.

God had seen fit to bring Margaret and her children safely to Springfield.

REMINICENT OF A day from her childhood, Mary helped her mother work in the garden. Her eldest child, young Joseph, had been given a spot in the dirt to dig as his little brother toddled around in the grass in pursuit of a kitten. It was too late to plant, but root vegetables, late lettuces and spinach were ready to harvest.

Margaret was delighted to have her daughter living next door. Nathaniel, his wife Katherine, and their two children lived two doors north, on the other side of the Langtons. Six of her children still lived at home, while Lawrence, who had come ahead, dwelled with Nathaniel.

Talk of the Pierce scandal had reached all the way to Hartford, and Margaret, eager to catch up on Springfield news, asked Mary about the village "witches." Mary looked up from where she knelt. "They have been questioned by Mister Pynchon and the magistrates. Joseph says they are gathering depositions. Some hope they will be sent to Boston for indictment and trial."

Margaret bent to cut parsley. "Are you acquainted?"

"I know them by sight—they dwell near here. Folks are certain they are devils." Absent-mindedly Mary yanked at a weed.

"And you, Mary? What think you?"

"They frighten me—just to look at—and the tales I've heard." She tossed her weed onto the compost heap. "But they've done nothing to us. I do pity the wife."

"And Sarah Lyman? What of her?"

"She has three children now, two daughters and a son." Mary commenced to pull up carrots and lay them in her basket. "James Bridgeman has done well enough for himself."

"In what way?"

"He was made constable a few years back, and I'll warrant there's carpenter work aplenty." Mary got up and brushed the dirt off her hands. "He added a lean-to to the back of the house, giving his wife the kitchen she desired. Joseph said he also bought into the toll road to Boston—surely that's to his advantage. Sarah wishes he'd been asked to stay on as constable."

"Do you and Sarah visit?" Now Margaret was wielding a hoe.

"One another? Nay. Now and then we gather with friends—Goodwife Branch or Goodwife Langton—and at meeting, of course."

Tiring, Margaret straightened to ease her back. "Have you spoken of past troubles, after her mother died? Has she forgiven us, forgiven you?"

"Nay, of that we do not speak. I have forgotten her foolishness, and I hope she has too." Mary eyed a long row of beets ready for harvest.

Her mother said, "You do know, don't you Mary, that when forced out of her father's house, she became exceedingly angry and turned the blame on you? You would do well to speak with her about it, see that she harbors no ill will. As I remember, Sarah oft liked to blame others for her woes."

Mary shook her head and got down onto hands and knees. "I'll not mention it. I think it best to let sleeping dogs lie."

"I'm not asking you to brazen her out, Mary. Just to have sympathy with her memory of that time, and to say you wish it had been otherwise."

"Her claims were foolish and unfounded. I'm sure she would rather not be reminded of that. Truly, Mother, we've done enough here for the moment. We deserve a rest." Mary clearly wanted an end to the discussion, and Margaret, believing she had said enough, let the matter drop.

EVERYTHING ON TOWN Street looked in order. The sky was blue, the day warm, goodwives and their daughters and grand-daughters sat in the shade of trees, carding wool or quilting, talking as they labored. Their children worked or played in the sun. On that part of Town Street the houses were humble, but neat and well kept. Some nearby apple and pear trees still clung to the last ripe fruit. But watching eyes lurked all around, and wary folks took care to keep their secrets locked up, shut tight behind their doors. Often the victim of rumormongers was unlucky. Gossip could lead to charges and an appearance before the constable, or the magistrate, William Pynchon.

When James Bridgeman saw Hugh Pierce breaking the law by smoking his pipe on Town Street, he reported him to Con-stable Ashley, who ordered the bricklayer to pay a fine of ten shillings. Hardly a month passed before Hugh Pierce saw James Bridgeman taking tobacco in the yard outside his own house, so he evened the score by reporting Bridgeman, and Bridgeman likewise was fined. After three men saw Thomas Miller hit an Indian, Nippinnsuite Jones, with the butt-end of his gun and reported that to Pynchon, Miller was given a choice of a whipping or paying the Indian four fathoms of wampum. Miller chose the latter.

The previous year, during one of Mister Thatcher's long sermons, the canoe man Samuel Terry was seen standing outside with his face to the Meeting House wall, according to his accusers, "chafing his yard to provoke lust." Both Hugh Pierce and John Lombard witnessed this self-abuse but kept it to themselves—for a while. Finally, though, they reported him to Pynchon. The magistrate gave his canoe man private correction with a rod across his bare back—six hard lashes, well placed—and no one else in town was the wiser.

In Springfield it was best not to invite suspicion. All were mindful of the witchcraft executions: Mary Crespet of Hartford, Alice Young of Windsor, Joan and John Carrington and Mary Johnson of Wethersfield, and Goodwife Bassett of Fairfield. The Carringtons and Goodwife Bassett had been hanged only a few months before.

NEITHER THE GARDEN nor the brightness of the day helped Mary to a cheerful state of mind. She still grieved the loss of her father and her son Benjamin. For the thousandth time, she remembered holding the babe in her arms as he quietly slipped away to travel alone to the country beyond sight. During her time of sorrow Mister Thatcher had reminded the grieving ones from the pulpit that their little ones' souls had flown to their appointed fate and that it served no purpose, spiritual or temporal, to mourn beyond a reasonable period of time. Mary chafed at the idea, for her heart had no calendar. She was in awe of the preacher's propensity to scold—even those who mourned. He also had suggested that those of the class to possess mourning clothes should remove them, being a counterfeit form of sorrow. "We are not Catholics," he abjured them, "committed to traditions that are of no use to the dead and harmful to those left behind." Mary had no mourning clothes to remove. On some days, though now less and less, it was her spirit alone that wore black.

Many days Margaret came to help Mary with the garden, and on one of those days when Margaret had done all the work she could physically manage, she scooped up little John, took young Joseph by the hand, and headed toward the front door. "I'll take the children in for food and rest."

Mary didn't want to leave the garden yet, for the hard physical work kept her thoughts at bay. She tried to think only of her blessings and her love of the soil, to divert her mind from painful memories and her fear that Joseph no longer cared for her—and to distract herself from the knowledge that she was up against forces beyond her control.

"THIS VILLAGE REEKS with evil," Mister Thatcher cried from the pulpit one Sabbath morning not long after Margaret moved upriver. "Surely one of you is a devil!" Everyone knew of whom he spoke. Only Eunice Pierce appeared to close her mind to the preacher's obvious reference to her husband.

The next day Joseph bought a lock and key from George Langton. "You cannot lock a witch out with iron," Langton warned.

Mary watched Joseph install the lock. "Can that be necessary?"

He regarded her with sudden disdain, a look she would long remember, for it was then that she first feared he had seen her leave the house at night. "With all that's loose in this town," he said coolly, "we'll do well to lock the door." No more about the need was said.

That night before he went to bed Joseph turned the key in the lock and put it on the mantel. From their bed Mary watched her husband as he sat late by the fire with a tumbler of wine, staring at the glowing embers. He's waiting for me to fall asleep, she thought, and then he will hide the key.

IN DEPOSITIONS TAKEN in the case against Hugh Pierce, people came forward to testify to his threatening speeches and the strange things that happened to them afterward: a little boy in the night with a face as red as fire, a cow's tongue disappearing from the soup kettle, unexplained pains in the belly, an enchanted pudding, three knives vanishing and reappearing like magic. Fear of Hugh Pierce had also spread to Mister Thatcher. The bricklayer had refused to finish the chimney he had started at the minister's house, and when Thatcher threatened to sue him, Pierce had said, "I will be even with you—you shall get nothing by it!"

For weeks of Sabbaths the very Meeting House walls were charged with enmity and mistrust. The Branches and the Bedorthas looked with fear and hatred at Hugh Pierce. Sarah Bridgeman regarded Mary in a far from friendly way. Eunice Pierce, lost somewhere in her beset mind, seemed to notice no one at all, and Hugh Pierce was often missing.

One morning Margaret, Mary and her little boys sat down beside Mister Thatcher's adolescent daughters, Honor and Union. The Thatcher girls' young faces were blanched by winter's pallor, their heads covered with white coifs, bodies wrapped in heavy woolen cloaks. While waiting for meeting to start, the two girls shivered in the cold, exchanged whispers about something Mary could not hear, and looked warily at Eunice Pierce who sat nearby. Sarah and Joanna Branch sat directly behind Mary, who had opened her Bible for young Joseph to see.

"Look who's reading the Bible." It was Sarah Bridgeman's voice, just loud enough to be deliberate.

"Aye, hypocrite, that she is," Joanna Branch said. "You won't believe what I saw last night."

"Do tell."

"I saw her on Town Street in the dead of night wearing naught but her shift," Mary's onetime friend said. "No cloak nor shoes did she wear, though 'twas colder than a witch's tit."

Rejoicing to have an ally, Sarah said, "This much I know—God's work is not done at night."

Mary had heard enough to make her head spin, and a heat rose in her face. To comfort herself, she reached to take little

John's hand. As for her mother, she seemed not to have heard them.

Mister Thatcher's sermon topic was "Satan's Anger," and he got to it with passion. Nearly foaming at the mouth with his own wrath, he shouted, "No matter how hard he tries, the Devil finds no rest. Satan's kingdom is supported by enmity, malice, the utter destruction of mankind. He loves human suffering and sacrifices of human blood as he himself boils in the everlasting wrath of God. 'He loosens the chain of the roaring lion so that the Devil is come down in great wrath to set up his kingdom amongst us,'" he ranted. "The Devil wants you for his subjects!" With one sharp finger he stabbed the air all around the room, piercing the hearts of each member of his flock. "You! You! You!"

From her seat on the bench near Mary, Eunice Pierce stared at the minister, her blue eyes immense with faith and fear. Like a young tree in a breeze, her thin body swayed from side to side as she hugged and rocked herself.

"Be sober! Be vigilant!" Thatcher roared. "'The Devil goes about as a roaring lion, seeking whom among you he may devour.' Witches throw our children into the water and drown them, they make horses go mad, and brew tempests and dangerous lightning. They cause unfruitfulness in men and alter the will of judges and magistrates so that they cannot hurt them. They cause themselves and others to keep silence even under torture."

Seeking to steady herself against his terrifying rant and stem her sudden nausea, Mary lifted her toddler onto her lap.

"Watch! Watch! Seeking whom among you has opened his door to the Devil and invited him in—" Thatcher paused, took a deep breath to renew his vigor, then took up his rant again. "The Devil is our neighbor, just as sure as we are neighbors!" And he looked straight at Hugh Pierce seated among the men.

Pierce let out a loud sardonic laugh, chilling the whole room. He stood and pushed his way past the men who shared the bench. When he reached the center aisle, he turned toward the rear of the room and walked out the door, letting it bang with a terrible crash.

White-faced, Mister Thatcher paused. The sound of the door

banging shut seemed to shake the room. Everyone trembled at the blatant disrespect shown the minister. The silence that followed was quickly shattered by screams. At first no one could be sure of the source, for they seemed to come from every corner of the room. Mary felt besieged, overwhelmed by horrendous screams. All that she would remember later was her astonishment to see it was the Thatcher sisters, shrieking and thrashing about on the floor beside her. And then Mary fainted.

Wild with terror, Honor and Union lay in the aisle tearing at their clothes. Swept away in the frenzy, Mary came to moments later, with a pressure like a hand at her throat. "I'm strangled—strangled!" she cried, as the sisters' bodies lurched and heaved against her. In a very few strides Joseph got to Mary and his terrified children. He picked her up and held her quaking body, as Margaret raced from the room with her grandsons.

The Thatcher sisters were carried home. After prayers, and a complete herbal fumigation of the house, Honor and Union recovered. With the support of Joseph and her brother Lawrence, Mary walked home, going to bed where she lay feverish for hours. Joseph sent for the Widow Marshfield.

When Mary awoke it was dark outside and the room was bathed in firelight. Joseph sat by the hearth, her little boy lay asleep in his bed, and her toddler slept beside her. Her first thought came like a flash of lightning—I am tainted, stained, ruined. Joanna Branch saw me.

When she stirred, Joseph came to her, took her hand, and touched her forehead. "The fever's gone," he said, as if to reassure her. "You fainted. The widow says you must rest. Sleep. I will come to you soon." When little John stirred, his father lifted him from Mary's bed and put him in bed with his brother. Joseph then reclaimed his seat by the fire across the room.

She closed her eyes, but could not sleep. He watches. He's afraid to sleep. He knows. He knows.

After a time passed, Joseph spoke softly. "Mary, are you asleep?"

Saying nothing, she watched him through half-closed eyes as he tiptoed to the door and locked it. He turned to look at her, then hid the key inside one of the boots standing beside the door. After he crawled into bed and turned his back to her, Mary smelled strong drink on his breath and knew that he loathed her. Her mind raced. I am a burden to him. She longed to leave Springfield, but where could she go? Back to Hartford? That seemed impossible, unless Tom would take her in. Fear piled upon fear. Will Joseph cast me off? She thought of escaping to England. I'll not live with him if he hates me. She thought of raising her sons by herself, of Joseph disappearing into the wilderness, of his dying. Forcing back sobs, she remained silent and still, afraid to breathe, afraid to wake her husband. Finally, after what seemed like hours of hideous thoughts, she had to use the chamber pot and slipped out from under the covers.

But when she sat up and put one foot on the floor Joseph, instantly awake, grabbed her arm. "Caught!" He pulled her toward him across the bed. "You won't find the key this night."

"Joseph!" she cried, as he got to his feet to haul her out of bed. "Joseph! I have to— ."

Keeping a firm grip on her, he retrieved the key, unlocked the door, then pulled her outside and dragged her across the yard toward the edge of the woodlot and the root cellar.

She knew she mustn't scream and risk waking the children. "Joseph, have you gone mad? Let me go!"

"Where do you go, Mary?" he choked through his teeth as he pulled her on. "Who is it you meet at night?" He yanked at the root cellar door till it flew open.

"No one! I meet no one! Have mercy, Joseph, I beg you!"

Pushing her inside the cellar, he slammed the door and bolted it.

"Let me out!" she begged. "Please, Joseph, let me out! I'll freeze to death!"

When no answer came she knew he had left her. The cellar was cold and black as death, but like the winter vegetables stored there, she would not freeze. She huddled on the dirt floor, grateful for thin stripes of moonlight seeping through cracks in the door. Suddenly filled with rage, she kicked at the door with her bare feet till they were near to bleeding. When it did not budge and she had exhausted herself, she withdrew, feeling her way along the stone wall, panting in terror.

All of a sudden the door opened. Joseph's bent form filled the void, his face eerily lit by the lantern he carried.

"Joseph!" she cried out, reaching for him. He evaded her grasp to throw a pillow and blankets at her, then set the lantern just inside the door.

"Please, Joseph, please," she pleaded.

He said nothing, and after he closed the door Mary heard the bolt fall into place. The lantern flame danced living shadows around the cellar walls, lighting herbs hung to dry on the low ceiling and barrels of grain and vegetables stored on the floor. Mary crept into a corner and relieved herself in the dirt, then crawled back to the blankets and wrapped them around her. All around the small enclosure, weird shadows came and went. The barrels seemed to swell, then recede, like dark bubbles bursting. Hanging herbs took the shapes of grinning birds in a blighted sky.

"He knows," she spoke aloud. "He knows my shame." Her mind ran in wild circles. 'Tis the end of his trust in me, for he thinks I'm a wanton—or worse, a witch. She listened to the sound of her own panting, sure that some horrible being watched her from the darkest corner. Pressing both hands over her mouth, she barred the scream she knew would unleash the thing that watched her. The lantern flickered wildly and went out. She held her breath and waited. Her tormentor pushed close, enveloping her, then broke into a thousand pieces of light. Glowing white, like poppets thrown into the air, they descended. Mercifully, she fainted.

IV

. . . I prize thy love more than whole mines of gold,
Or all the riches that the East doth hold.
My love is such that rivers cannot quench,
Nor ought but love from thee give recompense . . .

—Ann Bradstreet (1612–1672)
To My Dear and Loving Husband

THE MORNING AFTER Joseph locked Mary in the cellar, the cooper John Dover arrived to finish the barrels Joseph had ordered. Joseph had freed his wife from her prison soon after dawn, commanding her to make breakfast for her family. Half mad with grief, Mary had managed to dress herself and feed her husband and sons. Her pleas to Joseph for reconciliation had fallen on deaf ears, and immediately after breakfast he left for William Pynchon's house.

In harsh sunlight, Mary wandered around the farmyard beside the jumble of board fences—one barring the pigs, another the goats, another defining the line between Joseph's land and the land belonging to the Widow Bliss. Mary's herb bed was a tangle of withered leaves. The sage and thyme, browned from winter storms, looked as though they would never resurrect. Numbed with shame and cloaked against the cold, Mary moved unconsciously from chore to chore as young Joseph and little John followed, whimpering for attention. She noticed John Dover at his work, and now and again he raised pale eyes to look at her. She did not speak to him, and he said nothing to her as she walked past him to the well to draw a bucket of water for the chickens.

When Joseph returned, the boys were playing with the cats. He crossed the yard toward Dover and asked him to leave. The startled cooper withdrew, taking his tools. Joseph looked around the yard for Mary. Their eyes met as she let the cows into the pasture. He called to her.

When she came to him, he took her arm to draw her to the sunny side of the thatched storage shed. Though exhausted and dazed, Mary spoke first. "How could you? Why did you lock me in the cellar last night?" She was crying.

"I was afraid for you—afraid you were led by evil spirits. Everywhere there's talk of witchcraft. This morning Hugh Pierce and his wife were taken to Boston—to be tried, Mary. Folks are looking for witches, and oft I saw you go out at night." He stood stiffly, staring into her eyes. "I saw you hasten into the shadows where a woman waited. Was it Eunice Pierce? Have you followed evil spirits?"

"I met no one!" Her voice was emphatic. "You saw no one, shadows perhaps. I saw no evil spirits, not until you locked me in the cellar and left me alone in the dark. Oh, Joseph, the cellar was full of spirits. I threw my pillow at them, yet they would not be gone from me." She was still shaking with remembered terror.

"You say you met no one, Mary. Then why did you leave my bed, and how did you find the key no matter where I hid it?"

"Joseph, I have walked out in my sleep from the time I was a child. Ask Mother. I don't know why I do it. It vexes me terribly—waking at night to find myself in the middle of a stream—my feet wet—or outside in winter in the freezing ice and snow." Surely he would understand. "When I was a child my father feared the wolves would devour me during my night travels. I thought I had left all that behind—and I had. I did not walk in my sleep again until after Benjamin died, here in Springfield. You know what sore grief I have felt."

"Perhaps. But I know not what that signifies—sleepwalking."

He gave her a puzzled look. "And the key? How knew you where it was hid?"

"I saw you hide it—in your boot—and before, on the mantel." She was sobbing, hands clasped at his shoulders.

He heaved a deep sigh, shook his head, and seemed to soften toward her. He reached to take her in his arms. "Oh, Mary. You should have told me."

"I was afeard, ashamed. I thought you loved me no more," she wept.

He lifted her face to his. "Be not ashamed, Mary, not with me. Be always truthful, else I cannot protect you. If our neighbors see you walking about at night you know what they'll think. I must lock you in every night, until this evil passes from the village. I shall wear the key around my neck on a rawhide, and you shall be safe."

SPRING CAME GENTLY, with moderate rain, sweet days filled with tender breezes and sun. Mary's withered sage and thyme greened up. She planted parsley for her broths and meats, dill for her fish and cucumbers, dandelion for her sallets, and tansy for its clustered tufts of button flowers that would live through winter in a vase.

Sarah Bridgeman, great with child, stood in the middle of Town Street. She had packed a dinner of pork, bread and cider for her husband and sent it off with her children. She watched nine-year-old Sarah and six-year-old John, with little Martha between them, walk north on Town Street toward the Thatchers' house, where James was doing repairs. The sight of them made her heart glad. They were everything to her. And to think, she reflected, if I hadn't talked to that old witch I might not have children at all. She patted her full belly and laughed to herself. It was a memory she guarded and would never tell anyone, for it linked her to Goody Crespet. Only her husband knew about their brief encounter. Lost in a sweet memory, she looked again at her children, growing smaller on the road, as they were about to pass out of sight.

Just then Blanche Bedortha, leading a white goat, and Joanna Branch, carrying a heavy basket, came along Town Street past her door. They looked as merry as young maids without a care in the world.

"Good morrow, Goodwife Bridgeman, have you heard?"

"Good news, I hope." Content with the world, Sarah wanted none other.

"Eunice Pierce is dead!"

"Mercy! They hanged her?" Sarah knew the woman had been sentenced to hang, not for witchcraft, but for the murder of her child. Hugh Pierce, acquitted, had run off to Rhode Island, leaving Mister Pynchon to try to sell his land for him.

"My husband has been over the river to the store," Joanna said. "He heard that when the jailer went to fetch her for the hanging she already lay dead in the straw."

"Lord, have mercy!" Sarah shuddered. "What a strange turn."

"Well, ye ought not look so sad, if I were ye," Blanche said. "She deserved to die. How could any woman with a heart do what she done?"

EARLY THAT WINTER, before Joseph Parsons left for the northern forest, he hired the cooper John Dover to help his wife around the farm. Even in winter there was work to be done: animals to care for, wood to split, and trips over the Connecticut to the general store. Certain that he had taken care of everything to do with his family's safety and well-being, Joseph and two of Pynchon's canoe men packed their dugout with barrels containing bolts of trading cloth, English knives, trading beads, and Jew's harps, a favorite of the Indians. They pushed off from Springfield wharf and headed upriver into the land of the Nonotucks.

Mary and her sons were left snug and warm by the fire. It was too cold for the children to play or work for very long outdoors. As soon as they could understand spoken commands, she and Joseph had given them work—small jobs like fetching things, keeping the chickens watered, collecting eggs and kindling. Young Joseph, who was six, knew how to shine his father's boots and, if his father must be away from home at dinnertime, carry his dinner to him all the way across town or out to the woodlot.

"If a child's tongue can speak," Margaret had told her, "his ears will understand the rule of a parent."

After the work was done, Mary read to them. Even little John, who was four and blond like his father, was trying to learn his letters. Sometimes she taught them from a primer.

"A. In Adam's fall we sinned all. B. Thy life to mend this Book attend," she read slowly so the boys could memorize the verses. "C. The Cat doth play and after slay."

"Ask us, Mother," red-headed Joseph begged.

"Very well. I'll say the letter and you say the verse. You first, John. N."

"Uhhh," he said, rolling his brown eyes to the top of his head.

Joseph jumped up and down. "I know! I know!" Even his freckles looked excited.

"Let your brother answer."

Just then the door blew open, letting in burly John Dover on a gust of icy wind and dry leaves. Mary shivered as he closed the door.

"Goodwife Parsons, the sheep are in and the chores done." Dover gazed boldly at her as she sat beside the fire with her sons, arrested in her reading by the surprise of his sudden entrance. Her face was flushed from the warmth of the fire, and her copper curls hung uncoiffed around her shoulders. She was big with child, her full breasts straining against her bodice. He ate her up with his eyes, knowing he would think of her again as he finished his own chores, as he took supper with his wife and children, as he tried to fall asleep that night. He had never seen a woman as beautiful as Joseph Parsons' wife, and he could not take his mind off her.

"That's fine, Goodman Dover." She seemed uncomfortable.

Embarrassed because her hair is down, he thought.

"Will you come tomorrow?" she said.

"Aye, in the morn—soon as milking's done."

"Well, then thank you and good afternoon. Please remember me to your wife."

She wants to be rid of me, he thought, ready to back out the door.

"Lads? Coming then?" Earlier Dover had told the boys that when he was done, if their mother agreed, they could follow him down Town Street to go sliding on his frozen pond, and Mary had said that they could. The boys jumped up to go.

Mary called out, "Wait, children! Your cloaks and mittens." They dashed back and pulled their things down from the pegs by the door.

V

This Blazing Star being in conjunction with diverse other awful Providences and Tokens of Wrath, calls upon us to awake out of security, and to bring forth fruits meet for Repentance.

—The Rev'd. Samuel Danforth
An astronomical description of the late Comet or Blazing Star; As it appeared in New-England in the 9th, 10th, 11th, and in the beginning of the 12th moneth, 1664

IN THE FAR north, a beaver pond lay frozen in the wilderness, surrounded by sentinel pines, its banks buried in drifts of snow. The beavers' dam held back the stream so perfectly that not a trickle of water escaped beneath the surface ice. Humped up in the middle of the pond like a stick-and-mud haystack was the beavers' lodge. Mated for life, the beaver pair protected two generations of their young from the cold, as a third generation waited to be born.

Six men—four Indian trappers and two Englishmen, all clad in heavy winter garb and snowshoes—had come upon the southern edge of the pond. Sunlight glinted off the ice. Joseph shaded his eyes as they made their way toward the beaver dam. They stopped at the end of the long straight dam of sticks, sapling logs, mud and stone. After a brief consultation, one of the Pocumtucks walked out onto the dam and hacked at it with a hatchet.

Everything was frozen silent and the air was still, but soon after the hatchet sounded a seep of water was heard, a trickle followed, then a steady flow emptied the pond into the streambed.

Now the beavers' lodge sat high and dry among sheets of cracked and broken ice. All four Indians went after it with hatchets. As panicked beavers tried to escape, they were netted and clubbed. The trappers would eat the meat and add eight more pelts to their take for the day.

So great was the European desire for beaver hats and coats that farther south the animals had been hunted nearly to extinction. Joseph had come for a look at the north country, hoping to persuade Pynchon to sell him the rights to the fur trade. He'd been here a month, and it looked more than hopeful. No shortage of beaver here.

The Indians' winter camp lay to the west of the great river. As night approached, the hunting party entered a bark-covered longhouse where two fires burned under smoke-holes, one at either end. Joseph and the others bedded down for the night on platforms built against the walls and lined with fur robes. He lay in the dark hut watching the fire, glad for the warmth, enclosed by the pungent odor of smoke, the smell of the bear robe tucked under his chin, and the stink of grease off roasted meats coating the ceiling. He was as warm as if he were home in bed with his wife, and well satisfied with the day's take. They had bagged twenty-eight beavers and ten mink.

He loved the wilderness: waking in the morning to the cold air, the frost on his breath, the thrill of fresh mink or wolf tracks in the snow, canoeing through the ice floes with a boatload of pelts. And he loved the peaceful nights, dark and starlit, or bright as day under a full moon gleaming on white snow; the silence shattered by sounds made brilliant in the utter quiet: the rush of owl's wings diving through the canopy for mice and moles tunneling under the snow, the crack of snow-laden limbs crashing to the forest floor, the beautiful haunting cries of wolves calling to the moon.

Everything was going well for him. He had two fine sons, another child on the way. He'd taken his oath as a freeman and could vote. He'd been elected selectman at Springfield and accumulated a number of decent-sized parcels of land. His direction in business was now clearer. Things were falling into place according to his plan—even Mary. For a time during the witch excitement at Springfield, he had thought he had reason to fear for her life and her soul. Out there in the dark and alone, she might have been seen and suspected. She might have fallen prey to evil hiding in dark places. And in truth, she had looked guilty, trying to keep her night prowling secret from him. He had watched her and had begun to suspect that she had fallen in with the others: Eunice Pierce, Bessie Sewell, and that Merrick woman, who said they built fires in the woods at night and danced with Satan.

Finally he had locked her in the cellar. The memory choked him with shame. And when she explained, he had seen the truth in her eyes and had been sorry. Later, he had spoken with the Widow Bliss about Mary's night walks, and she had reassured him that Mary was still the woman he had taken for his wife. How I love her, Joseph thought, shuddering at how near he had come to destroying it all with his fear and cruelty. Joseph thought softly of Mary. Mindful that she was soon to deliver, he longed to return to her and his sons. He had vowed to himself to make everything up to her. He would make them rich, build her a large house, give her beautiful things. He had promised all this to her, though she told him she cared for naught but his love and good opinion. He pulled the bear robe closer around his back, wishing it were Mary snuggled against him, and fell asleep with her on his heart.

As the night sky sparkled with fairy snow, a bright object stood in the heavens over Springfield. The starry blur stained the sky, its long tail arching over the river and the forest. James Bridgeman knew it as a bad omen—one of the worst—and Sarah was in the midst of her travail. While she labored, he had shuttered the windows and forbidden the women attending her to speak of the comet. With all his heart he prayed that God would spare his wife and child.

And God did, for Sarah gave birth to a girl-child whom James gave the name Rebecca. For as long as Rebecca Bridgeman lived, everyone in Springfield would remember that from her birth she was star-crossed.

The great malediction in the heavens lasted thirteen days, and with that sign still blazing in the night skies, William Pynchon packed up and left Springfield. Traveling with him were George Thatcher and his family. Some would say that Thatcher fled because in the eyes of the town his daughters had been tainted ever since that morning at meeting when Hugh Pierce bewitched them. No one knew for sure why Thatcher went, but the town would be left without a minister and would remain so for the rest of the decade.

In spite of his temporal authority, Pynchon had to flee or be tried for heresy. Though he had endeavored to recant some of what he had written, his conscience would not allow him to repent it all. His liberal views were not forgiven, and the old gentleman was stripped of all rank by the General Court. When word came that his enemies were prepared to try him for the crime of heresy, wisely he fled, leaving his lands, indeed everything that was his, to his eldest son, John. In very short order the folks of Springfield would elevate John Pynchon to the station his father had held, for many were in debt to him or earned their living at his will. Those who knew Old Pynchon best would miss him. No one in the town would take the side of Pynchon's enemies in Boston, for not one had read his book or understood the complaint against him.

With her children tucked in bed for the night, Mary Parsons sat beside the fire with the mending. Joseph was somewhere in the wilderness with the Indians, and she wondered what it would be like to be with him now. Some fur traders didn't make the great effort Joseph made, going on the hunt himself with the trappers. Other traders let the Indians bring the furs to them. But Joseph fancied the outdoor life and the hunt. He'd often entertained her with stories about his adventures, and he was teaching his boys to speak Algonquian. Mary was feeling secure in the fire's warmth when suddenly she heard a soft knock at the door. It was too late for visitors.

"Who knocks?" She asked quietly so as not to wake the children.

"John Dover," came the voice.

She opened the door a crack. "What brings you at this unseasonable hour?"

"Let me in and I will tell ye." He pushed his way inside. "'Tis cold out there, and I have something to say." His breath reeked of alcohol.

Mary was more annoyed than frightened. "Surely it can wait till morning."

"Nay, it cannot, Goodwife." He reached behind him to shut the door. "For a long time now I have wanted to ask if ye are safe."

Mary frowned. "What makes you think I am not?"

His lids half-closed over cold blue eyes, the man slurred his words. "I were there, the day after he locked ye in the cellar. Yer husband dismissed me, but I stayed behind. I hid in the shed and heared him accuse ye. I could not hear all he said, but I heared enough to know he is cruel."

Stunned speechless, she stared in disbelief.

"And during the witch excitement I seen ye out at night in the wet meadow, aye, walking alone in yer shift. Does he drive ye from the house? Does he make ye wander in the dark? I love ye well, Mary. I can think of naught else." He reached for her, but faltered and put a hand against the wall to steady himself.

She backed away several steps and raised her voice. "Dare not call me Mary! I am Goodwife Parsons to you. Leave me at once! You know nothing about my husband or me!" She glanced hastily around for some way to defend herself and, finding nothing else, put a chair between herself and the man.

Dover made no move to go. He stood there looking shocked, staring as if he did not believe her, as if he'd expected her to rush into his arms.

She backed toward the fire. "You are wrong to say these things. My husband is not unkind to me." Taking the poker in hand, she raised it, ready to strike. "Leave me this moment, or I will do my best to kill you!"

Dover looked deeply wounded. When he blinked back tears, Mary saw that he had truly hoped in vain. He turned away, managed to wrench open the door, and staggered out, letting in a blast of frigid wind.

Two days later Mary was delivered of another son. Her mother and sister Hannah came to care for her and the child, who had a lusty hunger and a fuzz of red hair. Mary counted her blessings—three sons—but she told no one about John Dover. When Joseph's new son was a fortnight old, Joseph returned from the wilderness and named him Samuel. Other changes had taken place in his household as well. Mary had hired Jonathan Taylor's son Peter to help with the chores, and a serving girl to work inside the house. Mary answered his questions about John Dover with lies, saying that the pressure of his own business had forced him to ask for release from his chores. Though Joseph did not take well to the new arrangements, Mary insisted that if he would leave her for months at a time, she must be free to make her own decisions.

He laughed at her choice of a housemaid. "She's naught but a child! Why, Mary, I see you waiting on her—not the other way round."

Mary had to admit he was right. Elspeth was like a stray cat. A tiny, almost black little thing, whose age she had guessed was not yet thirteen. She was recently orphaned, the daughter of the blind peddler. Mary had found them sleeping in the hay with the sheep and cattle, and before she could offer much in the way of help, the old man had died, leaving his daughter bereft. Elspeth, having spent her life leading her blind father around the country, knew not the first thing about housekeeping. Though she was little help yet, Mary could see that she was bright, and given time would learn. Besides, Mary felt motherly toward her, and alone in a household of males she enjoyed the company of a creature of her own sex—even a needy child.

Though Elspeth had little to say to adults, she was animated enough with young Joseph and little John, herding them around the house and farmyard like a shepherd with her flock. She was as quick with her affections as she was her scoldings, and with the new babe she was gentle as a little mother, singing strange new songs to him until he fell asleep in her arms.

From the first, Mary was fond of the maid. And when Elspeth had turned to her, with black eyes full of unspoken questions and unnamed fears, Mary found her heart quite bursting with love for the child. Elspeth had never been taught to read, or anything else that Mary could see, but when Mary read to her boys the girl listened eagerly and joined in their lessons.

From the looks of her, one might think she was an Indian or a blackamoor. Her father was a Scot, her mother a mystery, having died giving birth to her. The blind peddler had raised up Elspeth on the road. Together they had traveled the river valley from town to town, peddling his wares. He filled his pack with things new and used, always able to mate a handful of nails or an old costrel with a settler who had need of them. For a hot meal or a few pennies, he traded for almost anything: a burning glass, a pouch of seed or nails. In summer they camped out at night between villages and, it was rumored, sometimes took shelter with the Indians. In winter, a kind soul in Windsor took pity on them and put them up for as long as it was cold, but the blind man would grow restless and set out again on Indian trails and English cart-ways.

Some nights, when Mary could hear Elspeth crying herself to sleep by the kitchen fire, she would go to her and offer comfort. But now that Joseph was home, he insisted that she leave her alone. "You cannot treat her better than your own children—she must learn to comfort herself."

One night after Joseph had been home for a few weeks, Mary again heard whimpering in the kitchen. She slipped out of bed and went to Elspeth, who lay on her side facing the fire.

"Now, now, why weep, my child?" She knelt down, taking her hand as she brushed dark wisps of hair from her eyes. "Tell me a tale—about a happy time with your father," she said.

"I grieve my father," Elspeth cried, rolling to her side, bracing her head with one arm.

"Aye, I grieve mine too. We always shall, but our heavenly Father is beside us now and loves us well."

"But the Lord has eyes to see and no need of me."

"Your father is with God now—his eyesight restored. 'Tis I who needs you. Look at me, Elspeth." Gently she stroked the child's cheek. "Here I dwell in a house full of sons and a husband, and no woman to talk with. I was lonely until you came."

"Were ye?"

"Aye, child, and now you are here. Look what I have for you." Mary opened her hand. "This was given me when I was a maid."

Elspeth sat up, eager to see what her mistress was holding. Her eyes grew wide. "What ever is it?"

"Take it."

The girl lifted the silver amulet and chain high, dangling it in the light of the fire. "Ah, so fine a thing for me?"

"Aye, Elspeth, for you. Now put it around your neck and wear it under your shift always close to your heart. When you are afraid or sad, you must look at it and know that all will be well. Now, will you tell me a story?'

"Oh, thank ye, Mistress, I thank ye." The child's face brightened as she settled back on her pillow. "Shall I tell ye a story about the Indians, or fishing on the great river?"

"I've been fishing many a time. Tell me about the Indians."

"Did ye know they make everything from the animals?"

"Nay, I did not."

"They use skin for their shoes and clothes, the hair is like thread to them. From the deer horns they make tools, and the hooves make rattles for their dances."

"Have you seen them dance?"

She nodded. "I did, once—a night before they went to battle. They painted their faces, and around the fire they did dance, making a fearsome noise with their drums and rattles. And they did sing—not like English songs at meeting—but their song came like the drum beat. The first man to dance—my father called him a shaman—and when each man got up to join the dance he did agree to fight in the morning."

214

"Then only those willing to join the fight would dance?"

"Aye, and those who would not sat around the fire and sang to lift the warriors' spirits. What a terrible sound it was, and how fearsome a sight to behold. Though Father told me we had nothing to fear, I could not sleep that night."

"Nor could I, had I seen such a thing," Mary said. "You told me something I've never seen, Elspeth. Thank you. But now it is late, and we have work in the morning."

Seeming at peace, the girl nestled into her bed and closed her eyes, one hand on the amulet around her neck.

In the days that followed John Dover's drunken visit Mary was thankful for the closeness of her mother and Elspeth, and watchful when she left home. She did not want to chance a meeting with a man who would ruin her. A man's lewd advances were no light matter, for the crime of adultery was punishable by death, though rarely was the full extent of the law applied. Already she had seen him in the village, and as she crossed the road to avoid him he had watched her go with a loathsome smirk on his face. At meeting she felt his lustful stare and was afraid his wife would notice.

When the long winter was over and the soil was ready for her hoe, she worked it for her early crops: peas, lettuces, onions and spinach. As she worked, she thought of her ambitious husband and his latest inspiration. He and other venturers were making plans to move north to settle a wide meadow the Pocumtucks had sold them. John Pynchon had advanced the money for the venture, and Joseph could talk of nothing else. Mary was not wedded to Springfield, though if they left she would miss her extended family and her garden, where she had a mind to transplant blue and white violets near the daisies and yarrow around her door. Soon when it was warmer she would plant foxgloves, hollyhocks, vervain and gillyflowers. Come summer Mary's garden would be the prettiest in town, just like the year before, when goodwives stopped to notice and mumble enviously under their breath.

"Vanity! Planting like that! Good thing every flower's leaves or root are useful for meat or medicine." Those envious goodwives grew the same flowers, but none planted with the eyes of a painter.

Gardening plans overran Mary's thoughts of Joseph and his venture, for she was wondering about the lush ferns in the woods, whether she could transplant them to a shady spot under the trees. As she knelt in the dirt with her hand on a weed she was suddenly startled to find John Dover standing a few feet away. He was staring at her, saying nothing, and she had no idea how long he'd been there.

His boldness enraged her. "How dare you! Leave me alone!"

"Meet me at the river," he said, looking her square in the eye.

If he had been frightening when drunk, his lustful sobriety was terrifying. "Be gone!" she commanded, surprised by the strength of her voice.

"Ah, ye must have kept our meeting secret," he said, "for yer husband is sociable enough when we meet. 'Tis a good thing. Now I won't have to say that while he was away, ye asked me to come to ye." He grinned suggestively and walked away.

Mary wasn't sure why she had kept Dover's lewd behavior a secret, and his mention of it left her feeling unsettled and guilty. Was she afraid of what Joseph would think? Afraid that, as Dover said, she had somehow encouraged him? There was only one thing for her to do—talk to her mother.

She looked across the yard toward her mother's house. Since Thomas Bliss had died, Margaret had managed his meager estate to her advantage, enabling her to buy more land. She had also moved into Springfield society with ease. Widow Bliss, as she was called, was nobody's fool. When a few tried to make her so, she filed complaints and won civil suits against those trying to cheat or take advantage of her. In several cases, the court's award enriched her coffers. Though six of her children were married and had homes of their own, she still had three nearly grown ones at home. When Mary asked her why she hadn't remarried, Margaret had laughed. "I'm not looking for a master!"

Sure that her resourceful mother would have good advice, Mary dropped her trowel, walked across the yard and stepped onto her mother's land.

VI

White Hellibore, which is the first Plant that springs up in this country, and the first that withers; it grows in deep black Mould and Wet, in such abundance, that you may in a small compass gather whole Cart-loads of it . . . the Indians cure their Wounds with it, anointing the Wounded first with Racoons greese, or Wild-Cats greese, and strewing upon it the powder of the Roots . . .

—John Josselyn
New-Englands Rarities Discovered, 1672

Nonotuck, 1654

HAVING CROSSED THE great river at Springfield, Joseph Parsons and his fellow adventurers journeyed north with two oxcarts filled with supplies and weapons for protection and hunting. The old Indian trail ran along the river through a wide forest valley surrounded by wooded hills. Though only twenty miles long, the march would take the nine men, their oxen, and their horses more than five days through spring mud on the narrow, rocky trail. In the years to come Joseph would say that they should have waited until later, for the melting snow left mud everywhere in their path. But of more concern to them was the time it would take to build shelters before winter set in.

A year before, John Pynchon had advanced the money to procure a hundred fathoms of wampum, ten English coats, and a number of small gifts—the price the Indians had asked in exchange for fifteen thousand acres of prime meadowland and timber forest. Having never used the meadow, they thought they had the better end of the deal.

As the party advanced, the air buzzed with gnats and smelled of damp decaying wood. Water dripped from ledges and ridges, forming little rivulets that turned the ancient footpath into a wash. But the men struggled on, pushing and pulling their cumbersome carts, sometimes quagmired in mud ankle deep. The travelers had no time to notice the shining white of bloodroot growing in masses along a hurrying stream, bronze and yellow trout lilies, and white hellebore lying low along vernal pools in the leaf litter. Spider webs glinted in the sun, and here and there trees uprooted by winter storms had left deep black pools of water on the forest floor. These venturers were fully aware, however, of the swarms of flies biting the backs of their necks and hands, and tormenting their beasts of burden.

"Ha, ox!" the driver ordered.

"Whoa!" another man yelled as the cart began to tip.

As a large stone jarred loose by a horse's hoof took flight down the trail, Joseph yelled, "Look out below!"

Their shouts flushed birds into the sky to sing in another part of the forest. Before long, the men concluded that they might have made faster progress had they left their horses at home, for their mounts had to be led up rocky inclines and down mud-washed slopes.

At night they camped in the forest, aware of being watched from a distance by a small party of Indians. They were, in fact, being given a secret escort. Having discovered this early on made the trek all the more anxious for them.

"They are harmless," Joseph said, for he knew them for what they were. "They want to make sure we settle the right land."

Most of the men were from Hartford, where the venture was first conceived. Robert Bartlett, who brought his son Samuel along, assumed the role of leader. Besides the Bartletts and Joseph were Edward Elmore, William Holton, the Lyman brothers, both John and Richard, John Stebbins from Springfield, and Thomas Bascom from Windsor. They would be the cast of characters for a new town: the future owners of gristmill and sawmill, a mason, a shoemaker, a deacon for the church they would establish, commissioners and constables, and one who had made up his mind to become the richest man in the new territory.

Some of the travelers spent those nights in the wilderness in fear. Unlike Joseph, they had little knowledge of wild places, the Indians, or the animals living in the deep wood. They had heard that lions had been seen north of Springfield. Nowhere did they see signs of their God as they traveled in a kind of purgatory, through which they had to walk if they were to conquer the country and claim the land and its riches. At night Goodman Bartlett led prayers and the singing of psalms.

> Jehovah feedeth me: I shall not lack.
> In grassy fields, He down doth make me lie:
> He gently leads me, quiet waters by.
> He doth return my soul: for His name-sake.
> In paths of justice He leads me quietly.
> Yea, though I walk in the dale of deadly shade,
> I will fear no ill, for with me Thou wilt be:
> Thy rod, Thy staff, they shall comfort me.

Joseph reassured them they would be safe if they took turns keeping watch and stoking the fire. "No bear, lion or wolves will come within thirty feet of a good roaring fire," he said. But only he slept peacefully, his long gun clasped in his arms like a wife.

When mornings dawned, the fire was refreshed and the men breakfasted, each from his own sack of provisions. At night they roasted the meat of animals and birds they had killed on their way. After the first three days of travel, the settlers made better time on higher ground through a stand of white birches, a small river running below. Soon they left the birch wood to enter a marsh where geese flew straight as arrows toward a distant pond. The adventurers marveled at the large number of waterfowl in the mud flats: ducks, whooping cranes, herons, loons, cormorants and geese. The morning of the next day they climbed a high ledge overlooking the forest. In the distance they saw two dark-green mountains with a narrow passage between.

"Nonotuck lies just beyond those mountains," Joseph said. "We should arrive long before sunset."

Having glimpsed their goal so early, they thought the day dragged endlessly. The men pushed and pulled their horses and oxcarts over the rocky landscape as Indian scouts in plain view watched from the mountain ledges. The venturers stopped at the northern end of the passage for a first look at the valley below, where the wide river snaked through a bright-green meadow, lush with spring grasses and wildflowers and rimmed by the never-ending forest.

When they reached the meadow they spread out to explore as far as they could before regrouping to make camp for the night. Building fires for warmth, they bedded down in the open meadow, feeling thankful and more at home. As he fell asleep, Joseph thought of the advantage he had over the others, for on his last trip to the great meadow he had spotted the piece of land he wanted. It lay on the east side of a stream, just above where it forked to feed a small river running east to the Connecticut.

The next day the men began to explore to the edge of the forest, where they stood in awe of the park-like woodland, acres the Indians groomed by burning the underbrush each spring. With only mature trees left standing, hunters had a clear shot at deer moving under the canopy. With spring floods in mind, the venturers decided to settle a good mile from the great river. They marked off the town's main street and named it Bartlett Street. It ran southeast from the foot of the hill, where they planned to build a meeting house, toward a small river—a perfect spot for a mill. Finally, each man chose a house lot of fifteen acres. Most wanted to be on either side of Pleasant Street, a second road that would run south off Bartlett Street. Joseph moved a quarter of a mile to the northeast and took the land he wanted. Over the spring and summer more settlers would come, and the first houses would be built, but few would spend the winter on the new frontier.

WITHIN DAYS OF her arrival at Nonotuck the following spring, Mary knew she had come to a place of blessings: rich soil, freshwater springs, rivers, streams, vast forests. She thought of her father, who had struggled so hard with little success. This was the land of his vision. Except for missing her mother and siblings in Springfield, Mary was glad to be away from that dreadful place and skulking John Dover.

She marveled at Joseph's plans to enlarge their house. Before she came to live there he had created, around a great central chimney, rooms for them to winter over in, including a front room and a kitchen with its large fireplace and beehive oven, and upstairs chambers for sleeping. Pleased with what he had already accomplished, Mary recognized in that first dwelling the beginnings of a much finer house than any she had admired in New England except for the grand Pynchon mansion in Springfield. Though some of the men had warned Joseph that his first house was too ambitious, he went confidently ahead.

Mary watched as proudly he paced north off the present dwelling to show her its future and final dimensions. This would be the house she had hoped for as a child leaving England: gables, a large garret over the second story, casement windows, a keeping room, buttery and borning room. The first floor would have an entrance hall, and the upper story would overhang the first by nearly two feet, giving the house a much more imposing appearance than the flat-faced houses most of the others had built.

"I'm bringing up three men from Springfield to help me build the rest of the house this summer, Mary," he promised her, "and we'll have every piece of timber and every nail in place before winter."

While she and Elspeth tended children and kept house, Mary got to work planning her kitchen garden and had the raised beds built and filled with topsoil. The following year she planned to put in an apple orchard, raspberry canes and gooseberry bushes. And by October, Mary was once again with child.

MORE MEN HAD arrived that spring to claim house lots and build houses, among them the carpenter James Bridgeman. Ann Bartlett with her three youngest children came as well and settled into the house her husband had built on land facing Mill River. In early September, Sarah Bridgeman and her children arrived with her brother Richard's wife Hepzibah and their five children. Sarah was delighted with her first view of Nonotuck's meadow, the uplands to the west, the gentle curve of Bartlett and Pleasant Streets, and groomed woodlands to the north. Her family was growing, and she hoped her husband would find new opportunities to increase his income by building houses on the new frontier. Her eldest daughter, Sarah Jr., was eleven, and though plain, pious and quiet, she was a great help to her mother. Her boy John was eight years old, a cooperative and pleasant lad with a mass of tousled blond curls and bright blue eyes like his mother. Martha, at five, resembled her father, except for hair spun of Lyman gold. A precocious child, from the age of three she had adopted the role of little mother to Rebecca, now two, whose temper and will were as strong and great as her beauty.

Yet from the moment Sarah saw the house her husband had almost finished, at some distance from the main settlement, she complained. "Oh, no, James. My brothers and all the others live on Pleasant Street."

"But we'll have more room here. 'Tis as if the whole meadow belongs to us."

"I'm not a savage, James. I don't like being so far out in the meadow."

His face and whole body seemed to sag with disappointment. "Ah, well, 'tis too late now. Besides, we shall have neighbors before you know it."

Ignoring his attempt to reassure her, Sarah bustled from room to room, shaking her head "It's clear the house is too small," she said.

"What's here will keep us warm over the winter, and next spring I can enlarge the house to please you."

At length she softened. James was a good husband, and she had been too hard. "Ah, well, 'tis a goodly enough place. We shall make of it what we want."

Throughout the fall Joseph stayed close to home. He had work to do inside, plastering and whitewashing, adding finishing touches. On the night of the first snowfall, after the children were asleep, he and Mary sat by the light of the fire. Wrapped in a bearskin robe, she had an open Bible in her lap. Joseph put down his pipe and took a long deep drink of strong beer.

"I have news," he said.

"From John Pynchon."

He stared in amazement. "How did you know?"

"Just now, I was thinking on him as you sit there so quiet, your face all dark and full of mystery."

"He's agreed to sell me the northern fur trade."

She had dreaded this conversation. "Has he?"

"We talked about it in October, on my trip back to Springfield," he said, ignoring the edge to her voice. "But today I received his reply in a letter. His holdings have grown too vast; his interest in the fur trade has dwindled. 'Tis a fine opportunity for me."

She heaved an impatient sigh. "You'll be gone away among the Indians, Joseph, and I shall spend my life awaiting your return. What good is this fine house if I must dwell here alone?" She put down the Bible and stood up, green eyes ablaze. "You would leave me to take care of the farm all alone, when I have the children and God knows what work to do?"

Joseph downed the last of his beer. "'Tis settled, Mary."

"How will I manage?" She pressed her hands to the sides of her head, feeling utter distress. "You know I'm with child."

"I won't be away so much, except during winter, and I shall hire an extra hand." He scowled at her. "In any case, woman, you have Elspeth. Now stop complaining. This is what I've waited for. This will make me rich."

Seeing it was useless to object further, she left him at the fireside and went to bed.

IN DECEMBER, JOSEPH joined the other leaders of the town for their first official meeting. Being the northernmost settlement in the Bay Colony, they agreed to name the place Northampton, after Robert Bartlett's birthplace in England. They also began plans to build a house for the town—a combination meeting house for religious purposes and public gathering place. Joseph, along with Sarah's brothers Richard and John Lyman, William Holton, and Edward Elmore agreed to supply the timber and the labor.

The building would measure 26 feet in length, 18 feet in width, with four pair of rafters. Every other detail was specified at that meeting, down to the size of the laths, spars, collar beams, windows and chimney pieces. These were useful men, ready to provide for their neighbors' needs, used to putting their hands to work when required. The volunteers would be responsible for everything except the nails and the raising of the roof, when everyone in town would be called on to help.

ON A FOGGY morning in April following days of rain, young John Bridgeman set out into the meadow with a rope, in search of his father's cow. Trying to keep his feet from getting soaked, he gingerly lifted his boots from one clump of dry meadow grass to the next. In the distance, through the fog, he saw the cow in the swamp at the edge of the forest. Forgetting his boots, he made a beeline for her.

He thought he could make out the solitary figure of a woman in the meadow ahead, her head bent in thought as she went toward the river. She seemed to look his way. He slowed his pace and stared. Was it Goodwife Parsons? The woman's belly appeared to be swollen with child, and her ghostly image frightened him so that he stopped in his tracks to consider his fear. Afraid to walk forward and approach her, he stood still, waiting for her to go on her way, but to his dismay she seemed to be calling to him, though he could hear no voice.

Suddenly his fear changed to terror, for the sky above filled with the sound of great flapping wings. Something struck the youngster a brutal blow on the head, knocking him face down in the grass. He pulled himself up to run but tripped over a log, cutting his knee badly. Barely able to get to his feet, he staggered toward home. His leg felt as though a knife stuck through to the bone, and blood soaked his torn pants. In his shock and fear he glanced back over his shoulder as he limped on, to see if the woman was following him, but the meadow was empty. He was alone.

He made it home, though Sarah could scarcely believe he'd been able to walk at all. The boy's leg was strangely contorted, and the cut on his knee bled profusely. Sarah, big with child herself, was terribly afraid. Fortunately James was close by, and once the bleeding was staunched, he determined that the wound was so bad he should go for the doctor. With that, he left for Springfield, promising to return the next evening. Fortunately, over the past year many improvements had been made to the trail. Now a man on horseback could cover the distance between Northampton and Springfield in a day.

Each hour he was away seemed to last forever as Sarah sat with her wounded son, hearing him moan and whimper. At times the pain was so great he cried out in anguish. She had made a plaster and dressed the wound, and to ease his suffering gave him strong drink to help him sleep. Having done everything she knew to help him, she agonized over her poor boy, drunk and half mad with pain.

When the surgeon arrived the next day, he needed James's help to yank the boy's knee back into place. Sarah turned away as the men set to their task, covered her ears and wept. Straightening the misaligned joint was so painful that the boy fainted. But that would not be the end of John's agony. Though the surgeon stayed on at the Bridgemans' house for two days, the boy's pain never let up.

"I am filled with wonder," the surgeon said, "by the state of your son's health. "Never, in twenty years of practice, have I seen a worse case. Something unnatural has possessed him." He stroked his beard thoughtfully and looked pityingly at the boy. "Though his leg has been returned to its proper place and his cut is healing, his mind remains grievous affected. I look to the Devil for the cause, and so should you." Seeming eager to return to Springfield, he shook both the parents' hands and bid them farewell. "I've done what I could for your son. The rest is up to God Almighty."

A week went by, and still the boy suffered. At daybreak one morning, John's screams woke both his parents and, as they had done many times before, they hurried to his side.

"Goodwife Parsons will pull off my knee!" he cried.

"What say you, child?" Sarah laid a shaky hand on his tear-stained cheek.

"Ah, look!" he screamed, "she pulls off my knee. See her there?" He pointed to a shelf on the wall that held pewter vessels.

James was exhausted by the boy's unrelenting torment. "He's out of his wits," he said to his wife.

"See her there?" John shrieked. "Goody Parsons sits on the shelf! Can't you see?" Their inability to see what seemed obvious to him merely increased his frenzy.

"Nay, John," James said, "there is no one." He took the boy onto his lap.

"There she goes!" he screamed. "See? A black mouse follows her!"

"Stop that, John!" Sarah demanded, for he frightened her.

"Yea, there she is! Don't you see? There—she runs away!" he yelled, burying his face in his father's shoulder and sobbing.

Powerless to help their suffering child, the Bridgemans regarded each other with utter bewilderment.

On the first day of May, Mary gave birth to her fourth son, Ebenezer, the first child born in Northampton. On the thirtieth day of May, Sarah gave birth to her husband's namesake, James. His birth had followed weeks of nursing her older son back to health, and Sarah was exhausted. Fatiguing her further, the infant James was small and required frequent feedings. Constantly on the brink of tears, she held her babe for hours, rocking him. The newborn took up so much of her time that her daughters were left with the housekeeping and care of little Rebecca. Often she rested the baby's small body across her knees and massaged his back, barely able to hold up her own head. One day, at about an hour past noon, she was just so employed when a loud blow sounded on the front door. She nearly jumped out of her skin, and her startled babe began to cry again.

"Martha!" Sarah called to her daughter in the next room. "Answer the door."

Dutiful Martha ran to the door and opened it, but no one was there. That revelation sent Sarah into a tailspin. She began to shiver. "There is wickedness in this place, and I fear your baby brother will die."

"Nay, Mother," Martha cried, running to her side. "Don't say it!"

"Then run outside and see who knocked."

Martha obeyed. She was gone for a while, and when she reappeared in the doorway she said, "I looked first right, then left, and saw no one, Mother." Coming into the room, the girl hurried to look at the baby and reached out to fondle his soft fuzzy head. "He will be well, Mother. Worry not."

Just then Sarah looked toward the open door and saw two women passing by with white shawls on their heads. "Away! Martha, ask the white-cloaked women who they are, for I've never seen them in this place before."

Martha looked mystified. "What women?"

"Do as I say, quick, before they are gone from the road."

Martha ran out the door again as Sarah laid her sleepy baby in his cradle. Going to the door herself, she saw Martha running back and forth, looking up and down the way, and called to her, "Pray, who were the women I saw pass by?"

Martha was weeping. "There be no women on the road, Mother."

Sarah screamed and ran to the cradle, lifting baby James into her arms. Though he had already passed from this world, he still felt warm and sweet, a tiny bit of life gone in two weeks. His would be the first grave in the new burial ground.

VII

*Experience shows that it is an easy thing in the midst of
a worldly business to lose the life and power of religion
that nothing thereof should be left but only the external
form, as it were the carcass or shell, worldliness having
eaten out the kernel and having consumed the very soul
and life of godliness.*

—Richard Mather (1596–1669)

WITH GLASS INSTALLED in the front windows of his
house, Joseph Parsons had finally added most of the finishing touches. The remaining windows would have to wait for
glass to be shipped from England. He had built the front door
in the Dutch style, one door above the other, and over the top
door six square panes of glass. Joseph had had the blacksmith
in Springfield fashion a beautiful iron latch and four long strap
hinges, giving the door a look of permanence and dignity.

The front chamber upstairs, where Joseph and Mary slept, ran
the whole width of the front of the house, a great luxury of space
with a fireplace and four windows looking out over the road and
the stream. The other chambers also had windows and fireplaces
and room for all the children. Elspeth had a garret chamber to
herself, with space enough for two other servants, if they could be
had. It was the finest house in town.

Through Pynchon, Joseph had ordered bolts of fabric for
Mary: woolen kersey in sadd red, steel gray, and olive green

from Devonshire and Hampshire, Antwerp duffel and Taunton serge, satin ribbons, gold buttons, silk and crewel lace. In Boston he bought his wife a fine red- oak chest with double hearts carved on three panels, rope moldings, a scalloped skirt. He also bought a chair upholstered with Turkey work and, for himself, a great oak chair with a wicker seat and turned posts and finials. Mary was making comfortable cushions to fit. For delivery the following year he ordered a blanket chest, a turned oak highchair, a long trestle table and chairs, a chamber table, a joined stool, and a great bedstead befitting his wealth. The town honored Joseph by making him Clarke of the Band—the keeper of the muster rolls and inspector of arms and ammunition for the local militia.

More settlers had arrived at Northampton, now making more than thirty households living on new streets as the town spread north and south of Bartlett Street. The Pocumtucks had also moved to town, scattering their wigwams in all directions around the edges of the settlement, as close as they could get to the settlers' house lots.

Sarah's difficult brother, Robert, and his wife Helen moved in next door. They were a constant source of embarrassment for her, though she felt obliged to take his side in squabbles with neighbors and be kind to his wife who, from the day she was born, had one short leg and an awkwardly twisted back. Helen's otherwise pleasant appearance became grotesque the moment she began to walk. Sarah could not see past her misshapen body to value Helen's gentle, sweet nature, and she punished herself for her revulsion. Wondering how her brother could love such a creature, she forced herself to be outwardly kind, at least.

It still rankled with her, not living on Pleasant Street. Though she now had neighbors up and down the street, including George and Hannah Langton from Springfield, Sarah still wished for more, or for the other. Both her Pleasant Street brothers were better off than her husband, and when it came to visiting her brothers' wives—John's Dorcus and Richard's Hepzibah—she felt like a poor country relation. As for Mary Parsons and her husband's grossly obvious wealth, Sarah consoled herself with the knowledge that Mary was nothing but a serving girl in disguise.

Sarah's most cherished new friend, Honor Hannum, was slightly older and had a son and four daughters. Coming from Windsor, where she and her husband had lived for fifteen years, they had a house built two lots north of Joseph Parsons. Honor was a congenial sort of woman with like-minded folks, plumpish, with brown hair, apple-red cheeks and skin that looked so well scrubbed that it shone. Never introspective or serene, she craved the company of women who found her a fount of exuberant conversation and a storehouse of gossip. When she and Sarah met at meeting, they were quickly drawn to one another by shared mutual loss, including Sarah's recent one.

When the two met on Bartlett Street one day on their way to the mill, Honor confided, "As many has died as has lived. Five in all, I have carried to their graves." She shook her head decisively. "But no more."

Sarah chided her. "You cannot know what will be."

"Nay, I do know. For six years," she said behind her hand, "I've kept that man on his own side of the bed and made him forswear his pleasures."

Sarah gasped. "'Tis a sin to deny your husband." She could not understand her friend's willful disregard for her husband's needs. "To be sure, yet more afeard am I of birthing another babe than of going to Hell." Honor appeared to mean every word. "I say that the Lord put the fear in me for good reason."

Sarah's eyes welled up with tears. "Though I've had three sons, only one lives. And she—*she*—has four, alive and strong. I cannot bear that bravely."

Honor looked puzzled. "Who has four sons?"

"Mary Parsons. She's not right with the Lord, you know. She comes from naught—was once in service in my father's house, and look at her now, her husband the richest man in town. I do wonder what help she's been given and whence it came. She's always been envious of me, and now, I'll warrant, she seeks to destroy me."

"Why, Sarah, what has she done that you blame her so?"

"She caused my son John an injury, a grave injury. In his fever he said the same. He was like to die in our apprehension, but God looked kindly on him. She hates that any of my sons have lived. In my heart I know it is not God who punishes me, for I have committed no great sin. I look to Satan as the cause."

They had reached the mill and were no longer alone. Honor whispered, "Goodwife Parsons? And Satan?"

Honor Hannum's mind was always busy. She kept her hands just as active at the spinning wheel and quickly piled up stores of yarn, which she offered for sale to her neighbors, Mary Parsons among them. Not one to turn away a good customer, Honor nevertheless regarded the goodwife with careful suspicion after what she'd heard.

Honor's eldest daughter, Abigail, was sixteen, a pretty maid filled with curiosity and blessed with a happy nature. Unlike her younger sisters Jane and Elizabeth, who were choleric and dull, Abigail was outgoing and eager to please, rarely a trial to her mother. Honor still had hope for her youngest daughter, Lydia, who was only six, but found the middle daughters too troublesome to train.

"'Tis easier to do it myself than move your lazy bones!" Honor railed, hoping to shame them into cooperation. Her least painful course was to pile most of the work on Abigail, who was quick about her chores. Carrying a basket of her mother's yarn, Abigail set off to Goodwife Parsons' house. She loved getting out and away from home, away from her bickering mother and sisters. On the road she could hear the stream babbling along on the other side of the way and the birds singing in the meadow. By the time she reached Bartlett Street she could see the Parsons' large dark house in the distance. She stopped to look with wonder at the complicated lines of its roof, chimney and gables. She liked the way it lay nestled in gardens planted with young trees growing behind a low fieldstone wall. When she reached the house she stopped to stare at the dazzle of the fine diamond-shaped windows in front, the garden filled with more flowers than she'd ever seen planted in one place. Elspeth was sweeping the front step, and Goodwife Parsons, who looked to be gathering herbs, waved to her.

"Good morrow, Goodwife Parsons," Abigail called as she walked up the garden path.

Mary greeted her with a smile. "How fortunate. I see you have the yarn I ordered."

"Aye, Mother said to tell ye it is her very best."

"Come inside, I'll get your due." Mary took the yarn and removed her broad beaver hat as she disappeared into the house.

Elspeth ushered the girl into the sunny front room. "Wait here, if ye please," she said, before disappearing into the kitchen at the back.

Abigail surveyed the grandest room she'd ever seen, with its round, well-polished table gleaming in the sun. She hardly had time to look around before Mary appeared with a small boy clinging to her skirts. Abigail looked more closely at Mary—at her gown of drab green, white apron edged in lace, her red hair fastened and covered with a laced coif. She felt honored just to be in her presence.

"Abigail, this is our son Samuel." Samuel looked shy and disappeared behind the goodwife, who was obviously delighted with him. "Now let's see what you brought," she said, her green eyes sparkling as her little son peeped around the fullness of her skirt. Taking the buff-colored yarn in hand, she examined it and sighed. "Oh my, there is fault with the yarn. Look here, at the threads. There are too few threads in a knot. And see—this has more defects. I cannot accept this—it wants weight."

"I would fain ask your pardon, Goodwife, but that cannot be."

"Trouble not your head, child, 'tis not your fault. Have your mother send me a new lot."

"Oh my, Goodwife Parsons, I am sorry—did ye have need of it today?"

"Nay, child, but soon I shall. Come, sit you down. I want to ask you something."

Comforted by Mary's friendly expression, Abigail sat on the Turkey-work chair. She found her hostess charming and comely and could not take her eyes off the gold thumb ring she wore.

Mary offered her hand for a better look. "I see you notice my ring."

"A gift from your husband?"

"Yes. Do you fancy it?"

"'Tis extraordinary fine—one day, I pray, I shall have a rich husband."

Mary's cheeks colored when she laughed. "Abigail, I have observed you close, and I see a good girl in you."

"I try to be good," she said, feeling warmly blessed.

"My husband is oft away on business, and I and Elspeth are left alone to care for the house and children. There is much to do with four sons and no daughters to help. Presently I hope to find a young maid ready to go into service. If you should like to come here, I shall speak to your father and offer a wage."

Abigail could hardly believe her good luck. She would love to live and work in such a fine house for such a kind woman. "Aye, Goodwife, please speak to him. I am well learned in cooking and cleaning, and I enjoy minding little children."

Honor Hannum was furious. "Nay! I say, nay! How dare she speak to my child before she speaks to me—to *you*!" she shouted at her husband.

"Ah, woman, calm yourself or you'll melt your grease," William Hannum said. She's made a generous offer. Besides, 'tis time ye stopped relying on Abby and get those good-for-nothing daughters of yers up off their arses. Ye do them great harm. What good will they be to their husbands?"

"Do, Mother," Abigail begged, "do please let me go to work for her. She is kind, and I would learn much in her service."

"You shall not go hither to dwell if she gave you ten pound a year! I have been warned, by those who know, to beware of how I have to do with that woman."

"She's good enough to buy yarn off ye!" Abigail howled.

"Hold your tongue, child, or I'll have your father whip you," Honor said, looking unkindly at her husband.

Abigail wept. "She found fault with your yarn—that's why ye won't let me go."

"She witched it," Honor hissed, lifting the offending yarn from the basket. "This was my best yarn, yet you bring it back to me wanting. Mercy me," she gasped, examining the yarn once more. "Now there are but eighteen threads in a knot of forty, and here twenty-eight for forty, yet I swear it was my best—till she got her hands on it."

Struck dumb, Joan, Elizabeth and little Lydia huddled in the corner as their usually obedient sister stood up to their mother. "'Tis excuses ye make for yourself," she cried, stamping one foot. "Ye want me to do all your work. Ye don't care if I ever have a chance to be glad."

"Listen, how this wicked child speaks to me," Honor wailed at her husband, striking the girl across the face. "And what shall you do about it, pray?"

"I'm going to see my cow." William raised his lean body off the settle and ambled out the door.

Honor Hannum spun more yarn for Mary Parsons and decided she would deliver it herself. Though the walk to the Parsons' house was short, she arrived out of breath and in a sweat, finding Mary at work on a patch of ground by the road. Without a word of greeting, Honor said, "I spun more yarn, Goodwife, to recompense the defect you found in my yarn."

"There was no hurry, Goody Hannum," Mary said, unaware that the woman was fuming.

"No one ever found fault with my yarn before, and I am here to tell you that it is against my wishes that you speak to my daughter again." Red-faced, Hannah was shaking with anger.

"Hold your peace," Mary said, taken aback by the woman's anger. "What have I done to offend you?"

"No offence. I need the girl myself."

"Of course, and I'm sorry to hear it." Mary was looking closely at the yarn. "She is a fine young maid of whom you may be proud."

235

She held the yarn up to the light, hardly believing what she saw. "Nay, but this will not do. 'Tis as short as the first."

"I believe it is not." Honor yanked the yarn from Mary's hand to examine it herself. "By the universe, it was fine until you touched it," she gasped.

"Nonsense. I believe you've brought me the same lot as before. I have no use for it," Mary said, as she let her hoe drop and turned to go.

"I am a Christian woman," Honor yelled, "yet to you I appear a thief. I am no cheating slut."

"I never said so." Mary was anxious to get away.

"I shall spin for you once more, and it shall be examined by an honest witness. My yarn is the finest in the village, ask anyone." Honor turned on her heel and headed home.

What a mountain from a molehill, Mary told herself, surprised that she trembled inside and out. As she entered the back door to the kitchen she found young Joseph looking for something. "What's amiss, son?"

"My shoe. I've looked all around and 'tis lost. You've put it someplace?" He was obviously upset.

"Nay, child, I have not seen your shoe. Somehow I keep mine on my feet. Where did you last see it?" Mary laid her hat on a chair.

"In the barn, I think, but I looked there." The lad sounded cross with himself.

"By my troth," Mary said, "I have enough on my mind without keeping up with your shoes. Go look again."

Joseph, just back from Springfield, walked in the back door at that moment, frowning at the harsh sound of his wife's voice.

"I have! I have looked!" young Joseph yelled, crossing his arms on his chest, unaware that his father had come up behind him.

"Don't talk like that to your mother." Joseph's command startled the boy.

"Oh, Joseph, he's lost his shoe," Mary said, "and I haven't time to search for it."

"His new shoes?"

"One of them, at least. The ones with the brown bows."

"Where?" Joseph demanded of his son.

He struck an impudent pose. "I know not, Father, else I would go and fetch it."

Joseph grabbed the boy and shook him. "How dare you speak so!"

Frightened, the boy cried out and ran through the house and out the front door, both parents in pursuit.

"Wait, Joseph!" Mary shouted after her husband, hoping to avert violence. "I have already whipped him!" she lied. But Joseph caught the boy before he reached the street and, holding him by an arm, beat his backside with one hand as Mary pulled at Joseph's coat, crying, "Pray, stop, Joseph, he's but a child!"

"I'll teach him who rules here!" Joseph delivered his last blows as the child cowered on the path, his face streaked with tears and dust.

Mary knelt and reached for her boy.

"Leave him be!" Joseph ordered.

She regarded her husband with utter disgust and took the boy by the hand. "Come, I'll help you find your shoe."

Joseph shouted, "I said, leave him be!" He grabbed Mary by one wrist and yanked her around to face him.

"Nay, Father!" young Joseph cried, "I am sorry. I am sorry!"

"Woman, I forbid you to coddle this boy!" Joseph yelled, pushing Mary onto her knees. "Do you understand me? DO YOU UNDERSTAND?" he shouted, again and again, until she cried yes, her eyes streaming with tears.

The next morning, about a half-mile up the road from Joseph Parsons' house, there was no peace at the Hannums'. William Hannum, a thin, wiry man, sat at table with one hand supporting his chin, his small eyes closed, his pointed nose poking over the hand that covered his mouth. He felt greatly overlooked by his robust wife, who still raved about Mary Parsons bewitching her yarn. She had talked of nothing else. He had hardly listened to a word and had nothing to say to her. Having finished his breakfast, he stood up and walked out the door.

Despite his size, Hannum was a strong, hard-working man. He had two oxen but needed to borrow two more to make a team of four. On his way to see if John Bliss would lend him his team for a couple of days, he walked down the road past William Miller's house and found both Goodman Miller and Sam Wright conversing by the side of the road.

"Good morrow, Hannum," Sam Wright said. "Miller here was telling me he seen Joseph Parsons beat his wife yesterday—right out in front of his house for all the world to see."

Miller chimed in. "And I was just telling him that's what comes of managing family business on the road."

Hannum nodded and laughed, figuring Miller referred to Joseph's many trips away from home. "Indeed, my intelligence tells me Mary Parsons *wants* a beating." It was good not to have the only troublesome wife.

"Aye," Wright said. "She's a high-spirited woman—too comely for her own good."

Hannum had his final say. "One of ye, being her next neighbors, must also ride on a broom staff." He chuckled to himself and went on his way, having no more time for gossip.

Wright frowned, puzzled. "What's he mean by that?"

"Ah, just nonsense." Miller shook his head. "Some of the foolishness I heard before—folks be saying Goody Parsons is a witch—that she rides on a broom staff." When his neighbor's eyebrows made for his scalp, he hastened to justify himself. "In my estimation, though, folks that say such things on no better grounds are naught but fearmongers and jades."

Within a few days Mary welcomed Goodwife Margaret Wright into her front room. They had much to talk about, for Margaret's daughter Lydia had married Mary's brother Lawrence at Springfield, and Mary was fond of the girl.

The Wright family had been through very recent troubles. Margaret's 24-year-old son, Samuel Jr., married about a year, had been found guilty at Springfield of wickedness with his wife's sister Mary Burt. Ordered to support the resulting child, the young husband had also taken twelve lashes on his naked body. Though horrified and embarrassed by their son's shocking behavior, the Wrights were grateful to the magistrate, John Pynchon, for keeping it quiet. Mary, aware of their troubles through the family connection, was thankful not to have heard anyone in Northampton mention their shame, for if it were known, Margaret Wright would be an outcast.

After she offered Margaret refreshment, the two women caught up on the news. Lawrence and Lydia were now settled in their own home. Goodwife Wright described the house, its location, and how Lawrence had worked to build it. Then she lowered her eyes, and put down her cup. "My dear Mary, may I speak as if I were an elder sister?" She didn't wait for permission. "I'm afeard I've come with evil tidings. My husband has heard ugly gossip." She looked kindly at Mary. "'Twas just the other day Goodman Hannum said to him that you be a witch, and my husband being your neighbor, should ride on a broom staff. This he said in jest, I believe, but I've heard such things from women in the village as well, and I know for certain Goodman Hannum's wife has talked in the same way."

Mary frowned and shook her head. "What foolishness. Truly, I am embarrassed. I'm sure I know where this all started. After Honor Hannum quarreled with me a few days ago about some yarn I asked her to spin, she left here in a fury." Though alarmed, Mary did not wish to show it.

Margaret took her hand. "Do not allow them to speak that way, for 'tis a slander on your good name and a shame on this town."

"Ah, my friend you have my thanks. I must think what to do."

When Margaret got up to go, Mary said, "Wait. I know your eyes trouble you. Let me send you home with clary and sage. Steep them together in boiling water and when the potion is cool use it to wash your eyes."

Appreciative, Margaret went on her way as Mary closed her door on the world outside to sit safe by her kitchen fire. Elspeth was at work making vinegar. Glad to be distracted from her thoughts, Mary helped her pour ale into a strong vessel and seal it. Afterward they carried it into the garden, where it would rest in the sun for weeks, the first stage in a long process.

That task accomplished, Mary pondered what she should do about the Hannums. How cruel and unfair! It seemed everything had gone wrong. She was still angry with Joseph for losing his temper, though she understood that she and her son had provoked him. It had all been a horrible mistake, because in a very short time they'd found the boy's shoe in the barn. He'd decided to go barefoot, took them off and left them, then came back to find only the one. And now this morning, like a piece of magic, there sat the shoe in plain view. Mary felt ashamed to have had such a violent quarrel over nothing.

Thinking carefully about Goody Wright's warning, and her scene with Honor Hannum, Mary decided to speak to William Hannum herself, and set out to walk to his house. She would plead her case with him and ask him to reason with his wife. She found Hannum plowing his fields with a team of four oxen and immediately recognized the two front beasts as her brother's young whites. John Bliss was building a house on land between the Parsons' house and the Hannums' and had evidently lent his team to Goodman Hannum who, in her estimation, was driving the beasts too hard.

"Goodman Hannum!" she called from the road.

When he did not respond, Mary supposed he hadn't heard. She watched as he cracked his whip over the heads of the oxen, and when the beasts moved no faster through the dank heavy earth, he lowered it, letting it fall across their backs.

She winced and cried out, "Goodman Hannum, have mercy!" Lifting her skirts high, she headed through the plowed field, calling at the top of her lungs. Either he still did not hear or chose to ignore her, for he whipped the oxen hard, again and again. With each step she took her fury deepened. At last she reached him and, out of breath, shouted, "My good man, I beg you, stop abusing my brother's oxen!"

Startled by her sudden appearance, he took a moment to

answer. "'Tis no abuse I give. Ye are but a woman and have no knowledge of these things."

"Please, come away from your plough and listen to what I have to say."

Though he looked surprised, he obeyed. She stood taller, and as she looked down on him, his eyes traveled up the front of her ginger-colored gown to stop at her breasts.

"Goodman Hannum, your wife and I have had words about her yarn. She tells lies about me, that I ruined it with my touch or some such rubbish."

"Aye, she's said the same to me." He fairly devoured her with his eyes.

"Just today, I learned that you had made a rude remark at my expense. Now I find you brutalizing my brother's oxen. I have not spoken with my husband about this, yet, but if you do not find it in your Christian heart to cease these cruelties, speak to him I shall."

Hannum stood dumb.

She had worked herself into a state of righteous indignation. "Beyond that, I demand that you require the same of your wife. Do this right away, or pay dearly." Without waiting for his answer she turned and walked away, leaving the little man with his boots buried to the ankles in the fresh-plowed earth.

When Hannum thought back on his encounter with Mary he had to admit that he could put up with her yelling at him every day—and every night. He had watched her walk away, unable to explain to himself how strange she had made him feel. He could not remember ever feeling so enthralled by a woman.

VIII

In New Haven there was a sow, which among other pigs had one without hair, and some other human resemblances had also one eye blemished, just like one of a loose fellow in the town, which occasioned him to be suspected, and being examined before the magistrates, he confessed the fact, for which, after they had written to us, and some other places for advice, they put him to death.

—Governor John Winthrop
The History of New England 1630–1649

ONE AFTERNOON THAT summer, Ann Bartlett invited Mary to pay her a call. With Joseph in Boston all week and not to return for another, Mary was lonely and looked forward to seeing Ann and her other guests. The boys came along, expecting that while Mary enjoyed the women's companionship they and Nat Bartlett would go fishing at Mill River, with Elspeth to supervise.

Mary and Elspeth, who carried baby Eben in her arms, set out on the long walk to the far end of Pleasant Street. Young Joseph and little John marched ahead of little Samuel, who was still in his skirts. At the corner they could see the Meeting House on the hill, its bare yard sloping down to the Common where cattle grazed. Goodwife Sarah Edwards was outside sweeping her stoop, and Mary greeted her with a friendly smile.

The goodwife glared at her and retreated into the house.

"Well, I never!" Elspeth grumbled as they walked past the Edwards' closed door.

Mary said nothing, for a stab of pain had stuck in her throat, and she knew she could not speak without a catch in her voice.

While Elspeth and the boys fished, Goodwife Bartlett poured a glass of sack for her guest. Her daughter made a brief appearance with a pound cake and a gooseberry pie fresh from the keeping room, but Mary, puzzled by the absence of other guests, wanted no food. "You invited no one else?"

"None of the others could come." Ann averted her eyes as Mary set her untouched dish of pie on a table.

"Hepzibah Lyman?"

"She declined."

"Sarah Edwards? I just passed her house, and she was at home."

"Nay, she could not come," her hostess said, clearly aware that Mary had sensed the trouble abroad.

"Could not, or would not?"

"My dear, ordinarily I would counsel you to trouble not your head about the idle talk of brainless, jealous women, but I'm afraid there be dangerous gossip abroad."

"Goodwife Wright has recently warned me of the same." Mary stood and walked over to look out the window, for suddenly the room seemed close and her hostess too observant. She turned back to Ann. "Have I only two friends in town?"

"Though I am your friend," Ann said, clasping her hands, "I ask you not to bring me into this. "You must tell no one what I am about to say." She looked intently at Mary, her normally cheerful face sad and pale.

"May I tell my husband?"

"Yes, if he agrees to the same."

"I understand. Now tell me, for I feel myself shaking with apprehension." Mary returned to her seat.

"First, I shall say I believe not a word of it. Sarah Bridgeman is the source of your bad name. She says 'twas you who caused the injury to her son John, and 'twas you who took her infant's life. Now that she is with child again, she fears you greatly."

Mary opened her mouth, but no words came.

"She believes, and says so, that you keep company with the Devil, who has given your husband wealth and all the healthy sons you desire."

Gasping, Mary covered her mouth with both hands, then dropped them to her lap. "Surely none believe that!"

"I do not. Others, especially Goodwife Hannum, are not so sure."

"Then a pox on them both!"

"Mary!" Goodwife Bartlett cried, frantic. "Curse not! Should either one sicken, I should be bound to say that I heard you cry out against them."

The reproachful look on her friend's face frightened Mary.

"You cannot but admit that from girlhood you have spoken too much your mind, and this is what comes of it. Keep your thoughts to yourself. Speak words that cannot be twisted into something evil, else you may pay dearly."

Chastened, Mary hesitated, then blurted out, "I'm to be afraid and cannot speak my mind?"

"No woman who is wise speaks her mind. A mind is a secret place, my dear, not to be shared."

"I cannot brook it, Sarah Bridgeman taking that liberty—and those fools, the Hannums."

"Ah, Mary, it does you no good to quarrel with me about these things."

Mary softened as she grasped her friend's true concern for her. "Nay, I am sure yours is wise counsel—that you give it like a mother to her daughter. But I cannot allow it. I would rather forsake all company, to live lonely with only Elspeth and my mother for comfort. Here I boil in my own resentment and cannot easily see my way to another state of mind."

"I know not how to advise you, Mary," Ann said sadly, rising from her chair. "However hard this talk, it seemed to me I ought to tell."

Feeling dismissed, Mary thanked her and said goodbye. Too soon for their liking she claimed Elspeth and her disappointed boys from the riverbank to head back up Pleasant Street toward home, the boys grumbling about not being given time to catch the first fish. Folks on the street saw Goodwife Parsons walk by with her head held high. She looked at and greeted no one, leaving the impression that she was haughty and much too sure of herself.

A week later Joseph returned from the city with the latest news. A third woman, Ann Hibbins, had been executed for witchcraft in Boston. City folks had found it ironic that the former governor and now deputy governor, John Bellingham, had been forced to officiate at the trial of his sister-in-law. Even more shocking, he was among those who found her guilty. Her husband, dead for two years, was no longer around to protect her.

Some time before this, Joseph Parsons had briefly had business with William Hibbins and had heard the rumors about his wife. Famously difficult, she had been censured by the church, and it was common knowledge that her husband had been embarrassed by her self-government, her quarrelsome relationships, her unbending will. Some said she had turned him into a wisp of a man. Her neighbors had feared her and set up such a clamor with the authorities that she was charged, tried, and condemned.

Her trial and immediate execution were the talk of the town. As far as Joseph knew, never had a woman of her elevated station come to such an end. Most of those found guilty of witchcraft were poor, old, and friendless. Around the town, on street corners, in taverns and keeping rooms, gossip spread like wildfire. The authorities had searched her body for signs of witchcraft—marks of the Devil or tits fit for familiar spirits to suck. She had claimed her innocence to the very end and had put her case to "God and his Court" but all she got was the hangman. It was true, however, that several prominent, well-placed citizens condemned the tragedy. They saw Ann Hibbins as having far greater intellect and importance than the neighbors who had damned her.

. . . . .

Mary trembled at the very thought of sitting amid her hateful neighbors at meeting next Sabbath. After a sleepless night, she decided to tell Joseph what the goodwives Wright and Bartlett had said. As he listened, the color rose to his face until it was so red that Mary's soul cowered, fearing he'd direct his wrath at her.

"I'll not stand for slander!" he cried. "I'll put a stop to Sarah Bridgeman's evil back-biting tongue. Holton and Pynchon will help me see to it in court. God damn her to Hell!"

Mary gasped at his curse, though relieved by her husband's strong declaration. "If there's to be a fight, Joseph, then I shall lead it." Simply knowing he would support her gave her courage.

"This very morning," he said, looking at her as if she was about to be taken from him, "I shall file suit against her." With that he reached out and took his wife into his arms.

"And I shall go with you!" Mary declared.

For once he smiled down at her, though Mary knew he had not always found her strong will amusing.

In short order, Commissioners William Holton, Thomas Bascom and Edward Elmore went to work gathering depositions for a slander case: *Joseph Parsons, plaintiff, against Sarah, the wife of James Bridgeman, defendant, for slandering Parsons' wife.* The three commissioners now had the job of interviewing witnesses, those who had heard slanderous words from Sarah Bridgeman herself. Because the Court of Assistance had no members yet in Northampton, the nearest being John Pynchon and Elizer Holyoke in Springfield, local commissioners had been sworn in and empowered to hear all cases too small for the court.

William Holton decided to commence his inquiry by talking to Robert Bartlett. He approached the constable's door, glad for a chance to see his good friend. With both surprise and a friendly twinkle in his eyes, Bartlett invited him inside and gave him a tall cup of beer. At first the two exchanged views on matters to do with the administration of the town, then Holton got down to business. "Joseph Parsons has accused the wife of James Bridgeman of slander," he said, "and the commissioners and I are about the business of collecting evidence for the case." He downed the last sup of his beer with obvious satisfaction.

Bartlett looked thoughtful. "What sort of evidence?"

"Have you ever heard Sarah Bridgeman say anything she shouldn't about Mary Parsons?" Though Holton felt a bit like a petty gossip, he had to ask.

"What I've heard is hearsay, for she ne'er said anything direct to me."

The commissioner frowned and pulled on his short beard. "Where did you hear it, then?"

"From George Langton, and from my wife, who's heard the backbiters often."

"And Goodman Langton?"

"Well, he said the gossip began last spring when William Branch's wife Joanna came up from Springfield to visit. In the presence of Langton's wife, Goody Bridgeman and Goody Branch spoke about Mary Parsons being a witch. When Langton's wife said she could not think so about Mary Parsons, Goody Bridgeman seemed disgusted with her. According to Langton, these women had hard thoughts of my own wife as well, because of her friendship with Mary Parsons. The two have known each other since Mary came to Hartford little more than a girl."

"'Tis as I feared," Holton said, having made mental notes he would later commit to paper. "I find no pleasure in this business, but I must thank you and take my leave, for I am on the noble mission"—his lips curved upward in a grim smile—"of going round town talking to folks about women's gossip."

At the Langtons' house, next door to the Bridgemans', Goodwife Langton welcomed Holton and asked if he would take some refreshment.

"A sup of beer would be welcome," he said.

She brought him a drink and sat down, then confirmed Robert Bartlett's story. "Sarah Bridgeman told me that when her boy's knee was hurt, he cried out against Goodwife Parsons, saying she would pull off his knee. At first I believed the story, but soon after God helped me over such thoughts and I changed my mind. I am sorry I should have hard thoughts on no better grounds," she said. "I would not wish to be charged with slander myself."

Nervously straightening her apron over her lap, she went on. "Goodman Holton, you ought to talk to Hannah Boughton up the street. She too has heard talk straight from Goody Bridgeman's mouth."

Women! Holton groaned to himself as he trudged three house lots north to call on Goodwife Boughton, another Bridgeman neighbor, who welcomed him inside with a glass of sack. He thanked her and sipped as he explained why he had come.

"By my life," she said, "I am sorry to tell you that it is true. Sarah Bridgeman has slandered Mary Parsons within my hearing. One day when she came to visit she mentioned that they had both lived in Springfield before they came here, and that John Pynchon himself had told her that he did not think Goody Parsons could be right—right in the eyes of the Lord, is what she meant."

Holton left the Boughton house feeling he'd put in a hard day's work. Though the sun was still overhead, he went home for a nap.

Word that Joseph Parsons had filed suit against her came to Sarah's ears the very same day, filling her with terror and shame. She could not understand it. To the best of his ability, James explained the slander laws and tried to reassure her that they could turn this to her advantage. "We must show, Sarah, that what you have said is true."

Soon news of the slander case spread to Springfield and all the neighboring towns. One day not long after, Sarah opened her door to find Margaret Bliss standing there. She wanted to flee but was too proud to show it. "Why, Widow Bliss—I knew not that you were—"

"May I come in, Sarah? I think it would be to your benefit if we spoke."

Though Mary's mother was the last person she ever expected

to see, Sarah invited her in and apprehensively offered her a seat beside the fire. The moment she studied the woman's gentle face, though, she remembered that Margaret Bliss had always been kind to her. "Would you take refreshment? I have some fresh-made cider."

"Nay, I thank you, Sarah, but I would take it kindly if you would sit down here beside me."

Unable to think of a response, Sarah took a chair near the fire and gazed at her uninvited guest.

"I've come about the trouble between you and my daughter's husband. I recently heard that he brought a suit of slander against you, and that brings me upriver to see you."

Margaret's demeanor seemed so calm and charitable that Sarah clasped her hands together and, close to tears, thought back to the day her father died and the kindness Margaret Bliss had shown.

"'Twas a great sorrow for me to hear that such a thing had come to pass," Margaret said. "'Tis hard for me to fathom, Sarah, for I remember you as you were, years ago, and in that memory wish to think of you warmly."

At last Sarah found her tongue. "And you cannot, knowing that your daughter and I are at odds."

"Have you slandered my daughter, Sarah? Surely you do not believe the things people claim you've said." Margaret's countenance was as open and gentle as ever.

No longer able to look the widow in the eye, Sarah turned her gaze to the fire. "I am not alone in my estimation of your daughter."

"And what is that?"

"For a long time, even before I believed it, I heard your daughter was a witch. In Hartford she befriended Mary Crespet. In Springfield, it was said that she caused the blind man to die and took his daughter for a servant, and that Elspeth, who was then an innocent child, suffered from swooning fits caused by the nearness of the Devil."

Margaret shook her head sadly. "Ah, Sarah, that is all quite untrue. The blind man died from the cold. I was there often, and not once did Elspeth suffer fits. She has been like a daughter to Mary and is now deeply cared for by all the family."

The widow's composure unnerved Sarah—the quiet strength with which the woman defended her daughter while appearing to be a friend. "Some say your daughter has what she wants because she entertains the Devil himself."

The Widow Bliss looked stricken. Her hand closed tight over the arm of the chair as she leaned forward to peer into Sarah's face. "And you believe that? Oh, Sarah, how can you?"

"Indeed I do, for she caused the death of my son."

"My daughter would not harm a child," Margaret said, in earnest. "She would not harm you, nor any one of your family or another. You must know it, for you've known her most of her life."

"You don't know the worst, Widow Bliss."

Her visitor stood up to leave. "I see, then, that nothing will change your mind. There is no hope for you. 'Tis a great pity. I hate to see you laid bare by the law, Sarah. You must believe me when I say that this slander suit will be your ruin."

Sarah cried, "Your *daughter* has been my ruin!" She jumped up and flung open the front door. "Widow Bliss, you are quite mistaken. The town will support me, for behind every door on every street here dwells a goodwife who *hates* and *fears* Mary Parsons."

For a moment Margaret closed her eyes and drew her lips inward as if fighting back tears. "Then I shall leave you. I am sorry you are so wrong. You will be chastised for it."

Free of the noxious atmosphere of the Bridgemans' house, Margaret walked in cold terror to Commissioner Edward Elmore's house, where he took her deposition confirming that Sarah Bridgeman had once more slandered Mary Parsons.

IX

*Thou shalt not go up and down as a talebearer among
thy people: neither shalt thou stand against the blood of
thy neighbor: I am the LORD.*

*Thou shalt not hate thy brother in thine heart: thou
shalt in any wise rebuke thy neighbor, and not suffer sin
upon him.*

Leviticus 19:16-17
The Holy Bible, King James Version

WILLIAM HOLTON PRESENTED the collected evidence
in the case against Sarah Bridgeman to Joseph Parsons,
who came away satisfied that the testimonies taken on his behalf
would show Sarah as both a liar and a slanderer. He hurried home
to find Mary walking alone in their young orchard, her head bent
in thought as she wandered through the grass. Knowing her fear,
he called to her in good cheer, and she turned, eager to see him.

"Mary! I've just come from Holton's." He strode swiftly to
her side and laid an arm around her waist. "Several women will
testify that Honor Hannum's yarn was defective in their hands,
too. Others will say the Bridgeman infant was unwell and died in
consequence of it. And one has heard an outright lie from Goody
Bridgeman—that John Pynchon, while gossiping with her about
you, said he thought you weren't quite right." Joseph managed a
rueful smile. "A shame she wasn't more discreet."

"More discreet?" Mary looked only slightly relieved.

"Not discreet at all. She's shamelessly babbled her slanders all over. She was a fool to say that the *great man himself* was her confidant. Pynchon will never testify to that, and now she shall be punished."

Mary seized both his hands. "But, Joseph, I cannot bear the things she's saying. "I could not have dreamed such things myself! What if people believe her?"

"We shall prove slander. No one will believe her ever again." He looked deeply into her eyes, now rimmed in red. "Never fear, Mary, I shan't let anyone harm you."

How comely she is, he thought. He could not forget that once he had hurt her, but now he was moved to pull her toward the shed. "Come, my bliss," he said, his voice choked with desire as he took her in his arms and carried her inside. There he set her feet on the ground and pressed her against the wall.

"Joseph, someone will see us."

"Nay, we are alone," he said with urgency, his lips to her throat. In that moment he felt her body release its tension as she yielded fully to his kiss. Her mind full of fear and worry for weeks, Mary had not wanted to lie with him, but now she gave herself to her protector, her love.

SARAH BRIDGEMAN WAS pregnant again, and once more she hoped for a son. Her husband James knew as well as she that Holton and the other commissioners had collected evidence against her. Her paranoia grew to the point that she was afraid to go out. "I've said nothing but the truth," she told him. "Prithee, how may I endure in silence all that Mary Parsons has done to me?"

"Aye, Sarah," he took her in his arms to quiet her trembling, "but they will fight back. You may depend upon that."

"Believe me, James, you must believe me." She pulled away from him, too distraught to be still, and began to pace.

He was at a loss to calm her. "Aye, that woman has done evil, as you said."

"Then you must help me." Her voice was like iron. "You alone do I trust. Go to see the Hannums, the Bartletts, go everywhere in the town and ask around. Go to Springfield. Find out who else has been hurt by Goodwife Parsons. Surely I am not alone. Find out who will testify on my behalf."

"Oh, Sarah, my dear." He shook his head, almost cringing. "I am not good at that kind of thing. I don't know—if—"

"JAMES!"

He winced at the sharp command.

"You *must* find those who will help me, those who know that Mary Parsons is a witch."

His eyes scanned the room as if searching for something. "*Someone* must, I know that. I've said this before, but if it means *I* must solicit the testimony, I'm afeard I am not up to the task. What should I say? How would people receive me?"

You sniveling fool, Sarah thought. She could not stand the sight of him. "You are useless—no man!" she cried. "Think you that Joseph Parsons hesitated to come to his wife's defense? Think you that he now stands dumb and useless in the midst of the room? Ooh!" She threw up her hands as she ran out the door.

Though he spent the rest of the day looking over the meadow, into the woodlot and on the streets of the town, James Bridgeman could not find his wife. At last, at dusk she reappeared and went straight to the great bedstead where she remained for days.

While Sarah lay in her bed of woe, taking only sack and broth and bread, James wandered from house to house in Northampton knocking on doors, talking to townsfolk over back fences, even picking his way across a field to talk with William Hannum. There he found that the Hannums had evidence worth mentioning. Honor Hannum already had promised to tell the story about Mary bewitching her yarn. Now she further agreed to say that ever since she had refused to allow her daughter Abigail to go into service at Goodman Parsons' house, her formerly healthy, tractable daughter had been sickly and unhelpful. The goodwife was certain that Mary Parsons' spiteful witchery had caused the change in her child. Beyond that, after Mary had cursed Hannum for driving her brother's oxen too hard, his own ox had died, and he agreed to put that loss at Mary's feet.

With this news Sarah revived, for her husband had given her hope. Thereafter they worked on her defense together. She would testify about the death of her last child, and how her son John had been struck down by Mary Parsons' familiar spirit in the form of a large bird.

GOSSIP HAD TRAVELED downriver, infecting Springfield. At every house along Town Street, in every alley and byway, people talked about Sarah Bridgeman and the trouble she was in. Middlesex County magistrates had asked John Pynchon to gather depositions there. No fire burned in the ordinary on the hot, humid day when Pynchon went in search of information. The room was dark and smelled of rancid smoke and spilled beer. John Pynchon's face was remarkably like his father's. But unlike his broad father, he was tall and slim. He was also fairer, but with the same large eyes, prominent nose and sensual mouth, all fitting his large frame more handsomely. Local gossip had led the richest, most prominent man along the Connecticut River to the ordinary in search of one man. He found that man sitting alone in a dark corner—as far away from a window as possible. Pynchon approached the lonely figure huddled over a tankard of strong beer.

"What possesses a man to come to the ordinary alone in the bright of day?"

Quite still except for his pale, deep-set eyes, the cooper John Dover glanced briefly at Pynchon then looked away. "What possesses ye to speak to the likes of me?" His voice carried no trace of humor.

"County business."

"I have naught to do with the county." Dover shifted his weight, resting his chin in the cup of one hand. "All the same, sit ye down, Mister Pynchon."

Pynchon took a seat, placing his leather satchel on the floor beside him. "A man cannot live in Springfield and be unaware of what's going on upriver. I am sure you've heard of the slander case."

"There ain't been no slander," Dover growled, taking a pipe from his pocket.

"Charges of slander have been filed," Pynchon said. "Just tell me what you've heard Goodwife Bridgeman say."

"She's said naught to me, but she's right about the wife of Joseph Parsons." The cooper tapped his pipe against his open palm.

"Right, you say? Then you know what she has charged?"

"Aye. Witchcraft." Dover regarded Pynchon as if he was a naif.

"Tell me what you know."

With a sly smile, Dover put down his pipe. "Back during the witch excitement, I went to Parsons' house to finish up some barrels and heard him tell his wife she was led by an evil spirit."

Pynchon was dubious. "What prompted this speech?"

"I know not, but she did not deny it. She said that he was the cause of it because he had locked her in the cellar and left her where it was dark and full of spirits. What's more, Sarah Bridgeman ain't alone. I've heard others say things about her. Are ye going to arrest them?"

"The court will want to hear from them. May I have their names?"

Dover snorted, looking deep into his nearly empty tankard. "George Colton told me that one night under the full of the moon he seen her go through the swamp in her shift. He followed her, and though he were wet to his knees, her shift was dry. Now, how did she walk on water, if she ain't a witch? And 'twas William Branch who told me Joseph Parsons hisself suspected she be a witch. I tell you, Mary Parsons ain't no ordinary wife, and Goodwife Bridgeman should not be punished for speaking the truth."

Once Pynchon determined that Dover had given him all the information he could, he took a quill pen, a small pot of ink, and a sheet of paper from his satchel. After writing a brief summary of Dover's testimony, he read it back to the man and asked if what he had written was accurate. When Dover affirmed that it was, Pynchon wrote, "I hereto set my mark" and asked him to sign.

Dover made his mark, a swirl like a seashell, and handed the quill to Pynchon, who signed and dated it himself. He thanked Dover, and with a heavy heart set out to find William Branch and George Colton. Joseph Parsons was an old friend, and it weighed heavily on Pynchon to think that he might be headed for serious grief.

As he walked away from the ordinary, Pynchon counted it good luck to see the carpenter William Branch across the street with his wife. They appeared to be on their way to the wharf. "Goodman Branch," Pynchon called. "A word with you, if you please."

Joanna Branch was no longer content to send her husband shopping. No matter how well she described what she wanted, he always came home with something inferior. She was not sure if this was a plot against her, or if he was simply witless. For weeks Branch had promised her a trip across the river, and they were on their way to the store. Both Branches looked surprised to see John Pynchon beckon to them, though Joanna was thrilled by the great man's notice. For years she had admired Pynchon and his beautifully dressed wife at meeting. Though long ago she had admonished herself for it, her worldly desires had led her to stare and to covet Amy Pynchon's wardrobe. Quickly she straightened her shawl and corrected her expression to one of delight.

Pynchon crossed the street to explain his mission and asked Branch what he had heard about the goodwives Bridgeman and Parsons and the quarrel between them.

Joanna began, "As I am Goodwife Bridgeman's closest friend—"

But Pynchon ignored her, speaking to her husband instead. "Goodman Branch, I must hear from you on this matter. Your neighbor John Dover declares that Joseph Parsons told his wife she was led by evil spirits, and beyond that stated that you bear out his opinion. How say you?"

"Aye," Branch said, "when Goodman Parsons lived here he himself told me he suspected her. He had to hide the key from her, or she would go out at night, and he told me that wherever he hid the key his wife, like magic, would find it. And he said, in my hearing, 'God preserve her with his angels.'"

Joanna could not keep silent. "Hear me out, sir," she broke in eagerly, "for there is more to tell." Pynchon barely listened to her prattle on that she knew firsthand many telling things about Goodwife Parsons. Something about the woman made him want to be on his way. He thanked them and bid them farewell.

For some time George Colton had had business dealings with Pynchon, as had most everyone else in Springfield, but Colton was hardly reliant on Pynchon for his bread. Other tenant farmers rented land long-term, leaving Pynchon with most of their profits, but Colton was an independent renter who leased land short-term, and then only when it lined his own pockets. Also militia quartermaster, he dealt with Pynchon for supplies and provisions and was in his sixth term as selectman. Unlike John Dover and William Branch, Colton lived near the top of Town Street, where he welcomed Pynchon into his front room, offering him a seat on a handsome paneled chair.

Pynchon commenced by reciting the story he'd heard of Colton's claim that after seeing Mary Parsons in the swamp at night, wading in her shift, he'd followed her through the water and seen her come out dry.

Colton snorted. "What twaddle. You may rest assured, I've never waded through the swamp at night, nor did Goodwife Parsons, I'll warrant you."

Pynchon wanted to be sure. "I have a witness who told me you said you did."

"Confound him, he's either mistaken or a liar, and I'd like to know the scoundrel's name."

"I cannot say, 'twould be against my oath. Surely you have heard that Joseph Parsons has charged James Bridgeman's wife with slander. Some folks in Springfield think she may be telling the truth."

Colton shook his head. "I doubt it—though, years back, I did see Mary Parsons act strange at meeting, in the same way as the daughters of Mister Thatcher. People did say, you know, that the girls were, for a time, possessed by the Devil."

With all the information he'd collected, John Pynchon sent Joseph Parsons a letter. "You must strike against these charges, Joseph. Everything they said sets the course for an indictment of witchcraft against your wife."

James Bridgeman traveled downriver to Springfield and, like Pynchon, made visits to households up and down the streets of the town. He visited old friends, talked about Sarah's troubles, and enlisted support for her cause.

Joseph also went to work immediately, calling on witnesses who could refute the testimony taken in Northampton and Springfield. Within a few days he filed a response with the Northampton magistrates, for witnesses had signed and given him eleven new depositions refuting the Bridgemans' depositions. The three women who assisted at the birth of Sarah Bridgeman's last child testified that the child was born small and sickly, and Sarah herself had said she thought it had taken cold. John Boughton said he'd skinned William Hannum's cow and found four or five gallons of matter in its belly—enough to cause the cow's death. And, he said, when he showed this to Hannum, he had called out to his wife saying that they need not fear witchcraft. George Alexander and Samuel Allen, who were present when a snake bit Hannum's ox, declared, "We saw nothing but what might come to pass in an ordinary way and we killed the rattlesnake." Both Ann Bartlett and Margaret Wright said that they too had purchased yarn from Honor Hannum and found it defective. Goodwives Edwards and Alexander said in their signed depositions that the Hannums had told them "that they had nothing against Mary Parsons."

Joseph took these collected testimonies to the Hannums' house and showed them what their neighbors had said. Both Hannums then swung over to Parsons' side, accusing James Bridgeman of having coerced them into testifying against Mary. Joseph also traveled to Springfield to talk with Pynchon, and there he explained to his business associate and friend his side of the testimony Dover had given. He persuaded Pynchon that he himself had been wrong to worry about Mary's soul, and that he now had full confidence in his wife's innocence.

At last, when John Pynchon finally read the depositions gathered in Northampton, not at all pleased to be included in the affair, he denied ever saying anything to Sarah Bridgeman about Mary Parsons "not being right."

If the whole business had been a nightmare for Mary, it had been a wild ride on a runaway horse for Sarah. At first Sarah was exhilarated by the hope that she would, at last, make people understand, but when the last depositions were taken and holes punched in every one of her accusations she fell into the depths of despair.

On September 8, after the deliberations of the court, a warrant was issued in Springfield for the arrest of Sarah Bridgeman, demanding that her husband put up £100 as surety for her personal appearance at the next county court, to be held at Cambridge on October 7. There she was to answer to the complaint of Joseph Parsons for slandering his wife.

Though Sarah had known it was coming, James tried to explain the warrant to his grief-stricken wife, who once again had taken to her bed, ill from shock and disappointment. She was five months along in her seventh pregnancy and had been unable to keep food on her stomach for two days. "How can they arrest me?" she asked in tears, for she knew how ill she was and swore she could feel her baby spinning inside. "Ah, James, though I lie still as death, the child will not rest."

"I don't have a hundred pounds, Sarah," James said, ashamed and helpless.

Constable Alexander Edwards soon came for Sarah and took her to his house, where both he and his wife could watch over her until she could appear in court. Her health did not improve, and Goodman Edwards soon filed a document with the court saying that she was weak and with child and unable to appear without hazard to her life.

Without Sarah Bridgeman in attendance, the Magistrates'

Court convened in Cambridge as scheduled, and after due delib-
eration the Honored Bench of Magistrates rendered the following
decision:

> The court having read the attachments and pursued the evi-
> dences respectively ... do find that the defendant hath without
> just grounds raised a great scandal and reproach upon the
> plaintiff . . . and do therefore order that the defendant shall
> make acknowledgement before the inhabitants of the places
> where the said parties dwell: vizt: North Hampton and also at
> Springfield at some publick meeting at each place by order of
> Mr. Pynchon or Mr. Holliocke ... within 60 days next ensuing
> and in case of default having notice of the time at each place
> the said defendant, vizt: James Bridgeman shall pay damages
> to the plaintiff: ten pounds sterling: Also this court doth order
> that the defendant shall pay to the plaintiff his cost of court,
> vizt: seven pounds one shilling and eight pence.

Sarah's punishment was cruel. Like other slanderers, she
was ordered to proclaim in a public place that she was a liar. But
Sarah was deathly ill. To save her the shame of chastening herself
publicly in both Springfield and Northampton, her husband paid
Joseph Parsons the equivalent of seventeen pounds, one shilling,
and eight pence in corn and cash.

X

This evening, if my heart deceive me not, I had some
sweet workings of soul . . . an encouragement unto
me to look unto Christ, that he would do that for me,
which he has promised to do for some, nor dare I exclude
myself; but if the Lord will help me, I desire to lie at
his feet, and accept of grace in his own way, and with
his own time . . . Though I am dead, without strength,
help or hope in myself, yet the Lord requireth nothing
at my hands in my own strength; but that by his power
I should look to him, to work all his works in me and
for me. When I find a dead heart, the thoughts of this
are exceeding sweet and reviving, being full of grace and
discovering the very heart and love of Jesus.

—Eleazar Mather (1637–1669)

Northampton, 1657

EVEN THOUGH THE town fathers made it their business to
exclude undesirables—Quakers, Jews, Baptists, and single
men of unknown origin—the town's population reached nearly
two hundred in the first three years after Northampton was
settled. The laws required each new settler to prove his moral
status and ability to support himself and his family. Any man

who appeared in need of assistance, financially or otherwise, was asked to leave. Visitors to the town could stay up to thirty-one days without having their characters and pocketbooks inspected, but after that probationary period they were invited to a meeting of the selectmen and had better have a way to show that they would be an asset to the community.

Early on, the village set aside a common ground for grazing cattle, with a fence to keep the cattle and sheep out of crops growing in the meadow. A cowkeeper was employed to look after the cattle, and village children were made responsible for the rounding-up and herding, for cows were milked at home where they were housed overnight, safe from wolves. Until breeding time, the highly prized town bull was kept separate from the cows in his own shed at the edge of the meadow. The cowkeeper watched over him, fed him, and was expected to capture him when he escaped.

The Meeting House dominated the crest of the hill, its yard the center of town. Next in importance was the ordinary, so vital an institution in the colony that fines were imposed on towns without a tavern. John Webb, town blacksmith, land surveyor, and famous wolf hunter, was offered land, pasture and tax exemptions to entice him to become the publican.

There was no mistaking The Wolf's Head, for the ordinary was flagged by a grisly sign depicting in relief the carved and painted head of a dead wolf, eyes closed, red tongue hanging out. The building had two public rooms on the ground floor and a brewhouse in the rear. A huge fireplace took up the center of one wall of the barroom. Webb served beer, ale and rum drinks, the latter potation being imported from Barbados and very expensive as a result.

While the fellowship offered at the tavern was important to civilization on the frontier, drunkenness was strictly forbidden. Drunkards went around town with a label sewn on their coats—a large red D on a white background. Never was the publican allowed to serve Indians. Should he break the rules, his license was revoked. The gristmill and sawmill were the only other public buildings in town.

Every citizen—only men were citizens—was expected to hold public office of some sort. But after the slander trial, Joseph's business endeavors were too pressing to allow it. He had no time to give to the town and paid twenty shillings in lieu of public service that year. At the next election he was once again made selectman, a vote of confidence from the town, leaving his enemies without a doubt that the majority of important people supported the verdict against Sarah Bridgeman.

Joseph Parsons' acreage sustained a fine young orchard, a fenced field adjoining the house where he grew crops for household use, grazing pastures for his horses, a kitchen garden, a barn, smokehouse, and brewhouse. His wife was among the best-dressed women in town, her gowns purchased on his many trips to Boston. His four children, all sons, owned books of their own and dressed in fine clothes for the Sabbath. Joseph owned more cattle, sheep and horses than any man, along with dogs for hunting and protection. But unlike John Pynchon, who was revered like royalty, Joseph was an object of envy and suspicion. By regularly performing his public duty, however, and attending meeting every Sabbath he was in town, he kept gossip and complaints about his worldliness and ambition to a minimum.

Mary expected her sixth child in June. Though married to a wealthy man, her days were filled with hard work. Together she and Elspeth cared for four boys, the kitchen garden, certain of the smaller animals on the property, the production of necessary household items such as soap and candles, plus all the laundry, sewing, mending and cleaning. At harvest time they helped Alice, the cook, dry fruits and vegetables and pack the cellar full of dried beans, onions, squash, pumpkins and other less-perishable produce. Though the cook was also in charge of the brewing and the smoking of meat, she could not do it alone.

IN SPRING THE meadowland filled with the sounds of meltwater trickling out of the forest and down the banks of the river, loosening the ice at its edges. Slowly the ice let go with sighs, creaks and groans. When warm days brought more meltwater, great blocks of ice broke loose and piled into screeching ice jams. At last the floes exploded in a deafening rage as huge blocks of ice careened downstream toward the sea, uprooting trees, eroding the riverbank and reshaping the river.

The sound of the ice floes filled most hearts with joy, for it meant spring would soon follow. But for Sarah Bridgeman the rumbling sounded like the Horsemen of the Apocalypse riding up from Hell. The Bridgemans were now regarded warily by most in the town. Sarah had been shamed, labeled a liar and slanderer. Her neighbors, afraid of becoming her next victims, steered well clear. After her allies betrayed her, Sarah would not even look at Honor Hannum. Friendless, she did not know what she would do if not for her sister-in-law who lived next door. Helen was the only woman in town willing to befriend her. As for her other brothers' wives, Sarah had never liked them. Whenever she went out, Sarah walked with furious footsteps and appeared in meeting like a stone.

In January she gave birth to a daughter, and in February the little one died. Folks shook their heads and thought more softly of her. As for Mary Parsons, she shuddered when she heard the news and, like others, pitied Sarah. In her prayers she asked God to give the Bridgemans a son, a healthy child who would live and grow and give aid to his parents.

When Sarah's babe was born, she had asked James to let her name the child Patience, and he agreed. "That is what I must have now," she had added. I am good, she thought. I have not excited God's wrath. Only patience and persistence will help me unmask Mary Parsons, who offers my flesh and blood to the Devil.

Yet another torment came upon Sarah—her fascination with Joseph Parsons. He was a striking figure, virile, the father of sons, and every time she saw him she could not help wondering how it would be to lie with him. But then she would admonish herself with reminders that he was, after all, too fixed on his own aggrandizement and shameless ambition. And yet she dreamed of him, of his taking hold of her with his generous hands, his caresses, his entering her and moving against her until her body shook with a pleasure she had never known outside her sleep. She would wake in a sweat, still enthralled, sure she must have conceived a son. This, she knew, was also part of Mary's mischief, for Sarah was a good woman who would never fall to that kind of sin, and she was horrified that she had to endure it in her sleep.

When Mary gave birth in June, Sarah said to her husband, "Another son—now she has five and I but one."

"But Sarah, my dear, yours are the most comely daughters in Northampton, and beyond that, they are good children. We have much to be thankful for. Have faith, the child you now carry will be a son."

Sarah was disappointed in her husband, for he had fallen even farther behind her brothers. Richard and John had married women from prominent families with substantial dowries, giving them a head start in life. Her own dowry was better than some, but James had not used it well. Her brother John also had a thriving business as the only cobbler in town. Two of her brothers had been voted selectmen, while her husband had not. James was asked to do less important jobs, such as sealer of weights and measures, supervisor of highways, and other minor offices.

She recognized his kindness and knew he was a good father and husband who would do anything he could for her, but in her mind he was meek and of no consequence. There was nothing remarkable about his square face. He was of average height and build. His eyes were neither blue nor brown but hazel. His almost colorless hair did not hang perfectly straight, nor did it curl. While most men wore their hair long enough to just miss the shoulder, James wore his cropped just below his ears, blending with his beard. Though the ruling ideas behind Bridgeman's life were reliability, loyalty, humility, endurance and patience, he bored his wife. She chided herself for all her wicked thoughts about the man who adored her. She wished to adore him too, but she could not overcome her disappointment.

In early summer, while gathering wild strawberries, Sarah saw the Indian women working in their cornfields. Some years they moved from their winter quarters to other planting grounds, but that year they'd come to Northampton and set up summer wigwams at the back of the Langtons' and Hanchets' lots, not far from the river. They would spend the summer catching and drying fish.

The Pocumtucks were friendly, and sometimes came into the village to hide from their enemies. One day during the previous summer Sarah had been frightened out of her wits when she walked in from the garden to find two Pocumtuck braves squatting on her kitchen floor. They had dodged a small band of Mohawks in the meadow to take shelter inside. In response to her terrified screams, they sprang up hastily and backed out the door, for they were a most unwarlike people.

Sarah had seen Indian women, shamefully bare to the waist, working in their fields. "Thank God, we made a law against that," she sighed aloud as she carried kitchen scraps outside to the pigs. And what colorful fools they made of themselves, dressed in a mixture of English and Indian clothing. She had seen the strangest things: their painted faces worn with powdered hair, and beads, shells, and feathers pinned all over their waistcoats and skirts. The men, being fond of English coats, wore them with their breechcloths in summer and under their animal-skin robes in winter. But Sarah was most terrified by the braves' bizarre heads, plucked of all hair except a fringe down the middle.

Remembering the two braves who had made themselves at home by her fire, Sarah looked up from the farmyard toward the Indians' cornfield and shuddered. She looked to the left toward the cowshed and to the right at the house. They might come again, she thought. Ah, the endurance and resolve it takes to have savages as neighbors. Should a cow break out of the common fence and wander into the forest, she's fair game for them. They had never tasted beef until we brought our cattle, and now they want it at every meal—that and spirits. They cannot restrain themselves from taking beer and rum, the stronger the better—that and desecrating the Sabbath. No matter how often we notify them it is against the law to powwow on the day of rest, they beat their drums and chant, despoiling our ears with the sounds of Devil worship.

THE SELECTMEN OF Northampton, Joseph among them, met to consider another serious threat to their community: violation of the sumptuary laws. These were laws first put in place long before, in England, as a way to keep the classes distinct in appearance. But the Puritans had embellished the law to include virtue in dress. As a safeguard against vanity, Saints must appear pious and be modest in dress. Still the law held close the notion that one ought to be able to judge a person by the way he dressed. Those of high income or class did not want to be fooled by a peasant in disguise. Young people were the chief disregarders of the laws, and the selectmen met to put a stop to it.

"Charges of dressing in a flaunting manner have been brought against the daughter of John King, the daughter of Widow Walford and the wife of Walter Lee," Robert Bartlett said, casting his eyes around the room. "Please come forward."

Slowly three embarrassed young women approached the selectmen, properly dressed for the occasion in modest, somber-colored woolen skirts and waistcoats with white aprons and coifs.

"Women of your condition should not garb yourselves like gentlewomen. Do you know what is forbidden you?" he asked.

"Well, yer honor," said Goodwife Lee, "I ain't allowed gold or lace or ribbons. That much I know."

"You are charged with wearing silk. Did you know that is against the law?" he said, regarding the young woman who stood humbly before him.

"I may know—but 'twas a weakness in me that I have ever since repented. I were tempted by the green silk given me."

"Priscilla King, have you repented of your crime?" He looked at the deposition lying on the table in front of him. "You were accused of—"

"Ringlets, Goodman Bartlett," Priscilla said, her hair tucked neatly inside her coif.

"So it is—ringlets. Pray, what have you to say for yourself?"

"Well, sir, I shall never do it more. My father's already whipped me. Methinks I have learned my lesson."

"And you?" He gazed into Katherine Walford's comely face. "What vanity did you affect?"

"None!"

"None?" He looked amused. "What say you? Do you stand before me defiant, or falsely accused?"

"Falsely accused of wearing ribbons at my sleeves," she said. "Ye may search my mother's house. I own no ribbons."

"Were they lent you, then?"

"Nay!" She tossed her head with vehemence.

Joseph was riffling through his papers. "Who accused this woman?" When no one answered, he called, "Who reported this maid?"

"There is no name on record here," John Lyman said.

"Let the maid go," Joseph said, for there was something in her manner that made him believe her.

The men all nodded, and Bartlett spoke for all. "Go in peace, Katherine Walford."

She smiled her thanks at Joseph, gave a curtsy, and turned to go, impressing him with her neatness and pluck. Joseph made a note to himself to keep an eye out for the daughter of Widow Walford. The selectmen fined the other women ten shillings each and instructed them to go and sin no more.

FOR THREE YEARS the people of Northampton had gone without spiritual leadership in the form of a minister, but by summer they called Eleazar Mather, the twenty-one-year-old son of the first minister at Dorchester, Richard Mather, and elder brother of Increase Mather, who would one day make a great name for himself.

The young minister, who had come to the frontier on a trial basis, had graduated from Harvard at the age of nineteen. At the time of his arrival in Northampton he had neither been ordained nor married. He was given a four-acre house lot at the top of Bartlett Street, next to John Lyman's, along with forty acres of meadowland to farm.

Sarah Bridgeman listened to Mister Mather's first sermon

believing his arrival was a sign of good to come, for as he spoke she proudly held an infant son in her arms. As the minister's voice filled the room, she looked at her daughters sitting beside her: Sarah Jr., nearly a woman and the apple of her father's eye, young Martha, her own help and comfort, and little Rebecca, the star-crossed beauty whom Sarah could not look at without a stab to her heart. James sat across the center aisle with their thirteen-year-old son John. For once Sarah was feeling thankful and at peace, until she looked at John, who still walked with a limp. She did not permit herself to look at Mary Parsons, who sat a few rows forward, though she had already noticed her dress of blue brocade, a two-tiered gold and pearl necklace over a lace collar, auburn curls peeking from underneath a lace coif, and a gauzy white hood.

Years had passed since Sarah's conviction of slander. Following the trial she had been regarded in the town with suspicion and caution. As time passed, new people moved in, old residents forgot their hard feelings, but Sarah did not forget. She had learned her lesson. She watched her tongue, careful of what she said.

In the days immediately following the new minister's arrival in Northampton the town enjoyed a time of general well-being. Life went on unperturbed by major catastrophe, uneventful, except in small ways, for its citizens. Mister Mather would marry a minister's daughter and be ordained at the end of his probation. Following his term as Clarke of the Band, Joseph Parsons would be elected to another term as selectman. After his election to the office of constable, James Bridgeman's stock would rise in the town. A ferryboat moored at last on the banks of the Connecticut would become a great convenience. But at the end of winter Sarah and James Bridgeman had to watch helplessly as their nine-month-old son Hezekiah died with a fever.

XI

Moses describeth a woman thus: "At the first beginning,"
saith he, "a woman was made to be a helper unto man."
And so they are indeed, for she helpeth to spend and
consume that which man painfully getteth. He also saith
that they were made of the rib of a man, and that their
froward nature showeth; for a rib is a crooked thing good
for nothing else, and women are crooked by nature, for
small occasion will cause them to be angry.

—Joseph Swetnam
The Arraignment of Lewd, idle,
froward, and unconstant women . . . 1615

. . . woman was made of a rib out of the side of Adam; not
out of his feet to be trampled upon by him, but out of his
side to be equal with him, under his arm to be protected,
and near his heart to be loved.

—Matthew Henry (1662–1714)
Commentary on the Whole Bible, 1706

WHILE THE COOK was busy over the breakfast fire Joseph poured his own cup of beer, unmindful of his sons gathering for the morning meal. Impatient, he looked out the window at snow still falling from a white sky and wind-drifts pushed against the north side of the barn. Done with his early chores, he was eager to be out in the woods with his sons and his dogs.

"Yer food is on the table," Alice said, her voice utterly cheerless.

Joseph sat down between his namesake and young John. Both boys looked as though one day they would be as tall as their father. He was proud of his boys, and whether at work on the farm or hunting, kept them with him. Joseph studied his plate full of johnnycakes, baked beans and roast venison. He downed his beer, poured another, and seasoned everything with maple syrup.

Elspeth and the younger boys, Samuel, Ebenezer and Jonathan, had taken their places at the table. Mary, who was four months pregnant, took her place beside her husband and bowed her head.

Joseph, with his mouth full, said the grace. "O Lord, we thank you for your loving provisions. Amen."

His shaggy-haired deerhounds, painfully alert to the smell of food, licked the drool off their chins. They dared not approach the table or the children's laps, for as pups their poor manners had led to beatings, and now, their wills tamed, they did not stir. Tormented by their own keen sense of smell, they settled themselves by the hearth hoping that one of the children would drop a tasty morsel.

The meal progressed without conversation. The only voices were those of the youngest children, who burbled childish demands, silenced by stern looks from their father. The eldest children and Elspeth were not allowed to speak, and Mary had nothing of import to say. Sharing her meal with two-year-old David, who sat in his highchair, Mary knew where Joseph would spend his day and had plenty to think about in organizing her own.

Joseph had given up complaining about Mary and her behavior at mealtimes. Though he believed Elspeth should be the one to have her meal interrupted by the baby, Mary insisted on feeding her own tiny son, offering him bits of food and a small sip of watered beer, delighting in him. Joseph was quite aware that Mary hoped the child she carried was a girl. She had taken the trouble to make sure her wish would come true. Last June, just as the sunset filled the sky with a rosy glow, he had watched her gather

274

wild lupine from the meadow. She dried the blue-violet blossoms, and with a prayer on her lips, ate them. A few hours later, in the dark warmth of their bed, she roused him and he gave her a child. And after six sons, Joseph hoped for a daughter himself.

He devoured the last of his food. "I'll be off," he said, rising. He grabbed his cloak off the peg by the door and motioned to his two eldest sons. "You've eaten your fill, come along." Joseph Jr. and John scooped up what was left on their plates and clambered out of their chairs as their father laughed at their puplike eagerness.

Eight-year-old Samuel begged, "Let me come hunting, Father. I'm big enough now."

Joseph regarded the boy, cocked his head, then smiled. "Very well. Get your cloak." He turned to John. "You, son, shall be in charge of your brother."

"Ah, Father, I'm big too," chimed Ebenezer, a six-year-old with bright-red hair and a freckled face.

"Nay, Eben, you'll slow us down." The head of the house had spoken. The disappointed boy lowered his eyes and backed toward his mother.

Joseph's three eldest sons rushed to claim their cloaks as their father took the long guns down from the rack. He handed one to each boy and, shouldering his own, whistled for his dogs. They headed out the door. Joseph couldn't help laughing at little Sam as he labored manfully to shoulder his weapon. At the barn they took down their snowshoes from the wall and lashed them to their boots, then made for the woods. Excited to do what they were bred for, the long-legged dogs raced ahead, bounding like deer through drifts of snow. Squirrels leapt up the trees, rabbits scurried for cover. Looking for bigger game, the hunting party plodded on, intending to bring back a buck.

From her chair Mary had watched them go through the door. In Joseph she saw a man she hardly knew at times. His body had broadened through back and belly, and his face was no longer fresh and young but red from the sun and wind beating upon it all year round. Only his brown eyes and head of blond wavy hair had not changed. He was a man of great appetites, and she worried about the long hours he spent away from home and the farm. He had made his portion of the fur trade easy to manage, hired a number of hands to do farm work, taken over the ordinary, and opened a general store.

Looking worried, Eben sidled up to his mother. "How can it be, Mother, that I'm too big for your lap but too small to go hunting?"

His younger brother Jonathan empathized. "I can't go hunting either, Eben. I'll play with you."

Eben began to cry. "But I'm bigger than you."

Mary took the older boy's hand and pulled him into her arms. "You *are* a big lad, Eben, just not big enough to hunt. This is the first time for Sam, you know, and he's older than you. Your turn will come, dearest child." She cuddled him to her breast. How she loved this little boy. She knew why she favored him, for he was very like her brother Lawrence. She couldn't look at Eben without thinking of Lawrence at that age and remembering the early days in Hartford when she and her brother were always hungry. Like wild birds, they ran off to the sunny side of a hill to eat their fill of blueberries. Long ago days when her mother made her do the laundry with only Lawrence to help. She remembered how they had dropped the laundry basket beside the river where a still pool had formed, how she had raged about her terrible life so far removed from Painswick Parish, how hard Lawrence had tried to change her mood. While she scrubbed clothes clean on a low flat stone at the water's edge he had implored her to tell a story. For the most part all the other children ignored Mary's temper, but Lawrence found her rages fearsome.

"Tell me about the crossing, Mary," he'd begged. "I like the part about the great storm. You remember better."

She could not resist. Though she loved telling that story, she wanted to turn the occasion to her advantage. "I'll tell the story if, all the day long, you promise to be my slave."

"Aye, Mary. Now tell me."

While her little brother settled himself to listen, she picked up a flat chunk of dead wood. He lay flat on his stomach on the river bank and trailed his fingers in the water.

"We boarded our ship with all that we could carry and many chickens, the goats, and the cow, and did set sail on a bright sunny day in June." She leaned forward to lay the chunk of wood on the water, guiding it gently along as though it were a ship bobbing over the ocean. "That was many years ago," she said, capturing it with her fingers. "You were very small, and Mother kept you on a leash so that you would not be swept away into the sea. At first the wind was calm, so calm that the pennons hardly flew from the masts. But then up came a great wind," she said, dramatically. "And the seas did storm, and we were wonderful sick as we came. On and on the winds did blow, and the waves rose up, near over the ship they did ride, and the salt spray blew, stinging our eyes and making us cry because we were so afeard."

The boy's eyes sparkled with excitement. "Make the seas storm!"

She became very serious, like God himself, splashing the water with the flat of her hand, making waves for her little ship to ride. With a turn of her wrist, she twirled her fingers around it, creating a whirlpool into which it sank and disappeared before it bobbed up again. The two children had watched as slowly it floated toward the middle of the river, and then, as the make-believe ship picked up the current and was carried away, Lawrence had hooted and yelled. Leaping to their feet they ran along Little River, following as far as they could to watch their craft float away on its course to join the Great River.

Now, for Mary those memories of the past seemed ever dearer. She knew she had been part of a great adventure, and that coming to New England had brought her to the man she loved. She looked happily at her little boys, felt a faint stirring in her womb, and was thankful.

REBECCA BRIDGEMAN HAD confounded her mother by surviving well into her eleventh year—the lustiest of all the Bridgeman children. While both Sarah Jr. and Martha were quiet, sweet, obedient daughters, Rebecca was willful, filled with boundless energy, and cleverer than anyone else in the household. Sarah had begun to wonder if the comet fixed in the sky on the night of this daughter's birth might have signaled not the child's doom but a rebellious spirit. Though Sarah had yet to interpret it fully, Rebecca seemed unlike any of the women in the family, indeed any child she had ever known or heard of. And James, the girl's father, agreed, while commenting on her remarkable intelligence. They watched Rebecca grow, dazzled by her beauty, hoping she would escape Satan's greedy notice.

Sarah tried to keep Rebecca close to home and away from danger, but the child's spirit would not allow her mother to suffocate her. She found ways to claim her freedom, and when her mother's back was turned she often slipped away to explore the meadow and the edge of the forest, where she came to know the birds. She whistled to them, watched how they flew, listened to their songs, searched for their nests. She knew their favorite trees and asked around about their names. Watching them fly away in autumn and return in spring, she wondered where they had gone. Wishing she could fly too, she asked anyone who would listen to tell her why the birds went away but returned in spring. She was told that, like bears, they hid in caves and other secret places in the woods where they hibernated for the winter.

In search of fresh air and quiet, Mary Parsons returned to the spring woods. Soon after her arrival in Northampton she had found the perfect spot, not unlike the glade she remembered from childhood where she'd first met Goody Crespet. The formation of both glades had begun many years before, when heavy snowfall broke the uppermost branches of the forest canopy. Through the opening, sunlight had stolen in to the forest floor, and with the arrival of light the nearby trees had leaned in, throwing themselves off balance. Along came the winds and more heavy snows, adding weight to the branches of the unbalanced trees, toppling them. Year after year the cycle recurred, and more sunlight came into the forest glade where the dead trees at its center crumbled into nourishment for insects and new vegetation. The glade would not last forever, for young trees would grow strong in the sunlight and tall enough to shade the ground, eventually returning the glade to dark forest.

But for the moment Mary's glade was carpeted with grasses and rimmed with bracken ferns, wild herbs, ground pine, wild-flowers and sedges—all plants for Mary's larder, for her infusions and decoctions. She found peace in the glade, where she came to be alone and sleep in the sun. Here, and in the surrounding woods, she found goldenrod for treating fevers and to make a yellow dye, the red berries of squaw-vine to make an astringent and speed the process of childbirth, and lady's-slipper, whose roots she crushed to make a sedative and remedy for insomnia. Though she grew many of the herbs she needed to run her household, the forest added to her stores. And, as much as it was her pharmacy, it was her cloister.

In June, when wild strawberries were ripe in the meadow, Rebecca walked alone near the edge of the wood eating her fill. The moment her mother's attention turned from her to the laundry she had run away. Rebecca knew that when she returned she would be punished and made to stay indoors, but she wouldn't mind terribly, because she had a book hidden under her mattress— *Orbis Pictus* or *Visible World; or A nomenclature and pictures of all the chief things that are in the world.* It belonged to her brother and was designed to teach science and Latin. The day before, she had stolen it. As to other books, she had long had *The Primer, or an easie way to teach children the true reading of English, With a necessary catechisme to instruct youth,* a book that had belonged to her sisters before her. Of course, she was always welcome to read the Bible, and did. She loved Genesis best, her favorite stories being the Great Flood, especially God's granting of the rainbow as a sign, and clever Jacob and his simple, hairy brother Esau. She loved the adventures of all the wives and maidservants and young women, and how they got their husbands and babes from God. Her most favorite story was about her namesake, Rebekah, especially the part where she was given jewels and found true love.

The sun shone brightly, though a cool breeze made Rebecca pull her cloak tight. From the corner of her eye she saw the cloaked figure of a woman and guessed she was gathering strawberries on the sunny rise just above a birch grove. Curious, she walked in among the birch trees to see Mary Parsons sit down on a large flat stone, resting what looked like a full basket beside her. The child knew who she was—the beautiful lady her mother had warned her about.

"Don't go near her, my child. Remember what I say, no matter how she tempts you."

Rebecca was tempted only to look. As a breeze played about her head, the goodwife removed her coif and let her hair fall free. She pulled off her boots and stockings and wiggled her bare feet in the grass. She stretched and sighed and let the sun fall on her face. Rebecca knew she should go away, and she would, but first she had to study the woman's enviable clothes. Her deep-green cloak was of softer, lighter fabric than any Rebecca had ever seen, and the red skirt peeking from underneath looked merry and bright. She moved a bit closer and hid behind a bush—too late, for the object of her fascination looked startled and called out, "Who waits there?"

"Only I, Goodwife," Rebecca said timidly, stepping out from behind a tree. "Methinks I have troubled your solitude."

"Ah, Rebecca, good morrow," Mary said, recovered from her fright. "How came you so far on the meadow?"

"Picking strawberries," the child said, glancing over her shoulder.

"Your mother would not want you here—especially with me."

"Phoo! Don't trouble your head about that," she said, "for to be sure I shan't tell her."

Goodwife Parsons chuckled and smiled warmly.

Rebecca dawdled a moment then went to her knees. "When will your baby come, and what lies in your basket?"

"The child will be born very soon," she said. "And how lucky I would be to have a girl just like you." She smiled.

Rebecca's face brightened as she leaned over Mary's basket for a look. "I see all the berries you found, but what are these plants you carry, and how do you use them? Do you know everything about how to make simples?"

"Mercy, child, do you always ask questions in droves? Let me answer one before another is asked."

"Then what have you found?" Rebecca teased, dragging the words out.

"Ah, quite an array." Mary lifted one of her finds. "This is fairy wand, and here is vomit-root and colt's-tail—good for my children's cuts and bruises. The others I'll use for Eben's cough."

"How did you learn? Did your mother teach you? I don't think my mother is skilled in simples. Do you suppose I'm too young to learn?"

Though charmed, Mary felt painfully aware of whose child sat beside her. "I was a little older when I first took an interest, but not nearly as clever, I'll warrant. Now, you must away, or your mother will worry."

"I shall, Goodwife, but first hear this. I find you exceeding fine—not like the village women, for they find little to think on but all the things they hate about one another. Pray, may I visit your house so you can teach me?"

"Nay, Rebecca," Mary said, "your mother would not approve. I cannot go against her wishes. Now, away with you before you get me hanged."

Puzzled, the child backed away. "I dare not think on such a thing as that. Goodwife, you have made me sad, for methinks I need to learn. We could keep it a secret."

"No secrets, child. When you are a mother you will understand. One mother must not go against another. Now away," she shooed with her hands, "before we both regret this day."

Rebecca turned away, tears welling in her eyes, and without another word ran toward home. She was hurt and did not understand why. At first she felt the fault lay with her, then she decided it lay with her mother. With that, she promised herself to learn everything she could about Mary Parsons.

XII

From the altar I turn mine eye and behold
How Harry hath a new coat, and his wife another;
Then I wish it were mine, and all the web with it.
At his losing I laugh, in my heart I like it;
But at his winning I weep, and bewail the occasion.
I deem that men do ill, yet I do much worse . . .
And whoso hath more than I, maketh my heart angry.
Thus I live loveless, like an ill-tempered dog . . .

—William Langland (1332–1386)

BIG WITH CHILD, Mary sat among the village women at meeting, dressed in silk, a gauzy tiffany hood covering her head. Some wondered, silently, how she got away with it. Joseph, on the other hand, enjoyed seeing her thus. He did not worry about common pettiness, for his wife was kind to her neighbors, bought their wares, and gave generously to the poor and the sick. Ann Bartlett had warned her to be careful. But Mary loved beautiful things, and what was she to do with the gowns her husband brought her from Boston—throw them on the kitchen midden, out with the shattered plates and broken windowpanes?

She had asked Goodwife Bartlett, "Should I pretend that I do not share his wealth?"

"By my troth, I would," Ann warned, "and then I'd tell my husband to stop flaunting it."

"Is it too much to ask Christians to love me no matter how I dress?"

Ann had rolled her eyes, shaken her head and told Mary she tempted fate.

Mister Eleazar Mather was aware of the divisions among his flock—feelings against both Joseph and Mary Parsons, as well as against the Hendricks family. The latter were Dutch, spoke thickly accented English, and practiced strange customs like excessive scrubbing of their floors and personal bathing. The minister had written a covenant for his people, quite similar to covenants used by other gatherings of Saints. In it, he pointed to the importance of Christ's love. And it was to this purpose that he finally came at the end of his long sermon.

"Christ Jesus asks us to keep one unto another in brotherly love, each of us seeking only the spiritual *good* of the other—each of us subject to one another."

Sarah Bridgeman, who sat with other women in front of Mary Parsons, had other things on her mind. "I'll have no truck with Goodwife Parsons and her airs," she whispered to Goodwife Elmore, casting a snide look over her shoulder.

"Indeed, I do find it odious," Goodwife Elmore said, "to worship with a peacock."

Goodwife Lyman added her own barb. "The harlot of Springfield would do well to have that gown on her back."

"And as for *this* particular company and society of Saints," the minister went on, looking directly at Goodwives Elmore, Bridgeman and Lyman as their heads bobbed together and back, "we must promise to cleave one unto another in brotherly love and seek the best spiritual good, each of the other, engaging in mutual subjection one to another."

Mather's voice was no more than a distant rumble to Sarah Bridgeman. She had other thoughts. The women of this town do not love Mary Parsons, that much I know. With all her fine clothes and her wealthy husband, I have more friends than she. I'm glad I'm not her. I do thank God for that.

Mather read the covenant aloud, then placed it on a small table at the foot of the pulpit. He turned to face the congregation. "These things we shall promise in the sincerity of our hearts before the Lord, the examiner and trier of all hearts. And when we, through weakness, shall fail then to wait and rely upon the Lord Jesus Christ for pardon, acceptance and healing, this, and the worship of God, is the highest purpose of our coming together. Brothers and sisters, cleanse your hearts, and if you are moved by the love of Christ, sign this covenant today." He took up the quill, signed his own name, replaced the quill in the inkpot, and beckoned the faithful to come forward.

Sarah's eyes flew to Joseph Parsons, who stood among the men moving into the center aisle, which now began to fill also with women—among them the same women who had whispered against Mary during the sermon. Getting up to follow, Sarah looked contemptuously at her enemy, who kept to her seat. She watched just long enough to see Mary look up from her Bible, when it appeared to Sarah's prideful heart that the woman had tears in her eyes.

Except for the Hendricks woman, an Indian servant renamed Peggy, the feeble-minded beggar woman, and most of the children, Mary alone remained seated on the women's side. Everyone noticed. Hostile eyes probed the unrepentant figure sitting apart. Sarah saw Joseph look toward his wife, his face coloring, and she thought surely he was embarrassed. Victorious, she knew what the villagers saw—a defiant sinner callously refusing to covenant with them.

Joseph held his tongue all afternoon and evening until that night when they were alone.

"'Tis a dangerous folly, Mary," he said, his voice rising. "By not going forward to sign, you foolishly inflame your enemies. Do you mean to flaunt defiance?"

"Will it never end?" Mary cried. "It took every power within me not to stand and shout, 'Hypocrites!' They would see me burn in Hell, Joseph. Nay, I'll not be subject to those who do not love me. With my heart full of anger, I could not, in good conscience, sign that covenant."

He all but yelled. "What a fool's game you play!"

"I cannot love them!" she answered heatedly. "I am not sainted. It pains me, Joseph, that you signed, for you know them as well as I."

"I signed because I must. I have significant business interests in this place. I cannot turn my back on the people here."

"Is that the heart of a covenant? To aid Joseph Parsons in his business dealings? To promote your prominence in the country? The covenant asks that we be converted to love."

"You think you know everything." Furious, Joseph threw on his cloak, grabbed his broad hat, and left the house, slamming the door behind him. Sabbath or not, he headed for his office at The Wolf's Head where he could work off his anger. Papers awaited him on his desk.

At midnight, Joseph returned to find Mary awake, propped up on pillows, reading her Bible by candlelight. She wore a veil over her head and a long white nightgown trimmed in lace. Her heart leapt as he entered the room, for she hated their quarrels and was eager to tell him she understood his disappointment. She craved peace, and the comfort of his arms.

"Joseph, you are home at last." She did her best to make her voice cheerful.

He said nothing as he threw his hat toward a chair. It landed on the floor. He let his cloak fall, then, removing his shirt, turned to look at his wife. "Ah, she takes to her bed to read God's word." He was slurring his words. "I am free to sign or not to sign. The Lord would have me follow my conscience," he mocked.

Her heart sank. "You're in drink—full of rum."

"You'd rather I drank poison?"

Knowing her hope for an understanding was now impossible, Mary ignored him, closed her Bible, and blew out the candle on the bedside table. The moon lit the room.

"The proud one does not deny it," he mumbled, trying to pull off his boot. "The defiant one thinks not at all of her husband." His boot came off at last in his hand, and he tossed it on the floor.

Mary was disgusted. "What nonsense."

Joseph pulled at his buttons, flopped on the bed, and held up his other booted leg for Mary's assistance. Aware that he expected her to tend him like a babe, she climbed out of bed to oblige, and when the boot was in her hand she let it fall to the floor and settled herself back under the covers. He stood up, struggling to remove his breeches. She wanted to laugh at his clumsiness but feared to offer more offence. Once his breeches lay in a puddle on the floor, he stepped out of them to climb into bed next to her. He grabbed a pillow from under her head and cuddled it.

"Ah, my pretty maid," he cooed, kissing the pillow.

Still Mary pretended to ignore him, until he reached across the pillow and tugged at a lock of her hair.

She shoved his hand away. "Stop that."

Joseph laughed and tugged again. Again, Mary pushed his hand away. He tugged again.

At that, Mary forgot herself. "Damn you!" she blurted out.

He threw the pillow across the room and planted his head on Mary's breast, reaching up to stroke her cheek. "You're more beautiful than when I first saw you," he said, suddenly serious.

Knowing he was not himself, Mary was unmoved by his attempted seduction. Revolted, she pushed him away. Joseph, suddenly enraged, grabbed her arm and pulled her to him. "You'll not defy me again! Kiss me!"

"Nay, let me go!" she cried.

Struggling free of him, she jumped out of bed and ran for the door. Joseph leapt out of bed, seizing the tail of her nightdress and tearing it. Enraged beyond reason, he picked her up and flung her onto the bed, looming over her, his breath rank with drink.

"Joseph, are you mad? You know I'm with child. You'll kill us!" She cowered under him in a panic.

Unmoved by her tears, he ripped open her gown, revealing her nakedness—the distended belly, the painfully swollen breasts. Helpless in her terror, Mary watched as shame overtook him and his anger ebbed. Sobbing, he covered her body with the remnants of her nightdress and fell to his knees, burying his face in his hands.

WHILE THE WOLF'S Head was the essential meeting place for the men of Northampton, the women and children met at the general store. It was a place to browse, have chance meetings with friends, and buy longed-for things. Trade and barter were also an acceptable form of exchange, and one often heard voices in the midst of lively negotiations and dickering. Joseph had entrusted the day-to-day management of the store to young Jonas Walford, who had for a time been apprenticed to him at the gristmill.

Joseph had built the general store, a simple one-story clapboard with four windows facing Bartlett Street, directly across from the Meeting House. Inside, people could find barrels and bushels filled with flour and oatmeal, flitches of bacon, Holland cheese, loaf sugar, pepper, nutmegs, cloves, such dried fruits as currants and prunes, and other foodstuffs for the housewife's larder. The shelves were lined with aquavit, books, honey, and bolts of fabric—Dutch serge, cotton, broadcloth, flannel, canvas, linen, wool, even silk. Here men found tools and gunpowder, and women sorted through gloves, sewing supplies, stomachers, combs, ready-made cloaks, stockings, and other temptations. The well-stocked store had hardly any room left over for customers to gather.

One afternoon Jonas Walford walked out of the stockroom and greeted young Rebecca Bridgeman, who leaned on the front counter, engrossed in a small book. She did not immediately look up to greet him, for *A Mother's Legacy* had her complete attention. The book had been popular among a generation of women. At the time it was penned, the author was a young wife, pregnant with her first child. In advance of the birth, she had purchased her shroud and written detailed instructions on how she wanted her child reared, for she had rightly predicted that the birth would end her life.

When Jonas spoke again Rebecca mumbled absently, "Good morrow, Jonas." She had little time to chat, for her mother expected her to return with stockings for Martha, white thread and almonds for the sweets she would bake. Only recently had Rebecca been granted the freedom to go to the store alone, and that only after threatening to stay in her bed forever unless her mother gave her some room to grow up. Her father had come to her aid.

"You will handicap the child, Sarah," he'd said. "'Tis time that she learn something of the world."

Jonas liked the girl and found her amusing. "Ye came in here yesterday—leaned on that same counter and read that same book. Pray, do ye love it enough to buy it?"

"Nay, Jonas." For a moment she looked up. "I've nearly finished it. Don't misunderstand me, 'tis a wondrous fine book, but not one I'll read again."

"Rebecca, most folks *buy* a book before they read it."

"I shall buy, you may be sure, but only after I've read every word and am sure the book is worthy."

"Hmph! Joseph Parsons won't grow rich because of the likes of you."

She rested the open book face-down on the counter. "Jonas?" A brilliant idea had just crossed her mind. "Does Joseph Parsons' wife frequent this store? I've never seen her here."

"That's because ye come afternoons. Besides, she was just delivered of a child."

"Mornings are when I have my chores. I can't come then."

"Well, she always comes of a morning, or else sends Elspeth."

"That explains it," she said. "And the babe? Mother says *she* can't have any babes but sons."

Jonas said, "Not this time, Rebecca. She had a girl."

But Rebecca made no comment, for she had more pages to read.

Jonas went about his dusting and restocking, glancing at Rebecca from time to time. The book was open on the counter next to her elbow, her chin resting in her open hand as her eyes followed every line on the page. Now and then she stopped to rub her elbow or switch arms, but she looked riveted.

"Jonas," she called finally, "I want to ask you a question."

He moved closer. "Rebecca, ye are a fine comely maid, but far too bossy. One day ye shall be a handful for yer husband."

"Jonas, I don't *want* a husband. Now tell me, what does Goodwife Parsons buy when she comes here?"

He shrugged. "I don't know. The usual things."

"Like what? Does she buy books?"

"Nay, not that I remember. She takes buttons and thread and such things as sugar and salt. 'Tis her husband's store, ye know, so she doesn't have to pay."

"Is she very rich?"

"Aye, she is that, and a fine woman, too. Kind to a fault. I pay no mind to what some folks say against her."

"I quite agree. It has come into my head how uncommon she is—singular in kind."

"Singular, indeed. Like ye!"

MASSASOIT, THE GREAT Sachem of the Wampanoags, was dead, and rumors had spread throughout the colony that his son and successor, Alexander, who ruled the Pokanokets, had conspired with the Narragansetts to make war against the English. From the 1620s onward Massasoit had carefully nurtured friendships with Plymouth Colony governors Edward Winslow and William Bradford, among other powerful English leaders, and folks still held his name in high regard.

Robert Bartlett, having both his thirst and the death of Massasoit in mind, stopped by The Wolf's Head. He hadn't seen Joseph Parsons for weeks, at least not to talk to. He asked the barmaid if her master was in, ordered two glasses of rum, and knocked on the office door.

Joseph was glad to see his old friend. They raised their glasses in good cheer and settled in to discuss the old days and the role the benevolent Massasoit had played in the settlement of the new land. "Has it been so long?" Joseph said. "Thirty or forty years? In those days we struggled."

"Aye, we thought we would surely starve." Bartlett relaxed into his chair.

"Some did—especially the first to come. The natives, led by Massasoit's example, lent us a hand. Now that he's gone, we don't know what we have in his son."

Bartlett was packing his pipe. "Some say he's not to be trusted."

Joseph nodded. "Alexander has shown some sovereignty in the land deals he has struck with Governor Williams of Rhode Island, though Plymouth has asked that they not sell to those rogues."

"'Tis too late now." Bartlett pondered for a moment, drawing air through his pipe. "The Indians cannot destroy us. We are too many." And in that surety he lit his pipe.

"That's as may be," Joseph said, "though I'd surely not fault them for trying. They see their kingdoms reduced to, dare I say, a quarter of what their fathers enjoyed. Why, there's precious little good farmland left, and both we and the Indians need land for our crops. Then, too, our sons shall soon desire land as well."

"In contrast to the old days," Bartlett puffed a cloud of smoke over his head, "wampum has lost value."

Joseph stroked his graying beard. "Aye, Bartlett, all is change, is it not? For the fathers of the first generation will pass away—*are* passing away, like Massasoit. Though I've sought to teach my sons, our sons know not the Indians as we know them, nor do the Indians' sons know the English as Massasoit and his kind knew us."

Bartlett tossed down the last of his drink and shook his head sadly. "Truth be told, my sons don't seem interested. They care little for the reasons this colony was founded."

"Truth to tell, good friend, I can't say I care either—never have." Joseph regarded Bartlett warily, awaiting the man's reaction. "It goes against nature. Men like John Winthrop and Thomas Hooker were dreamers. They thought they could build a nation where Saints would live by God's law, in brotherly love. Ha!"

Bartlett frowned. "Dreamers indeed, I fear, Joseph, for it seems we're naught but a nation of quarrelsome rogues."

"Aye, I know we're taught not to be worldly. But no man in his right mind will pass up the chance to make his fortune where he can."

"Even so, 'twas a fine dream, and 'tis a shame we have lost it. In the end we shall surely be punished for falling away from the covenant our fathers made with God."

Joseph leaned forward to make his point. "If the Indians want war, then, aye, we shall be punished. But they cannot defeat us now. Their opportunity? They let it pass."

XIII

At this court of assistants one James Britton, a man ill affected both to our church discipline and civil government, and one Mary Latham, a proper young woman about 18 years of age, whose father was a godly man and had brought her up well, were condemned to die for adultery . . . both died very penitently, especially the woman, who had some comfortable hope of pardon of her sin, and gave good exhortation to all young maids to be obedient to their parents, and to take heed of evil company . . .

—Governor John Winthrop
The History of New England 1630–1649

IN THE HOUR before sunset, four men walked out the front door of The Wolf's Head, merry from their hour together. Inside, Katherine Walford bent across a long oak table with a damp rag in her hand. She rubbed at wet rings left by mugs of ale, careful not to soil her apron. Katherine had worked for Joseph Parsons from the day the ordinary changed hands.

The daughter of Widow Walford, who lived in a small house on the banks of Mill River, Katherine had first come to Joseph's attention at the meeting of the selectmen where she had been wrongly charged for wearing ribbons. Struck by her from first sight, he took an interest in her family's welfare and found them barely scraping by, for the mother had been widowed nineteen years, since her two children were small, and the heartless husband had left the whole of his small estate to his business partner. As the selectmen did not want responsibility for the widow and her children to fall on the town, they disrupted Walford's cruel plan by dividing the £97 estate between the widow and Walford's disgruntled partner.

Katherine was a hard-working girl. She spent her mornings helping her mother at home, her afternoons and evenings working at the tavern. Joseph had also hired her brother Jonas to work at the general store. With Jonas's and Katherine's wages and the widow's homemade sweets, featured on the front shelf at the store, the small family had been saved from poverty.

At the moment, Katherine found satisfaction in polishing the table, now burnished and glossy from fat dripped off the greasy meats men preferred with ale. She wore an old-fashioned brown wool gown, identifiable as the uniform of a serving girl, with a straight white apron over her skirt and a gathered white linen kerchief covering her shoulders. Each day she tucked her fine light-brown hair inside a close-fitting white linen cap, making her whole appearance neat and chaste.

Three strangers entered the tavern. Katherine stopped polishing and looked in their direction. A lock of hair had fallen from her cap, and she tucked it neatly back. "What may I get ye to drink?"

"Flips all round," one said, smiling in an overly familiar way as they took seats at one end of a long table.

Past random benches and stools scattered round the room Katherine walked to the wooden bar lined with pewter mugs, pots and basins. She took a basin from the shelf and broke three eggs into it, whipped them up with sugar and cream, and divided the mixture between three mugs. She uncorked a bottle of rum and tapped the beer casket, giving each mug a long draught of each, then carried them to the fire. Resting the mugs on a hearthstool, she retrieved a red hot flip-iron from the coals and plunged it into one of the mugs. A burst of steam escaped, setting the whole concoction to boil.

The men eyed her closely as she brought the first mug to their table, and with an evil leer, the oldest one reached out to give her a smart pat on the behind. "I'd like to stable this two-legged mare," he told his friends, with a wink.

"Aye," said another, "she's a comely lass." He grabbed her by the waist and pulled her toward his lap.

"Behave yourself!" Katherine squirmed out of his grasp. "I am not yours to handle. Ye are some poor woman's husband, I'll warrant, and she's welcome to ye." She turned and went back to the hearth, where she steamed the next drink and laid the flip-iron back on the fire. Her face burning with shame, she kept her eyes on her work.

The third man tried his luck. "What name do ye go by, lass?"

"Goodwife Walford," she lied, steaming the last drink.

"So ye be a married woman?"

"Aye, and I'll thank ye to give my husband your respect," she said as she brought them the last two mugs.

The men all leered and laughed at her. Seeking refuge, Katherine headed for the back room and went in, closing the door quietly behind her. There she started, surprised to find Joseph Parsons behind a pile of paperwork at his desk.

"Oh, I'm sorry to intrude without knocking. 'Tis not yer customary hour."

Joseph smiled and put down his quill pen, sipping from the glass of rum on his desk.

"'Tis growing dark, Katherine. Will you light the lamps?"

"Aye," she said, taking a wisp from the hearth broom and setting it alight it in the fire.

"Just now, when you came into the room, you looked distressed."

"Well, Master," she said, lighting the lamp on his desk, "I was. Them men I made flips for, they said wicked things to me."

He chuckled. "No wonder. You're a comely lass. You tempt them."

She felt color rise to her cheeks. Her master had never said such a thing to her before. Not knowing how to respond, she folded her arms and moved toward the door. "Well, I'd best be getting back to work, as that's what ye pay me for. I only want to do my work and go home to bed."

"Ah, to bed—how sweet. Would that I lie with you, Kate." Joseph stood up, as though he meant to approach her.

"Why, I dare not think such thoughts." She was flattered, though, excited by compliments from a rich man. In spite of nearly twenty-five years between them, Joseph was a desirable man, still handsome, and richer than any she had ever talked to. "If ye say these things to me, ye must be in great need. Make haste, go home to your wife, for ye have a comely wife." She smiled at him and opened the door to the tavern.

His voice followed her. "Aye, comely indeed, but where the grass grows green the steed starves. Now off with you like a good girl, before I get into trouble."

One day that spring when the cook was ill with the flux, Elspeth was busy with the children. That left Mary to wash and peel the last of the Jerusalem artichokes, a knobby tuber with crisp white flesh that the Indians had taught the English how to use. They were highly valued, because they could be stored over winter and used when there were few vegetables for the table. Mary cut rotten spots from the surface of those left from last summer's harvest and sliced them into a pot of boiling water.

Happy any time she was working with her hands, she remembered her childhood and how hard she had worked to learn all she needed to know. She prided herself on how well she handled the knife, how swiftly and skillfully she worked, and while the vegetables cooked she turned to make Indian pudding. In time, she tested the white flesh of the chokes with a fork, found them soft, and poured them into a colander to drain. She slid a large slab of fresh butter into a hot skillet and watched it melt, then froth into bubbles. With a fine whisk of twigs she blended in flour, salt and pepper, and when it was cooked she poured rich cream over the mixture, stirring quickly to make the sauce smooth. She had ready a small bouquet of parsley and chopped it fine, added it to the sauce, and poured the whole over the chokes, wrapping the dish with a clean towel and setting it aside.

Mary stepped back to survey the morning's production. On

her table was a platter of roasted squash, a skillet of cornbread and crocks of Indian pudding and baked beans. Loaves were rising on the hearth, and her masterpiece was ready to remove from the oven—Joseph's favorite, chicken and almond pudding. That morning she'd waked eager to begin cooking, to hold vegetables and fresh poultry in her hands, to take eggs, sugar, flour, salt, butter and cream and turn them into luscious food for the mouths of those she loved. She wanted to be in her kitchen alone with the elements of her art and was glad Elspeth was away with the children.

Contented, she knew that Joseph, Elspeth, and all the children would soon be home for the midday meal. She set Joseph's place at the head of the table, remembering the previous night with a thrill. Her husband had come home later than usual, after she had gone to bed early. He woke her, smelling of liquor, so she knew he had come from the ordinary. Lately he had moved the files and papers from all his businesses into one office there. For months Mary had been worried about her husband. She was used to his abruptness by day, but it was usual for him to warm to her at night. It was in their bed that their marriage lived, yet of late he had shown little interest.

"I try not to trouble my head about his drinking or his lack of pity for me," she had confided to her mother one day when the Widow Bliss had come up from Springfield. "Of late he does not lie with me—not since little Mary was weaned."

"'Tis the fault of strong drink, Mary—a common weakness in men at his time of life."

"Father never drank."

"Aye, Mary, by my troth, he did so."

"I swear, I never noticed—well, perhaps on occasion."

"Most all men do in their middle years."

"But why?"

"Despondency."

"Despondent? Joseph? I cannot bear bravely the thought that a rich man with six sons and a daughter has any reason for melancholy."

"No reason, 'tis true, but hear my words, the attainments of men do not bring them contentment. In that way they are far different from women."

Now Mary folded her lover's napkin, remembering last night when he had reached for her, taking her to him, covering her body with kisses, staying with her for what seemed like hours. Surely her worries were at an end, and all between them would be well.

Joseph headed home for dinner, hungry in two ways. His stomach was empty, his mind full of lust for his serving girl. As he rode out of the town he thought again of the night before. After all the tavern customers were gone, he had held Katherine and kissed her and told her to lock the front door, but she would not let him lie with her. For an hour they had kissed, and he had caressed her, driving himself mad with desire. He felt contempt for himself now, having taken his lust home to Mary, who seemed eager to relieve him of his affliction. He cursed himself in one breath, in another longed for the day to end. Surely tonight after closing Katherine would yield to their shared desire, and he would have her.

That night after supper, he rode back to his office and set to work, waiting for closing time. But as the evening wore on he grew impatient. Though men of the town still sat by the fire, drinking and talking, he told Katherine to finish her work, then lock the door and come into his office. He waited for her there, sipping rum, watching out the window as the moon rose behind the trees. After she locked the front door Katherine cleaned up, wiping the tables, waiting for the last customers to leave.

Goodmen Lyman and Edwards still sat talking about the recent death of Alexander, the Indian chieftain. Massasoit's eldest son had had a very short reign, and the English found it worrisome that the Pokanokets were now led by his brother Philip, a very young man with a reputation as a rogue. Philip was known to be no friend of the English, who he believed had poisoned his brother.

Hendricks the Dutchman sat alone near the window. He

finished his drink and paid Katherine before he left, but the town elders ordered another round. Katherine served them, walked to the door of the back room and opened it a crack. "Master?"

"Come in, Kate." He half rose from his chair, eager. "Have they all gone?"

"Nay, Goodman Lyman and Goodman Edwards stay on."

"Close the door."

She lingered at the threshold. "I dare not."

"Please, close the door. What troubles you?"

Katherine obeyed but stood with her back pressed against the door.

"Last night. I fear I tempted ye."

"Aye, Kate, and you were tempted as well." He moved from behind his desk to take her in his arms.

She stepped away. "Please, let's forget," she said, opening the door. "Now I must away." She rushed into the barroom, and Joseph walked to the open door to watch as Lyman and Edwards paid her. She went to unlock the front door so they could leave, and he heard them say, "Good even," as they went out. Hurrying back to work, she forgot to lock the door, and as Joseph watched she wiped the last table clean and picked up the used mugs, ready to carry them behind the bar for washing.

He strode into the room. "Put those down," he said, grasping her waist from behind with both hands.

She froze, bracing herself against the table, closing her eyes. Letting the damp cloth and mugs lie, she felt Joseph press hard against her. With her head bent low, she began to cry.

He turned her to face him. "Ah, Kate, what ails you?" He covered her mouth with his own. As they kissed, she warmed to him, her tears stopped, and she grew breathless with desire.

"'Tis a sin!" she cried, pulling away, moving toward the door. "If ye care for me, ye must let me go."

"I need you, my love."

Sobbing, she ran to the fire and took up the flip-iron by its handle to thrust its glowing end at him. "Here! If ye love me, ye will hold this burning thing in your hands for one minute!"

"Don't be a fool, Kate."

"For me ye will not burn one minute, yet if I lie with ye I shall forever burn in Hell!"

She dropped the iron on the floor, narrowly missing Joseph's boot, and ran out the door.

XIV

. . . Capt. Underhill, having been privately dealt with upon suspicion of incontinency with a neighbor's wife, and not harkening to it, was publicly questioned, and put under admonition . . . the woman being young, and beautiful, and withal of a jovial spirit and behavior, he did daily frequent her house, and was divers times found there alone with her, the door being locked on the inside. He confessed it was ill, because it had an appearance of evil in it; but his excuse was, that the woman was in great trouble of mind, and sore temptations, and that he resorted to her to comfort her; and that when the door was found locked upon them, they were in private prayer together.

—Governor John Winthrop
The History of New England 1630–1649

IN THE HOPE that her mother would send her to the store early, Rebecca Bridgeman hurried through her chores. She plotted to chance upon Mary Parsons, certain that once Mary got to know her she would agree to teach her all she knew of remedies and herbs.

"Why make haste, Rebecca?" Sarah asked, as her daughter raced through washing the dishes.

"I'm trying not to linger, Mother, to forswear my lazy ways. Do you think I like it well when I hear you say what fine daughters Sarah and Martha are, and no mention of me?"

"Where did you get such a notion? I've never said that either was a finer daughter than you. Sarah is swifter and more cheerful at her work, and Martha has a great desire to please. You are an extraordinary fine daughter in many other ways, except for the saucy things you're wont to say."

"Then tell me the ways I am fine," she said, wiping the breakfast plates one after another with a clean white towel.

Sarah, sweeping kitchen litter out the door, paused. "Rebecca, I think very well of you."

"Just why, Mother?"

"In my good judgment 'tis not something you should know."

"I should not know how it is that I am a daughter you think well of?"

"Nay, you should not know it. It will swell your head and make you saucier than ever. Pride is a sin, Rebecca, a sin with which you are well acquainted. Now hush your mouth and help your sisters with the laundry."

"After that may I take your list to the store?"

"After that you may sit and sew—in silence, if you please."

"Ah, Mother, let me sew in the heat of the day and go to the store while it's cool. Please, I promise not to be any trouble if I can go to the store before it gets hot."

Weary of debate, Sarah gave in, and Rebecca happily headed outside to help her sisters finish the washing. Soon after, she took her mother's list and headed for the village, arriving out of breath and full of excitement. But Mary Parsons was nowhere to be seen. Goodwife Bartlett was at the store, chatting so intently with Rebecca's Aunt Dorcus that they did not notice her come in. While his customers browsed, Jonas swept the back room and did not see Rebecca either. She ran to the door and looked up and down the road, but Mary Parsons was not there. She heaved a sigh of disappointment just as Jonas appeared.

"Good morrow, Rebecca." He propped his broom against the wall. "You're getting an early start."

"Good morrow," she answered in her most grown-up voice. "Mother wants lamp oil, a small amount today, and twelve quarter-inch hair buttons."

"What color?"

"Dark—black or brown. Has Goodwife Parsons been in today?" She kept her voice low, not wanting to be overheard.

"Nay, she sent Elspeth."

"Ah, well—my mother wants two pounds dried peas, some wick, and brown thread," she said in her normal voice.

He smiled at her as he filled her sack. "Tell me, Rebecca, what's your interest in Goodwife Parsons? You ask me about her every time you come in," he said quietly, glancing at the older women.

"Why, 'tis only that she is a friend of mine."

"That will be six pence. Next time she comes in I'll tell her you asked for her." He took the coins she held out to him.

"Thank you, Jonas, please do that." She favored him with her most gracious smile.

"Ain't you going to read a book today?"

"Nay, I haven't time." And she was out the door.

JOSEPH HAD BROUGHT another kind of trouble on himself, this time with Robert Bartlett. Their falling-out had occurred when the county needed a team of oxen to work on the roads. Constable Bartlett had appeared at Joseph's door and asked to borrow his team, though Joseph did not want to part with them just then. When Bartlett made demands, the men came to blows and parted both bloodied. Following this act of aggression, Joseph had been charged with high contempt of authority. The court reprimanded and fined him for resisting the constable. Because Joseph had admitted his guilt, his fine was lessened by twenty shillings. But the damage was done. He had soured a longtime ally.

After Sarah had heard that Joseph Parsons and Robert Bartlett came to blows, she had been tempted to talk with Ann Bartlett— to feel her out. Maybe Mary's old friend would finally understand. Was Ann Bartlett still friends with Mary? If not, was there a chance for an alliance? Goodwife Bartlett, she thought, might be privy to Mary's secrets. Though Sarah, like any woman, needed to talk with a friend now and then, never had she told anyone her own secret thoughts, nor unburdened her soul about a recent dream. Dreams came either from God as portents, or from the Devil as temptations, and were not to be ignored.

It all came about after she had walked home one day by the road at the back of the Parsons' house. As she passed the little thicket, she saw Elspeth hanging Mary's linens out to dry. All through the trees floated white shifts and petticoats trimmed in lace, fine things blowing in the breeze. Sarah had never seen such a collection of lovely things, the sun brightening them in the prettiest way. When Elspeth went back to the house Sarah felt safe to stand and gaze for a moment. She found it the most curious thing, concealed there under the trees, looking at another woman's underthings charged with the breeze, all lacy and white, moving as if alive.

That night she dreamt again the things she was ashamed to remember. In remembering, she was overcome with longings she dared not have, thoughts she liked to linger over, for they gave her pleasure. In her dream Mary appeared naked under her lacy shift. Joseph kissed and caressed her, and when he penetrated her, Sarah felt Mary's pleasure, her ecstasy so real that she was disappointed to wake and find it was only a dream. Such thoughts she never would have allowed herself, but they were forced upon her against her will, and she knew then beyond any question that Mary's breeze-filled clothes had bewitched her.

Sarah pondered these things. I have better thoughts to occupy my mind—the state of the world, for one thing, this vale of tears. Three years had passed since her brother Richard died, leaving his well-dressed Hepzibah and eight children behind. Sarah still grieved for him and for all her dead.

In England, Cromwell was dead, the hope of the people dying with him. Now they had King Charles's son to rule, and a plague spread throughout England. Thousands had died, all fevered and swollen. This punishment from God puzzled her not, for surely God was displeased with the world's wickedness.

And here in New England, she mused, we have witches. James Wakeley of Hartford was indicted two or three years before and escaped. Who knows where he hides now, or what mischief he's up to? And we executed others—I think I can say all their names. There was Mary Stanford, and Rebecca and Nathaniel Greensmith of Hartford, and that woman—from some little village in Connecticut—I remember that from last year, or was it the year before that they hanged her? The earth and skies have shuddered and glowed with signs of woe—the terrible earthquake felt here, and just last fall the comet hanging overhead. Terrible times, for that comet brought war to the Pocumtucks. And this summer no rain here. These great crushing things must I pray about, ask God's mercy on us, and—she all but shouted it aloud—stop thinking about that wicked dream!

IT WAS STILL summer when Mary decided she must tell Joseph she was with child again. She had seen little of him for weeks. No wonder, it was the busiest time of the year. Added to the management of all his business affairs was the work of the fields and the struggles the drought had brought upon them. Ordinarily Joseph had three men in his employ full time in summer, toiling in the woods, orchards and fields, but this year they had lost half their crop, and he let two men go.

The children were abed. Mary knew Joseph would be late, but she waited for him all the same, windows flung wide to let in the breeze and with them moths that fluttered at her candle's flame. The day had been hot, but the night came on breezy, driving the heat from their room. She waited in a cool white shift, finding her Bible good company. After nearly an hour by the glass Mary felt sleepy.

She put down the book and lifted a small wooden flageolet from a table under the window. Pressing the mouthpiece to her lips, she blew a few notes, then stopped to listen. Would her music wake the children? When none stirred, she went to the window to gaze at the great milk-white moon. From her perch she saw how the road came out of the meadow through a break in the trees, the flat meadowland shining in the moonlight beyond. She breathed in the cool night air and gasped with delight as a sparkling cloud of fireflies flew just below, across the fragrant masses of rocket that filled the night air with the scent of violets in spring.

It was four years before, after the birth of her first daughter, that Mary had first wanted music. The idea struck her as she sang lullabies to her children and realized that her song soothed them far more than her words. Humming quieted their fears and comforted them in a most magical way, and when she sang her heart filled with joy. For months after little Mary was born she sang happy songs. She asked Joseph to buy her a flute, and he came home from his next trip to Boston with a small, ornately carved flageolet. Mary taught herself to play it by ear and now could play several familiar tunes and hymns, even a few of her own composition. The children picked up her flute and liked to play, so Joseph bought recorders for them.

But the town would have none of it. A neighbor complained of the un-Christian sounds drifting across the road. Soon Mister Mather suggested that Mary not teach her children frivolous, idle pastimes. So the recorders were packed away in a wooden chest in the barn, where the more mulish children found them and sneaked a few notes when no one was around. Thus the Parsons' house harbored a number of clandestine flautists.

When a rider approached on horseback, Mary stopped playing. He came on the road out of the town, moving at a steady walk. She watched, knowing it was Joseph, glad she had stayed awake. In bright moonlight she saw him disappear behind the house, where he would stable his horse in the barn for the night. She climbed into bed like a young girl with a wonderful secret to tell.

At last Joseph entered their room, surprised to find her awake. "'Tis late for you, Mary."

"I waited. You must be bone tired."

"No more than you, I'll warrant," he said, taking a chair.

Mary went to assist him with his boots. She pulled them off and set them neatly beside the chair.

Joseph watched as she removed his socks. "You look like the fair maid I used to know," he said, smiling at her.

Mary blushed, charming him. "I have something," she said, "something I've been saving to tell you."

"Then tell me now."

"You haven't guessed?"

"Are you teasing me? If you are, I like it well." He grabbed her wrist, pulling her into his arms, kissing her.

"Don't you recognize me?" she said. "I've felt like this at least once every two years since we've been married."

"Ah, then you are with child."

She nodded, flirting with him. "I remember the night you gave me this child. You came home late and woke me. 'Twas a night I shall long remember."

Joseph's heart sank. His nights of passion with Katherine had time and again led him straight to Mary, as if she were Kate. Forcing Kate from mind, he looked to his wife. "Ah, Mary." He kissed her tenderly, then led her to their bed where he exhausted himself in Mary's embrace, passing into a guilty sleep imagining Katherine in his arms. How the maid had captivated him with her simplicity and honesty, her passion and strength of will. Her purity in the face of her desire tempted him fiercely. If patient, he believed she would be his. Hating his weakness, he pitied both his serving girl and his wife, who carried the fruits of his lust.

SOON JOSEPH WOULD have another day in court. He was charged with breach of the law for allowing Hendricks the Dutchman to spend his time and estate in the ordinary. Hendricks was one of Joseph's best customers. Every day he left the ordinary for home just before sunset. Never did he show the slightest sign of drunkenness, yet his wife had complained to the town, blaming Joseph for luring her husband into his place of business so that Hendricks might squander his earnings. The selectmen agreed, found Joseph guilty, and fined him forty shillings.

But the townsmen had more serious things to worry about. The Indians wanted land to build a fort near the town. The natives suffered constantly from attacks by Mohawks and had no trouble arguing the case for their own defense. In anticipation of granting their request, Joseph, John Lyman and David Wilton were appointed to deliver the town's rules to the Indians: **No working or gaming on the Sabbath, no powwows, no liquor or cider and getting drunk and killing each other as is your custom, no foreign Indians taking sanctuary among you, no breaking down of fences, no welcoming the murderers Calawane and Wurtowhan and Pacquallunt among your numbers, and no hunting English cattle, sheep, or swine with your dogs.** If the Indians were willing to agree to all these rules, they would be allowed to build on a hill southwest of the Meeting House. The Indians agreed and the building began.

The time came when Joseph avoided late nights at The Wolf's Head, leaving Katherine to close up on her own. Her brother Jonas would see her safely home. Joseph had solid reasons for going home to Mary. All this traipsing about to treat with the Indians had kept him from his work; then there was his harvest-time exhaustion and his guilt. He found Mary nearly as desirable as Katherine and wondered why, at this time in his life, he was consumed by the same desire he'd had as a youth, to have a woman every day.

Another idea began to intrigue him. By appearing to lose interest in Katherine, would she be driven to make her own advances to him? Recently, when he saw her in the late afternoons, her sad, puzzled expression gave him hope that this strategy was working. One evening, a week after his calculated behavior began, Mary baited him in a quarrel, and he decided it would be practical to punish his wife and work late at the ordinary. Two things might be accomplished thereby. He would give Mary pause, should she think to be defiant again, and Katherine, who looked more and more forlorn, seemed ready for the taking.

When he entered the tavern by the front door, he found Katherine busy serving two tables. He greeted all present and headed for his office. Hanging his great hat on a peg by the door, he slipped inside, waited a moment, then opened the door again. "Bring me rum, Kate!" he called with a smile. After a few minutes she entered his office looking dejected, his drink in hand. "You look pale," he said. "Are you ill?"

"Nay, not I, 'tis mother who is ill. I've lost sleep over it."

"Is it serious?" He moved close to her side, thinking she looked miserable.

"I know not—she has a dreadful cough and has not risen from bed for a week."

"Has the doctor been sent for?"

"Nay, Master, we cannot afford the doctor."

"Nonsense, Kate." He reached into his pocket and withdrew a small bag of coins. "Here, take these."

"No! I won't take a thing from you," she sobbed. "I'll not be your whore!"

"Ah, Kate! Your words are unfair. I would not make you a whore. 'Tis precious little I give to help your mother. If you will not accept this small kindness, I shall give it to your brother, or the doctor himself. I ask nothing in return."

"Nothing?" She looked unconvinced.

"Naught. You shall see. I have repented. Daily I chastise myself for the grief I have caused you and my wife—if she knew. Would that I had not been so weak to cause you pain. Please accept my apology and my coins." He extended his hand once more, pleased with his little speech, almost believing every word.

"For Mother, then, I'll take it."

He laid the coins in her palm, then took her hand in his, closing her fingers over his gift. He bent his head, kissing her wrist lightly, then raised his eyes to look into her lovely face.

"I feel so ashamed," she said, as tears streaked her cheeks.

"Ah, there's no shame on your shoulders. The shame is mine." He was admiring his new role as a penitent.

But her tears continued to flow. "This sinful desire is not yours alone. I am guilty as well." She wept, burying her face in his chest.

"Then you do want me, Kate?" He lowered his head to kiss her.

"Aye, God help me, I do," she said, as his lips stopped her words.

They stood in the middle of the room, kissing long and rapturously, his heart soaring with joy as he went to his knees and lifted her skirts. Thrusting his hand inside her thighs, he gently forced his fingers up the furrow between her legs and heard her moan with pleasure. He felt her skirts close about his head, and when he pressed his lips to her soft young belly she cried out. Thrilled by the maid's excited outburst, he reached a hand to unbutton his breeches, but her body stiffened. She pressed her hands hard against his head and pulled away, leaving him alone on his knees. She backed off a few feet, staring toward the door, her face white with terror. Turning to look over his shoulder, Joseph came face to face with her brother Jonas, who stood agape in the open doorway.

"Jonas!" Katherine cried, and turned away from the sight of him.

Joseph said nothing as he got to his feet, fumbling at his buttons.

Jonas, face white with rage, his tears overflowing, fists clinched as though he would pummel his employer, shouted, "A pox on you, stinking whoreson! I've come to tell my sister that our mother is dead!"

Katherine reeled and spun round crying, "Nay, nay, don't say it! Oh, Mother!"

"Be glad!" Jonas commanded. "She'll not suffer from your sin."

As she fled to run out the back door of the building, her agonized scream shook Joseph to the core. "Listen, Jonas," he said, trembling with shame, "we didn't—"

"Save your lies for the magistrates!" Jonas spat as he left by the same door he'd come in.

After adjusting his clothes, Joseph, left alone with his puzzled patrons, announced he would close up for the night, explaining that his barmaid had just had word of a family tragedy. After saying good night to all and locking up, he headed home to his wife, not knowing how much his patrons had seen but certain that Jonas would not keep his secret. It would be worse should Mary learn of it from someone else. He found her getting ready for bed and told her straightaway what had happened, leaving nothing out. She listened in silence, one hand clutching the other, her eyes never leaving his face, her own face full of questions that would wait, her strength holding him on course.

When he finished, her eyes welled with tears. "You have brought shame on yourself, Joseph. My heart is sure to break," she wailed. She got up and left the room, closing the door behind her.

Joseph knew she would rather keep private the sight and sounds of her grief. He heard her footsteps on the stairs to the kitchen, where she would spend the night by the fire, awake, wrapped in a blanket. In the instant when he first knew Mary's pain, Joseph saw himself as he had never seen himself before. Yes, he'd punched the nose of a friend, a respected personage in the town. Yes, he was thought of as the man who'd enticed the Dutchman to drink. Yes, he made a spectacle of his wealth. Yet for the first time Joseph felt naked with shame. His weakness, his lust for a mere maid not yet twenty and with no prospects, had been exposed for his wife to see. Soon the whole town would know.

Although it wasn't the first time such a thing had happened in Northampton, that was no comfort to Joseph. Soon after the settlement of the town Robert Bartlett himself had been tried by the General Court for a "great misdemeanor"—the attempted seduction of Christopher Smith's young wife. The court got a signed confession from Bartlett. He gave a detailed account of how he lured her into a swamp while she was looking for her calf, threw her down, restrained her, kissed her, and put his hand up her skirts on her naked private parts. When she begged him to release her, to his credit, he let her go, saying, "I will not do it without your consent." Later, as he led her out of the swamp, he had said, "I could have done it whether or not you wanted." Misdemeanors done out of lust for women were understood by most men, though not condoned. But other more righteous men did not so easily forgive their lusty brothers.

IN JOSEPH'S DREAM the judge looked at him with un-Christian satisfaction. "Goodman Parsons, you have Jonas Walford to thank for saving you from the sin of fornication." The judge laughed, an ironic grin distorting his face. "Had he not opened that door, you and Katherine Walford might face a capital offence."

"Show her mercy," Joseph wept. "I pray you, show me none."

"Do I hear repentance from this proud man?" the judge asked the bench of dark-faced magistrates.

Still weeping, Joseph confessed, "She was my victim and is blameless."

"Your regret shall be endless," said the judge, "for you are hereby sentenced by this body to everlasting Hell. There you shall be chained to a lust from which you shall never be free, never to be fulfilled, never to be released from it."

XV

I have seen the extreme vanity of this world: One hour I have been in health, and wealthy, wanting nothing. But the next hour in sickness and wounds, and death, having nothing but sorrow and affliction.

—Mary Rowlandson (1637–1711)

FOR NINE YEARS James Bridgeman had been sealer of weights and measures for the town of Northampton. Only once did he move to higher office, in the year that he was voted constable, a job he was made for. To the bone, he was a man of law and order, conscientious to a fault, strict, unbending in his defense of right over wrong. But never again was he asked to hold the office he so loved. Instead, he became Northampton's first man to have a hand on the scales of exchange. As sealer of weights and measures he was responsible for making sure the scales used in commerce had not been tampered with and were in good working order. Unfortunately, it wasn't much of a job, the only places in town where scales were used being the gristmill and Parsons' store. Only once had someone complained that Jonas Walford put his thumb on the scale. James investigated, Jonas would not admit to having done so, and that was the end of it.

At this advanced stage in life it was evident to Sarah that her husband would never be anything other than what he was. In the past, she had encouraged him to let the selectmen know he wanted to be constable again, but James did not feel he should make his desires known. "I shall serve where I am asked to serve. Service, Sarah, is just that—for the good of the town, not the good of James Bridgeman."

Often she had reminded him that if one had little in the way of wealth, one ought at least to have some power. Both wealth and power were great levelers in this world. Aware that her husband was well liked and respected by most everyone, Sarah could not understand why he had been overlooked for higher office. But the carpenter remained staunch in his belief that God, or the selectmen, would put him where he should serve. A quiet, humble man, James let Sarah have her say and her gloom. Her grief at the loss of her babies was so formidable and unrelenting that he had never been able to feel his own. Loving Sarah with all his heart and soul, he longed for nothing but his wife's happiness and saw her as a hapless victim of extreme adversity, a fate he shared because of their union. While she looked for someone to blame, he secretly blamed himself, wondering what he had done to attract such extravagant wrath from God.

As for Rebecca Bridgeman, during her sixteen years of life she had learned not to cross her mother, for doing so came with grave consequences. Not to Rebecca, or so it appeared, but to her mother. Any conflict with her children, her husband, or her neighbors plunged Sarah into despair. Following the initial outburst of rage, hopelessness descended. She became silent and gloomy, unable to perform her duties. The pitiful sight of her mourning bathed the entire household in guilt so mighty, no one wanted to add to her suffering. From babyhood, Rebecca had learned to predict what would upset her mother. She watched and listened as her siblings fell from grace, and learned well those things that sent her mother over the brink.

The household's constant concern for Sarah went unaddressed by James, however. His silence on the matter of her grief left Rebecca uncomforted. As the most challenging child in the household, she feared she was to blame. She was not pious like Sarah Jr., nor compliant like Martha, and where her mother was concerned, she had become a practiced liar, nimbly outwitting her with hidden thoughts, passions, and movements. The survival of her young spirit depended upon her cunning. Always it had been a contest between mother and daughter. The battleground was Rebecca's heart and mind, and she resolved to win. She could not shake the feeling that if only Goodwife Parsons would befriend her, she would learn. She saw nothing in her mother that could teach her how to lead a contented life. The irony did not escape Rebecca. Often she wondered about it and made mention of it in her prayers.

"Forgive me, O Lord, my deceits and diverse wickedness. My mother has commanded me to be afeard of Goodwife Parsons, yet I am drawn helplessly to the one she hates. I do not believe Mary Parsons is wicked, for there is nothing in her countenance that says so. I must know Thy will."

Over the span of a year Sarah had slipped into a deep melancholy. Sarah Jr. and Martha ran the house. Fortunately for Rebecca, her eldest sister was more malleable than her mother, and she was able to get what she wanted more often, including visits to town and the store. But Mary Parsons was as elusive as a will-o'-the-wisp. By leaf-fall, Rebecca decided she would take matters into her own hands. One sunny day with her chores well done, she set out for a walk to the Parsons' house. She took the road by the meadow, hoping to see no one along the way, but was soon halted by two wives who had stopped to gossip in the road.

"Good morrow, Rebecca," Goody Boughton called.

Goody Wright had a smile for her. "Where are you headed on such a pretty day?"

Rebecca kept walking, but spun her heels to say, "Nowhere special—just out to take the air."

"How is your mother? We see so little of her."

"Ah, thank you for asking," the girl said, eager to be on her way. "Mother is busy, what with the putting by almost done." It wasn't true, but excuses were needed.

"Remember us to her, child."

"I shall," Rebecca called as she gave a little bow. She turned and walked quickly, eyes straight ahead, then looked over her shoulder. The women still watched her. She turned left on the road to the Meeting House and walked past Joseph Parsons' fields and orchard. Through the trees, she saw the handsome large house with its second-story overhang and windowpanes shining in the sunlight. Mary Parsons was outside at work in her garden. At the sight of her paragon, Rebecca's pace quickened. "Goody Parsons!" she called out.

Mary straightened up for a look, shading her eyes to see who had called. Seeing it was Rebecca, she waved her on and returned to her work. Rebecca called Mary's name once more and turned on the pathway to the house, walking unafraid through the herb garden, past the spent asters that had bloomed in profusion the week before.

"Good morrow, Goody Parsons. I've come to see you."

"Why, good morrow, Rebecca, so you have." Mary brushed her hands on her apron, taken with the boldness of the slight young woman planted amid her lettuces. "What brings you so far from home?"

Rebecca dropped a hint of a curtsy. "If I may be so bold to ask, would you invite me inside? 'Tis best, perhaps, if your neighbors don't see Sarah Bridgeman's daughter idling with you in your garden."

When Mary hesitated the girl met her gaze squarely. "I confess a desire to see your fine furnishings, and I shan't refuse refreshment should you offer it."

Mary laughed."Ah, well, come along, then if 'tis youthful curiosity." Taking Rebecca's hand, she led her through the door to the front room.

The richness of the interior made Rebecca catch her breath. "Oh, my!" After scanning the room she turned back to Mary. "How kind you are. And soon you shall know the reason for my visit, for I have not come out of frivolity."

"Of that I am sure, Rebecca. I never took you for a frivolous girl. Sit you down." Mary went to the cupboard for a bottle and poured a small glass of sack, then offered a plate of apple suckets. "There, sip that and help yourself to some sweets."

Appearing more relaxed, Rebecca took two of the delicacies. "Mmm!" Mary's mere presence seemed to lift an invisible weight from her young shoulders.

Seeing the girl more at ease, Mary seated herself. "Pray, Rebecca, don't keep me waiting. It took some courage for you to come here, knowing how your mother loathes me, and most particularly after I myself asked you to keep away."

"'Tis true, yet I must not ignore the one person who can help my mother."

Mary shook her head decisively. "I care not for your mother, nor do I wish to help her."

"Oh, Goody Parsons, I come to you in earnest." The girl's eager face said the same. "It is taught that we all sin, and that we must forgive if we are to be forgiven. With all my heart I believe it, just as I believe you are a true Christian."

Mary's hand flew to cover her lips, then dropped to her heart. "Child, you put me to shame. I am not worthy of such high elevation, but your honest words have softened my heart, and I am willing to listen."

Rebecca took a deep breath and abandoned her glass to the nearby table. She leaned forward in her chair. "Mother is gripped by a melancholy so strong I fear she may die."

"How long, child?"

"Months. All summer I begged her to tell me why she was so distressed, but she would not answer." Rebecca's voice trembled with unshed tears. "She hardly speaks and takes no interest in her work. My sisters and I do everything in the house and the garden, while she stares out the window or resorts to her bed. For hours she sleeps." She looked imploringly at Mary. "Truly, I despair of her, and ofttimes feel I'm to blame."

Mary took her hand. "The blame is not yours, child. 'Tis in your mother's nature to be melancholic, for she is lunar in kind, like her mother before her. I knew your grandmother, you see."

Rebecca's face brightened. "Did you? She died before I was born. Did you know her well?"

"I saw her often, but no one knew her. She seldom spoke, and, like your mother, was given to fits of melancholy. I was then in service at the Lymans', and 'twas I who found her dead." Mary sighed and shook her head sadly. "Never have I seen anyone more at peace in death than your poor grandmother."

Rebecca tightened her clasp of Mary's hand. "Your words fill me with apprehension. Am I the daughter of the daughter of woe?"

"Nay, but I fear that your sister Martha may claim that inheritance. You are like the sun, not the moon. Your face is round and jovial. Put your fears away, for your life is not your mother's. Now, tell me, what do you want of me?"

"A remedy—a remedy against melancholy. Is there something I may give her?"

Mary loosed her hand from Rebecca's, rose from her seat, and walked to the hearth where she stared for a moment at the fire. "Aye, Rebecca, there is help, yet I'm afeard to give it."

"But why? If you know, you must help."

She turned to look the girl squarely in the face. "Your mother once accused me of witchcraft, and though years have passed, it stings me still."

Rebecca got up and went to Mary's side to touch her shoulder. "Mother shall never know where I got it. I will give it in secret."

"How can you?"

"Of late, it is I who fixes her breakfast. I could give it then. I beg you."

For a moment Mary regarded the girl thoughtfully. "My heart tells me to trust you." She went to a wooden cabinet with many little drawers, opened one, and took out a handful of dried herb, opened two more and took a similar amount from each. She heaped her harvest onto a clean square of linen, brought the corners together, and tied it up with string. "Take it, then. This is for you." She handed it to Rebecca. "It should last you a fortnight, and when it is gone, if need be, come for more."

Rebecca hugged her benefactress. "Oh, I am forever in your debt. Now tell me how I must use it."

"Set water to boil, put three large pinches into a cup, and a fourth pinch in time if she be not renewed. Pour boiling water over it and let it steep a few minutes before giving it to her to drink."

Rebecca nodded eagerly. "Boil water, three pinches, let it steep. I can do that." She made as if to leave.

"Stay, Rebecca, there is more you should know. Lest you take pride in the success of these herbs or claim these powers as our own, remember always to offer a prayer before you give it, for 'twas God who made the herbs for our use, and God who shall heal your mother. If you are to be wise one day, you must never forget that."

"How shall I pray?"

"Holding the herbs in your hands, say, 'If it please Thee, Lord, make Mother well.' Then as you pour the water over the herbs say, 'In the name of Jesus,' and let the infusion steep. If there be others present, say it all in your heart, but if you be alone you may say it aloud. Either way God will hear. Now go on your way, and trust that your mother shall be well."

Rebecca released a great pent-up breath. "I give you heartfelt thanks. I knew you were the kindest of women."

Mary allowed herself a little laugh. "Pray tell me how you knew that, with all you've heard in your father's house against me?"

"'Twas something I knew when first I saw you. Will you teach me more?"

"Nay, child, we must not tempt fate. Now go home to your mother."

Rebecca smiled broadly, then pecked a kiss on Mary's cheek. "I'm not afeard of fate, for if God wills all things, my fate is meant for me, and I shall put it on and wear it with a smile. God keep you, Mary Parsons." And home she went, determined to see her mother cured.

· · · · ·

Rebecca cut a thick slice of bread, put it on a plate and took it to a small table by the window where a crock of fresh butter, a plate of cheese and a bowl of apples waited. Returning to the table by the fire, she slipped a bag of herbs from her apron pocket, untied it, and dropped three pinches into a cup before she carefully retied the bag and returned it to her pocket.

"Mother," she called, walking to the foot of the stairs. "Mother, your breakfast is ready."

Hearing no answer, Rebecca climbed the stairs and tapped on her mother's door. "May I come in?"

"Come."

"Breakfast is waiting in the kitchen," she said as her mother rolled over and put her feet on the floor. "I set the table by the window for you, where you may watch the sun fill up the meadow. 'Tis cool—the prettiest of days."

Sarah slowly stood up and steadied herself against the bed. "Let me dress first." Her voice seemed to come at great expense.

"Nay, Mother, come in your shift. There's no one about, and you'll feel stronger after you eat. Let me put this shawl around your shoulders."

"Very well." Sarah looked relieved not to have to exert herself.

Rebecca watched as her mother inched her frail body down the stairs. How changed she was. Her hair, now mostly gray, fell over her shoulders, which were rounded not from age but from the weight of her burdens. At forty-six, she looked like an old woman, with sorrowful blue eyes, her mouth down-turned, her face lined from years of worry and fear.

"Here, come and eat, Mother. I've made something nice for you to drink." As Rebecca poured steaming water into the cup she had already prepared, her lips moved in silent prayer. "Here's a nice warming cup, and do eat all your bread and butter. You'd feel so much better if you put some meat on your bones."

Sarah sighed and sat down, regarding her youngest daughter. "Ah, Rebecca, what would I do without you and your sisters to help me?" Her eyes filled with tears as she buttered her bread and cut a slice of cheese. "A God's send, you are," she added, sipping from her cup. She swallowed and sipped again. "This is special good. It has the pleasantest taste. What is it?"

Rebecca turned away to wipe down her work table. "I made it myself with a few herbs," she said, easy with her lie. "I thought they smelled good."

"Don't forget how you did it, child," Sarah said, sipping again. "I like it well."

WINTER SNOWS WERE deep and covered the ground until late March, when early signs of spring came to the forest and meadow. Unbeknownst to the local Indians and villagers, a small band of Mohawks had moved out of their winter quarters and headed south.

An hour past dawn, Joseph rode out to inspect his outlying fences. In the near distance he saw nine Mohawks, their hair cut for war, riding toward the forest with four of his steers. He was alone and knew it was useless to give chase, for the braves were armed and making good time. Surprised by the brazenness of the daylight raid, he knew that after the hard winter the Indians were hungry. His theory was confirmed when he came upon a dead steer, butchered right there, the best cuts of meat gone; the rest left to rot in the grass. The braves had eaten the meat raw. Remembering Mohawk treachery at the end of the Pequot war, he rode off to inspect the land.

The Mohawks were the most powerful nation in the northeast. Over the last fifty years they had exterminated entire rival tribes in order to monopolize the fur trade with the Dutch at New Netherlands. Three years before, they had attacked the Pocumtucks north of Northampton, destroying everything, leaving the land free for the English to settle the new town of Deerfield.

Joseph headed out across the meadow and west toward a round, low hill not far from Nathaniel Clark's land. A gust of cold wind from the north sent a chill through his cloak. He rode past a thicket of naked birch and out onto a plain of dry grass that usually was filled with grazing animals. Though he could see a plume of smoke coming from Clark's chimney, there was no one in sight. Then, up ahead, some thirty yards from the barn, Joseph saw something on the ground. He spurred his horse and drew near to a body. It was Nat Clark's Indian shepherd, scalped and lying in a river of blood. Joseph's steer had not been the Mohawks' only victim. Greatly alarmed, he rode off to find his neighbor.

THE PARSONS' COOK Alice had been in bed for a week with the rheum, and Mary's youngest son, David, suffered from a sore throat his mother had been unable to cure. Letting other work go, Elspeth and Mary nursed both patients. Usually an illness like David's responded to goldenrod, but when his nose began to bleed, Mary worried.

That morning Joseph had gone out near dawn, she knew not where. Their town had a surgeon by now, and she sent Eben all the way across town to Elm Street to fetch him, sending Jonathan to look for Joseph. And then she waited, holding her child close. For the moment he slept, blond curls resting on his forehead. In a house full of red and brown heads little David and John were the only blonds. They looked like their father.

Soon Eben returned with the surgeon. Their talk woke David, and Mary put him down on the bed. Eben sat on the bed and touched his little brother's cheek fondly. "How's my little lad?"

Normally a bright, cheerful child, David gazed at him dully.

"He feels fevered again," Eben said.

The surgeon lifted the child's shirt and looked at his belly, then asked him to open his mouth. "This I do not like to see," he said, almost under his breath. "His throat is spotted white. How long has he been like this?"

"A week, ten days, perchance," Mary said. "What does it portend?"

"I have not seen this before." He looked again at David's tongue and throat.

Mary's heart sank. "Nor have I," she said, watching the surgeon. "Just this morning he's had trouble breathing, and he had a nosebleed."

"His throat is nearly swollen shut." Slowly the surgeon stroked his beard, sadly shaking his head. "We can treat the fever, but only that."

Mary wanted to cry, but seeing little David's large brown eyes full of pity for her, she smiled for him and took his hand.

After meeting with Goodman Clark and the magistrate, Joseph returned home in the afternoon. The men had gathered to consider the Mohawks' raid and the death of Nat Clark's shepherd boy. Joseph had convinced them that the unlucky boy had surprised the Mohawks in the midst of their raid and felt certain the savages would not trouble the English again, for they had driven the cattle north to their winter camp to feed their starving people.

When Mary told her husband about the doctor's visit, Joseph was silent. She saw a shadow fall over his whole body as he lifted his youngest boy into his arms and sat down beside the kitchen fire. He held his child for hours as the boy slept, rocking him, kissing his forehead, not speaking. Mary asked if he wanted supper. He refused, and stayed with his son until twilight, when little David died.

XVI

Mr. Hopkins, the governour of Hartford upon Con-
necticut, came to Boston, and brought his wife with him,
(a godly young woman, and of special parts,) who was
fallen into a sad infirmity, the loss of her understanding
and reason, which had been growing upon her divers
years, by occasion of her giving herself wholly to reading
and writing, and had written many books. Her husband,
being very loving and tender of her, was loath to grieve
her; but he saw his error, when it was too late. For if
she had attended her household affairs, and such things
as belong to women, and not gone out of her way and
calling to meddle in such things as are proper for men,
whose minds are stronger, etc., she had kept her wits . . .

—Governor John Winthrop
The History of New England 1630–1649

FOLLOWING JOSEPH'S BETRAYAL with Katherine Walford, Mary faced a long period of sadness mingled with anger. Shortly after his dalliance was exposed, however, she became fully aware of her husband's deep regret and shame. Joseph's faithless behavior had created terrible problems for both Jonas and Katherine Walford. He wanted to do something for the orphans, suddenly unemployed and nearly penniless. He felt the importance of including his wife in deciding what he should do, and Mary had good counsel to offer.

The Walfords had relatives at Windsor, and Mary thought it prudent that they remove there. She asked Joseph to give Jonas and Katherine £30 each to assure their futures. Well did she recall Rebecca Bridgeman's words—"It is taught that we all sin and that we must forgive if we are to be forgiven." Those words had brought Mary a new freedom. Forgiving Sarah enough to help Rebecca had healed something wounded in Mary's heart. She said nothing to Joseph about her heart's opening to him, but he gradually saw a change in her and rewarded her with extravagant lovemaking, sweet attention and gifts. By the time their daughter Abigail was born that spring, Mary's heart was full of love for her husband, and Joseph knew without a doubt that he would never turn to another again.

HER HEALTH IMPROVED, by virtue of Rebecca's potations, Sarah began to reenter village life. Her most constant friend was her sister-in-law Helen, wife of her wayward brother Robert. For more than a year Robert had been in an unheard-of phase of reform, promising his wife not to drink, and working hard, mostly at hunting and fishing to bring in enough game to sell for a profit. Robert had waited until he was thirty-three before he had married his very young wife. At first Sarah did not like his choice, for she was only a year older than Sarah's eldest daughter. Helen, though blessed with a comely face, was deformed, her back twisted in an accident of birth. Sarah reminded herself of that, and trained her eyes to look only upon her face. Helen had a wounded but open heart. She had given birth to three children, and though not one was alive today, she remained ever hopeful that the one she carried would live.

With the passage of time, Sarah guided her eldest daughters into marriage. Sarah Jr. married Timothy Tileston and moved to Dorchester, and Martha married Samuel Dickinson of Hatfield, youngest son of a wealthy family there. Sarah's son John married Mary Seldon of Northampton. She liked her daughter-in-law well enough, though she'd had someone else in mind. The marriages of her siblings left Rebecca at home with a mother who had little to think about save her youngest daughter's future. From early childhood, Rebecca had believed she would never marry. As the vision she'd nurtured of her life did not include the burden of motherhood and the drudgery of housewifery, she came up with a different plan. If all over town she was famous—or infamous—for her tough pie crusts, her fallen cakes, her knotted stitchery and her poorly seasoned stews, no man would ask her to marry. At seventeen she was about as clumsy as she could be without attracting a whipping. Both James and Sarah shook their heads and pitied the poor girl.

Sarah walked into the front room and once again found her daughter reading by the light of a window. "Rebecca, put down that book and listen to me."

Saying nothing, Rebecca marked her place, lowered the book to her lap, and watched her mother sit down on the settle near the hearth and take a moment to calm herself before she spoke. "You are more interested in books than your own future. Why, I've never heard you ask about the day you shall marry."

Rebecca's face remained blank. "'Tis not something I think about. Besides, I am too young." She opened the book again and looked at the text.

Sarah shook her head in disbelief and reached to snatch the book away, but Rebecca resisted, pressing it to her breast.

"One is never too young to prepare. You know that, child. Think on your sisters—both married and soon to have babes. 'Tis something to be glad of. And you shall be especially blessed in marriage, for I have thought of the perfect husband for you."

Rebecca sighed and laid the book aside to study her mother's smiling face. "If *someday* I am to take a husband, then I should like to do my own scheming."

"Rebecca." Sarah frowned. "Once you hear, you will agree that I have thought of the best man in the world for you."

"Pray tell?" The girl reopened her book.

"Why, the Bartletts' son, Samuel." Sarah thought it a brilliant idea.

Apparently Rebecca did not, for she shook her head. "He's old. A widower. Why, he could be my father."

"Nay, foolish girl, he's not that old. And as far as I can tell—you being such a childish creature—you'd best have a guiding hand. I can see you trying to keep a household together with a young man. Why, you'd starve to death. Samuel is recognized, he is well off. I wish I'd done so well myself."

A loving glance from Rebecca made Sarah think she had either convinced her daughter or Rebecca had decided not to argue.

"You have considered my happiness most kindly," the girl said. "Now pray let me age a bit longer."

"Ah, Rebecca, you charm me," Sarah said, delighted.

THE PREVIOUS WINTER Samuel Bartlett's wife and newborn had both died in the childbed. At twenty-nine, he was respected in the town, as Sarah had said. The elders had made him the youngest constable ever appointed in Northampton. He had served the year before, while managing his farm and Bartlett's mill. Sarah's brainstorm was not unique. More than one mother hoped he would notice her daughter. Others had greater portions to bring to a marriage, but when Ann Bartlett told her son what Sarah had in mind, he took a serious look at the youngest Bridgeman.

He watched her at meeting. She seemed always alone but happy in the company of adults. Her face was charming, her lips full and rosy, her pale complexion unmarked by freckles, though tinged pink at her cheeks and violet around her magnificent eyes. She was too young to marry, but he was in no hurry.

As for Rebecca, after her mother's declaration she cast a wary eye in Samuel's direction. He was handsome enough and would make a good husband for a maid with a mind to marry. Young men nearer her own age seemed boyish. Perhaps her mother was right. I might benefit from a worldlier husband, were I to have any husband at all. She'd had enough of penny-pinching, something that would not be a problem with Samuel Bartlett. Still, Rebecca held back, afraid to tell her mother she was afraid to marry.

THE BANNS HAD been posted on the Meeting House door. Young Joseph Parsons was to wed Elizabeth Strong. In Northampton, when the eldest son of a wealthy man married the daughter of a church elder, the whole town was invited to the celebration. Because of its nearness to mown meadowland with room enough for the townsfolk to ramble, all parties agreed that Joseph Parsons' house was the best location for the wedding feast, though some in town planned to stay away in protest. Word had gotten out that there would likely be round-singing and country dances, and fears were expressed that an overabundance of wine and the proximity of young men to young women while dancing could lead to promiscuity. It certainly had done so, on occasion. While none of the New England towns had banned dancing, it was regarded as risky.

The bride's family was not opposed to a little merry-making. Elder John Strong had answered complaints with a reminder that of course those present would not dance to wanton ditties or jigs, adding that all dancing should not be forbidden, as it is a wholesome form of exercise. Besides, he counseled, both Moses's sister Miriam and later King David had danced in praise of God. Because Mary knew the blessings of music she agreed to allow her son's marriage to be celebrated with moderate abandon.

Both Joseph and Mary had come to know Elizabeth Strong in all her goodness, modesty and temperance. "A crown of glory!" Joseph had said of her. "She shall serve my son well. Her mother is a good example and a prudent helpmate to her father." Her mother, Abigail Ford, came from a large land-holding family at Windsor and had given birth to sixteen children. It did not skip Joseph's notice that Elizabeth's dowry included a fair piece of land. Her father was a prosperous tanner and the first ruling elder of the church at Northampton.

The wedding day dawned with a light fog over the meadow, the trees in the orchard budding pink and white, and grass already green. As if God was happy in the expectation of a wedding, the spring rains had come and gone. At the Strongs' house, all but the youngest children were awake and busy. For a week Goodwife Strong and all the women in her extended family had baked cakes and rich pastries and hidden them away to keep cool. On the eve of the wedding, the final stitches and application of the last pale silken bow were made to Elizabeth's gown.

At the Parsons' Mary Jr. helped her brothers Eben and Jonathan bring branches of apple blossoms into the house, while their brothers John and Sam struck the fires in the outdoor pit where eight geese and four fat pigs would roast on spits. In the kitchen Alice and Elspeth were in a sweat over the puddings, while six-year-old Hannah leaned on the high-chair enticing little Abigail to eat her egg. Mary was everywhere at once, trying to remember to send someone to cut some jonquils in the meadow, while Joseph, her stalwart spouse, rolled over in bed and covered his head with a pillow. When he finally got up he reminded Mary to see to the preparation of sack posset, his favorite drink.

Elder John Strong would make four trips to the Parsons' with carts full of his eldest daughters, their cook, the amassed pastry, roasted vegetables, salad makings, cold roast chickens, wine and beer barrels—enough for the whole town. Following the early afternoon wedding at the magistrate's with only the families in attendance, guests were expected on the meadow where they would find a long table groaning under a more than bountiful feast.

The sun shone on a meadow swarming with villagers, everyone in their finest. Excited children romped among the jonquils Mary forgot to cut. The smell of roasting meats wafted onto the breeze, making mouths water. The bride, who could not let go of young Joseph's arm, glowed in her pale-blue gown with a white laced cap covering her black hair. As cups clinked at the end of a toast, Mary could not look at the couple without a smile on her lips and a tear in her throat. When the music began—Samuel and John on flutes, William Hannum playing the fiddle—couples gathered for a round of dancing.

The light happy notes of "Rose is White and Rose is Red" brought all hands to the center of the ring and back, turning and turning, then forward and back as wives and maids bounced in and out under their partners' arms.

Eben, whose freckles had never left his handsome face and whose chin now sprouted the first soft hairs of a beard, asked his mother to partner him in the dance. When they joined the circle, Mary was suddenly visited by a memory of the last time she had danced, at her brother's wedding in Springfield, months before little David had died. The little boy had asked her to let him join the long line of dancers, and Mary had lifted him into her arms and carried him through the first steps.

"Let me dance by myself," he'd demanded, and she'd put him down with a kiss. He seemed to wink one brown eye, as if to soften the blow, then watched the other lads and tried his best to follow. She had taken his hand and led him forward and back to a bow, changing places with him in the line. Flushed with happiness, he had skipped and laughed, dancing in his new breeches, his curly blond head bobbing out of rhythm, in and around the dancers. She knew he would be her last son, for with the birth of Abigail the year before, she believed her child-bearing days were over.

Today as she danced with Eben she was fully aware that some of the maids bouncing past had an eye for him. He hooked arms with her and gave her a turn. "You, my mother, are the most beautiful."

She laughed at him. "You, my son, are a blessed liar. Soon I shall be a grandmother."

Sam Wright had dashed across the road and come back with his militia drum, and George Alexander had gone home to find his cittern hidden away in a wooden chest in the attic. When George returned, all smiles, they struck up the old tune "Parson's Farewell." Everyone laughed at the pun, and groups of four gathered to touch left hands and step to the right. Eager to dance with her husband, Mary went in search of him, and as she did, out of the corner of her mind's eye she caught a glimpse of little David as he ran off alone to play in the meadow.

Feeling a tug on her sleeve, she turned to see Honor Hannum's smiling face. Though it had been years since the Hannums had recanted their testimony against Mary in the slander case, Mary had maintained little more than a nodding acquaintance with her neighbor.

"What a glorious day! What a fine couple—your son and the comely Elizabeth." Honor Hannum took Mary's hand. "Glad am I to know we have put the past behind."

"I too," Mary said, giving her neighbor's hand a friendly squeeze.

"I had wished to see Goodwife Bridgeman and her family here today," Honor said, sending a chill to Mary's heart. Clearly the woman had used this ploy to provoke a reaction, perhaps to gossip. "What a great shame," she went on, "a pity she will not soften her heart toward you." She smiled triumphantly, her tongue fairly dripping with spite.

"So we may hope," Mary said, her anger rising, "though I'm sure I would rather not see her standing here like you, pretending friendship with me."

In another part of town, Rebecca Bridgeman worked alone in the garden, hoping sounds of wedding revelry would come her way. She leaned on her hoe, closed her eyes and listened, imagining the winged sounds of flutes, a fiddle and drum flying over the farmyards and houses: over the Fitches', the Boughtons', the Bascoms' to sing in Rebecca's mind where dancers decked in ribbons and laces were free to frolic on the meadow. Rebecca's heart and head yearned for the joy of it all.

Shortly before the wedding she had called on Mary, tearfully explaining that her mother had forbidden her to attend the feast.

"I fear time has not softened your mother's feelings toward me," Mary said. "We must pray that one day she will be free."

Dropping her hoe at last, Rebecca ran down the road past the Bascoms' and the Boughtons'. She slipped stealthily inside Joseph

Fitch's barn and climbed the ladder to the loft, planting herself in the shadow of the hay door. From there she could see the Parsons' house across the road and watch the dancers. She smelled pigs roasting and studied the maids' gowns as they danced. She could taste all the fun she was missing, just because her mother hated Mary Parsons and always would.

XVII

My young Mary does mind the dairy,
While I go a howing, and mowing each morn;
Then hey the little spinning wheel
Merrily round does reel
While I am singing amidst the corn:
Cream and kisses both are my delight
She gives me them, and the joys of night;
She's soft as the air,
As morning fair,
Is not such a maid a most pleasing sight.

"The Happy Husbandman"
A spinner's poem

THE BARTLETTS AND the Bridgemans agreed that Samuel could come to call. The young couple would be allowed to meet in their respective homes and take walks together, to talk privately and begin to know one another. Rebecca would not be ready for marriage until she was older and more practiced in all the domestic arts. Samuel, already in love with the sprightly young maid, was willing to wait. In the meantime he worked long hours enlarging and improving the house where he'd lived with his first wife, longing for the day he would bring Rebecca home.

Rebecca liked the way Samuel looked at her, the way he made her feel when he took her hand. And while she liked it that her mother insisted she have two new gowns, she still felt in control of whether or not she would marry. Two or three years must pass, and that seemed a long time. She was prepared to tell him that she did not intend to slave over fires baking or do laundry until her knuckles bled. If Samuel wanted her, he would have to take her with all her faults and provide her with a servant.

After several months Samuel proposed, and Rebecca, who believed that he fully understood her conditions, accepted. That night she was struck with terror and could not sleep. The next day her heart sank into the depths of fear that sent her to Mary Parsons' door. Mary listened to Rebecca's fears, spoken in a torrent of words as the girl wrung her hands and wept, but Mary could not put her finger on the problem. "What exactly do you fear, child?"

The question surprised Rebecca. "For all the world, I know not."

Mary took her hand. "Are you afeard you cannot run a household?"

"Nay, Samuel knows I'll need help." She stood up and began to pace.

"It is the marriage bed you fear?"

"I know nothing of it. How then could I fear it? Yet there is something fearsome at the back of my mind." Rebecca hastened back to her chair, closed her eyes a moment, and rested her chin on her palm. She was quiet for a time, then her face told Mary that she had made a discovery. "I fear bearing children," she said, filling up with tears.

"'Tis a common fear, but with a babe at your breast the pain is soon forgotten," Mary said, hoping to comfort her.

"Nay, 'tis not the birthing that fills me with apprehension, 'tis the dying!" she cried.

Mary knew that from an early age Rebecca had watched her mother mourn the death of every infant born in that house and never recover from her grief. She drew her young friend close and patted her back. "Ah, child, 'tis the way of the world, and as women we must bear up. Once again I will say you are not your mother. God has a different plan for you."

Rebecca looked at her through tears. "How can you know?"

Mary saw that the girl wanted to believe her. "I know it, sure as I know my own name. Dry your tears and fear not. Samuel will make a fine husband."

As time passed Rebecca began to feel some comfort, knowing what it was she feared and that Mary thought God had a different plan for her. She knew that since Grandmother Eve, God had much the same plan for all women—bringing forth children in pain. Many suffered, and there were numerous deaths in childbed, but what of Mary, who had lost only two? In her prayers Rebecca asked God to let her be like Mary Parsons. She was happy to know that the man who wanted to marry her was handsome, kind, and well placed in the town. Her affection for Samuel grew steadily, and she looked forward to their meetings with excitement.

One day as she walked with him along Mill River she felt so light-hearted that she couldn't stop herself from prattling on, her thoughts coming as if to bare her soul.

"I know a place where wondrous fine herbs do wildly grow," she said. "'Tis the prettiest place on earth!"

"Nay, Rebecca." He stopped to gaze at her. "Your face be the prettiest place on earth."

"I want to learn about all herbs," she said, wishing he would take interest in her words rather than her looks. "Did you know that God has made a thing to cure every ill?"

"Of course, he gave you to me." He reached to draw her close.

Rebecca settled into his arms. "But think on it, Samuel. If we put the herbs to a trial, then we may know. Would that I might learn to rid the world of sickness."

He bent to kiss her lips, saying afterward, "Hush, and let us talk of the day we shall marry, or I'll believe what Father says, that a woman's mouth is never still."

Briefly silenced, Rebecca moved away then turned back to face him. "I want to tell you my thoughts and if you listen well, I'll let you kiss me some more after."

He took her hand and kissed it. "Be quick, then, and say what burns to be said."

"Samuel!" She snatched her hand back and stood with arms

akimbo. "If you don't want to know my thoughts, then you don't love me well. I'll not marry a husband who leaves me to talk only with women."

Her betrothed looked chastened. "Do pray forgive me."

"I have always had something to say, and I always shall. If you want a silent wife, well, I'll not be that wife." She was near to tears.

"I could not bear silence from you, Rebecca." He took her into his arms again. "Now tell me, tell me everything."

She stamped her foot and pushed away. "You've driven all thoughts from my head, and now all that comes to mind is a secret I cannot tell."

"Ah, Rebecca, if we're to wed, there shall be no secrets between us. Remember? Those are *your* words."

She pondered a moment. "Aye, there shall be none, but we may have secrets *kept* between us."

"I'll not tell your secret," he said, confident as he pulled her back into his arms.

"Do you promise? No matter who pleads with you?"

"You have my pledge."

"No matter if you be tortured?"

He laughed. "Tell me, minx, or be still."

"I shall tell you because I love you well and want you to know." She pecked a kiss on his lips. "The wooded place I tried to describe belongs to Mary Parsons, for she found it first. One day I came upon it by chance and found her there."

He scowled. "She's not well liked among the women of this town."

"They're jealous. I consider her a friend."

"Hmm. A strange alliance indeed." He let fall the arms that held her. "What does your mother think of you and your friend?"

"She knows not. 'Tis my secret, and now 'tis yours to keep. You will change your mind when you hear all the comfort she's given me and the many useful things she's taught."

He looked skeptical. "What things?"

"Remedies and cures. Ah, Samuel, I want you to know her too. It was she who taught me how to make my mother well." Rebecca slipped her arms around his neck. "Had she not done so, we should not be able to marry."

"How so, my precious?"

"With prayer and herbs. She says I have great skill with remedies."

"Well, then. I'll keep your secret. Now, give me a kiss." He pulled her close and tipped up her face with a finger under her chin.

ANN BARTLETT, ON her way through the meadow, saw a young woman standing at the edge of the woods. Changing course for a closer look she saw Rebecca turn, then disappear into the underbrush. She should know better than to go into the woods alone, Goodwife Bartlett thought. With the best intentions, she decided to investigate.

In the shade of tall chestnuts and oaks she found a well-trodden path. Seeing no one, she followed it toward a clearing, approaching with care, ashamed of herself, not ordinarily one to do something so impulsive. As the path passed through underbrush at the edge of the clearing she came to a sunny glade in time to see Mary Parsons greet Rebecca with an embrace. Ann could not believe her eyes. The sight of those two together shocked her breath away. She tried to hear what they were saying but dared go no closer. Mary pulled something from her apron pocket and handed it to Rebecca, then took Rebecca's hand to lead her to the edge of the glade where they seemed to study something growing there. All the while Mary talked, Rebecca listened intently. Nodding from time to time, she appeared to ask questions. Ann hurried away, overcome by sudden panic, sure no good could come of such a meeting.

Sarah had just finished drinking her warm healing cup and was doing the dishes when a knock came at the kitchen door. She dried her hands on her apron and went to answer, opening the door on Ann Bartlett. "Why, Goodwife Bartlett, welcome."

Ann was out of breath, her face flushed with heat and glistening with sweat.

"My goodness, you look quite beside yourself. Come, sit. I'll make you something flavorsome to drink."

Winded, Ann could barely speak. "Nay, I want nothing to drink," she gasped.

"You must taste it. It lifts the spirits in the pleasantest way. 'Tis Rebecca's invention. I know not what I would do without it, for it keeps me from melancholy. Now sit yourself down, I insist."

Ann sank into a chair as Sarah went about making the drink, busy with a steaming kettle of water and measuring herbs. "Catch your breath. What possessed you to hurry so?"

"I couldn't believe my eyes. I saw—you won't believe what I saw," Ann said, still breathless. "Here, Goody Bridgeman, stop all that nonsense over that cup, and come sit down." Ann's voice quivered with anxiety. "I have something of great import to tell you."

Sarah stopped short, kettle suspended over the cup. After a lifetime of practice she could smell bad news, and Ann Bartlett reeked of it.

"On my way through the meadow just now, I spied our Rebecca as she entered the forest."

"Dear God! I've told her not to go there." Hot drink forgotten, Sarah hurried forward to sit near her friend. "How many times I've forbidden it I cannot say."

"Aye, well, I followed her and saw with my own eyes that she had gone there to meet—Goodwife Parsons."

"What?" Sarah fell to her knees, hands to her head. "God help her!"

"One day, when Samuel and Rebecca marry, we shall be sisters, my dear. Already I think of Rebecca as my own, and now I am filled with apprehension, for it looked to me as if they plotted a secret."

"Nay, not Rebecca!" Sarah's eyes overflowed with tears. "Mary Parsons means to have my daughter's life, I'm sure of it."

"Ne'er was I afeard of Mary Parsons until now." Ann, too, choked back sobs. "I had to see it to believe the worst."

Sarah rested her hands on her friend's knees. "I vow, I shall go to my grave if Rebecca is taken from me."

"It shan't come to that. Something must be done."

Just then the door opened and a surprised Rebecca walked into the room. Seeing her mother kneeling on the floor, she went to her and helped her up. "What's amiss?" she said. Her question fell on icy silence as Sarah got to her feet and Ann rose from her chair.

"I'll be on my way now," Goodwife Bartlett said. And in seconds she was gone, leaving Rebecca and Sarah alone. Sarah turned to her daughter, wiping her tears with a corner of her apron. "Pray, where have you been?"

"I went for a walk." Rebecca seemed put upon by her mother's constant hovering.

"With Mary Parsons?"

Rebecca paled.

"Goodwife Bartlett saw you. She followed you into the forest and saw you talking to that woman. Tell me, Rebecca, what would the daughter of Sarah Bridgeman have to say to Mary Parsons?"

"Naught of import, Mother, I assure you. Why, I just followed her into the forest, as Goodwife Bartlett followed me."

"I cannot believe that." Sarah began to pace. "You met her there. It was arranged that you should meet, was it not?"

"Nay, it was not."

"Well, 'tis plain to see that I waste my breath. If I stood here all day begging for the truth I would not hear it. You have no pity for me, none at all." Sarah headed for her bed, turning for one last word. "I'll ask no more questions now, but I swear to learn the truth. I'll know what's going on between you and that woman, Rebecca. I vow it!"

PART THREE
Not the Sins of a Witch

I

It was not long before the Witch thus in the Trap, was brought upon her Tryal . . . when she did plead, it was with Confession rather than Denial of her Guilt. Order was given to search the old womans house, from whence there were brought into the Court, several small Images, or Puppets, or Babies, made of Raggs, and stuff't with Goat's hair, and other such Ingredients. When these were produced, the vile Woman acknowledged, that her way to torment the Objects of her malice, was by wetting of her Finger with her Spittle, and streaking of those little Images.

—Cotton Mather (1663–1728)
Pastor, North Church, Boston

Northampton, Massachusetts Bay Colony, 1674

FOR A FLEETING moment Mary felt alone in the wilderness, set down on the frontier of the New World as she had been so long ago, a child torn from England. On a rainy summer day in the dim light of her kitchen she suckled her last, her eleventh child. Though birthdays were of no import among the Saints, Mary had lived forty-six years. Out of those, twenty-five had been given to childbearing. Releasing her mind to wander outside the window,

345

she looked out at a black-and-blue sky hanging over her husband's green fields. Wind stirred the nearby forest and drove the rain against her windowpanes. The storm whistled through the apple orchard, but no rumbling carts or pounding horses' hooves troubled the road, no outlanders passed on their way to town. She stared at torrents of rain washing her windows as thunder rumbled and a bolt of lightning struck nearby.

The tempest did not frighten her, but something else did—a fearsome shadow flickering at the back of her mind. She was alert to signs, used to harbingers, preludes, portents of good and evil. She shivered, then closed her eyes and tried to bring into focus something dark and powerful stirring through her consciousness. When the misty warning would take no shape, she chided herself for being foolish. Brushing aside her fears, she gazed down with pleasure on her pretty child, plump and rosy in a little gown styled like her own.

The storm passed as quickly as it had come. Shafts of sunlight raced through breaches in the clouds to gild the orchard. But, sunlight or not, the murky vision came back to tug at her reason. Mary closed her eyes. Whatever it was, the obscure danger loomed, ominous as a dark and whistling wind or a pelting gale. Not like drumming hooves or creaking wheels did it come, but it pummeled the road like the pounding of heavy boots. Hoping the sound of her own voice would quiet her mind and relieve her fears, she spoke to Elspeth, who was at work by the hearth.

"Ah, my poor little Esther. Her father chides me so for keeping her too long at the breast." The toddler had stopped suckling. Mary brushed a kiss against her wispy curls.

Busy over several small fires in the great fireplace, Elspeth felt comfortable enough in the household not to hide her disapproval. Turning a strict countenance upon Mary, she shook her head. "In my estimation Esther's too old for a sucking child. You'll hasten her ruin."

Though neither the meaning of Elspeth's words nor her pointed look escaped Mary, she made no effort to argue her case. As Esther slipped off her knee and toddled across the room, Mary turned her attention toward the window. A woman was coming on foot up the road. Not eager for a visitor, she asked Elspeth if the latchstring was out. Since the death in early spring of Alice, the Parsons' cook, Elspeth had most everything to do by herself, and Mary could see that she looked harried.

"Busy as I am," she said, "I'm not apt to keep my eye on the latchstring." She darted a glance at Mary and went on bustling over her preparations for the midday meal.

Poor Elspeth. She wonders why I dally with my child and don't give her a hand. "I'll see to it myself," Mary said. "'Tis an unseasonable hour to come calling."

She opened the door to a somber-faced Margaret Wright. Suppressing an impulse to send her away, she invited her in, for Goodwife Wright was dear to her.

The breathless visitor blurted out, "Have you heard the news?"

"I've heard no news, not since the Indians shot at the Hewitts' son."

Margaret hurried into the room. "Cry you mercy, something worse, oh, something so terrible has happened, and none can make sense of it."

Mary guided her toward the settle. "Elspeth, fetch a glass of sack."

The goodwife fanned herself with one hand. "Ah, I thank you, for in faith I could use something to steady me."

"Come, Margaret, you frighten me. I should be shrieking with terror at this moment, did I not know my husband's and children's whereabouts."

"Forgive me," the visitor said, accepting the small glass of amber liquid Elspeth brought her.

"No, 'tis not your family's loss, but the Bridgemans' and the Bartletts'." She paused for a sip of her drink. "Rebecca is dead. That lovely creature, less than two years a wife."

Mary clutched the table's edge as the room revolved at a dizzy speed. Feeling as though she would vomit, she could not stop shaking or stop repeating a single word. "Rebecca? Rebecca? REBECCA?"

She felt hands take her by the shoulders and guide her to a chair. Elspeth embraced her a moment and whispered, "For God's sake, hold on to yourself." She made her mistress sit down and returned to the cupboard to pour two more glasses of sack—one for herself, one for Mary.

"Aye," Margaret said, "I am certain. My husband told me, just now. He was at the ordinary last even, where everyone spoke of it. He got home so late I didn't learn till this morn."

Elspeth's eyes brimmed with tears. "What happened?"

Margaret shook her head. "No one knows. When Samuel came home for dinner he found her in bed, as though she had gone to lie down and never got up again."

The glass of sack trembled in Mary's hand. "I can't believe it! She's so young, so dear. Dear God, have mercy on—"

"Have mercy on Rebecca's soul," Elspeth said, giving Mary a sharp look. "Drink your sack, Mistress," she commanded.

What does it matter now, Mary thought, if Goody Wright or the whole town knows that Rebecca was my friend?

But Mary obeyed Elspeth and lifted the glass, emptying it swiftly. Elspeth poured her another and downed her own, as Goodwife Wright looked back and forth between them with questions in her eyes.

"I came to you to comfort myself," she said, "not to give you sorrow. But now I see you both greatly grieved. I did not know that you—that you and Rebecca—were friends."

"She is *my* friend," Elspeth said firmly, as Mary stared past her neighbor at the whitewashed wall. "She'd make a disaster of her baking, then come round my door with shillings in her hand for my master." The servant smiled, remembering. "And she would beg me for a pie or bread. She'd let her husband think that she'd learned to bake. At other times she'd ask to come in and watch me work so as she might learn. But she was near hopeless as a cook and—dare I say it?—lacked most every skill needed by a wife."

Margaret's eyebrows had risen half an inch. "I wonder what Sarah Bridgeman thought of that?" she said to Mary. "*Her* daughter in *your* kitchen?"

Again, Elspeth answered. "Rebecca kept it secret from her, just as she kept it from her husband."

Mary still had not rejoined the conversation. She rose from her chair. "Please excuse me. I am unwell." She held a hand to her mouth as she hurried from the room.

The goodwives vowed they had known all along that Rebecca's life would be short. They remembered her birth twenty-two years before, under a night sky marked by the largest comet ever seen over New England. With Sarah Bridgeman's husband praying outside the closed door and the curtains drawn tight to hide the heavenly portent, the women had helped Rebecca into the world. She had been with them only as long as fate allowed. And now the women prepared her body for burial.

An investigation into her death found no reason for a young woman in the prime of her life to die. Rebecca had no symptoms of illness, and nothing on her body indicated an injury. Most believed it was a simple matter of fate, while others contended something more sinister had helped her death along.

To no one's surprise, Sarah Bridgeman took to her bed—not the best bed in the house that sat proudly in the front room, but one upstairs away from the rest of the household where she could mourn alone. She was close to sixty years old. Her milky skin had soured, her blue eyes gleamed pink, her once-golden hair lay lifeless, nearly white, on her pillow. Rebecca's demise would be the death of her, she was sure.

Throughout a life that her recall marked only as tragedy, she had never felt less willing to go on. She shifted to her side, readjusting her bolster and pillows so she could face the window. A stripe of bright sunlight cut through a break in the closed curtain to disturb the gloom, falling rudely across her feet like merry laughter. She turned away. "Ah, if just once more I might behold her!" she cried out.

She slept for awhile, then woke remembering her daughter's wedding, how lovely she had looked in her gown, the happiness on all their faces. Rebecca had been slow at the spinning wheel, her stitchery was childish and she cooked like a mad alchemist, imprecise in her measurements and wild in her inventions. At almost any time of day she could be found sitting in a cluttered room or beside a fire gone to coals with an open book.

After their first weeks together, Samuel had arranged for a servant, and Rebecca had welcomed Henrietta Negro, a mature black woman who had come from Barbados to live in Springfield before moving to Northampton. Samuel Bartlett had accepted her fine references from the Wiltons, whose grown children no longer needed her. She seemed at home almost immediately, taking over like a warm, resourceful mother, making the little household hum with efficiency. The servant had taken delight in watching the newlyweds, so in love with one another. Sarah remembered how Rebecca, with her household now settled, had wanted a child.

THE DOOR OPENED a crack. Afraid to disturb his wife, James Bridgeman peered hesitantly into the room. Though long accustomed to such a sight, seeing her still in tears pained and alarmed him. Hurrying to her side, he took her in his arms, for he had news he hoped would cheer her. "My poor wife," he whispered, kissing a damp cheek.

"I cannot bear it." She clung to him. "Gladly would I suffer her stubborn childish ways, if I could only hear her laugh once more. Rebecca was so young, James, no more than an innocent child."

The whole house seemed to groan under the weight of her mourning. "James, today I did the wickedest thing, as I apprehend. But surely God will forgive a grieving mother." Sarah seemed to try to compose herself. "Six weeks have passed since Rebecca's death, and already her face has faded from my memory. Hoping to see her again, I closed my eyes and, in my fancy, began a walk to her little house. Have you ever let fanciful wishes lead your mind to idle wanderings?"

"Nay, Sarah," he whispered, "I've no gift for imagination."

"At once I found myself walking past the tavern and the town's bullpen. It was harvest time—like now—a bright afternoon. Close your eyes, James. See what you see. The street was crowded with goodwives carrying baskets full of things to barter."

James looked at her, her face as animated as a child. He closed his eyes, ready to play her game.

"I could see yeomen on their way to the blacksmith and the tanyard, housemaids gossiping outside the store, and field hands hauling their harvest to market. I could see them all plain as day—and a flock of swans, like a slow-moving arrow, flew across the sky of my mind."

"I see it all, as you tell it," he said, blinking. "Why, when I closed my eyes, everything came to me just as you told it."

"Remember how Samuel stopped by in the morning to say that Rebecca wasn't feeling well? How he asked me to look in on her while he met with his father at the mill?"

"Aye, Sarah, my dear, now let's talk of something else." He feared her morbid fascination with everything leading up to Rebecca's death would plunge her into an even deeper downward spiral. "We've spoken of this many, many times before, and in my estimation dwelling on that day is of no—"

He might as well not have spoken, for she droned on. "In the distance I saw the little alley and the house where Rebecca lived, the house where Samuel took her as a bride—better than any house we lived in for many a year," she said reproachfully.

"Sarah, let's think on something else. I have news—"

"But then, as I came upon the front gate, my feet turned to lead. My heart stopped still in my breast, and I turned and ran away. In my mind I could not approach her door. The alley grew too narrow and dark, the house too fearsome a place for my mind to venture."

"Sarah, come." He took her hands as if to raise her from the bed. "Let's think on today. God's been good to us this day."

Her dark-circled eyes harbored doubts. "What possible good is left to me in this life?" She pulled out of his grip to wipe her red nose with a handkerchief.

James knew she depended upon him for his steady attendance, as God had left her little else for comfort. He had never recovered from the day thirty-five years ago when he first laid eyes on his blue-eyed Sarah. Through the years—hard years—she had remained the same fragile, golden angel he'd adored at first sight. And now he had news that would cheer her. "Sarah, the most astounding intelligence has come to my ear, straight from Rebecca's husband, Samuel. He stopped at our door and told me to expect a visit from his parents this very—"

She didn't let him finish. "Not today, James. You'll have to entertain them alone. I'll not be put out of my bed."

"But, dearest, I know you'll recover when—"

"Recover? I shall never recover. I don't *want* to recover."

"Sarah, please try to calm yourself. If you will just listen a moment."

"I'm not up to visitors," she snapped through her pinched mouth. "How can you talk about good news when our poor Rebecca lies in her grave? Visitors are not good news to me, James!"

At a loss how to extricate himself from this misunderstanding, he began to pace the room. "Sarah, let me begin again. My news has naught to do with the Bartletts paying a call. It has to do with the *court*. There's to be a hearing at Springfield." He swallowed to moisten his parched throat. "And, Sarah, John Pynchon and the magistrates want to look into Rebecca's death. *They suspect witchcraft.*"

Sarah sat straight up in bed. Suddenly full of life, she flung off the covers. Her face alight, she cried, "Praise be! When?—Tell me everything, James. Tell me every word of this blessed good news."

James had never seen her so lively, so delighted. Her ashen face was suddenly pink, glowing with expectation. He beamed at her, exalted to be the bearer of such thrilling news. Sarah hung on his every word. They must prepare the evidence against Mary Parsons, he told her, the hearing was set for September 29th. Samuel had been to Springfield to plead his case to Mister Pynchon, who subsequently ordered a search of Mary Parsons' body. Their visitors, the senior Bartletts, would arrive at any moment to help them begin.

II

*. . . they found a strange place in her legs being a con-
junction of blue veins which were fresh with blood . . .
which was provable where she had been sucked by imps
or the like.*

—Mary Perkins of Eunice Cole, 1673

*. . . when she came in hott one day and put off some
cloathes and lay upon the bed in her chamber. Hanna
said she and her sister Elizabeth went up to the garet
above her roome, and looked downe & said, looke how
she lies, she lyes as if sombodey was sucking her, & upon
that she arose and said, yes, yes, so there is . . .*

—The examination of Elizabeth Godman,
May 12ᵗʰ, 1633

BENEATH A COLD and luminous sky Joseph Parsons' fields lay covered in snow just deep enough to bury the stubble of last summer's corn. No wind stirred the naked forest, and the tranquil waters of the great river passed quietly under a thick layer of ice. A number of darkly cloaked women followed behind a tall man tramping slowly along the road out of the town. Toward Joseph Parsons' gabled mansion they marched, their boots crunching deep tracks in the new-fallen snow.

From her kitchen window Mary watched their approach with mounting dread. The sight of this dark-clad party seemed entirely familiar, for the previous summer she had sat through a rainstorm with the sound of these very boots pounding in her head. "I do say, Elspeth, you'd think I was about to deliver and had sent for the neighbors." Fear thinned her voice, though she tried to make light of the approaching delegation. "Make haste here to the window. They are coming."

Hurrying to Mary's side, Elspeth squinted through the snowy glare. She was afraid for her mistress. Things had not gone well for Mary at the hearing in Springfield. Samuel Bartlett had made his case, and old slander-trial evidence against Mary was also reexamined as the court looked into the possibility of both past and present witchcraft.

According to Magistrate John Pynchon, the evidence was too compelling to ignore. Pynchon had told Joseph that while he regretted what had come to pass, he could not forbid further inquiry into Mary's involvement in Rebecca's death.

Elspeth still stood at the window. "I'll warrant 'tis Goodman Bartlett in the lead," she said.

"Aye, that's Bartlett to be sure, but the balance is the jury of women."

Under their dark hooded cloaks, the women's faces could not be seen from a distance. Elspeth counted eight of them, marching solemnly through the snow.

"The latchstring," Elspeth said, "shall I let it out?"

"Nay, leave it," Mary said, as if a little piece of rawhide could keep this formidable committee at bay.

Mary's eldest daughter and namesake burst into the room, out of breath. She had run downstairs to tell her mother they were coming. Hannah and Abby, their hands still clutching the mending, appeared behind her. Ever since the hearing they had dreaded this day. No one had known when the jury would come, only that they would. The girls knew they must let them in. Still, their questions came in a torrent.

"Why so many?" Hannah cried, running to the window.

Abby followed, crowding her sister. "Who is among them? Oh, do let's hope for friends."

"Patience," Mary said, taking Esther, who had started to fuss, onto her lap. "We must wait and see."

With her nose pressed against the icy window Hannah said, "Where's Father, John and Eben?"

Her sister Mary answered. "They left just after dawn, on horseback. I saw them head north."

Their mother pointed at the door through which her daughters had come. "Girls, I want you gone from this room before Elspeth lets them in."

"Oh," Abby begged, "let us see who comes."

"You heard your mother," Elspeth commanded.

Disappointed, all three walked out single-file. Mary's knees trembled as she continued to stare out the window. The delegation advanced slowly, like grimly shrouded pallbearers. Without a word to her worried servant she left the kitchen, stationing herself just inside the hall where she could lurk unseen. Pressing her ear against the kitchen door, she waited for the sound of Bartlett's huge fist, sure she would feel his knock like a gunshot to the head. Powerful instincts told her to run, but there was no escape.

At last a harmless, slightly muffled knock came at the door. Mary could hear Elspeth welcome the visitors, inviting them in out of the cold.

"We've business with your mistress," Robert Bartlett said, stamping the snow off his boots. "Surely she knew we would come." His broad shoulders sagged under his heavy cloak. Age had bent him, and he no longer had to duck to enter the room. He motioned for the procession of women to follow him.

Elspeth motioned him toward the fireplace. "I shall tell her you are here. But come, I beg you, warm yourselves, while I get you something to drink."

Bartlett hadn't budged. "Rouse your mistress, Elspeth. We shan't keep her long." His voice was calm, matter-of-fact.

Mary admonished herself for acting like a fool and, reassured by Bartlett's voice, emerged from behind the door to open it with a smile on her face. "Good morrow, my friends, I saw you coming by the road and hastened down to welcome you. Goodman and Goodwife Bartlett, it's been such a long time since you've honored this house. Welcome, Goodwife Lyman and Goody Lewis." She welcomed them all, Goodwives Janes, Miller, Lee, Woodford and Smead. "Come sit you down. Elspeth will prepare a cup to warm you."

Mary's eyes burned with curiosity, amazed to see the younger women, Ann Bartlett and Sarah Bridgeman's sister-in-law Hepzibah Lyman, among the very old women from the village. Though Elspeth motioned for them to sit, the women stayed on their feet as Elspeth collected the cloaks that had covered their somber woolen gowns. To a one, the old women wore old-fashioned capelike collars, white and bereft of lace, their skirts protected by long white aprons, each smoothed gray head covered by a plain white coif.

"This is not a social call, Elspeth," Bartlett said, refusing the refreshments she offered. Though he looked and sounded remote, Mary detected regret in his voice as he handed Elspeth his cloak. "Here, Mary," he said, "I have the order to search your body."

"I have no need to see it. I'm sure all is in order."

"These women are a jury," he said, "garnered from the village—chaste and sober every one. Do I not speak the truth? Are they not worthy women?"

"Of course, each is a paragon," Mary said, terror gripping her belly. She knew she must submit. She spoke slowly, her voice surprisingly strong. "Being innocent, I have nothing to fear from your search. You shall find no signs on me."

The paragons stood still as stones. Goodwife Bartlett said, "Then let us remove to the privacy of the bedchamber."

Elspeth lifted little Esther into her arms as the women guided their object hastily up the stairs. Mary felt as if a sudden stiff wind had seized her, whisking her away in a storm. From the corner of her eye she saw her daughters, wide-eyed at the doorway, and tried her best to look brave and in control. Robert Bartlett stayed behind in the kitchen with Elspeth.

The swarming hive of righteous women swept Mary into the room she shared with her husband, and Ann Bartlett closed the door behind them. "Off with her clothes," one aged voice croaked, as a dozen hands reached for her.

Mary pushed their greedy hands away. "Do not touch me. I shall do it myself."

Ann Bartlett reached out to touch her cap. "Here, let me help—"

Mary recoiled, her voice louder. "I beg you, take your hands off my coif." She reached for her cap as Ann withdrew her hand, then unfastened her bodice and pulled open her shift, offering her shoulders for their inspection.

Goody Janes looked skeptical. "That will hardly do. Remove yer gown."

Hope Miller shook her head sadly. "If you don't submit, what should take a few minutes will take all day."

"Have I refused to submit? You know I have not."

Ann Bartlett said, "Mark you, Mary, 'tis no pleasure of mine to be mixed up in this business, but you'd best remove every stitch and lie down on the bed."

It was not modesty that made Mary want to cling to her clothes. Every two years for the past quarter century these women, or others like them, had assisted her in childbirth. There was nothing on her body they had not seen. Hands like these had laid hot poultices on her sore breasts. Following Esther's birth, when the bleeding would not stop, they had packed her with clean rags and bound her belly tight. She knew many of them had long borne her malice, yet when she was in the throes of labor they could not think of withholding their care. As women they were bound to help one another.

She sighed, knowing it had to be done. After removing her clothes, Mary accepted a shawl from Ann Bartlett and clasped it to her breasts as she lay down on the bed. Wordlessly, they prodded her to turn onto her belly. She closed her eyes as rough hands crawled like ants down her back, over her buttocks.

"Turn over," a solemn husky voice ordered.

Mary complied, hating every second of her ordeal as coarse

icy hands lifted her heavy breasts and searched through the hair under her arms. The room was warm enough from the fire burning on the hearth, but she shivered and closed her eyes as cold indifferent hands goaded her to separate her legs and probed the folds of her privy parts. She obeyed, thinking how strange that her stomach rumbled hungrily. Downstairs, venison was roasting on the spit, peas simmering with onions and thyme, fresh bread baking in the oven. Soon these women would be gone, and the menfolk would come home to a table laden with good food. The boys would flock into the kitchen and the girls would leave their sewing and come down. Everyone would laugh about the silly women who had stripped off her clothes in search of Satan's marks.

At last Goody Woodford admitted, "I ain't seen nothing out of the ordinary."

Goody Miller concurred but asked Mary to stand and unpin her hair. Reaching for her shawl, Mary wrapped herself before unpinning the russet knot at the back of her head. Her heavy hair fell to her shoulders like spun copper. The women gasped with awe and reached to touch it.

The sight of these old paragons playing with her hair made Mary smile, and she wiped tears from her eyes. Giggling, Goody Smead ran her fingers close against Mary's scalp as Goody Miller and Goody Lee sighed wistfully, toying with her curls as if they were the locks of a bride. Mary couldn't believe it, amazed at these ancient women tittering like virgins, whispering behind their hands. Were they delighting in long-ago memories of their own lusty uncoiffed nights in the arms of their men? At last the women reined themselves in and withdrew, satisfied that Mary's body was clean, free of fiendish marks or tiny tits fit for demons to suckle.

Ann Bartlett had the first word of reassurance. "Mary, I am relieved to see that there is nothing on your body to show that the Devil is in your acquaintance."

With a hairpin in her teeth, Mary lifted the hair off her neck to mutter, "Of course there is none. Surely you never expected such."

But just at that moment Goody Janes began to shout.

"Behemoth! Zabulon! Balam! Isacaron! Whore! Filthy whore!" She was pointing at the back of Mary's head.

"What's wrong?" Mary cried. "By all that's holy, tell me what's wrong!" The women were whirling around her like a screaming tornado, their awful railing unceasing as each paragon, like children lined up at a keyhole, pushed past for a closer look at Goody Janes's monstrous discovery. Mary's neck seemed to burn from the fire in the old women's eyes. She raised a shaking hand to the place at the base of her skull where a familiar brown mole lay half-hidden by her hair.

Goody Lee shrieked, "She's a pretty deceit! Could trick the Devil hisself!"

Ann Bartlett's kind face had turned white with shock.

"Goodwives!" Mary commanded. "All this fright over something I grew as a child? It got large with age, but 'tis no sign of witchcraft. Look you at your own bodies, I'll warrant you shall find just such marks."

Chilled by what they saw as evidence, the women would not be turned from their discovery. Goody Janes declared, "Thou shalt not suffer a witch to live!"

And calling on God to protect them, they flew from the room.

JAMES BRIDGEMAN WAS thinking about the previous summer, how the Indians hadn't come back to the meadow to fish or plant corn. He hurried home through the snow, wondering where they had gone. No longer did a row of wigwams rim the meadow in back of the houses facing Hawley Street. Five years before, the town had made the Indians tear down their fort and withheld permission for them to rebuild anywhere in the area, but until last spring they had stayed on in the meadow. This sudden vacancy struck him as strange and unsettling. Where could the Indians have gone?

But this was no time for worry over such a thing, for he had wonderful news to carry to his wife. A decision had been made in the case against Mary Parsons, and he wanted Sarah to know that the magistrates had now seen all the evidence. They had looked at the mark of the Devil on her skin, and she would go to Boston jail to await her trial.

"Is it true?" Sarah cried from her bed. "May I believe it at last?"

"Yes, Sarah," James said, almost giddy," the judges will sift it out, to be sure, but till spring when the roads are passable she has been given into her husband's custody." Happiness was a stranger in James's house, and he felt drunk, like a man with an empty stomach who'd just downed a cupful of rum. No matter that his happiness came at the expense of someone else's freedom. He did think of that.

"And then, by my life," he cried in triumph, "Joseph Parsons— the great whoreson himself—has been ordered to deliver his wife to the authorities in Boston. She'll go to jail as soon as the river thaws."

"Ah, James," Sarah said, her face a mask of twisted glee, "I shall dance a jig round the jail that day." But then, suddenly alarmed, she jumped out of bed. "How could those fools turn a clever, unshriven witch over to her husband when everyone knows he's not to be trusted?"

"Parsons will do as he's told, else 'twill cost him fifty pound."

Sarah scoffed. "Is that all? And he a rich man?" Still, when she turned her mind back to the good news Sarah was delighted. She pulled on a dark-gray skirt over her white shift. "Oh, James, everyone must believe me now." She buttoned up a brown woolen doublet and reached for her apron, fairly dancing on her feet.

"Aye, my dear, now everyone will know what you—what we—have known all along. Every last one of them will hang their heads in shame." He got up to stride back and forth, hands clasped behind his back. "She should have been stopped twenty years ago."

"In that way they're all to blame, are they not?" Sarah tied her apron strings around her narrow waist, and then, apparently fully restored, she hurried downstairs to the kitchen.

III

A Traveller, beareth on his shoulders in a Budget, those things which his Satchel, or Pouch, cannot hold. He is covered with a Cloak, he holdeth a Staff, in his hand wherewith to bear up himself. He hath need of Provision for the way, as also of a pleasant and merry Companion. Let him not forsake the High-road, for a Foot-way, unless it be a beaten Path. By-ways, and places where two ways meet, deceive and lead men aside into uneven-places, so do not [take]. By-paths and Cross-ways. Let him therefore enquire of those he meeteth, which way he must go; and let him take heed of Robbers, as in the way, so also in the Inn, where he lodgeth all Night.

—John Amos Comenius
Orbis Pictus, published in English in 1659

LIKE A CATHEDRAL'S vaulted ceiling, the curve of trees overhead blocked the travelers' view of the sun. Riding his favorite chestnut, Joseph led a small cortege toward Boston. Behind him his son John rode next to Mary, and their son Eben, mounted on a white mare, brought up the rear. All three men were armed and wore heavy dark cloaks, great boots and broad hats as protection from the March wind. Mary looked small, even frail, balanced atop Joseph's brawny bay. She kept warm inside a fur-lined cloak, her head hooded and her hands sheathed in a fur muff. They had ridden all day and would be glad for rest.

At the inn in Brookfield where they stopped for the night Mary would take no food and, shivering from cold, went straight to bed. She wanted extra blankets, which Joseph summoned, along with a warm and nourishing mug of flip. Joseph, Eben, and John dined in the tavern on pork roasted with winter squash, herring pie, bread and wine. Joseph had always enjoyed his sons' company, and now that they were men he reveled in these gifts his wife had given him. John, like Mary, was not easily impressed and had a strong, original mind. Eben on the other hand had a merry heart, was steady as an ox, as hard-working as his father, a solid, practical young man.

Over dishes of trifle and glasses of port they joined in the gossip with other diners. Rumor had it that King Philip, the Great Sachem of the Pokanokets, had been seen outside Springfield, Hadley, Brimfield and Shelburne—indeed as far north as Haverhill. The report seemed doubtful to Joseph, who knew more about Indians than almost anyone. He understood the Indians' fierceness of purpose. "But they are not birds," he said, "and not likely to have traveled so widely, especially in winter."

Eben drained his glass and set it firmly on the table. "As far as the natives are concerned, Father, the threat of war is real. The Indians have just awakened from a long nap to find their land gone, the beaver gone, the days of getting rich from the English over."

John had not yet touched his wine. "Aye, they have given their lands away too cheaply. As we all know, Governor Winslow has worked his fingers to the bone taking land from the Pokanokets, and now his greedy tricks and schemes have pushed them toward war."

"True," Eben said, "but King Philip is only a man, and our people have made him a devil, with enchantments and strengths beyond human power."

"Makes one think of a certain back-biting goodwife," John said, "one who's spent her life imagining our mother's marvelous powers." He picked up his glass for a long first drink of the sweet ruby wine.

"Nay, 'tis jealousy that's ruined Mother." Eben looked

aggrieved. "Tonight as she rests upstairs she may wish she had been plain, poor, and mild, more willing to forbear than to speak her mind."

"I know you speak aright, son." Joseph spoke sadly. As long as he and his sons talked of war he'd forgotten for a few minutes why they were so far from home on a heartrending mission. "In her discourse she has been more honest than prudent."

With morning, the travelers headed east on the road. Mary fixed her eyes on her husband's back, wondering what worries he kept to himself as he fulfilled his obligation to deliver her to the authorities. The magistrates surely had a cruel sense of justice, requiring a man, under conscience, to convey his own wife into the hands of her judges. She felt for her sons. John, who was betrothed and halfway through with building a house, had abandoned everything to do what he could for her. When she was first accused he had been active in her defense, and remained her staunch supporter yet—so much so that some of her enemies had tried to bring charges of witchcraft against him as well. Eben had delayed his plans to move to Northfield, although he was eager to live on the land his father had deeded him and looked forward to the adventure of settling a new town, finding a wife, making his own fortune. But for now as they picked up speed on the road to Sudbury, they both devoted themselves to their mother.

The day before, they had crossed the Connecticut River by ferry and set eastward on the road to Boston. Traveling through a spruce forest, they had come upon an abandoned beaver pond lying dark and still as a mirror. It struck Mary how dead her heart felt, even in the face of such beauty, with the scent of spring in the air. Here were the first signs of spring—the rocky slopes of unfolding bracken, swans flying north over meadows bare of snow—yet nothing quickened her heart. All winter she had craved the fragrance of spruce and pine, the earthbound smell of the forest coming alive. At a farmstead at Brookfield, Mary saw two women draping white linen shirts and shifts over the bushes to dry. A youth herded sheep through a broken fence as small children worked in the farmyard. She had seen a goodwife spading her kitchen garden and wondered if she might be too hasty. Wasn't the ground still wet and cold? And what of me? Will I ever again turn the soil in my own garden?

From the moment they'd left Northampton, Joseph hadn't known what to say to comfort his wife. All of the previous day she'd been quiet and withdrawn—as well she might, for in the past thirty years close to seventy men and women had been charged with witchcraft in New England, and thirteen of those lives had ended on the gallows. Joseph himself had knowledge of two who perished. With his family, he believed Mary Crespet had been the innocent victim of a mob, and the other, Ann Hibbins, was so full of herself, so outspoken and overbearing, that she gave her enemies rope with which to hang her. He refused to believe either woman had practiced wicked arts. Because there had been no execution since 1663 when three people were hanged in Connecticut—12 years—Joseph feared the time was ripe for another.

Believing himself a man of reason, Joseph Parsons despised superstition. In times of famine, plague, Indian troubles and the like, innocent people often stood wrongfully accused, as if a hanging would appease God and redirect the course of evil. He knew witches existed and that they had seriously meddled in good people's lives, but the guiltless had too often suffered for naught. And now all the signs were in place again. People were looking for someone to blame for the Indians' unrest. Many lived in dread, over-vigilant, afraid that every boulder or thicket hid a murderous heathen. And in Joseph's mind none of this boded well for his beloved Mary.

He turned to look over his shoulder at his sons. He knew that at present both young men thought only of their mother and the derision and cruelty she had endured. He could not bear to let his mind wander too far into the future, the possibility of her dying on the gallows. Were it not for Mary's oft-stated faith that God would preserve her, he feared that rage and despair would overwhelm him.

Concerned with their progress as the day wore on, Joseph worried that they might not reach the inn at Sudbury before dark. He was familiar with the byways in the western Bay Colony and, recognizing a grassy hillock with a narrow cart-way winding from its base, turned off the high road and rode north, signaling the other riders to follow. Thoughts of Mary came as fast as his horse could trot. I know her mind, he told himself. She mourns her babe—for all her children she mourns. She wonders if she shall ever see them again, at least in any place more commodious than the jail. There's precious little I can do to help her now.

In February, during a break in the weather, he had begged her to run, to sail from Boston for the West Indies, where he had connections at Barbados. She would be safe there, hiding until he and the younger children joined her. The court had remanded her to his custody, and a 50 pound fine hung over his head—so little to pay for her freedom. But no matter how persuasive his arguments had been she would not listen. "I am clear of this crime," she had said, desirous of facing her accusers, insisting she had naught to fear from airing of the facts in a court of law.

From the top of a rise Mary looked out at the soft pink glow of an impending sunset over a large meadow pond's dark glimmer. All day she had resisted thoughts of the morrow and their arrival in Boston. She forced herself to remember Elspeth, in whose care she had left her children. She looked back to the day she'd found her, like an orphaned kitten—a half-breed alone in the world at such a young age. How quickly the ragged little thing had captured her heart, how soon she learned to cook and to spin, so that today no more able or gentle soul walked this earth. Oh, Elspeth, how I miss you.

Mary watched the stars' first twinklings in the violet sky as a hawk circled overhead. She had spent the day traveling widely in her past. Every turn of the road through the forest led her back to the woodland glade, to Goody Crespet and Rebecca. She had loved Rebecca like a child of her own, a secret child she could not claim. Only Elspeth understood, for Mary had confided so little to Joseph.

Joseph's short-cut brought them in time to the inn at Sudbury, where Mary lay restless with her sleeping husband at her side. How odd it felt to be in an unfamiliar room, in a strange town, with an uncertain future. Tomorrow night she would sleep in Boston prison. For long moments she gazed at her husband's sleeping face, then watched the fire dwindle. Unable to rest, she closed her eyes, and let her mind return to Northampton and a warm summer day. "Think of something pleasant, Mary," her mother had taught her. She recalled kneeling beside the little spring in the woods to remove her waistcoat and peel her shift to the waist. Bending over the quiet pool, she'd washed her neck, her face, and her breasts in cool water, then rinsed the soot and dirt from her hair and let it dry in the sun. To rest in the woods unseen, luxuriating in cool water, to free her spirit to delight in the sun—these things, she knew, would astonish the goodwives of Northampton. In a village full of folks living crowded in small, ill-smelling houses, as far as Mary knew no one else ever did such a wanton thing.

From where she lay beside her husband, she felt the wholesome force of Rebecca's blue gaze upon her. A dark fist seemed to wrench her heart, and she tried to scream—It's not possible! She cannot die!

"Phoo! Don't trouble your head about it," Rebecca said. "Now tell me, did God make fairy wand for the use of mankind, or simply something comely for us to fancy?"

Rebecca is alive! Mary laughed with delight, her voice echoing through a rising passageway of light.

"May I see what you have in your basket—what have you harvested?" Rebecca called from a distance. "Mother is troubled with melancholy—will you help her? Will you teach me?"

Looking for Rebecca, Mary ran into the light. "Nay, child, your mother would not permit it. I cannot go against her wishes."

Sobbing little cries of woe, Rebecca's voice came weak, as if from a great distance. "You sadden me, Goodwife, for God has put it in my head that I have great need of you."

"You belong to your mother, Rebecca, not to me. No, not to me—now away—away—"

"Mary," Joseph whispered, nudging her shoulder. "You're talking in your sleep. Shhh." He reached out and wrapped her in his arms.

It was midafternoon when they reached the Charles River, which wound gently westward from Massachusetts Bay, its quiet reaches separating Cambridge from Roxbury and Boston. Since early morning Joseph had pressed eastward, leading them through the villages of Sudbury and Waltham. Except where there were meadows and cleared farmland, the high road was hemmed in by the forest. A light snow began to fall, leaving Mary numb with cold and sick with dread. All day she had traveled in silence. Soon she must face her accusers. Except for God, she thought, I am alone in this. Alone—like giving birth, like dying.

Joseph's own silence hid a racing mind. He was afraid for his wife, and for himself and the children. He had business to see to in town, as for more than a year he had negotiated to buy a warehouse with its companion wharf in Boston Harbor. If Mary were to be indicted and jailed, perhaps he should buy a house as well. If convicted—God forbid—she would hang. He broke into a sweat at the thought. And she might be jailed for months awaiting trial, then he would need a place to live. A house might be a good investment, he thought dumbly. He could well afford it.

John must go home to help Jonathan and Samuel manage, and Eben must leave for Northfield. Mostly he was exhausted and wanted the whole nasty business done with. Even the journey had been trying, for he felt pressed to establish his family at the inn before dusk. Joseph's small entourage, seeking shelter from the cold air and falling snow, disappeared on the cobblestone streets of the town.

IV

At this Court Mary Parsons the wife of Joseph
Parsons of Northampton in the County of Hampshire
in the Colony of the Massachusets being presented &
Indicted by the Grand Jury . . . for not having the feare
of God before hir eyes and being Instigated by the divill
hath at one or other of the times mentioned in the evi-
dences now before ye Court entred into familiarity with
the divll and committed severall acts of witchcraft on the
person or persons of one or more as in the sayd evidences
relating thereto . . . all this Contrary to the peace of our
Soveraigne Lord the King his Crowne and dignity, the
lawes of God and of this Jurisdiction.

The Court Orders hir committement to the prison in
Boston there to remaine & be kept in order to hir further
tryall.

This Court is Adjourned to the 13ᵗʰ of May next at
10 of the clock in the morning.

—Court of Assistants, Boston, March 2, 1674/75
Mary Parsons' indictment for witchcraft

ACROSS THE STREET from Boston Common, inside a tall
swaying fence, the prison stood at the center of the town on
the shadowy side of Prison Lane. Like a shout from the pulpit,
the rotting building towered above the street, a warning to all
who lived their lives outside the law. After forty years the wooden

jail was well on its way to ruin. Prisoners had given no rest to the floorboards and walls. Only the barred windows went unmolested in this tomb for the living, where fleas and lice did the job of worms.

Beside the prison stood the House of Correction; there the poor, drunkards, rebellious children, stubborn servants and slaves, vagrants, Quakers, whores, and petty criminals lived and worked. In this house inmates could learn a trade. There the unemployed had work and would earn by their labors, and the Word of God was taught with the same passion used to convert the Indians. Men from the House of Correction worked in the yard replacing old fence posts, in an effort to shore up the barrier and thwart the passing of escape tools to prisoners waiting at the windows. Newer than the prison, the keeper's humble clapboard dwelling stood among a cluster of young trees planted in the hope of privacy.

On the first floor of the keep the cells had been decimated by prisoners. In the grips of rage or boredom, they had chipped away at their small enclosures, leaving a ruin of jagged partial walls. Several rooms on the second floor served as cells for wealthy prisoners, those who could pay for special treatment, but most prisoners lived on the first floor, some shackled with leg or neck irons. Those with caring friends or family had straw mats to sleep on, while others slept on straw provided by the town. They were a filthy, ragged assortment of murderers, traitors—those who refused to take the oath of allegiance to King Charles II—men and women with all sorts of crimes on their souls. All were troubled with lice and fed poor rations. A good number were numbed by the strong beer purveyed by the jailer.

After her indictment, Mary was chained at the wrists and led from the court to the prison. A large crowd had gathered around the gallows, which was decorated with human skulls and a native's severed head. At the moment, a black woman with the hangman's noose around her neck was the object of their taunts and jeers, one Anna Negro, an unmarried servant who, in the words of her indictment, "did maliciously and willfully murder an infant child borne of her own body." Though Mary had not asked for an explanation, the jailer gave one. "See, that's what happens to blackamoors who murder their young." She had been whipped, and now she would stand on the gallows for an hour with the rope around her neck. From there she would be taken back to Charlestown for another whipping, then released with the certain hope that the next time she thought of taking comfort from a lover she would remember these lessons.

As he led Mary inside the prison she looked closely at her jailer. A remarkably short man, his neck seemed wider than his pointed bald head, his arms were covered by a mass of tangled black hair, and he reeked of yesterday's sweat and today's rum. It made no sense to her that he wore an old-fashioned leather jerkin around his stuffed trunk or spurs on his boots. They entered the main enclosure where his stench, compared with the stink rising off the slop-buckets littering the prison floor, was a sweet perfume. With human beings moaning, coughing and spewing, crying and cursing all around, the warder strapped her right ankle into a leg iron chained to a post. The gaping walls of her cell offered her the opportunity to see out, into a warren of half-demolished cells.

Taking advantage of the jailer's presence, a frazzled young woman dressed in stained yellow silk shouted, "Let me out of this hellhole!" The jailer seemed not to notice her, which enraged her further. "I am free to go and ye know it, base lying jade!"

"Rot here, Witch!" he said to Mary. "'Twon't be long 'afore you look like all them wretches." He laughed again, jerking his head toward the gaunt-faced prisoners in their filthy rags, all straining to see the new arrival in her clean, well-cut, brown wool gown with its spotless collar trimmed in lace.

The jailer sneered at the other prisoners. "Keep watch," he charged them. "As if yer lot weren't bad enough, ye have a witch to curse ye now."

"I am not a witch!" Mary declared, with hollow conviction.

He laughed with glee. "Aye, that's what they all say."

"Jailer!" Mary demanded, "when am I to be removed to my own chamber?"

"Why, Duchess, 'tis your chamber here."

Every prisoner within hearing distance laughed as Mary protested. "I'm to have my own—" When laughter turned to jeers, she addressed the jailer again. "May I know your name?"

The woman in yellow silk mocked her. "May I know your name?"

"This lady's no duchess," said a woman about Mary's age, nearly as clean and well-fed as she. "'Tis the Queen of England, Scotland and France who's brightened our dolesome prison. Welcome, Madam, to the suburbs of Hell."

"Blackbeard!" the jailer roared. "That's my name."

Most everyone laughed except for Mary and a pale young woman with an infant in her arms who lay in the cell to her right.

Mary sniffed. "A name well earned, I'll warrant. I expect my husband, and he shall see I'm removed from this pit."

The jailer heard not another word of Mary's demands, for he did not stay to listen. Roaring with laughter, he walked out the door into the fresh air.

The poor young mother lying in the straw looked up at Mary. "Yer in for a worse time, Mistress, if you put on airs." Propped against what was left of a wall, she busied herself picking nits from her babe's head.

The better-dressed woman in green chimed in. "Ye might as well get used to this stinking place, Queenie. Save yer strength for yer trial. If ye have something to give, I'll furnish ye drink."

Mary responded to neither, nor could she bear to take a second look at the young woman or her sickly child. Instead, she sank to the straw-covered floor and leaned back against the post to listen to the rain pelting the outside walls as a fierce storm blew in from the sea. The room darkened and gusts of wind rattled the shingles and shutters, stirring the stench inside. Mary shook all over, whether from the cold or from fear she knew not. I'll not weep, she vowed to herself. Never will I give these wretches the pleasure of my tears.

Through the twilight in the room Mary felt eyes upon her. She lowered her head and closed her own eyes. All my life, she mused,

I've lived with judging eyes upon me. She couldn't bear to think of her enemies knowing she was in this place. Sarah Bridgeman had triumphed over her at last. She forced her tormentor from her mind, aware that even this prison was a kinder place than her hatred for Sarah.

The cry of an infant woke Mary. Her back lay against something hard and pointed, her legs ached from the cold. The room had grown dark with night's approach.

The young mother fretted. "My milk does not come fast enough," she said, as she struggled to suckle her fussy child.

"What do they give you to eat?" Mary looked closely and saw that she was very young and thin as a blade of grass. She had no coif to cover her mass of black curls.

"Water, bread, sometimes gruel—that's all anyone gets here unless ye can pay for it."

Mary spoke half to herself. "A mother with an innocent babe to feed should have better."

"We're not innocent," the girl said, her eyes gleaming hungrily in the gloom.

"What is your crime?"

"I've no husband and no family. I bore this child in back of the prison—out in the open like a cow. I'd come to look for shelter at the House of Correction, but there wasn't no room. 'Tis only a fortnight we have to stay here, while they find me work and a place to live."

"How long have you been here?"

"I know not, it seems such a dreary long time," she said as her babe fussed at her breast.

"Have you asked the jailer?"

"I'll ask him on the morrow, but it does me no good to leave if I've nowhere to go." The girl shifted the babe to her other meager breast.

"Surely any place is better than this. Where is the child's father?"

"Dead, for all I know. He vanished before my travail. He was a fisherman. From Portugal he did come—here and gone. I wish

I'd never laid these sad eyes on him, but when we met he give me a warm place to lie down, and I cared for him, though I knew 'twas a great sin to live like that, unwed." She paused as if deep in thought. "I can tell," she said, "ye ain't no witch. How did a fine goodwife like yerself come to this pretty pass?"

Mary sighed. "'Tis a long, long story. I suppose you'll hear it before we say farewell, but for now I shall not tell it. What is your name, child?"

"'Tis Betty. What's yers?"

"Mary Parsons. Will they give us food tonight? I cannot believe my husband has not come. Will they let me see him?" Suddenly she feared that the jailer might have the power or the inclination to keep her from her husband's sight and counsel. "I had hoped to have a chamber, and now I'd gladly take a mat to lie on."

"Ye won't have a visitor tonight," said the woman in green, who'd been listening to the conversation. "Ye'll have no more comforts than ye have already."

"If I was ye," Betty said, "I would lie me down in the straw and pray for sleep. That's what I do."

Mary took Betty's advice. Fluffing the straw around her, she lay down on the bone-torturing floor and tried to calm herself. She could hear a woman in a far corner weeping. Except for the infant's whimpers, women whispering and the rude sound of snores, it was quiet. After a hateful day filled with anger and misery, no one cursed or raged; the only storm was outside in the dark.

IMMEDIATELY AFTER HER incarceration Joseph had tried to see Mary, but permission was refused. He had gone to the jailer's room to pay for her to have a room of her own. He brought a change of clothes, hairbrush and comb, cheese, bread, wine, and her Bible. He had wrapped everything into a bundle, rolled it up in a heavy blanket, and tied it with a rope.

"I've brought clothes and a blanket for my wife," he had said, slipping the jailer a few coins for his trouble.

"And who might yer wife be?"

"Mary Parsons of Northampton. Will you give her these things?" Joseph had handed the man his bundle, put off by the thought that his filthy hands held things his wife would touch.

"Aye, leave 'em 'ere. I'll see she gets 'em today. And, with haste, I'll move her upstairs."

Joseph had settled Mary's account with the jailer, paying him for her room and meals for every day until her trial—ten weeks' time. "May I see her now?"

"Not till she's settled in—and then not without special orders, ye can't."

Joseph wondered if the jailer was baiting him. "Whose orders?"

"The gov'ner hisself. Do ye know where the gov'ner lives?"

"I know it well. I shall go there now," Joseph said, eager to be away from the ruffian.

"Yer not apt to find him home at this hour." The jailer had sounded so smug, Joseph had the distinct impression that the man was being evasive.

"Then where shall I find him?"

"Who knows? He's a busy man. He *is* the gov'ner, ye know."

Joseph left before giving himself the pleasure of beating the jailer's face to a pulp. Through long life and trials, he had finally learned to keep his temper.

As soon as Joseph was out of sight the jailer had untied the bundle and helped himself to the food and Mary's change of clothes. The blue gown, he decided, would suit his wife well. Without delivering the rest or removing the accused witch to a private room, he pocketed the money and went home at the end of the day, leaving Mary to spend the night on the floor and Joseph confident that his wife was safe, well-fed, and sleeping comfortably under a warm blanket.

MORNING SUN BOLTING through the windows and the sound of angry voices woke Mary. Two men struggled with the slop-buckets. She stood to look around and saw that out of all the prisoners only she, the man with the red beard, and his dark companion were chained. Everyone else seemed to move freely in and out of their cells.

"Stop! You'll get us all whipped!" the woman in silk shrieked. The garish yellow of her gown seemed an odd highlight in the surrounding gloom.

"We'll be poisoned by the stink!" one of the men shouted as he lifted a bucket to the window and sloshed its contents through the bars.

"What's the fuss?" Mary asked Betty, who was nursing again.

"The jailer leaves the piss-buckets for days on end," she said, as if so used to abuse that it raised no indignation.

"Vile beast," Mary said.

"They'll get the whip sure, them what's dumped 'em," Betty said as a matter of fact.

Just then the door opened and the jailer and a woman entered carrying a large basket of rough brown bread and a bucket of water. They set their burdens down near the middle of the keep. The men and their slop-buckets went unnoticed, for they had quietly slumped against the walls onto the straw.

"I'll bring ye something to eat, Missus," Betty said, handing her infant to Mary and going to take her place in line.

Mary received the ill-smelling babe, her stomach wrenching with hunger as she watched the keeper's helper. There was something familiar about her. *Have I seen her before?* She was fair-haired, tall, and straight in stature, not young, much too decent-looking to be serving gruel in this place. But it was not her face that Mary knew—it was her ill-fitting gown. "Joseph!" she gasped, confused and angered by the sight of a stranger wearing her clothes.

The woman in green leaned near. "Did you call my name?"

"Nay," Mary said, shaking with disbelief. "My husband—he's been here—why—is that the jailer's wife? She's wearing my gown."

"Aye, 'tis her, but hold yer tongue. Ye are at his mercy here. Forget yer gown, or expect a whipping," the woman said as Betty hastened to Mary's side with a fair-sized chunk of bread in her hand.

Trading the infant for the bread, Mary sank to the floor. *My husband has come and gone and I was not allowed to see him.*

"Mary Parsons, your breakfast," the jailer's wife said, approaching with a steaming pot and wooden bowl in her hands. "Yer husband paid for this." Mary looked up at her in disbelief as she ladled hot porridge into the bowl. "Here, take it from my hand."

"My husband? Is he here?" Mary was bewildered.

"Nay, he's come and gone. Here, take it or I shall throw it out."

Mary took the bowl as the jailer himself approached. "'Tis for ye, Witch," he said, dropping a bundle on the floor.

Confused, she wiped the tears from her cheeks with both hands and looked up at him. "Did my husband bring it?"

"He left it yesterday and went away," he said with a grin.

"He didn't ask to see me?"

He turned to go. "Nay. Could be he's ashamed—or glad to be rid of ye—having a witch for a wife ain't easy on a man!" He laughed as he walked toward the door.

Struck dumb by the jailer's remarks, Mary put the food down. She was so sure of Joseph's love she had not considered his pride—his shame, as the jailer called it. *Is he indeed ashamed of my low condition? Was he glad, even a little, to be rid of me and the trouble I brought to his house? Why is the jailer's wife wearing my dress?* That question and others crowded her mind as the sound of a man's voice prodded her attention.

"Don't believe a word the jailer says." The voice was comforting, almost pleasant. "He's famous for a liar."

Mary turned to see that the man with a red beard had spoken. He looked younger than she had thought, seeing him chained by the ankle to the other man. Though not quite near enough to touch, he held out his hand as if in friendship. Through tears she tried to focus a moment on his dark brooding comrade, who lurked close by. "Ye don't look like a witch to me," he said, smiling.

"I'm not. I am a Christian." Her reply sounded lame even to her.

The small, swarthy man spoke up. "Aren't you impatient to see what's wrapped inside that bundle?"

"Ah, yes, I suppose I am," she said, untying the rope that bound the blanket. "I'll be glad for this, at least."

"Any food in there?" the dark one said hungrily. "'Tis our custom here to share."

"Then share I shall, if I find food." Mary unwrapped the blanket to find nothing but her Bible. "Ah, sorry. Perhaps my husband did not think what a blessing food would be." She wanted to cry.

"Are you sure, Missus? Look through the blanket—it may be hidden inside," the dark one said, as the red-bearded man looked over his shoulder. Mary turned the blanket for a look but found nothing. "You witched it away," he spat, disappointed.

"Let 'er be!" Betty shouted, frightening her babe to a howl. "Don't talk to those men, they're bloody ones—murdered their master."

Mary shivered and turned her back on their hateful gaze. She ripped off a chunk of her bread and ate it. Crude and coarse as it was, it tasted good. She swallowed the first bite but felt the men's eyes on her back. Spooning porridge into her mouth, she could hardly swallow, for Betty and the murderers watched hungrily. "Where is your porridge?" Mary asked.

"None of us can pay for porridge," Betty said.

"Then where is your bread?"

"We are chained and must beg it off someone," the red-bearded man said.

"Betty, bring them their share of bread. I'll take the babe."

"But them's murdering dogs!" Betty shuddered at the thought. "I won't put my hand out to them."

"They feel the pain of hunger just like you. Now away, before the bread is gone."

Betty handed her spiritless child to Mary and did as she was told. Slowly savoring the bread, Mary rocked the poor babe in her arms, lifting her eyes to study the assassins' faces. "What are your names?"

"Nicholas Feavour," said the one with the red beard, "and this hungry wretch is Robert Driver."

Feavour's face looked far too pleasing to belong to a murderer, but Driver looked as though he would kill at any moment. "Have you stood trial?" she said, glad they were chained.

"Nay, we await judgment," Feavour said.

"The divines came yesterday," Driver said, "to get our confession."

Betty returned with two lumps of bread, which the men ate greedily. Mary watched the food ease the lines on their foreheads and quench the fire in their eyes. Suddenly aware that Betty eyed her porridge, she said, "I saved it for you," and handed her the bowl.

"But your husband paid for it." The girl looked as if she'd been accused of stealing.

"I'm not hungry. Eat—it will help your milk flow."

Eagerly, Betty began to eat. When the murderers had seen the last of their bread, Mary asked them a question. "The divines—pray, were you sent into the company of ministers of God?"

"Aye," Feavour said, "that we were, and glad of it." He swallowed, wiping the crumbs from his beard with his sleeve.

"Speak for yourself," Driver sneered. "I had no pleasure in their company."

"'Twas not for your pleasure they came," Feavour said, "'twas for your soul."

Mary asked, "Were you with them long?"

"Aye, all the day long," Feavour told her, "and by the end of it I had repented." His face told her doing so had relieved his soul's burden.

"And you?" she asked Driver.

His eyes dark and deep-set, he had the look of a haunted man. "They'll send for me again today, I'll warrant, for I gave them no satisfaction."

"Yer pride will see you in Hell, Driver," Feavour said. "Pride was my bane. It led me to think that one so fine as I should not be a servant. While in service to my master I would sometimes say to myself, I am flesh and blood, as well as my master; I know no reason why I should obey him. Ah, see where my pride has brought me now."

Mary said, "You confess to your crime?"

"Aye," Driver said. As if meaning to frighten her, he continued, "In a bloody rage we knocked him on the head with an axe. And when it was over we saw lying at our feet as cruel a man as ever lived." His eyes sparked with fire. "I confess, aye, but I repent not."

"'Tis a bitter thing to have lived and worked under a cruel master, she said, finding sympathy with him, for he reminded her of a hurt and angry child. "But your crime was heinous, murdering him with an axe."

"Do not suppose I am glad of it, Missus," Feavour said. "Soon I shall suffer death. When I look to what led me to that despicable act, I can plainly see the path I took. While my father gave me good instruction when I was a child, I regarded him not. I would not learn my lessons, when my father would have taught me. I would not go into a trade, when my father would have put me to one. After my father was dead, I would not be subject to them that had charge of me. I ran away. And after that I ran away from several masters—straight into the jaws of death."

Their conversation was interrupted by a loud banging of the door and the jailer's jarring voice as he called across the crowded room: "Alice Thomas!"

As if it was her custom, the woman in green stood up, walked toward the door, and out into the prison yard. Mary was amazed, for as far as she could tell the woman had been given her freedom.

Betty ran her finger around her bowl and sucked off the last of her gruel. "Every day they let her go. Every night, back she comes to sleep."

"She's been here o'er a year," Feavour said. "They let her out to work."

"Pray, what is her crime?" Mary was amazed by what went on in the prison.

"Why, she's got many," Driver said, "most having to do with the use of her ordinary, where she entertains everyone from children to whores."

Feavour summed it up. "Aye, she's opened her house to notorious persons of both sexes."

"But they let her out to work?" Mary said. "They must be desperate for drink in Boston."

"She told me she served six months," Feavour said, "before they gave her liberty to be abroad from eight of the clock in the morning till six at night. That's how we tell time here and how we get the news."

Driver chimed in. "She comes back to us with all the gossip she hears at the ordinary, things folks tell her. Last night she said there's talk of war with the Indians. They found the body of that praying Indian—King Philip's interpreter. Why, he's a Christian martyr, no less. She said he'd gone ice-fishing in January and was never seen again till the thaw. They think King Philip or his lackeys murdered him."

Mary could not concentrate on Driver's story, for she was wondering why, when Alice Thomas had long been on her way into the streets of Boston, the jailer stood a few steps inside the door, hands on hips, staring at her. Had he called her name and she hadn't heard him?

"Get off your arse, Mary Parsons!" he shouted. "Yer time has come!"

She gave him the sternest look she could manage. "Time for what?"

The moment she spoke she regretted it. He crossed the room with purpose, his face red with rage. Raising her skirts with one toe of his boot, he looked at her ankles. Then he jerked her around by one arm and raised his hand as if to strike her. "Speak not, vile whore!"

"My, how brave!" Mary hissed, for he angered her very soul. "You aren't afeard of me, then?" With a bitter cackle she went on. "You'd best watch your tongue. Some say I can turn it black and wither it off to the floor!"

He let go her arm with a jerk and moved away. "I want no trouble with ye. Yer wanted upstairs." His voice was suddenly restrained as he tried to smooth her feathers and keep his tongue. Saying no more, he unchained her ankle. "The godly divines await ye," he said, locking her wrists together behind her back.

"Watch over my blanket, Betty," Mary said as she reached for her Bible. She turned to the murderers. "We shall pray for you." As the jailer led her out of the room she hoped with all her heart that prayer among men of God would ease her distress.

V

O they have laid them on the rack
They have tormented by degrees
And as they have done, so shall it be
Saith Christ, done unto these . . .

—Anna Trapnel (b. 1630s)

WITH NEW RESPECT for his prisoner, the jailer led Mary up the staircase to the second floor and into a small room under the eaves. Mary could at first see nothing but a blaze of sunlight washing the floor and a single chair in the middle of the chamber. Three seated figures sat in the shadows beyond the light.

"Mary Parsons, we've come to hear your confession," boomed a deep voice from behind the light.

She felt as if she'd walked into a dream. "I am glad of prayer and confession," she said, squinting past the sunlight into the gloom for a view of the speaker.

"The chair is for thee." It was the voice of an aged man, as a hand motioned for her to sit.

She obeyed, wishing she were not so uncomfortably situated in the hot sunshine. "Thank you. I have looked forward to prayer in your presence." She wondered why men of God appeared so remote and inhospitable.

"Witchcraft is a wicked treasure from whence proceeds evil alone." The voice seemed womanish, but this speaker had the form of a slender man.

383

She shaded her eyes with one hand. "I quite agree." It seemed prudent not to mention Goody Crespet.

"You seem not to understand, Goodwife," said the minister with the deep voice. "Unless you confess, you shall be damned to the never-ending tortures of Hell."

Before she could reply, the one with the womanish voice said, "As we speak, Thomas Bliss resides in heaven."

The invocation of her father's name made her tremble. "How do you—did you know my father?"

"Mary Bliss," he said softly, invoking her maiden name. "Please listen to me."

His voice, coaxing and sweet, enraged her. "Not once since my marriage has anyone called me by that name." She stood up as if to go. "Call me not the name of a child."

The divine with the deep, commanding voice stood to face her. Now she could see his unyielding visage over the stream of light. He fixed on her through narrowed eyes, demanding that she sit down. She obeyed.

Silence followed, then the old, unsteady voice said, "How will it feel, Mary Bliss, when thou art hanged, when at the moment of thy death, thou shalt see thy father at the foot of Christ, but thyself going away into everlasting Hell?"

"I shall not be hanged!" she declared. "I am innocent. Do not berate me. As men of God, pray with me for my deliverance from this prison." She forced tears from her voice. "Comfort me, I pray you, for I am wrongly accused."

"Stand up!" The shout was so frightening, she stood like a shot. In an instant the deep-voiced minister bent near, so close she could smell the sweat on his clothes. He reached out and released her wrists from the chain.

"Hold your arms in the sign of the cross," he commanded. "Raise them to shoulder height and hold them in place."

She did as he ordered.

"Now, listen to my words and think of the Christ who died for you. You are not worthy to die on the cross. You shall hang, and at your death descend into Hell."

The old minister's voice came with surprising strength and emotion. "Because of thy crimes, thou art sprawling in wickedness. Thou hast seen the Devil, yea, have known him well—keep thy arms out—unless thou confesseth, thou canst not be saved."

Shooting pains coursed through her shoulders as her whole body seemed to burn. "Sirs, what you ask me to confess is a lie." Sweat poured from her brow, dripping salt into her eyes as she panted. "Would you ask my heart to think of my Lord as my tongue tells a lie?"

"The fault lies with Satan," said the womanish voice, soft, almost sweet. "Satan never hesitated to assail you, to lead you into unpardonable crimes. It was his fault. Unburden yourself, tear Satan from your heart."

"I know him not! 'Tis God who resides in my heart!" she cried, her arms like heavy weights.

"Ah, but it is a sad, sad thing to be a sinner. Know you not that you must seek above all things to be saved from your sins?"

"I ask God daily to pardon all of my sins—but mine are not the sins of a witch," she gasped, unable to hold up her arms any longer.

"Hold up your arms. You may not lower them until you have confessed. Remember Jesus Christ on the cross," boomed the voice. "Before the sun has set on this day, you shall ask for mercy!"

Painfully Mary lifted her arms. She could not tell how long she had been in the presence of the divines, or if their words—which seemed to come in dizzying circles—had been repeated, for she seemed to have heard them a thousand times before. All she knew was that the sun had gone from the window and that the room was as cold as their tormenting words.

"Know thou art guilty of monstrous iniquity," the voice went on. "He that made thee will not save thee. He that formed thee will show thee no favor."

Mary blinked, then closed her eyes, concentrating, holding her arms aloft.

"Have you ever—in your prayers—asked that some gift of some object or thing be given unto you?"

"Aye, this I have asked," she said, her arms shaking uncontrollably.

"And was it given?"

"It was!"

"How do you know that God, and not Satan, heard your prayers?"

"I know my Lord well," she said.

"Satan is a wily one. Was it God or Satan who answered your summons?"

"I summon not the Lord—I am his servant. *He* summons *me.*"

"Ah, this witch is cunning as Satan himself," the cloying voice said to his colleagues. "She twists my meaning. She tests my knowledge."

Mary opened her eyes upon the old minister who had come very near, his face no more than a skin-covered skull. As his thin lips shaped his words, she saw a mouth full of crumbling black teeth. "Hell awaits thee, Witch. Thy flesh will blister and char for eternity. Thou shalt bear endless pain."

Furious, she let her arms drop. "A pain I shall welcome, after your cruelty!" she shouted.

"Ah ha! She admits to favoring the Devil over our presence. Hear that? She would rather rot in Hell than spend one day with those who would save her soul!"

The answering voices assumed a hollow, distant quality. As the room grew dim, she felt someone raise her arms for her.

"We offer you mercy, and you refuse it. We offer you the relief of sweet confession. We offer you the right to see your dead children at the time of your death."

"I don't want to die," she whispered, for she had no strength to roar.

"Christ shall hold thy hand forever. Thou shalt share in the glory of His light—but only if thou confesseth."

"I am not a witch" she gasped as the light went out and she crumpled to the floor.

When Mary awoke she was lying on the floor in a pool of cool light from the window, thankful to be alone. She rested there for a moment trying to collect herself, unaware that her forehead was bruised and bleeding. Freed from her chains, she rose and tried the door but found it bolted tight. She hurried to the window overlooking the street below. Long shadows crossed the yard, testifying to the late hour. Then, like something from a dream, she saw Joseph just below, his back to the prison, walking toward his horse. She pounded on the window and cried. "Look back, Joseph!" But he mounted and rode away. "O, Lord, have mercy!" she wept, her bones aching and cold, her heart broken.

She lay down on the floor again and remained so for a long while, her ear to the cold boards, listening to the voices of prisoners below. She was hungry and thirsty and wondered why Joseph had not been allowed to see her. Nicholas Feavour was right, the jailer was a liar. Joseph had come again. He had tried to see her and been refused. She wanted to pray but could not. She thought of her children, of life in Springfield, of Hartford and Goody Crespet, of Painswick Parish and her infant years, of her journey too far.

At last in the evening gloom Mary roused herself to stare through the window at the rising moon. Why was I abandoned here? Why wasn't I returned to the common room below and the company of other prisoners? She laughed at herself, longing for poor Betty and two murderers. Sometime during the night she was awakened by the sound of the door opening and the smell of the jailer.

"Mary Parsons, you had best get some rest." He threw her blanket and a mat on the floor and lifted her Bible high. "You'll need this before the godly divines are finished with you."

"They've come?"

He laughed. "They'll come every day till you confess. Ye may as well give in and save yerself the strain."

This time the jailer did not lie. The divines came every day. They used the same arguments again and again, trying to frighten her, to wear her down, to exhaust her. What she hated most was their cajoling and mock compassion, the way they pled sweetly, promising her everlasting life in heaven, the way they wept with mock sorrow at the horrible fate awaiting her. Unmoved, each day Mary grew stronger in her resolve to convince them she was innocent. She was tempted to confess—it was torture not to. The divines had promised that her reward would come in Heaven. With each fruitless day they slunk away, muttering their failure and her doom. She rejoiced in abetting their failure, for she loathed their persons and their hateful labors.

VI

There is no object that we see; no action that we do; no
good that we enjoy; no evil that we feel, or fear, but we
may make some spiritual advantage of all: and he that
makes such improvement is wise, as well as pious.

—Ann Bradstreet (1612–1672)

WEEKS HAD PASSED since Joseph went to the governor's
house, where he learned that Governor Leverett was away
and not expected back for at least a month. He had tried again
and again to get permission from the magistrates to visit his wife,
but no one had or would admit they had the authority to grant
that favor. He did not know that as part of their scheme to get
a confession, the divines had asked that Mary be isolated from
visitors and given no comfort or hope. Frustrated as he was with
the powers that be, he comforted himself with the knowledge that
Mary was at ease and well-fed in a room of her own at the top of
the prison. To support her further, he wrote to her nearly every
day. Almost daily he walked to the jail and offered the jailer a few
coins to deliver his letters.

One day, walking from the prison to the inn, he decided to
pass the Training Field to watch the troops drill. Along his way
he noticed numerous well-built and well-maintained houses,
stopping at one that appeared abandoned. The house was less
significant than its neighbors, but well-appointed and decorated,
with a small stable and extensive gardens, its back to a little hill.

His first sight of the house and its gardens made him think of Mary and, in an act of faith, quite soon he negotiated to buy it for her, with the hope and a prayer that one day she would enjoy tending the gardens there.

But once he had settled into the house and put it in good repair, his loneliness deepened. On occasion he climbed to the top of the hill behind the house to sit under an ancient spreading oak, gaze at the surrounding wildness—his own small patch of wilderness—and think of his hunting and trapping forays into the wilds. It had been a terrible time for him, softened only by the devotion of his son Eben, who stayed with him for many weeks. But finally Eben had to return to Northampton to help with spring lambing, fence-mending, and general cleanup before crops could be planted in late May.

The talk around Boston was of nothing but King Philip and his recent appearance in court at Plymouth, where he was questioned about the death of his former translator John Sassamon, murdered at Assawompset Pond.

It was known that in January Sassamon had warned Governor Winslow at Plymouth that King Philip was planning to wage war in the spring. Joseph could not imagine why the governor had ignored Sassamon's urgent plea to keep his visit secret. The governor had not kept his confidence, and now Sassamon was dead. An examination of his body had shown that he was killed first, then his body was pushed through a hole in the ice. Philip's henchmen were accused of the murder, and the authorities brought them into the presence of Sassamon's dead body and made them touch the victim. It was reported that the moment the accused touched him, his wounds oozed fresh blood—a sign that these men were indeed the murderers. Joseph was certain there would be war, and soon, for he could not imagine why Sassamon would have gone to Winslow unless what he said was true. Joseph reminded himself that he must now prepare for both Mary's trial and the war.

MARY REMAINED IN the upstairs chamber of the prison, often taking refuge in memories, transporting herself far away, back to the clearing in the woods, the little spring and the sunshine. Before long, Rebecca would come to mind and sadness would disturb her quiet daydream. What happened to Rebecca, Mary wondered? Why did she die?

The day after the divines paid their last unsuccessful call, the jailer returned Mary to the common room below, where she was chained by her ankle as before. In her absence some of the prison population had changed. The bawd in yellow silk was no longer there, nor were Robert Driver and Nicholas Feavour. Betty still lounged on the floor with her pale child asleep in her arms, more filthy, tattered and sad than before.

"Ah, Missus, they hauled ye away for a good long while. I wondered if I would see ye again," she said, laying her babe in the straw.

"They tried to get my confession. How long have I been away?"

Betty raised herself onto one elbow. "I pay no attention to time."

Mary sat down beside her. "Where are Driver and Feavour?"

"They took them to trial this morning."

"Praise be," Mary said, suddenly frightened at the prospect of her own trial. She had no idea how long she had been in prison, or when the thirteenth of May would come. It could be tomorrow. She spent the rest of the day waiting for Alice Thomas, who would know the date.

"The twenty-second day of March. I've been here less than a fortnight." The slow passage of time left Mary amazed and dispirited. She had seen much suffering and calamity and tried to remember how she had spent her time. Why did it seem to have been a year? Before the day was over, both Nicholas Feavour and Robert Driver were ushered back in their chains. Both looked like shipwreck survivors. The jailer chained them up as before, then left them.

The men greeted Mary eagerly. "Goodwife," Feavour said, "we were afeard they had killed ye!"

Driver sneered. "Are ye still glad of the divines?"

She shook her head. "No more." But let's not speak of me. Betty, here, told me that today you stood trial."

"Aye," Driver said, "they got me to confess."

"And sentenced us to hang." Feavour lowered his eyes.

"Ah, mercy!" she cried. "When?"

"Monday at dawn."

In their silence, how wretched they all were. No comforting words came to Mary's mind. She wondered if she too would hang, and hoped she would be as brave.

On the Sabbath, Nicholas Feavour and Robert Driver were delivered to North Church to hear Increase Mather preach. The court cared for the deliverance of their souls. The church cared for the deliverance of those among them who were tempted to stray. First, the sermon addressed the prisoners' lives: their ghastly crime described in detail, the dastardly course of their lives revealed, their going away from the Lord to sin, their honorable confessions and turning again to the Lord for succor, and the assurance that now they would be welcomed among the Saints in Light. The last portion of the sermon was directed at the full congregation. Here the minister told them of their good fortune. Though they could not talk to the dead, who would offer warnings against sin, they could look upon those sinners soon to die, and in fear and trembling take to heart a promise not to be led away from God. In case his parishioners did not know what to look out for, he followed with a long list of sins: cursing, drunkenness, fornication, lying, bestiality, thievery—his list went on.

That night as the moon rose into the heavens, the two condemned men looked toward the window from their places on the floor. "'Tis our last night on earth," Driver said.

Feavour leaned forward, hands clasped atop bent knees. "How shall we spend it?"

Driver gave a bitter laugh. "Ah, let's send for wine and a feast! And carolers, and dancing maids. All manner of celebration."

Before nightfall the jailer came for the murderers. Instead of a feast, they were led to prayer with the divines. The room was dark when they finally returned. Hearing voices and the snap of the lock on their chains, Mary spoke. "How fare you both?"

It was Driver who answered. "Mayhap we shall see one another in Hell."

"I shall pray for you." Mary spoke softly.

"Save your breath, or save yourself."

Mary supposed that during his life Driver had been shown little kindness, and therefore knew not how to receive it.

Then Feavour spoke up. "I wish my chain was long enough, for I would go to the window to see the moon for the last time."

"From my room high in this house," Mary said, "I saw the moon the other night. "I know how it would look tonight. Would you have me tell you?"

"Aye, Missus, if you would."

"Almost a half-moon, I saw, and by tonight it shall be a crescent, all silvery, cupped like the palm of a hand—a moon so bright, yet quiet in the dark sky," she said. "The sky was clear, the stars as bright as thousands of glowworms on the meadow. I am sure tonight is just like that, and so shall be tomorrow night as well. A thousand times again, there shall be nights like this." And with that she broke into tears.

Dawn brought the jailer and two divines to lead Feavour and Driver into the prison yard, now crowded with hundreds of onlookers. There was no time to say goodbye. Betty wept. "They weren't so bad—and I think they was truly sorry." Though other prisoners gathered at the windows overlooking the gallows, Betty did not join them. "I cannot watch." She wept, taking Mary's hand.

One prisoner called from his perch by the window, "They got nooses round their necks, and the preacher is saying a sermon."

Another remarked, "'Twill be their last—they won't sleep through this one."

The now-silent crowds gathered around to listen, but those inside the prison walls could not hear and soon grew bored with watching. Some sat down, while a few remained. The sermon seemed to go on forever, and Mary sat with her arms and head resting on her knees.

A call came from one of the watchers. "Feavour looks about to speak."

I know what he will say, Mary thought, for he told me the story of his prideful rebellion. As for Driver, she knew that when offered the chance to speak he would refuse.

"They have tied black sacks on their heads and sent them up the ladders," someone reported from the window. "See, one of them falters on the steps."

Mary knew it must be Feavour, for Robert Driver was glad to die.

The deaths of Feavour and Driver were not the last Mary had to bear. Betty's baby girl died a week later, and soon after Betty herself burned out with fever. What a strange young thing she was, thought Mary. She never talked about being free. She seemed content to spend the rest of her life in prison. Her crime did not warrant it, but no one outside the prison walls cared enough to pay her debt to the jailer.

Time lost form. No longer did Mary try to clean her teeth or comb her hair with her fingers. She stopped resisting the constant companionship of lice crawling on her head and body. She was no longer shy about squatting over the piss-bucket in front of the other inmates. She lived in her prayers and her dreams, for she had forgotten where she belonged and felt no better than the worst among them. And when she prayed, "Lord have mercy," she thought of Betty. She saw her face, as real as if she could touch it. And then the suffering of the whole world was laid out before her, and she, like a bird flying over the land, looked down on the hungry who fed her, the broken who offered her hope, the lonely who invited her in, and the hated who loved her. "Lord have mercy," she whispered. And Sarah Bridgeman sat down beside her on the prison floor and took her hand. Mary kissed her and said again, "Lord have mercy."

As the days passed she thought less and less of Joseph, of her home and her work. But she could not forget her children, and every day she prayed for them. She knew now that nothing short of God's own intervention would deliver her. She called out to Him in his temple, for He would not forsake her. With Christ, even here she was happy.

Within a week after Betty's death Mary, too, was boiling with fever. Whether it came from her raptures or from some contagion, she did not know or care. One day, from the furnace where she burned, someone called her name. Her forehead ran with sweat, but her mouth was dry as a desert. She tried to rub her brow dry with the back of her hand.

"Mary Parsons! Are you deaf?" The voice was unfamiliar. It wasn't the jailer. "Ye have a visitor." Afraid the divines had returned, she did not respond. Someone tall stood over her and yelled, "Stand yourself up! Are ye mad or deaf?"

"What visitor?" she gasped, as she struggled to stand on a heaving floor. "Who are you?"

He said nothing as he unfastened her leg iron, chained her wrists, and led her out.

"I will not see them," she cried. "I'll not confess!"

He laughed cruelly and led her up the stairs.

"My God, Mary, what have they done to you?" Joseph cried the moment the door was opened on a small room furnished with a chest, one chair, and a bed. She spun toward the voice as the chains were taken from her wrists. Through tears she saw her husband's face and the horror in his eyes.

Joseph was in a rage. "What have you done to my wife? Why, her clothes are filthy, and she is ill! WHERE IS THE JAILER?" he shouted at the creature that had brought her to him. "That swindler!" he yelled, grabbing the attendant by the throat. "He took my coins and left her to rot in that filthy dungeon. I'll have his job. I'll have his life!" Joseph roared as he pushed the startled man to the floor with a crash. "Who are you?"

"The j-j-jailer's h-h-helper." Shaken, the man cringed on the floorboards. "And now I know why h-he did not w-w-wish to see ye," he stammered. "I'm to tell ye that ye have one hour." He scrambled to his feet and hurried from the room.

"Joseph? Can it be you?" Mary stared blankly at him, as if she could not believe her eyes.

"Ah, Mary, my own Mary." His voice broke as he took her

hands. "You have suffered greatly." He could hardly bear to look at her. Her eyes gleamed a pink madness, blood seeped from her blistered lips, tears marked white lines down her dirty face. Her hair was wild, uncombed and uncoiffed, her dress ragged and filthy. She looked as distracted as a madwoman. She looked like a witch!

She clutched at his sleeves. "I thought you had forgot me."

"Never!" he declared, holding her tight as though she might be taken from him. "Did you never get my letters?"

She drew back to look up into his face. "I saw you ride away, Joseph. From a window, I saw you, and I cried out to you, but you rode away."

He held her burning face between his palms, his own face a mask of sorrow. "I've come often, Mary, to bring letters. They wouldn't let me see you without the governor's permission, and he is just back from his travels. I've brought clothes and food and—"

"Oh, Joseph, my children—how are they? My poor baby Esther, robbed of a mother."

"Did you never get any of my letters?"

She sobbed. "Nay, I saw no letters." She touched his face as if needing assurance that he was real.

He held her again, stroking her back, indifferent to the lice crawling in her hair. "Shhh, Mary, do not cry. We have so little time, and we must prepare for the trial."

"There was a young mother with a child here, Joseph. They both died. And they hanged the murderers."

"Mary, the trial is just weeks away."

"This place is a stinking Hell where lives are of no use—"

"Sit you down, my dear," he said, leading her to the chair, then seating himself on the bed.

She leaned forward eagerly, hands clasped, gazing into his face. "Have you heard of the godly divines? They sent them to me every day for a while, to berate me and promise everlasting life if I would confess, but I would not. I did not confess! For what had I to confess to? Oh, Joseph, how is the baby? Does she cry for me?" Mary wept.

"All the children are well, God be praised. I've been here, trying to see you, though John writes that they are well."

She sighed. "Ah, Joseph, then you did come to see me." She reached out to kiss one large comforting hand, devouring the sight of him. "I was so afeard that you had forsaken me—that you and the children believed I was guilty. That you were ashamed to call me wife. But I find God wonderfully supporting me, even in this place. He has helped me to pray for my enemies, for with their lies they harm their souls more than they harm me."

Joseph frowned, not in the mood for spiritual insights. "Their harm to you is real, Mary. We must be prepared."

"Nay! Can't you see, though I am a great sinner, I am clear of witchcraft and God knows it? That is what matters. This affliction upon my life sets me to examine my own heart and find Christ wonderfully supporting me. And now you bring me strength. You have not forgot me."

"Ah, Mary, how could I forget that my wife is in jail?" He turned away toward the window. Even he could hear the hollowness of his voice and feel the incline of his back. "I have suffered, too."

"I am sorry, Joseph."

He turned back to face her, burning with anger. "Your remorse is needless, for you have suffered more than I. Please, Mary, help me! Help me save you!" He went to her, fell to his knees, buried his face in her lap and wept.

VII

She said her first familiarity with the Devil came through discontent, and wishing the Devil to take this and that, and the Devil to do that and t'other thing; whereupon a Devil appeared unto her, tendering her what services might best content her. A Devil accordingly did for her many services. Her master blamed her for not carrying out the ashes, and the devil afterwards would clear the hearth . . . She confessed that she had murdered a child, and committed uncleanness both with men and with devils . . .

—Cotton Mather, on Mary Johnson, 1648

Northampton

JAMES BRIDGEMAN HEADED down the road to the Bartletts' remembering an old truism: A man is only as rich as the number of sons begotten—and I've but one and he married, looking to make his own fortune. He hoped his son-in-law Samuel would give him a hand. Then, out of nowhere, thoughts came to him of Joseph Parsons and one of his many sons. Pocumtucks with guns had shot at Eben last week, though he wasn't hit. The Indians had also shot at the town watchman in Hadley. Again, no one had been injured, but the savages' rash aggression had set everyone on edge.

Lost in his troubles, Bridgeman sidestepped a puddle and as he passed Widow Croade's dooryard absently returned her greeting. His mind was full of worry. How will I manage the planting, let alone the fence-mending, the pruning, and the carpentry work I've promised? What's more, old Bartlett will expect me to give him a hand with the repair of his barn—a favor he expects gratis, I warrant.

Bridgeman turned right onto the road to Mill River. The sight of Robert Bartlett's fine large house soon reminded him that in Rebecca's union to Samuel Bartlett she had climbed higher on Northampton's social ladder than ever he could have climbed himself. His daughter far surpassed her mother in her choice of a mate and he knew it. Used to humbling himself, Bridgeman felt no sting from the truth. Able to regard himself impartially, his thoughts shifted to his shortcomings, his awareness of them so deep-seated and palpable that he began to list them to himself. With clumsy manners, a modest intellect, always at a loss for words, how would he find a way to tell Bartlett what Sarah begged him to say? But he had promised his wife, and now it was up to him. She was too frail, too afraid, to tell what she saw on the day when they'd buried Rebecca.

Saying nothing, Robert Bartlett lit his pipe and leaned back in his chair, puffing a cloud of smoke above his head. Adjusting his wire-rimmed spectacles, he looked hard at James Bridgeman, who sat across the kitchen table staring at his hands as if they held the answer to a riddle. Bartlett had first made Bridgeman's acquaintance many years before, the same year in which the young carpenter married Sarah Lyman at Hartford. At that time Bartlett himself had been married for twelve years, was a father, and already respectably established. Bridgeman, in his mid-twenties, had not long before sailed from England. From the beginning Bartlett had seen James as an unremarkable man. He believed that if Sarah Lyman's father had lived to see his daughter married, he might well have been disappointed. Not that there was anything unseemly about the carpenter. Bartlett saw him as an average, decent sort, with a retiring, humble demeanor. Bridgeman never did less—or more—than he had to do to get by. He had barely made a passable living.

"My wife is ill," Bridgeman began. "She asked me to call on you, begged of me to tell what happened the day Rebecca was buried." He halted to drink from the cup of ale Goodwife Bartlett had offered.

"Well I remember how our angel looked," Ann Bartlett said, her eyes gleaming with tears, "that sweet, sleeping face, those two thin white hands folded across her breast."

"The whole town did come," Bartlett remembered, puffing his pipe. "She had been a joy to all who knew her, and to son Samuel most of all."

Goodwife Bartlett's eyes blinked back tears. "'Twas so strange—they did come so silently, afraid to speak, as if their voices might wake Rebecca from her sleep."

Bridgeman added his memory of the day. "So many came, we hardly noticed Mary Parsons among them," he said, and then Bartlett knew the man was coming to the point of his story. "She would not have come, had Rebecca been laid out at my house."

"Aye," Bartlett said, "she's always said and done what suits her." He knocked the ashes from his pipe. "'Twould not surprise me if she walked through the door this moment."

"I could never reckon why she thought to come," the goodwife said. "Though 'tis one more reason to believe that when I spied them in the woods—her and Rebecca—their meeting was no accident."

Bridgeman nodded. "My Sarah saw Mary Parsons lean over the coffin—this is the point of my coming here. I must know what you make of it. Now that the woman awaits her trial in Boston, we must prepare—we must make sure she goes to the gallows."

"Pray, Goodman Bridgeman," Bartlett said, "do not keep us wondering what it is you've come about." He had a full schedule planned for the day.

"Well—Sarah saw Mary Parsons whisper something over Rebecca and touch her cheek. Then Rebecca's cheeks did flush with fresh blood, and she turned her head a little away, as if to recoil from the vile touch of a witch's hand."

Ann Bartlett cried out, "Lord have mercy!"

Bartlett stood up from his chair and gave Bridgeman a hard look. He knew the carpenter was not the kind of man to draw attention to himself, especially not with far-fetched tales. The expression on Bridgeman's face sufficed to inform his host the man believed every shocking word he had just uttered.

"My wife insisted that I tell you," Bridgeman said, brooding, as he sipped from his cup. "I beg you, think on what I've said, for I know not where else to turn." His voice broke on his last words.

Thoughtful, Bartlett pulled at his beard, having no reply. He took his seat again, admitting to himself that he had always wondered about Mary Parsons—whether she was a mite more touched than the rest of the women in town. To be sure, every wife he knew, including his own, was slightly touched—beyond question less sound than their husbands. On the other hand, though she languished in prison awaiting trial, Bartlett had been among those who doubted her guilt.

Having spoken his piece, Bridgeman looked relieved. "Sarah told me—and these are her exact words—Rebecca recoiled from her touch, and before the witch turned away she smiled with satisfaction!" He let the impact of his words hang in the silence, then, shifting his weight, he cleared his throat. "Now, my poor wife must know if she's the only one who saw this evil thing. She begged me to ask around in the belief that surely someone else witnessed it too."

"Nay," Bartlett said, "I saw nothing like that—and God willing I hope I never shall."

Bridgeman turned to Ann Bartlett, who had risen as if to see to something in the kitchen. "And you, Goodwife, what did you see?"

Ann returned his gaze, though she did not answer his question. Instead she held out her hand. "Let me have your cup. Will you have something more?"

"I want nothing more—only an answer to my question. What did you see?"

She pulled up a chair and sat down again, but when she

opened her mouth as if to speak, no words came. At that she simply buried her face in her hands and wept.

"Ah, Goodwife, it pains me to see you so," Bridgeman said, "and that I may have been the cause of it."

Ann wiped her eyes with the hem of her apron. "Nay, I want to answer—'tis a pitiful sorrow comes upon me when I least expect it. Forgive me, I wish I could support you and your wife, but I have no recollection of seeing Rebecca move, or that pale face flush with fresh blood. Though I did see her lying there at peace, just now as you told it. On that day my eyes could not bear the sight of her in her coffin for long, nor the sight of my poor grieving son either."

The two men sat quietly as she composed herself. "Now, as I think back on that hateful day, I reckon I did see Mary Parsons standing over her. If I try to picture it, I can see her, her head bent down, looking properly sorrowful. But Sarah is right in one respect, for I'm sure I saw Mary Parsons smile. You know, the same little smile she's always worn, like a cat who's et a mouse for her supper. Now I wonder what could bring a smile to her face on such a dreadful day?"

Bridgeman's face relaxed. "Surely my wife has not smiled once since Rebecca passed into the arms of God. Will she ever smile again? Indeed, will she live? She has no will for it, lies abed all day, begging me to help her."

"'Tis too much for a woman of her nature to bear," Ann sighed.

"Far too much. Far too much, indeed," Bridgeman said. "But you understand."

Robert Bartlett studied his wife. She had lost four children of her own, though never one full-grown. Only two of her brood of six had lived to grow up and marry. Surely she understood Sarah Bridgeman's grief.

"What's to be done?" Bridgeman said. "I ask you, what's to be done?"

"Done in what regard?" Bartlett was packing his pipe. "Against Mary Parsons?" He watched Bridgeman stand and walk to the window.

The carpenter lifted the curtain with one finger and gazed vacantly upon the empty road. "Aye, that's what I propose. I beg you testify at the trial, Goodwife Bartlett. Go there and tell the court what you saw."

Sarah Bridgeman felt better, better than on any day since Rebecca's death. Her sudden calm spirit, her new hopefulness, sprang from the knowledge that James had finally answered her prayers. He was gone to see the Bartletts. She looked forward to the hour of his return, hoping he would learn something that would place Mary Parsons firmly on the gallows. Taking advantage of her rare frame of mind, Sarah decided to put herself to work. She was behind on her spinning and had her lettuces to plant, and it was the season to gather wild hellebore. But on that bright April day none of those tasks called to her. They would have to wait, forever if necessary.

Time and again since her daughter's death, her son-in-law Samuel had asked Sarah to remove from his house those things of Rebecca's that she wanted to keep. So on this morning Sarah asked her sister-in-law Helen Lyman to keep her company on her errand. They set out soon after her husband left for the Bartletts' and walked a mile to Samuel's house, abandoned the summer before when Samuel came back to live with his parents. The house where he and Rebecca had lived looked woefully neglected. Samuel kept himself sane by working hard at the mill and in his fields and orchards. He had no more need for the servant Henrietta Negro and had let her go.

With Helen at her side, Sarah felt no apprehension. Arriving at Samuel's vacant house, she opened the garden gate and approached as if on sacred ground, through the yard where a rosy crabapple tree stood alone in full bloom.

"How lovely!" Helen cried, her words cutting Sarah deep.

"'Twould be lovely were Rebecca here to see it," Sarah said.

Chastened, Helen felt apologetic but couldn't think what to say. Instead, she kept silent and limped along the path to the door in her usual way, sideways like a crab. Sarah put her hand on the latch and slowly opened the door. She had not stood on this threshold since the day when she found Rebecca's body. Quickly, she stepped inside the small foyer. A door on either side opened to another small, low-ceilinged room. The women walked first into the dark parlor to the left, greeted by a biting chill. Helen hurried to the windows and opened the curtains to let in the sun.

Sarah looked around, having momentarily forgotten the shocking clutter of her daughter's rooms. "Pray forgive the disarray," she said to Helen, who looked surprised. "Rebecca hated housework. Indeed, she seemed to thrive in what most folks could plainly see as disorder—flitting here and there, doing a little of this then a little of that—innocent of the jumble she left behind her. Even Henrietta Negro could not keep apace. Sometimes I wonder if I was the cause of it. I could never get her to take pleasure in her work as a child."

"Nay, Sarah, 'twas no fault of yours," Helen said. "From the day of her birth Rebecca was an uncommon child, meant for who knows what, but something wondrous, I know. I've no skill in reason. My mind is not so keen to know these things, but to me Rebecca was a regular little princess." She smiled. "And who ever thought of a princess sweeping up and scrubbing?"

"You are well intended, Helen, you always are," Sarah said, peering into an ancient blanket chest, "but I'm sure I don't know what you mean. Rebecca was a spoilt child. Hers was a presence to gladden the heart, to be sure, but she was badly spoilt by her father. That child, above the others, always had her way with him."

"Of course you are right, Sarah. You know your own child better than I, and I always think of such foolish things."

Sarah watched her sister-in-law limp around, mindlessly touching one object after another—an old oil lamp, a flax comb, two green glass bottles set carelessly on the hearth. Helen bent to pick up an open book. She closed it gently and retrieved a wooden bowl and spoon from the seat of a chair. As she carried them off to the kitchen, Sarah wondered why her sister-in-law was so silly.

In a moment Helen reappeared and went over to the bedstead. "My, what a large handsome piece, and how fine the coverlet." She straightened it, shivering. Sarah knew her thoughts, what she dared not ask. Is this rumpled bed where Rebecca died? Quickly Helen turned away from it. "May I help you, Sarah? Surely I can sort through things as well as you."

"Look here." Sarah lifted a long white petticoat from a chair. "'Twas Rebecca's very best. She wore it the day she was wed. And look, here's the little silver whistle that belonged to Father." She handed it to her sister-in-law.

"'Twas his from boyhood in England, I believe Robert said."

"Nay, I was with him when he bought it from a peddler on the streets of Boston, just after we came. He gave it to me before he died, and I gave it to Rebecca for her first child." Sarah reclaimed the whistle from her hand.

"'Tis a strange thing," Helen said, a sweet smile on her lips, "holding such things—the stories they tell."

Sarah slipped the whistle into her pocket and searched deeper in the chest. "Ah, look, here's Rebecca's Netherlands lace collar. 'Twas just made for her by her Mother Bartlett not more than a year ago. See how fine her stitches. 'Tis the latest fashion, you know. When Rebecca wore it over her green bodice, 'tis true, Helen, she looked like your princess." Sarah smiled, folding the collar and laying it atop the things she planned to take home.

The women continued their search through the chest, finding two tablecloths, two dozen napkins, three spare sets of sheets and pillowcases, an old petticoat, and baby things given Rebecca by her mother and her mother-in-law. They left all those inside, closed the chest lid, and stood up.

Sarah said, "There's a chest in the other room. The rest of her clothes will be found there."

Before they left the room Helen took a last look in the bottom drawer, quickly running her hand into its corners. "Wait, what's this?" She scooped something small into her hand and held it out—a fine silver chain.

Sarah examined it closely. "Something's writ on it. I've never seen this before. I'm sure Rebecca never wore it." She held it out for Helen to study.

"Why, 'tis the strangest thing," Helen marveled. "There's a silver disc, smooth to the touch and shiny. It looks like an amulet of some kind. On the other side 'tis gravened with strange figures, and there's writing here—words I've never seen."

Sarah took the chain. "There's a cross, and I know the letters, but they spell no words. Where would Rebecca get such a thing?"

"'Tis meant to keep off evil—a charm, I'll warrant."

"Open the lid to the chest again," Sarah directed, alarm in her voice. "Look in there, under the sheets. There's a small pouch at the bottom, full of old dried-up herbs. I didn't think twice when I found it."

Helen did as she was told, feeling around under the sheets till she put her hand on a small cloth bag. She opened it and lifted it to her nose. "Why, 'tis rue, Sarah. Rue is good for many things."

Sarah paled and snatched the pouch from her sister's hand. "I grant you, rue may be good for clysters and poultices and the wind colic, but remember, rue is given to our hands as a protection—a defense against witchcraft! Ah, my poor Rebecca! She was afeared and had armed herself against Mary Parsons!" She began to weep as her ungainly sister took her gently into her arms.

VIII

. . . The dust shall never be thy bed;
A pillow for thee will I bring,
Stuft with down of angels' wing . . .

—Richard Crashaw (1630–1649)

A T THE END of his first hour with Mary at the prison Joseph strode past the marketplace to Governor Leverett's dwelling on the south side of the Town House. The governor received him again and listened to Joseph's account of his experience with the dishonest jailer. Having pled his case successfully, Joseph felt reassured that never again would Mary be forced to lie in the cell on the first floor. He then returned to the prison to oversee his wife's removal to a small upper room with a window overlooking the keeper's garden.

To her amazement, Mary's small room had a chair and a warm bed, and soon a wooden chest was delivered. Inside it she found clean sheets, good clean clothes, a comb, a looking-glass and soap for bathing. The surgeon was sent for. He bled her and ordered her to eat nothing but cool herbs and lettuces. He administered syrup of mulberries and gave her a potion to rid her head of lice. When she felt well enough, Mary threw the brown wool gown out the window, ripped off her filthy skirts and shift, and threw them out too. Unconcerned that she briefly appeared naked at the open window, she watched her clothes catch the wind, billow and fall to the courtyard.

She felt giddy as a girl in the cool room as she hung up a clean gown for after her bath and poured still-steaming bathwater from wooden buckets into a tub provided for the occasion. First she rubbed her teeth and gums with a rough cloth till they were clean, then washed the prison off her face, body and feet. The fragrance of the soap brought tears to her eyes and memories of her babes at bath time, of rubbing clothes on river stones and rinsing them in the fresh clear water. The moment she was clean she emptied the water out the window and poured in fresh water to wash her hair. Kneeling beside the tub, she splashed the warm water onto her scalp, rubbing soap against her hair until it lathered. She massaged her head well, then rinsed and dried it, using a comb to remove all the tangles.

After she dressed, the looking-glass told her that though her face was no longer young and showed the ravages of her months in prison, her morning of pleasure had brought the light of hope to her eyes. All clean, there was little to do but lie down on her bed and watch the wrinkles fall from her gown. Mary laughed and snuggled under the covers. Her hands found her belly, sunk well below her protruding ribs, and she knew she was too thin. Soon she fell into a deep, delicious sleep, her heart filled with gratitude. When hunger woke her late in the day, she read her Bible to dull the pangs. Finally she heard a key in the lock, and a servant let herself in.

"Yer husband paid for this meal." The woman rested a cloth-covered tray on the table.

Mary lifted the cover to the mouth-watering smell of roast venison, beans and crusty bread. "Thank you!"

The servant handed her a cup of beer as well. "Yer husband is a generous man. He wants ye in good spirits for the trial."

Joseph visited her every day and, after they discussed their strategy, he lay with her and they were happy in one another's arms—so happy that Mary thought, if she must, she would be satisfied to die at the hangman's hands.

The day before the trial the heavens opened wide and washed

Boston clean, flushing the sewage off the streets into the harbor. Daybreak on the thirteenth of May brought clear skies. From her window Mary could see the row of trees in the yard, all sprouting tender new leaves. The sky was a pallid blue, the sun shone brightly. After breakfast she dove into her chest for clean stockings. Days before, she had hung out the gown she would wear at the trial, and the wrinkles had disappeared from its skirt and sleeves. Joseph had chosen well, she thought, fondling the lace collar that adorned the sadd-red gown of twilled silk.

Governor John Leverett would serve as the presiding judge at Mary's trial. He had heard numerous witchcraft cases, but there had been no such trials for nearly two years, not since the strange case of Anna Edmonds of Lynn. Known as Doctor Woman, she had been accused of witchcraft after curing a young woman of a severe infection. A highly regarded Boston physician had previously failed to cure the sick woman, making Doctor Woman highly suspect. Joseph had been relieved to hear that the Leverett court had dropped the charges for lack of evidence. Just possibly John Leverett had a level head. Certainly Joseph had found him reasonable, indeed helpful, truly alarmed to hear of the treatment Joseph had received from the jailer. He had promised to look into the villain's actions personally and relieve him of his duties.

On May 13 the courtroom was filled with folks from Northampton and Springfield. All the characters in Mary's life story were there: her mother and sons (her daughters kept innocent at home with Elspeth), the Bartletts, including Rebecca's husband Samuel in the leading role as plaintiff, assorted folk from Northampton including some who had given evidence in Springfield twenty years before, Sarah and James Bridgeman with their son John, even Henrietta Negro. For some it was their first visit to Boston, and they stood in awe as the governor and distinguished panel of magistrates entered and sat down behind the long table at the front. Once the dignitaries were settled, the governor enjoined silence on all present.

"At this court, Mary Parsons, the wife of Joseph Parsons of Northampton in the County of Hampshire, in the colony of Massachusetts," Leverett read, his strong voice carrying over the heads of the gathered witnesses, "stands trial for not having the fear of God before her eyes and being instigated by the Devil." He paused to regard the handsome woman whom, with her husband, the jailer had treated so ill. She carried her head erect, hands folded neatly at her waist.

"She has been indicted for entering into familiarity with the Devil and stands accused of several acts of witchcraft on one or more persons, contrary to the peace of our sovereign Lord the King, his Crown and dignity, the laws of God and of this jurisdiction."

Leverett was a handsome, broad-faced man in his late middle years. He wore his graying hair long but had been clean-shaven ever since his service in Cromwell's English court. In a time when pointed beards were in fashion, his old friend Cromwell had worn no facial hair at all, and Leverett adopted the same style. He looked again at the accused. "Goodwife Parsons, you may be seated."

Mary backed into a chair facing the bench, where Leverett sat with the aged deputy governor Samuel Symonds and the assistants, including John Pynchon of Springfield and William Stoughton and Thomas Danforth, the latter who would go on to prosecute some one hundred fifty people at the infamous Salem witch trials. Simon Bradstreet, widower of the poet Ann Bradstreet, had also taken a seat at the bench. A jury of her peers sat nearby, twelve men plucked off the streets of Boston, craning their necks for a view of the defendant's face.

The governor asked, "What say you, are you guilty of witchcraft?"

Mary's face was as serene as her words. "No, Your Honor, I am innocent."

John Leverett paused to look at his papers, then looked over the gathered assembly. "Who hurt you, Samuel Bartlett?" he called, to see who would respond.

A pleasant-faced man nearing his middle years stepped forward. The governor thought he looked quite respectable. "Mary Parsons. She murdered my wife Rebecca."

Leverett looked back to the accused. "What say you to this?"

"I am innocent, and the righteous God knows it." Mary's voice was strong and firm, her face free of guile or fear.

The governor studied his papers. "Others have complained as well. Goodman Bridgeman, who hurt you?" Again, he cast his eyes over the assembly.

A nondescript man of average height with a thin, pale woman at his side responded, calling out, "Mary Parsons. She murdered my daughter. No fever or flux did she suffer, no illness troubled her, yet she died."

The governor studied the gaunt woman at the complainant's side. "Are you Goodwife Bridgeman?"

"I am, Your Honor." She seemed eager to testify. "Mary Parsons has been a curse on me—and more. I need a space to tell it." Her voice shook with nervous emotion.

"What more?"

"She killed all my children but three, and she tried to kill John, here." She was wringing her hands. "She hurt him terribly. He still walks with a limp." She nudged a young man beside her. "Show them, John. Show them how you limp after all these years. How she maimed you. May he show you, governor?"

"Aye, he may. Come forward, young man."

Looking embarrassed, her son stepped forward and took a few steps for the governor to see. He had a limp, to be sure, but why was Goodwife Bridgeman cupping one hand like a blinder around one eye? Leverett peered at her again and decided the poor creature was afraid of the sight of Mary Parsons. How deathly pale and weak she looked, clinging to her husband's arm. Leverett pitied her. When he turned back to study the accused he saw that she looked strong and kept her gaze firmly on the Bridgeman woman.

Old Deputy Symonds, in his long pointed beard and skullcap, spoke with a wavering voice. "By what means did this woman murder your children?"

Sarah's answer sounded scornful. "How should I know? I am a Christian woman!"

Symonds clarified his inquiry. "I meant to ask how your children died."

"Thomas died of influenza the same year as Mister Hooker, I'll not put that on her. James and Patience died soon after they were born, and Hezekiah lived but nine months. When she tried to kill my son John, he was just a lad. She set a bird upon him, and he fell. He did call her name from his fever, and said a black mouse followed her and that she would pull off his knee. Rebecca died suddenly—a wife of two years—fell asleep forever, for no reason that any Christian can name. Only Mary Parsons knows what—" The woman choked with tears, unable to go on.

Looking impatient John Pynchon spoke from his place on the bench. "Most all this evidence was covered during the slander trial—twenty years ago."

The governor searched Sarah Bridgeman's face. "You were found guilty of slander, were you not?"

She countered with hitherto-unseen vigor. "Aye—*wrongly* accused and *wrongly* convicted!"

"Let us hear from the plaintiff," Leverett directed as he looked toward Samuel Bartlett. "Goodman Bridgeman has said that they could not find a cause of death. Why do you think your wife died?"

Samuel said, "The surgeon did not know. He said he was suspicious of witchcraft, for it looked unnatural to him."

"What made you suspect Mary Parsons?"

"Many signs."

"What signs?" Simon Bradstreet asked, smoothing his grey moustache with one plump finger and a thumb.

"My wife was troubled by Mary Parsons. Rebecca said that Goodwife Parsons taught her simples. She was enchanted by the woman, enthralled in a way that made me afeard. Most folks avoided her. Always I felt there were secrets between them and feared that Rebecca had been exposed to evil spirits. Your Honor, I must tell that many in the town are afraid of this woman. Many step across the road to avoid her. I am not the only one in Northampton to think these things."

"Nor in Springfield!" a voice boomed from the back of the room.

Mary gasped, turning to look for the person who had spoken.

Leverett, too, searched faces, hoping to find the speaker. Then a dissipated man with a venomous-looking mouth surged forward.

Symonds said, "Who is this man?"

Pynchon knew the answer. "John Dover, the cooper at Springfield."

Dover raised his head, as if to increase his height. "Mary Parsons is possessed of great powers," he declared, "ever since she be a young wife at Springfield. Over twenty year ago I heard with my own ears her husband accuse her of witchcraft." He glared at Mary as Joseph moved to slip his arm around her waist. "I should know, for she bewitched me and would not let me sleep. Though I lay beside my wife, *she*"—he pointed—"came over me every night and tempted me to lie with her."

A hushed cry and shocked, muted voices filled the room as all eyes went to Mary. She turned to her husband, who seemed surprised, then toward the governor as if asking for an opportunity to speak. Leverett deduced something had come between her and Dover of which she had not told her husband, for indeed, the husband looked shaken.

Not waiting for permission, Mary Parsons cried out, "I cannot bear bravely these lies! I had no power over this vile, lascivious man."

Pynchon asked Dover, "How did she come to your rooms? In the flesh or as an apparition?" He seemed not to trust the accuser.

"I saw her spirit sent over me."

Pynchon turned to the governor. "Are we to consider spectral evidence, then? For to put it mildly, such evidence is questionable."

William Stoughton spoke for the first time. "Pray, tell me why we should not?"

"Pynchon is right," the governor put in. "The Devil himself might have been responsible for the apparition, or this man may not be truthful. The jury may look at this evidence in part, but should not put too much weight thereupon." He looked back to Mary. "If we are to know the whole story, Goodwife Parsons, pray tell your side."

She took a moment to gather herself, remembering. "In those days," she said, "my husband traded furs with the Indians, and before he went away, he hired John Dover to help around the farm. One night Dover came in drink to my husband's house and pushed his way inside. He put his hands on me, saying he had loved me long and would lie with me. I told him to be gone and raised the poker to strike him—" Her voice faltered and she raised a hand to cover her lips.

Whispers rose to murmurs throughout the courtroom as Joseph took her other hand and pressed it close between his palms, as if to comfort her.

Stoughton looked down his long nose at her. "Did you report this outrage to the magistrate?" Slowly he entwined his long bony fingers, never taking his eyes from her face.

"No, I did not."

"Unwise," Stoughton said, "for had you done so, Mister Pynchon could confirm your story. Could you not, Mister Pynchon?"

"I believe Goodwife Parsons," Pynchon said, stoutly. "It is a sad thing to say of my own townsman, but John Dover is often in conflict with persons. He is a known drunkard, and some time ago I had to give him fifteen lashes on his naked back for contemptuous behavior toward Mister Glover."

Danforth spoke out sharply. "While you, Pynchon, work to prejudice the court against this witness, Goodwife Parsons has not yet told us why she failed to report this supposed outrage."

At that Mary spoke out again. "I was afeard and dared not tell, not even my husband. For John Dover threatened to tell my husband I had invited his attention, and I believed he would say the same to Mister Pynchon."

"*She told me!*" a woman's voice cried out from close behind the defendant. "She came to *me* for advice!"

Stoughton turned to see the speaker. "Who is this woman?"

"Widow Bliss, her mother," Margaret answered as she got to her feet.

"And what advice did you give your daughter?" Stoughton asked.

"I told her to say nothing, to wait for John Dover to come to his senses, for then he would have mercy on her."

"Hmph!" The long-nosed magistrate sniffed, and the widow resumed her seat. "A mother would tell lies to save her daughter."

Sarah Bridgeman waved her kerchief for attention. "Ask me about signs of witchcraft! The things I saw. Ask again what you asked, before John Dover interrupted."

Thomas Danforth nodded. "Speak, Goodwife. Tell us." He was interested, as the father of six infants who had died before the age of two.

Sarah looked happy at the chance for further accusations. "Here is one sign I'll tell. One day as I passed by her husband's house I saw her clothes hung out to dry. They did come alive and dance before my very eyes. They bewitched me, and every night after for a time, I dreamt unspeakable things."

"What things?" Danforth probed, for he, more than any other member of the court, had knowledge of signs.

She burst into tears. "I cannot think it and will not say it. Pray, do not make me say it."

As the courtroom erupted into loud arguments and general unruliness the governor banged his gavel. "Goodwife Bridgeman, you seek to inflame. Speak to these things with less fire, tell us something more verifiable than your dreams."

Sarah seemed to pull herself together. "While my soul rages against the evil in this room, I shall try to calm myself." She chanced a look at Mary Parsons, then taking a deep breath, began again in a more moderate voice. "We discovered evidence lately that my daughter was afraid for her life. In an old chest of hers, we found a silver amulet—here—I have it in my pocket for you to see, and with it a bag of dried rue to keep a witch away." She dangled her prizes in the air.

"Bring me the amulet," Stoughton said.

When Sarah came forward, the Governor saw Mary startle as Stoughton took the silver object from her. He studied it closely. "I've never seen anything quite like this. I shall describe it for the jury. Here is a cross with a circle over it, and words in Latin. Grace Alone, it says, with three small crosses under that. I'll pass it on with the admonition that this object looks dangerous to me."

The governor took it and examined it closely. "Mister Stoughton has described it rightly. But it is Christian, not pagan, and says what we here believe—that by grace alone we are saved. I see nothing sinister in the message here inscribed. On the contrary, I regard it as a token of Christian faith."

Danforth had seen it and passed it to Bradstreet. "But Rebecca Bartlett could have used it to pray for protection. She may have used it as an idol. It looks papist to me."

Bradstreet seemed concerned. "Effects like this are not allowed. Where did your daughter get it?"

"I know not," Sarah said. "I never saw it before her death, never saw her wear it. She would never do anything against the law."

Agitated, James Bridgeman bent to whisper in his wife's ear. Sarah listened, looking frightened, then cried, "I have seen Mary Parsons' familiar spirits!"

Stoughton looked interested. "Tell us, how do they come? What appearance have they?"

"Like creatures who suck her!"

"Creatures? What creatures?"

"A black dog comes on the road from her house. It hangs by my door, watching who comes and goes, and a large black mouse creeps about my husband's house and watches from the corner."

"Do they say anything to you?"

"They stare and say naught."

Danforth spoke to Mary. "What say you, Goodwife Parsons, do you know these creatures?"

"I have no black dog, though we have mice who come after the crumbs my children drop by the hearth," she said, adding, "Goodwife Bridgeman had best get herself a hungry cat."

When sudden bright laughter filled the room Danforth scowled, his face ablaze. "Silence! This is no laughing matter! I abhor the defendant's saucy remark and instruct her to keep a respectful tone while she is in the presence of this court."

"I thank you, good sir!" Sarah called out.

IX

Some are ready to say that wizards are not so unwise as to do such things in the sight or hearing of others, but it is certain that they have very often been known to do so. How often have they been seen by others using enchantments? Conjuring to raise storms? And have been heard calling upon their familiar spirits? And have been known to use spells and charms? And to show in a glass or in a show stone persons absent? And to reveal secrets which could not be discovered but by the devil? And have not men been seen to do things which are above human strength, that no man living could do without diabolical assistances?

—Increase Mather
President of Harvard College 1692–1701

"YOU HAVE ANSWERED some questions to my satisfaction, Goodwife Parsons, but I have more." The governor looked at his notes. "'Tis plain for this court to see that Samuel Bartlett and the Bridgemans have suffered. Why do they suspect you?"

"Long I have asked myself that question and can only wonder," Mary said, hoping to answer truthfully yet wisely. "I know not why Samuel Bartlett has accused me, except that in his grief he has been persuaded by his in-laws. And it may be—indeed is—as Goodwife Bridgeman herself suggests, I have been blessed with nine living children and my husband with wealth. If it is unfair

419

that I have these blessings when Goodwife Bridgeman has not, I am sorry. I too, have lost children—two sons. If the Devil does my bidding as Goodwife Bridgeman claims, why was I unable to prevent these most sorrowful losses?"

Leverett turned to Sarah. "What say you, Goodwife Bridgeman? Are those your grounds for fear of Mary Parsons?"

"Nay! She would make of it simple jealousy, and 'tis not. I would no more want to be her than a snake. It is because she did me harm that I accuse her. *She* envies *me*! She, for all her made-up grandness, was once a serving girl in my father's house. Why, Rebecca was the exact image of me when I was young, and *she*, who envied me then, *bewitched* her!"

"You say these things and they may be true, Goodwife," Danforth said, "but we need something more incontestable." He looked crossly at old Deputy Symonds, who slumped beside him snoring.

Sarah would not relent. "I can prove that my daughter had secret meetings with Mary Parsons in the woods."

"Ah," Danforth said. "No good comes of women meeting in the dark wood. What evil brought them there?"

"Rebecca would not say. Goodwife Parsons swore her not to tell, I'll warrant."

Samuel spoke up. "I know her secret. Rebecca asked me to keep it, though by her death I may break that promise."

What had Rebecca told him? Suddenly anxious, Mary glanced at Joseph, who seemed to steady himself against the next surprise. How she wished now that she had kept nothing from him.

"My wife spoke of a wooded place where they would meet," Bartlett said, "saying it belonged to Goodwife Parsons. Once she asked me to go there, but I never did see the accursed place."

Samuel's mother's voice rang out. "I saw it!"

"Who speaks?"

"I do, the wife of Robert Bartlett of Northampton. Rebecca was my daughter-in-law."

"Say what you will."

"One day on my way through the meadow I saw Rebecca at its

edge, just before she disappeared into the wood. I soon found the path she had taken and followed it to a clearing, where Rebecca and Mary Parsons stood. Alone, they were, with no one else in sight. I could not hear what was said betwixt them, but it looked as if Goodwife Parsons instructed her."

Danforth perked up again. "Describe what you saw."

"The goodwife pointed to the ground, then pulled a tare with its root and offered it to my daughter-in-law, gesturing o'er it—like casting a spell."

Pynchon craned his neck and turned his head, the better to hear. "But you heard nothing?"

"No. They meant no one to hear."

"What say you to these charges?" Danforth asked Mary, "and why do you frequent the dark wood where devout, obedient women are afraid to go?"

Mary cleared her throat, shaken by this testimony, though it was no surprise. Rebecca had told her about Ann Bartlett's discovery and the clash with her own mother that followed. "Goodwife Bartlett is an honest woman and believes she knows what she saw, but she is mistaken. Rebecca was eager to learn what wild herbs grow in the wood." As she spoke, Mary's voice grew in confidence and strength. "I taught her these things, for I use many healing plants found there."

"She confesses!" Sarah called out.

"Quiet!" the governor said.

Undeterred, Mary went on. "Since my childhood in Hartford, I have had no fear of the forest by the light of day. My mother sent me there to gather fiddleheads and hellebores. And when she was but a child, Rebecca first came upon me gathering strawberries in the meadow. I told her that her mother would not approve her being so far from home and sent her away. Some long time later, when she was grown, she came to my house to ask a favor." Mary paused, hoping the right words would come.

Leverett said, "What favor? Pray go on."

"She knew I was skilled with herbs and asked me to help her mother, who suffered from melancholy. I told her I would not aid her mother, for she had slandered me. But Rebecca insisted, and at length she prevailed."

Stoughton scoffed. "What art could an innocent maid use against you?"

"She said something to touch my heart. It is taught, she said, that we all sin but we must forgive one another if we are to be forgiven. These words I know to be true, and they softened my heart toward the woman who sought my ruin. I made an herbal infusion for Goodwife Bridgeman to drink, something to soothe her mind and lift her spirits."

Watching Mary intently, narrowing her eyes, Sarah whispered to her husband.

Stoughton said, "And what ingredients for your potion did the Devil provide?"

"None, sir. I gathered rose petals and added sugar, licorice and chamomile. Three pinches to a cup of boiling water, taken at night and in the morning, will cure even your ill humor, Mister Stoughton. "

Stoughton glowered as in vain the governor sought to suppress his smile and said, "Harmless enough, I'll warrant. And did you drink this infusion, Goodwife Bridgeman?"

Sarah looked as if she'd been struck by lightning. "Aye, I took of a healing drink *Rebecca* made, that's true. She gave it me twice a day at first, then I measured and poured boiling water for myself. But *she* made it, *Rebecca* did. She told me herself, and I believe that still. *She*"—she pointed at Mary—"LIES."

Pynchon said, "Were you healed by the drink?"

"Nay, I shall never be other than melancholy. Not after everything she's done to me."

A stunned Ann Bartlett whispered to her husband, who appeared to counsel and console her.

The governor posed another question. "Goodwife Parsons, why did you persist in this secret friendship with Goodwife Bridgeman's daughter?"

"As I said, Rebecca wanted to learn simples. She had the gift for it, and she plagued me to teach her. Always I told her that because of her mother's hatred of me, we could not be friends, but she insisted upon it. And, sir, Rebecca told me that the warm drinks had prevailed, that her mother's spirits had improved. I believe that is true, because for years Rebecca came to me every fortnight for a new supply."

Sarah cried out, "Once more she lies!"

Danforth addressed Mary again. "If you would have the mercy of God, you must confess to your craftiness as a witch." Though his voice was as soft as the all too familiar pleading of the divines, Mary would not be cajoled.

"If I confess to that, I confess to a lie." She directed her next remark to the governor. "Sir, Goodwife Bridgeman is already a proven slanderer. She harbors jealousies of me and has been convicted of slander in a court of law. Her lies have ruined my name. She will not let me be. 'Tis I who am the one molested."

Stoughton's long slender fingers had sorted through the stack of depositions on the wooden table. "Here's something," he proffered the paper to the governor. "A jury of women has examined Goodwife Parsons for marks of the Devil, and she was not clean. Let her show us."

Pynchon objected. "I have known this woman and her husband for many years and never thought ill of her. I would not wish to ask her to disrobe in public."

Stoughton seemed determined. "Ah, but if innocent, she should not be afraid to show us what the jury found. As well, the mark is not hidden under her clothes. It says here we need only look under her coif."

Her voice firm, Mary said, "I am not afraid to show it." She stood and walked to the bench, where she pulled off her hood and removed her coif. As she unfastened her hair, out of the corner of her eye she caught Joseph smiling. She shook her head and ran her fingers through the soft masses of her hair, and an audible murmur rose from the jury. Every man present looked as if he longed to touch it. Mary felt suddenly shy and girlish as with both hands she lifted her hair off her neck for the governor's eye.

"Look, here." She pointed. "Since childhood it's been there."

"Aye," Leverett said, leaning close enough to smell the fragrance of her just-washed hair. "It looks like an ordinary mole to me, and I deem it nothing. Do you wish to see for yourselves?" he asked his assistants. When none came forward, Mary returned to her seat.

"Your Honor!" Bridgeman got to his feet. "You have not yet heard all the evidence. We have something more to bring before the court."

"Then bring it, please."

"'Tis something—my wife—" Bridgeman motioned for Sarah to stand.

Slowly Sarah rose from her seat and raised her eyes to meet the governor's. "I am afeared to tell it, sir, for you do not seem impartial to me. But I have no choice, for 'tis the truth—what I saw the day my daughter was laid out at her husband's house, when friends had come to pay their last respects." She stopped and, swaying, leaned against her husband for support. Grim-faced, he braced her with his body. The whole gathering waited as Sarah regained her footing. "I am sorry, Your Honor, but I am not well. Never more shall I be well."

"You have borne a great shock, Goodwife. Would you like to sit down?"

"Nay, I shall stand." She took a moment to straighten and catch her breath. "As I said, folks had come, and I was astonished to see Mary Parsons there. She had come alone. I watched her, never did my eyes leave her. She spoke to no one but went straight to my daughter who lay in her coffin. She seemed to say something, and I thought she was casting a spell, then she touched Rebecca's cheek. At that, my poor daughter's cheeks flushed with fresh blood, and she turned her head away."

Stoughton frowned. "Who turned her head away?"

"My daughter, sir. She recoiled from the hand of the one who killed her."

As those present sought to fathom what Sarah Bridgeman had just said, a disorderly din filled the room. Judges and jurymen spoke up in disbelief as a bewildered Mary turned to Joseph. "This did not happen," she told him.

He said, "Did you go there, Mary?"

"Yes, but—I—"

He looked stricken.

As the governor's mallet came down hard on the board the room fell silent.

Pynchon said, "Mary Parsons, what say you to this charge?"

"'Tis true I was there. I knew I would not be welcome, but I had to choose. Go, or never believe that Rebecca was dead." Her voice broke. "I had to see her once more, for she loved me, and I owed her my tears."

Pynchon scanned the crowd. "Did anyone else see this abomination?"

Silence.

Adamant, Joseph half-rose from his seat. "You cannot take a slanderer's word alone."

"Your Honor," Sarah declared, "Ann Bartlett saw the same!"

The governor addressed the woman named. "Is that true, Goodwife Bartlett? Did you see what the goodwife described?"

Ann Bartlett exchanged a glance with her husband as she wiped tears from her eye, and when she spoke, her voice was firm. "I saw Mary Parsons pay her respect to the dead. No more than that."

Mary saw that Joseph's eyes were full of pity for her. He was glad Rebecca had been her friend.

Another woman's voice came from the back of the room. "Sirs, will you hear me?" As from behind the crowd Henrietta Negro pushed her way toward the bench, several of those present objected. "Keep your place!" "Who would listen to her?" "Shame, be still!"

Henrietta ignored the protests and moved to the front of the room, where she bowed to the governor. She spoke in a low voice. "Will you hear me? You looks and sounds like a even-handed man."

Stoughton cried, "Who is this blackamoor? Woman, what right have you to be heard?"

The governor banged his gavel. "Peace! I'll have peace! All be silent save this woman. Now, tell us who you are."

She was modest in her dress, respectful in her demeanor. "I be Henrietta Negro. I was in service at the house of Master Samuel Bartlett at the time Mistress Rebecca died, and I know for certain that some folks here have not spoke the truth today."

"Speak, then," Leverett directed.

All present fell silent and strained to hear, for Henrietta's voice was low. "As I say, some here has not told the truth. Mistress Rebecca was sickly—with a burning fever and the flux. I know this, for I nursed her. So that Mister Samuel Bartlett might go for a few hours to see to his mill, he fetched his mother-in-law to look in on his wife. But by the time she come—Mistress Bridgeman, that is—Mistress Rebecca would not wake up."

"Aye, and I heard another lie," Ann Bartlett called out. "Goodwife Bridgeman testified that the warm drink her daughter gave her did not make her well. This is untrue. Almost merry she was, after years of melancholy."

Sarah flew into a rage, standing up, shaking her fist. "You are all against the truth! You all want to kill me! Mary Parsons has put you into the hands of the Devil!"

The governor's pounding and her husband's urging finally got Sarah to sit down.

Until now, Simon Bradstreet had had little to say. "Where is the doctor who saw Rebecca? "May he testify to the cause of death?"

Samuel Bartlett answered. "You have his deposition. He is not here."

Bradstreet leaned forward, his face grim. "What do you say to the charge that you lied?"

Looking trapped, Samuel Bartlett muttered, "I only told what the doctor said—that it looked unnatural to him. That's what he *did* say."

Bradstreet directed a question to James Bridgeman. "Was your daughter ill that morning?"

"Not that I know of," Bridgeman ventured, looking to his wife to back him up.

Sarah shrieked, "She's *mighty*! A powerful witch! See how she twists the minds of great men? How she sways them to her?"

"Here, now, Goodwife!" Bradstreet commanded. "No one has twisted my mind. No one has taken it from me."

The governor spoke. "Methinks Mister Bradstreet is right. Is there a man here who feels his mind gone under the spell of Goodwife Parsons?"

Danforth answered. "Aye, I feel her power. Her nimble tongue entraps, she charms, she speaks as if to reason, but I see the Devil in her. It is the Evil One, not God, who aids her and beguiles all of you."

The weary-looking governor laid down his gavel and leaned back. "I shall leave that for the jury to decide. Have we heard all the evidence?"

No one replied.

"Mary Parsons, have you a final word?"

Joseph got to his feet. "Pray, sirs, hear me. I have not yet spoken in my wife's defense. My wife is innocent. Never would she harm a child. She has been a hard-working, faithful wife—always—even when I have not deserved it." He glanced at Mary, then went on. "If you would sit one hour among the gossips of Northampton and Springfield, you would pity her. Because of Sarah Bridgeman's slanders, this good and generous woman is nearly friendless. My wife is praiseworthy, blameless. She has been accused out of jealousies for her goodness, her beauty, her gifts as a wife and mother, her fondness for speaking the truth. I beg you, do not condemn her." Having said his piece, he sat and reached for Mary's hand.

Leverett addressed Mary. "Goodwife Parsons, you may speak to the jury."

Mary stood, her hand still enclosed in her husband's. She looked into the faces of the jury, men not unlike the common yeomen she had known all her life. She lowered her eyes, breathed deeply, and waited for the right words to come. When her spirit was sufficiently sure, she opened her eyes to gaze intently into their solemn faces one after another. "I am innocent, and the righteous God knows it. My fate is in His hands. I trust you, my good men, to do with me as my Lord wishes."

. . . . .

By day's end Mary stood in the garden of her husband's property in Boston. He'd proudly shown her the house, all its rooms furnished. John, Eben, Samuel and Jonathan were there with them. Her daughters and Elspeth would arrive in a few days with Joseph Jr.

Hardly able to believe their ordeal was at an end, she walked with Joseph through the grounds, where Mary delighted in mature apple and pear trees now in bloom. They climbed the little hill at the back of the property reliving together their moment of deliverance: how when the jury returned its verdict of not guilty the governor had looked Samuel Bartlett in the eye and said he had not proved his case, how Mr. Danforth had appeared crestfallen, shocked, and how Mary could not look at Sarah. Grateful for the chance to live, she would not revel in Sarah's crushing defeat. She took Joseph's hand as he guided her toward the spreading oak. They sat in the shade and Mary's eyes filled with tears of happiness as she marveled at the blessing of forgiveness Rebecca had taught her.

She looked below toward the garden and the house. It was May—time for planting.

Afterword

My grandmother loved to tell us stories—*Chicken Little* and *The Little Red Hen* when I was a four-year-old with my head on her shoulder, "true" stories about our ancestors when I was ten and sitting at her feet. I'd listen as she spun her tales, our hands entwined.

"As far back as we can trace our family history on both sides, we've found wonderful characters. Brave people who did nearly impossible things—some pretty radical." She laughed at the word "radical," for she was as conservative as they come. Her name was Marguerite Grace Parsons Vorbeck.

"Tell me about the ancestors who first came to America." I knew the question would launch her into my favorite story.

"I don't know when my mother's Scotch and Irish ancestors came and settled in Pennsylvania," she said. "I presume they came to escape religious persecution, like Joseph Parsons on my father's side, who first settled Connecticut in the 1630s—but Karen, I've told this story before."

"Tell it again." I never tired of hearing about the family witch.

429

"Well, he was among the founders of three towns—Hartford, Springfield and Northampton. That's where Mary Parsons really got into trouble with her neighbors, in Northampton—"

And then my grandmother was on her way, retelling the story of Mary Bliss Parsons, a woman with a wealthy husband who evoked jealousy among her neighbors in 17th-century Massachusetts. "Why, every time a farmer's cow died," she said, "they'd blame it on Mary." She told how Mary Parsons was accused of witchcraft, went to prison, and came to trial. How she acted as her own lawyer, defended herself, proved herself innocent, and after her acquittal went home to "lord it over her neighbors." My grandmother loved the lord-it-over-her-neighbors part, because she'd have done the same thing.

"You come from a long line of strong and unusual women, Karen. Don't you ever forget it! And don't forget your ancestors in Pennsylvania, who became a part of the Underground Railroad for escaped slaves trying to get to Canada. Or my father's grandfather, who took his wife and children out west in a covered wagon. What courage they had! On my father's side, one of my ancestors fought in the Crusades. John Calvin, on my mother's side, rebelled against the church."

And she would go on like that as long as I'd listen, telling stories that are now hard for me to believe. In her mind every one of our ancestors was a great hero, all brave figures out of the past who barely missed making it into the history books.

My childhood interest in Mary Bliss and Joseph Parsons stayed with me. Later, as a young wife and mother, I moved with my family to Massachusetts to live on seven acres of farmland in an old farmhouse built in 1710. I soon realized I was living in the same region where Mary and Joseph Parsons had lived, in a house quite similar to houses of their period.

I began to look into the story. That was in the 1970s, before the Internet. My research took me to libraries around the state but especially to Northampton's Forbes Library. I pored over old maps, read 19th century histories about the towns in the Connecticut River Valley. On one of the documents I found, I saw Mary's mark—the way she signed her name—and afterward wanted even more to know her. At first I was shocked to learn that she couldn't write, but further research revealed that in those times most girls were not taught to write, for they did not need it in their work. Reading, on the other hand, was important so that they could read the Bible. Later, with the help of the Internet and a host of new genealogical information, I found it much easier to flesh out this ancient story, its setting and its characters.

The legend of Goody Parsons the *witch* still lives in Northampton, where tourists may visit the Parsons House, built by one of Mary and Joseph's grandsons. The original house is gone, as are their graves in the old burial ground in Springfield. In the 19th century, when the railroad from Hartford to Springfield was built through a section of the old cemetery, the town moved what remains they could find to a common grave at the Springfield City Cemetery. What irony! Now what is left of their bones is mixed with the bones of the very neighbors who made their lives so difficult.

Mary and Joseph's story does not end with her trial. Both lived on. We know that following the trial they stayed in Boston for about five years. My grandmother got it wrong, for Mary did not return victorious to Northampton to "lord it over her neighbors." Two days after Mary's acquittal Joseph bought a warehouse and wharf in Boston. He also owned a house and land on a street that led to the Training Field.

In June, less than a month after Mary's trial, the first battle of King Philip's War began with an attack on Swansea in southeastern Massachusetts. On September 2 of the same year, Mary's son Ebenezer Parsons, who had recently settled in Northfield, was killed in the first battle there. In 1676 Joseph Parsons became a member of a military unit known as the Hampshire Troop of Horse. By 1678 Joseph and Mary became residents of both Boston and Northampton, and within the year they again made the smaller town their home.

Strange things continued to happen there, for early in 1679 John Stebbins, a Northampton man, was killed in an avalanche of runaway logs at the sawmill where he was foreman. Stebbins was the husband of Abigail Bartlett, daughter of the late Ann and Robert Bartlett and sister to Samuel Bartlett. Samuel Bartlett thought his brother-in-law's death was suspicious, so he called for an inquest into the death. Examination of the body showed "a warmth and heate in his body that dead persons are not usual to have." Stebbins's neck was reportedly as flexible as a living person's, and his body was covered with hundreds of spots that, after a scraping, "showed holes underneath." Although the jury reported back to the court in April, no further action was taken. The evidence gathered in the case is now missing from town records.

About that same time, Mary and Joseph Parsons left Northampton and moved to Springfield. Some historians believe gossip may have linked Mary Parsons to Stebbins's death, so that Joseph thought it wise to get out of Northampton and away from Samuel Bartlett, whom one 19th-century historian called the "local witch hunter." Who's to say? We can't know.

By then Joseph had moved up in rank to cornet of the Hampshire Troop of Horse, which was a British regiment, of course, under the command of Major John Pynchon. A cornet is the color-bearer, and Joseph was third in command. He must have been a dashing sight astride his horse, bearing the troop flag, dressed in his uniform with a silk scarf tied around his neck and his "cutlash" rapier in hand. From that time on he was no longer addressed as "Goodman Parsons" but "Mister" or "Cornet," making Mary eligible to be called "Mistress Parsons" in preference to "Goodwife."

Even after King Philip's death in 1676, which ended the war, Indian troubles persisted, and in 1681 Joseph was paid for "going after Indians." The following year he was elected selectman at Springfield. On October 9, 1682, Joseph died at the age of 62, leaving an estate totaling £2,008.09, making him one of the richest men in the territory. In contrast, when James Bridgeman died his estate was valued at £114.15.

Mary lived on to suffer the deaths of her grown son Jonathan and her adult daughters, Abigail and Mary. And on August 28,

1684, she lost her mother. In time, she would live to hear of the horrors of the Salem Witch Trials.

Old tales against Mary continued to circulate. In 1702, her daughter Hannah, along with her husband, complained to the court that Betty Negro had struck their son and told him that his grandmother had killed several people and that his mother, Hannah, was half a witch. But revenge came soon when John Pynchon and Joseph Parsons Jr. presided over the court and sentenced Betty to a lashing. The infamous witch trials at Salem had changed many people's minds about the ancient belief in witchcraft; by then people were less likely to jump to conclusions about their neighbors and never again was a witch executed in New England.

Mary lived to see the day in 1709 when her granddaughter Mary (daughter of Mary's son John) married Sarah Lyman Bridgeman's grandson Ebenezer Bridgeman (son of Sarah's son John).

Records still exist showing that when spirited Mary was in her mid-60s she bought blue calico, a scarf and two pair of red stockings. But alas, Mary could not live forever. After a life replete with struggle she must have been tired, and by the time she reached her mid-80s her mind had deteriorated. On December 4, 1711, at the Court of General Session at Northampton the following document was filed.

Whereas the Distressed Estate of Mrs. Parsons Widw of Springfield being as we have Good Testimony of so aged, Indisposed and Confused in her Understanding and Memory So that She is not fit nor in a Capacity to Manage her Self or Estate therefore this Court Considering the Premises do order that all acts bargains or Conveyances of her Estate Either former or Later while Indisposed as aforesaid Shall be Null and void and the whole and sole Care of her and her Estate for her Maintenance and Subsistance Shall and is by this Court Put into the Dispose and ordering of Capt. Joseph Parsons Esq. and Capt. John Parsons, her sons Giving in true Accounts of her Expense from time to time till Further Order from this Court and all others of the Children, or others, to have no Dispose of Managemt in the Premises besides what shall be Done and ordered by the sd Capt. Joseph Parsons Esq. and Capt. John Parsons.

Mary died on January 29, 1712. Five of her children survived her: Joseph Jr., John, Samuel, Hannah and Esther.

New names for some of the major characters were necessary. The real names of the Pierces—Hugh and Eunice—were Hugh and *Mary* (Lewis) Parsons, though no relation to Joseph and Mary. Rebecca Bridgeman's real name was *Mary* Bridgeman. Changes were made for the obvious reason that three characters named Mary and two Mary Parsons would have been impossible for readers to keep straight. Respect for a few characters portrayed as villains impelled me to change their names. Uncomfortably aware of their descendants, I did not want to tarnish anyone's memory to justify the characters I had created to act against Mary Bliss or Joseph Parsons. I did not change the Bridgeman or Bartlett names, because their characters were based on reliably strong historical evidence. A few characters were products of my imagination. Regardless of the historical background that exists to support the story, readers should know that they have a work of fiction in hand.

Reading and Discussion Group Questions

1. Why do you think the author chose the title, *My Enemy's Tears*? Did you empathize with Sarah Lyman Bridgeman?
2. Before reading *My Enemy's Tears: The Witch of Northampton* what did you know about Puritan life? Did the book change your view of these people? If so, how?
3. Did the Puritan theocracy remind you of any current-day societies? What about theocracies feeds the best or worst in human nature? How similar is the role of women in Puritan and modern theocracies? How is it different?
4. How close do you think Mary Crespet came to practicing witchcraft? Were you surprised by the charges against suspected witches in general? Why did early modern people believe in witchcraft?
5. What about the native peoples in this story surprised you? Did you see any connection between the belief systems of the Native Americans and the Puritans?

6. Compare modern people and those of the 17th century regarding their belief in miracles. Have moderns lost anything by their almost "religious" belief in technology and science?

7. Why do modern readers enjoy stories from the past? What liberties do you think the author took with history?

8. What are the major themes in *My Enemy's Tears*? Did you have a favorite character? Was it believable that Rebecca Bridgeman loved Mary Parsons?

9. How do modern men and boys' lives differ from those who lived in the 17th century? How did wilderness affect them? What, if anything, have moderns lost with the passage of time?

10. In the 17th century, parents wielded greater authority over their children than they do now. What effect did this have on the children? Do you think that sending children into service was harmful to their psyches?

11. Have you ever daydreamed about going back to a certain time in history? Do you have interesting ancestors? Are you surprised by the author's determination to tell this story even though it took her over 35 years?

About the Author

KAREN VORBECK WILLIAMS has lived more than thirty-five years in New England where she found the inspiration, settings, and spirit for *My Enemy's Tears: The Witch of Northampton*, historical fiction based on the life of her ancestor Mary Bliss Parsons. This is her first novel. She's been an editor for fourteen years and is a prize winning photographer.

Visit the book website at www.enemystears.com.

Lightning Source UK Ltd.
Milton Keynes UK
UKOW051037090912

198662UK00001B/16/P